WHINE

THE SEQUEL TO "*SEX & SANDWICHES*"

TRACEY L. DEBREW

herwritehand publishing, inc.

Washington, DC

Paperback First Edition 2014

Library of Congress Cataloging Number
available upon request
ISBN-13: (Pbk)
978-0-9832492-2-1

-to Mom & Dad
thanks for making me (write)

1

Camilla needed to get laid properly since every time with Bryan Bryant was unremarkable and flat. After several tears and boxes of tissue, she pushed through the pain and had finally gotten over him. Because the mothering thing was new to her, Camilla often felt bad for leaving her son Gabriel with Hailey or the babysitter so she could date. Camilla knew in her heart this could not continue, but she still had unfulfilled desires to be met.

When that man told Camilla he still owned a Polaroid Instamatic was when the red flags should have flown up the pole. Camilla thought that Felix would be a prime candidate. She had met him on a website after swearing she would never venture down that particular avenue to find a man. This site was different though. The men on the site had verified salaries in the neighborhood of three hundred thousand and above annually.

Camilla put off dating for over two years to raise Gabe and now that he could speak, she thought it would be a good time to get back into the dating scene. Felix was nice looking, with an extremely dry sense of humor. Frankly, he was corny and laughed at all of his own jokes unnecessarily. Of the hundred or so jokes he would tell in a short span, only three or four warranted a chuckle from Camilla. After a month of yakking it up online and on the phone, they decided that it was time to meet. After numerous rejections and feeling undesirable, Camilla had a newfound confidence. She worked out as usual, lost the baby weight fairly quickly and was blessed to not even have any stretch marks.

She met up with Felix at a happy hour. To her surprise he looked exactly like his photo. *Okay, he seems honest*, she noted to herself.

"Wow! You look . . . amazing!" Felix commented as his eyes bathed her body from top to bottom.

"Thanks. I try to look good whenever I'm having a night out," she said to him.

"Try? You are doing it . . . well. What are you drinking?"

"Oh, nothing just yet. I need to talk to you with a clear head my friend," she admitted.

"Okay, I respect that. After the day I've had, I hope you will excuse me," he guffawed. "I need Jack, Johnny and maybe Samuel!" his dry laugh matched his dry joke perfectly.

"Okay . . .," Camilla flatly responded. It was time for her to get down to brass tacks. "So what brought you to the money website? Or should I say MyMoneyMate.com? What do you do for a living?"

"I'm a club owner. Two in D.C., one in Princes George's County and another in Montgomery County. They all are doing very well. I thought the site would be a good way to meet women. I'm typically not in the clubs, I have promoters for that. I'm more behind the scenes. I chain myself to my desk and my secretary just throws me a few slices of bread every few hours!" he laughed again.

"Wow." Camilla said. Not in reference to being chained and thrown bread, but the fact that he laughed about it.

"What do you do?" he asked her.

"I hate telling people what I do. They always give me a strange look like I owe them something. I'd rather not say just yet."

Felix took a swig of his Jack and Coke and lightly nodded. He then looked at Camilla as if she were pulling his leg. He awaited her response.

"I'm serious," she reiterated.

"Oh come on. We're adults. What is it?"

Camilla gave a labored sigh, "I'm an auditor for the IRS."

"Ah, I see what you mean now. Luckily since I'm a numbers person too, the IRS has been a friend," he chuckled. "A damn good friend!" He laughed even louder.

"Well, I just have to ask. Being on a site that broadcasts your annual salary to potential mates, well . . . that doesn't make you . . . nervous?"

"How?"

"Do you think women will want you or your bank account?"

He sipped his drink again, thought for a moment then replied, "If I like her, my bank account won't matter and if my bank account matters, I won't like her."

The conversation continued and carried on in a light banter for another hour or so. Once Camilla felt as though she asked all of the pertinent questions, she relaxed and ordered a drink. It wasn't until after Felix's third drink that he mentioned that Polaroid Instamatic.

"For those intimate photos," he explained. "No photo shopping there!" he laughed again at his punch line. For whatever reason, that intrigued Camilla. She imagined that he had cameras mounted to the ceiling, bondage gear and attire, chains, gag balls and such. She never ventured that far into her sexual promiscuity, but was always fascinated.

"A Polaroid? I thought they stopped making those?"

"No, they're back. The pictures are clearer and they don't take as long to 'air dry' as I like to call it. It could be a lot of fun. You up for some fun?"

"Umm, let me think a second on it."

"Think long, you think wrong. Did I tell you how gorgeous you are?"

Camilla sipped her drink and shifted uneasily in her seat. She guessed this was the start of the campaign to get her to his house.

"No you didn't tell me," she said, "but it's cool. I know it already."

Felix reared back in his seat with a surprised expression. Obviously impressed with her confidence, he decided to push the envelope on their conversation.

"Okay, I hear you," he started, "I bet you'd look gorgeous naked in my Jacuzzi too."

"Jacuzzi?" she asked.

"It's square," he added as if it would firm up a commitment from her.

Like you, Camilla wanted to say but refrained from doing so. Even though he was a bona fide cornball, Camilla intuitively guessed that he was probably a freak. He may be just the sort of adventurous guy she needed to get her orgasms back into gear. *Freak from a geek.* That would be a perfect introduction back into the dating world.

"Where do you live?" Camilla asked.

"Mitchellville."

"Okay," she twirled herself around on the barstool to prepare herself to stand, "let's go. I don't have a swimsuit."

Felix looked at Camilla up and down before he seductively replied, "I said naked. You won't need one."

Camilla gave a sly grin and headed for the exit before she lost her nerve. Felix stared at her round ass that Camilla didn't always have before the baby. He could not take his eyes off of it, wondering how good it would feel cushioned against his pelvis when he would screw her from behind in just a few moments from now.

As Camilla drove behind Felix's car, she put on some soothing music to calm her jittery nerves. She had also packed along a flask filled with vodka. She took a moderate swig of that when they reached a red light before entering his neighborhood.

What am I getting myself into again? Camilla thought to herself. Her stomach curdled lightly, but she conveniently attributed that to the alcohol. She wondered what the sex with him would be like as she tried not to think how many times she had attempted to do this before. Camilla wasn't in love with Felix and need not be just to have sex with him. When they arrived, she noticed that he had an elaborate home with plenty of land surrounding it, although his neighbors still seemed close.

She parked her car behind his in the sloped driveway and noticed another vehicle but thought nothing of it. It wasn't uncommon for men of his financial caliber to have two or more cars. Camilla took another swig from her flask and left her wallet locked in her glove compartment. She quickly texted Josephine Felix's home address and his license plate number. With the press of the send button, she oddly felt safer knowing that her friend knew where she was. She let her hair down which had grown drastically during her pregnancy. It was always shoulder length, but was now to the center of her back. She gave it a gentle comb through with her fingertips and then applied some lipstick. The chime from the cell phone penetrated the silence of the car as it indicated that she had received a text message. Camilla glared at the phone, and debated indulging her instinctive reflex to check it. After a few seconds she grumbled, decided against it and tossed the phone in the glove box as well. Now feeling the effects of the alcohol, she hopped out of the car. Felix was standing nearby patiently waiting to lead her inside for a night of ecstasy.

"This isn't your friend's house is it?" Camilla asked with a smile. Felix laughed and shook his head. "You do know where everything is, right? And how to operate everything?"

"Will you stop, girl?" he teased. "We are going to have a great time."

They entered the large foyer and Camilla looked up and around at the art work and trim details – taking mental notes of what she could recreate in her home when the time came. She loved her condominium loft, but it was going to be too small in a few years. Even though Gabe was a toddler, they were already running into each other. As Camilla continued to look around, she noticed an abstract iron figurine on a pedestal that caught her attention. It was an odd-bodied woman with a cone shaped wiry afro holding the scales of justice. Perhaps he was a Libra. It fascinated her nonetheless.

"This is beautiful!" she complimented on the figurine.

"I got her in my travels to Europe. The sculptor is Roman Velihurskiy. He's very creative and very expensive," he told her.

"Is that right?"

"I had it appraised and apparently, this thing is damn near priceless. Would you like another drink?"

"I'm good. I'd rather hop into that Jacuzzi," she verbally nudged him.

Felix smiled at her enthusiasm and loosened his tie, "your hair is nice. I didn't know you had all of that packed in that bun. It is yours, right?"

Camilla averted her attention from his artwork and looked at him a bit perturbed. "Uhh, yeah . . . it is."

"Didn't mean to offend you with that. What I meant was you wouldn't want to get it wet would you?"

"I'll be fine."

"Okay sexy, let's go," he suggested.

Felix led the way to the rear of the house where the Jacuzzi was. It was one of those endless pools where you could swim laps in place but it also doubled into a whirlpool spa. That was why it was square shaped. Camilla mentally noted that swimming wasn't on his list of hobbies. There were large windows that surrounded the pool with several plants and about six lounge chairs. She guessed that he probably entertained in this area quite a bit. Above was a skylight and Camilla could faintly see the stars shining on the two of them. By now the alcohol from her flask had gotten her more than tipsy and she was ready to have a bit of fun with Felix. They embraced and kissed as if they had known each other for years.

Camilla was enjoying his touch and hoped to God Felix would not say anything else corny to wreck the flow of the euphoric mood she was in. Felix was handsome to her and stood at about six feet. He was in great physical shape, dressed well and had a laid back yet regal air to his demeanor.

"You comfortable?" he asked as he prepared the sound system with some soft R&B tunes. He dimmed the recessed lighting to make it romantic.

"Quite," she responded as she began to take off her shoes. The water looked soothing as the surface rumbled – she could barely wait to enter. When she unzipped the side of her dress, Felix's eyes were glued on her throughout the entire act. When she saw the pleasure on his face, she slowly stepped out of it to tease him a bit more.

"Wow. You look fantastic," he said as he continued unbuttoning his shirt and trousers. Camilla felt the need to dominate so she approached him and began kissing his neck and chest. He pulled her close to him and returned her affection. Camilla allowed him to grip her body with his firm hands. She looked around the room and noticed the Polaroid camera tucked away in the corner. Obviously this was not a first for him.

"So I see your camera over there," she noted.

He ceased kissing on her body for a moment and replied, "I won't take any pictures of you unless you want me to."

"I'd rather you didn't," she confirmed with a lighthearted smile. Taken slightly aback by her statement, he leaned backward to get a good look at her.

"You got it. I won't."

"Let's get in," Camilla suggested. This was just one night, she rationalized to herself. Then she recalled the one night with Steve that resulted in a child. She loved her son, but didn't want an instant replay of that again. Camilla had a NuvaRing, which could be inserted and removed like a diaphragm, was on the pill and stocked up on condoms.

The water temperature was perfect when she slowly stepped into the whirlpool. It enveloped her body like a soft, warm fleece blanket in winter. Felix stepped in immediately after Camilla and moved behind her. He massaged her shoulders and began kissing on her neck and upper back. To Camilla his touch felt better than the water. Gently, she closed her eyes and tilted her head backward to confirm her pleasure. His massaging reminded her of Bryan's touch, even though she knew full well that Felix was not Bryan.

Camilla shook the notion and concentrated on Felix's masculine hands as they rubbed her body sensuously. His hands went from her shoulders down her back to her waist and rested on her hips. He swiveled her around to face him and began kissing her lips tenderly. Camilla was thinking herself to orgasm, just based on his touch and the water lapping between her thighs.

A pleasurable moan oozed from her parted mouth. Feeling encouraged by that sound, Felix increased the movements of his hands and mouth across her body. Camilla was mentally engaged and close to climax. She stared into Felix's eyes before placing a French kiss upon his full lips. She gasped seductively when she felt his finger entering her. The sweetness she felt was escalated when he inserted a second finger in and out of her.

"Oh, Felix."

Camilla imagined that this was her man, her lover that she hadn't seen for months. She was fully prepared to toss all of her inhibitions aside for the next several hours. Any and everything that he asked her to do tonight, she was willing. She longed to be fucked and hoped that Felix possessed the stamina and drive that her body needed. Camilla still remembered all of the Kama Sutra tricks but hadn't been able to use them on anyone. Being more than ready, she'd exercised her pelvic floor muscles every day by doing Kegel exercises since Gabe was born. She was prepared to hold Felix's dick hostage in her tight love hole. The feel of his long thick fingers was enjoyable and she assumed his manhood would match.

Felix sat on the edge of the underwater bench. Camilla without hesitation straddled him. She lifted her body up and down on his midsection to simulate how she was going to ride him in just a few minutes. Felix squeezed her ass and spread her cheeks apart. Camilla bit down on his shoulder – the water from the hot tub was being lapped up with her hot tongue.

He gnawed and sucked gently on her neck as his fingers worked in and out of her. Camilla wanted to fast forward the foreplay and feel his pelvis pressed firmly next to hers. She whined in anticipation, unable to contain her lust any longer. It had been years! Camilla slightly flinched when she felt a different kind of sensation on her back. She ignored it and began massaging his hardness instead. The sensation on her back returned and she jerked a little. When the pressure on her back increased, it felt as though she was being touched by foreign hands. She turned to see and flailed about slightly in alarm while she pressed her tensed body close to Felix for protection.

"What the fuck?!" she demanded loudly.

Felix smiled and held Camilla close to his body and caressed her back. Although Camilla was holding Felix close to shield her frontal nudity from the stranger, her fist remained clenched just in case she needed to land two blows to someone's head. Camilla's eyes remained fixed on the woman as she made her way beside the couple.

"Camilla, this is Gia. I called her on the way here and asked her to join us."

Gia had to have been a 50 quadruple E, clearly outshining Camilla's dirty pillows. Gia even had the nerve to have a flat stomach and was ridiculously curvaceous. She looked like a horny teen drew her frame on a sketch pad one rainy afternoon and prayed that she'd become real. Camilla hunched her body closer to Felix's.

"I hope you don't mind," he said coolly.

"Are you crazy? Hell yeah, I mind!"

"You are gorgeous girl," Gia told Camilla as she caressed her some more. Camilla pressed her body even closer to Felix.

"I'm sorry, Camilla. Gia baby, can you give us a minute?" Felix asked her sweetly.

"Sure, Felix," Gia said as she casually stepped up and out of the Jacuzzi. She gave a sly smirk to Felix. Afterward, she winked and blew a kiss to Camilla on her way out of the sunroom. Camilla, clearly disgusted by the idea of an impromptu ménage à trios, waited until Gia exited and leapt out of the Jacuzzi. She began drying herself rapidly, barely listening to Felix's explanation.

"I thought you were into having fun?"

"With you, yeah! Not you and some damn chick who's got built in floatation devices. What the hell's wrong with you? That's not something you just spring on someone!"

"Camilla, I'm really sorry," Felix's weak apology was delivered from the Jacuzzi. He clearly had no intentions of ejecting himself from the endless pool to show her out, or offer her any sort of physical consolation.

Camilla fumbled awkwardly to toss on her clothes as quickly as she could. Although she was still wet from the pool, she zipped up her dress and grabbed her stilettos.

"You sure you won't change your mind? A lot of women become addicted to Gia. I don't know what she does to those girls, but they lose their fucking minds!"

"Uhh, I'll show myself out. You and *chesticles* enjoy yourselves," she told him as she headed out of the sunroom.

"Camilla? Camilla, wait!" he called to her. She turned to face him.

"What?"

"Can you send Gia back in?" he asked with a smile.

"Fuck no! You get your ass up and go get her!"

Camilla stormed out of the sunroom and through his home to the foyer. She doubled back and swiped the iron Libra sculpture from Roman what's-his-name and slammed the door behind her.

"Asshole."

She settled herself in the car, squishy ass and all, and barreled out of his driveway. She sped in the direction of the beltway. Her phone which was locked in her glove compartment was sounding off indicating she had more text messages. When she reached a red light, she retrieved it to check them. One was from Josephine, who obviously responded to her earlier text. Camilla read it aloud.

When are you going to stop doing this to yourself?

Camilla gave a labored groan and shook her head as she looked up at the red light. "When I'm tired," she replied. "And tonight, I just got tired."

2

Steve strolled slowly on the green at the ninth hole and looked down wearily. The sky was dark with a distant glow from the flood lights of the golf course's clubhouse. He peeled off his jacket and screamed as long and as loud as he could up toward the full moon. The nearby woods stirred with life as whatever inhabited them was disturbed. Steve laid flat on his back, arms outstretched beside him as he took a deep breath.

She knelt beside him and looked down on him with a gentle smile.

"I needed to do that," Steve told her. "That felt absolutely exhilarating."

"I think the wildlife running for their lives from your screaming was probably exhilarating for them as well," she giggled.

"Thank you so much," Steve said as he sat up on his elbows.

"And so this ends our therapy sessions. I'm really glad I could help you get over the trauma of breaking up with your first true love."

"Dr. Billingsley, I can't thank you enough."

"Please, our sessions have ended. You can call me Chase now," she assured him. Chase smiled and began to rise to her feet, but Steve reached his hand out to stop her. She remained and gave him a pleasant glare.

"So . . . Chase," Steve began, "since our sessions have ended, what else can I do?"

"I'm not sure I follow," she admitted.

"Can I just call you?"

Chase blushed and then smiled. In response to his request, she looked into Steve's boyish eyes and patted his shoulder gently. Steve sighed and then sat completely up on the green – his lips curled upward a bit to give soft smile of defeat.

"Oh okay, I know what that means," Steve told her. "Silence means no."

"I see you haven't learned too much from our sessions," Chase said.

"What?"

Chase tilted her head back and gave a light chuckle while she reached for his hand. As she caressed it slightly, Steve turned a little toward her, eager but somewhat confused.

"It's not a practice of mine to date my patients. During or after treatment."

"Oh," he nodded, "I see. I just wanted you to know that I do like you. It's not like I fell for you just because you helped me. It is genuine. Well, I guess I'd better go then."

"You are still proving you haven't learned anything from our sessions."

Steve tilted his head toward her a bit now, more confused than before. He wondered why Chase wore a sly smile across her lips. Steve felt rejected again and thought it was a bad idea to even mention that he liked her. Steve was attracted to her the first day he walked into her office, but his pain from the break up with Hailey made him view women differently. Sure, he recognized women and their beauty but dared not venture further than that. With each session, the more he opened up to Chase the more he felt as though he could trust her. Comfort came with confiding in her. But yet again, he had not chosen wisely.

"What do you mean? I remember everything from our sessions. Being assertive, recognizing what I want and regaining control of my destiny."

"True. So, what do you plan to do with what I've taught you?" Chase asked, still brandishing the grin.

"Well, having been rejected yet again . . . I'm going to take my ass home and wonder what the hell is wrong with me."

Chase laughed uncontrollably and fell back on the green turf. She placed her hands over her stomach and tried to catch her breath. Steve watched her giggle-fest with a stone face. Was she making fun of him after taking all of his money for the sessions?

"Why the hell are you laughing?" Steve asked.

"Steve calm down. You didn't let me finish. But the funny thing is," she said, "is that everything you learned from the sessions as you've just told me, you were *going* to do, but you doubted yourself. Why did you do that? Why is there always that doubt?"

"Because I had my answer!"

"You didn't let me finish. You have to listen more. What I was going to say was that I don't make it a practice to date my patients during or after treatment, but I was willing to make an exception for you. I really like you Steve."

"What?"

Chase laughed again. She sat up to look Steve eye to eye.

"Steve, I think you are a great man. It was just a bad time for you."

"It was," he admitted.

"I'd love to go out with you."

Steve smiled wide and gave her a hug that startled her a bit. He instinctively released her quickly in a non-verbal attempt to apologize for touching her without permission. Chase giggled again and gave him a peck on the lips to indicate that it was okay. Steve in turn leaned in to kiss her more slowly and passionately on her soft lips. The sensation that he felt was electrifying. He hadn't felt that chemistry since his last kiss from Hailey over a year ago. Chase was accepting and enjoyed the intensity of his kisses. While continuing to kiss her, he leaned Chase back down on the green as he positioned his body over hers. When he realized that he was on top of her, he stopped.

"I'm sorry," he said, slightly embarrassed.

Chase chuckled nervously and delicately wiped her moist lips with her fingertip. Steve moved back over to his side of the green and looked up at the night sky.

"It's okay," Chase told him. "You just got a little carried away. It's fine."

"I haven't felt that in so long, I'm sorry."

"Steve? Has it ever occurred to you that I may not have felt that in a long time either?"

"No. I just assumed..."

"Assumed what, Steve?"

"I just assumed that a woman like you, who's good at helping people make sense of their mess . . . I just thought you were taken."

"No, I'm not. I don't get the impression that a lot of guys would enjoy telling their friends, '*my girlfriend is a shrink*', ya know?" she chuckled.

"I wouldn't care what they thought."

Chase looked at him absorbedly. Steve sat up and kissed her again, more sincerely than the first time. Their bodies pressed together as they allowed each other to touch areas that just moments ago were off limits. Steve's hand went under Chase's shirt to feel her soft flesh. He squeezed her full breasts and covered her neck with kisses. Chase lifted his shirt to feel his bare back. If she had the strength, she probably would've ripped his shirt clear from his body. Sensing this, Steve removed it, flung it over his shoulder and recommenced tongue kissing and caressing Chase. She moaned and then stopped him by backing away. Steve looked in her eyes and waited for her to speak.

"I want you, Steve. Right here, right now."

"On the ninth hole?"

Chase pulled Steve closer to her, "Yes!"

"Well hell, let's do this!"

Chase pulled off her shirt and unfastened her pants. By the time she stepped out of her jeans, Steve was already naked. She looked surprised at how fast he had gotten undressed and giggled again. Steve felt a bit embarrassed not knowing why she was giggling.

"Oh no baby, I'm just . . . you got undressed fast!"

"Oh! Oh yeah! When it's time to get it in, it's time to get it in. I've got to be ready," he explained. "Speaking of ready..."

Chase looked down at Steve's erection and was impressed with what she saw. She smiled and reached for him to lay on the turf with her. Steve lay on his back, prepared for whatever was about to occur. Chase straddled him and pressed her body against his. She kissed his neck and down to his chest and nipples. Steve was trying to keep his load at bay because the kisses on his body from Chase were sending him into overdrive. He wasn't about to stop Chase when she went further and further down his body. The first sensation of her hot tongue on his tip was divine. Steve rolled his eyes backward and closed his lids tight. He sucked in the night air through his clenched teeth and blew the air out through his mouth. He lifted his head to see Chase swallowing him from that vantage point. He observed her for a moment, only to save the image for a later reflection, and then relaxed his head back on the green. Chase was good at what she did. Her therapy sessions worked wonders, and now it seemed as if her love making sessions would live up to the same reputation. Her mouth formed a tight suction around him as she slurped and moved her head up and down on him. Steve wanted to cum so bad, but he had to feel her. Under any other circumstance, he would've tasted her as well, but he wanted to feel her walls around him before he exploded. Chase didn't stop, she kept going. Her mouth moving up and down, her tongue swirling around his tip while his scrotum were being held gently in her hands. He loved this. He tried to focus on something else to keep him from cumming, but he kept seeing her smile and alluring eyes. He lifted his head and looked down again. He saw the top of her head moving up and down frantically while she pleasured him. With the most seductive glance, Chase looked up at Steve. To savor the visual, he immediately closed his eyes because he was going to bust. Just then – she stopped.

The crisp night air began to dry him. He looked down again and saw Chase reaching for her small clutch purse. She fished out a condom and put the tip of it in her mouth.

No she's not, Steve thought to himself.

Chase placed her mouth and condom on the tip of Steve's erection and began swallowing him. Simultaneously the condom rolled down on him as his thickness got stiffer. Chase deep throated him as the condom rolled down to the base of his hardness.

"Damn, Chase."

Chase straddled him without him entering her. She bent toward Steve to kiss his neck. After, she looked into his eyes.

"I like having my back touched. So I'm going to ride this in reverse."

"Shit."

Chase got up, turned around and stood over him with her back facing him. He looked up at her wonderful ass before she squatted down on him to position herself perfectly. Ready for this naughty cowgirl to ride him, he could not believe that he was about to bang his therapist! She lifted his stiffer than a 2x4 penis into position and sat gently on it. As it slid into her, she could feel her muscles tighten around him. She found a comfortable position and circled him. Swirling her hips around and around as she lifted and lowered herself back down. Steve eyed her ass that looked perfect on him. He wanted to cum so bad, but he didn't dare want to do that to Chase. Not after she spent the time to carefully put the condom on for him. Chase was clearly not about to stop until she got her first orgasm.

"Oh, ahhh," she moaned. She pounded against him harder and faster. Steve knew that she was almost there. He wanted to put her on her knees and go deep inside of her, but Chase was obviously taking control. She reached her first orgasm and then carefully turned to ride Steve face to face. She repositioned herself on top of him and bounced up and down on him, her breasts following suit. Steve watched her, his mouth agape as he saw beads of sweat forming between her breasts and on her flat stomach. He reached up and cupped her love lumps. Her nipples were hard, which aroused Steve. He lifted his body up and sucked on them, one to the other.

"Oh!!! I'm cumming!!!" Chase shouted.

At that moment Steve heard a light rumbling beneath them. He dare not take his off of Chase's bouncing breasts, but he heard what sounded like light hissing. His heart pounded faster as the sound alarmed him. He wanted to look in the direction of the sound, but couldn't tear his eyes off of her. The hissing sound intensified.

She was a beautiful woman, and looked beautiful while fucking him. Steve felt her muscles tighten around him as she bent slightly backward. He placed his hands on her waist to prevent her from leaning back too far. Just then, they were showered with water from the sprinklers. Chase looked down on Steve and smiled as her naked body was sprayed with water. Steve was about to blow, but he needed to deep stroke her before doing so. Chase made herself cum, now it was Steve's turn to make her. He lifted her by her waist and she moved her body off of him, wondering what he was about to do to her. He folded his soaked pants into a square and patted them.

"Put your knees on these," he told her.

"Oh anything you say wild man," she said. She bent over, putting her ass in the air and waited for him to enter her. Steve took in the view; she was waxed clean and had a pussy just as pretty as her. The water continued to mist on them. She got as comfortable as she could while being on all fours. From behind, he put his face in it and licked her slowly. He couldn't resist doing so.

"Yes," she moaned softly. Steve's tongue flickered very quickly. He knew that cunnilingus was one thing that he was a pro at performing. He gripped her hips to keep her from collapsing as her knees had begun to buckle underneath her. "Oh my. Oh my!!! Oh my *goodness*!"

Steve continued lapping at her clitoris, which sent her into a whirlwind of orgasms. She shimmied her hips and bucked in response to his feeding frenzy. He slapped her soaked behind to get her to behave and be still, but it only made her react more. Steve couldn't take it anymore. He wanted to feel her around his penis again. He lifted up and refused to ease his rod inside of her. As soon as his tip made the connection, he shoved himself perfectly inside of her. She responded with a low howl as she lifted her head upward toward the sky.

"Uh huhhh," Steve reaffirmed as to how good the insertion felt to him as well.

"I'm cumming!!!" she screamed.

"Go 'head, Chase. Cum all over me, baby." He gave her rump a firm, but sharp slap that made Chase melt all over him. "Ooooo, I like how that felt. Can you do it again for me, Chase? Come on baby, don't stop now. I'm gonna make her talk to me. Don't run from it, stay right there. Stay right there."

Chase was caught up in the orgasm that she didn't hear Steve's questions or comments. She concentrated on his deep strokes that filled her completely and erupted all over him again.

"Oh my gosh," she managed to breath out to Steve.

"You like that?" he asked.

She nodded, but Steve did not see because he was focused on how her narrow waist sloped nicely down to her ass. He was about to blow his load but wanted to make her cum at least seven or eight more times. Confidently, he knew he would have another chance to please her, so he climaxed right then.

"I don't want to cum yet, but I'm gonna!" he managed to grunt before exploding. He jerked her harder onto him by gripping her waist firmly. Chase's head dropped as she felt his final deep strokes and her pelvis pulsated in response. She observed the vision of his lean but muscular legs closely settled behind hers and closed her eyes gently for a moment. Steve breathed heavily and massaged the water from the sprinklers into her skin. He leaned his head backward as he kept his hands on her waist and hips. Water droplets extinguished the heat from his tongue while his mouth was parted slightly. He laid next to her on the green and she rested on his moist chest. The water from the sprinklers continued to cover them as they both exhaled deeply.

"Please tell me we can do that again soon," Steve muttered.

"Of course," she replied without hesitation.

Just then, they both saw headlights glaring against the trees in the distance. They both lifted up quickly then looked at each other, eyes widened.

"We gotta go!" Chase said.

They scrambled to gather up their soaked clothes and scurried off to the closest wooded area without being detected. Their giggles echoed in the night.

*   *   *   *

I stared at myself for a moment in the mirror. Although I wasn't developing wrinkles anywhere, I smoothed out my skin with my fingertips to magically erase them before they formed. I stared at the clock that hung on the wall and checked the time. It was 10:41. With a heavy audible sigh, I decided to play around with my hair for a moment to pass the time. I grabbed my wide-toothed comb and parted my hair to one side, brushing the long bangs forward to look like a young punk rocker. *No*, I thought to myself. 10:42. I inspected my teeth with a closed tooth, wide-mouthed grin. *Ah! I have a dental appointment next week*, I silently remembered. I tilted my head to one side, smirked and looked at my stomach underneath my black tank.

10:43. It's time.

I picked up the indicator with one hand and crossed my fingers with the other. I closed my eyes, took a deep breath and exhaled. I opened one eye, drooped my eyebrows and slowly opened the other eye. My shoulders slouched and my head immediately followed. I pitched the pregnancy indicator in the trash and placed my hand on the knob to prepare to let myself out of the bathroom. *I'm not going to cry*, I told myself, *I cried last time.*

This was the eighth test in five months. Failed again.

Ian was mixing himself a drink in the kitchen when I walked out of the bathroom. Slowly I crept up behind him and pressed my body close to his. He turned his head slightly in my direction and he smiled. I rested my head gently on his shoulder blade.

"It's okay, baby," he said.

"You are so sweet, Ian. But I'm getting concerned here. Why is this taking so long?"

"Jose', it will happen when it is supposed to happen. Don't rush it. Let's enjoy this time to ourselves because you know it will all belong to the kid when he comes."

"You mean when *she* comes?" I corrected him with a smile.

He turned around to face me and wrapped his arms around me. "When our *heir* comes, my Queen Josephine."

"My King Ian," I responded.

He took a quick swallow of his drink that he concocted and gave an affirming utterance of pleasure.

"Torture me, why don't you?" I stared at his drink.

"You want a sip?" he waved the rim of the glass under my nose.

"No, I'm okay. I just want to be pregnant!" I moseyed over to the couch and flopped down on it. Pouting over the results, I tilted my head back. Ian looked over at me and set the glass down on the counter.

"Babe, I want to ask you something, but I don't want you to get upset," he started.

"Uh oh. What is it?"

"Are you anxious to have a baby because Hailey and Camilla have kids? Are you trying to keep up?"

I looked Ian square in the eye with my mouth gaped.

"Are you serious right now?"

"See? I didn't want you to get upset."

"I'm not upset. And no! I'm not trying to keep up with them! It's just that we have been married for almost two years now. I thought we were pregnant before we even picked out our rings. Remember? This feels like a quest at this point. Don't you want to be a father? I know I want to be a mother."

Ian walked over to me and sat down. He placed a comforting hand on my thigh.

"And you will be a great one," he said. He kissed my forehead and squeezed me close to him with a one armed hug. "It will happen."

I patted his hand and nodded. He was right, but my impatience was beginning to take a toll on me and our relationship. I loved Ian dearly and at the very least wanted to show him just how much by making him a father. However, if this doesn't happen for us soon, I will be taking matters into my own hands.

3

Bryan Bryant had been back in the D.C. area for a little over three months now. After the devastating blow to his ego when he discovered that he was not the father to Hailey's child, he took a lengthy sabbatical. If one did not know him intimately, there was a distinct possibility that he may not be recognized right away. He looked completely different. Bryan had always kept his hair cut low with a manicured hairline. His hair had grown out wildly as did his facial hair, which encompassed an unruly moustache and matching full beard. His clothing had transformed from tailored suits and Italian shoes to deep V-necked pullovers, wide legged linen pants and sandals. He had spent most of his time in Jamaica and did an enormous amount of writing. He completed three self help books; one in regards to relationships, another on self publishing, and his last on building businesses from ground zero with minimal finances. Bryan also offered paid tours of the island, which had been highly successful. His touring company paid for his stay there. He had come to know so many people that most of his food and drinks were almost always complimentary.

The Jamaican women loved his debonair style and manly charm as did the Dominicans, whom he visited often. Because he traveled to the Dominican regularly, he also worked at a busy resort there. His frequent visits there allowed him to brush up on his Spanish.   He was also learning quite a bit of Patois in Jamaica. Several people from the U.S. visited and would fill him in on the latest and greatest. His talks were extensive when there were visitors from the D.C. area.   That was the only time he longed for home. It surprised him how much things had changed in more than a year. Thinking of D.C. made him think of his past life there. He still loved Hailey, despite her betrayal. Although Bryan had a modest share of Jamaican and Dominican women, he still craved Hailey. She was without a doubt the only woman that made him feel a sense of purpose in his life. Despite being without Hailey, he felt as though this chapter in his life had positively started over for the better.

Many times he toiled over going to see her when he returned to D.C. He thought it would only be fair to let her live her life since it had been so long since they spoke. Besides, Hailey was raising a son now. Bryan had no idea even if she and Steve had gotten back together. He didn't want to disrupt her life and wasn't confident he wanted Hailey to see the islander Bryan Bryant – whose nickname in Jamaica had become 'Wolf'. This was because he wasn't a Rastafarian and wasn't there long enough to have lengthy dreadlocks. Although he felt an unsurpassed amount of love and respect in Jamaica, when he returned to D.C., something seemed "off" to him. He found it hard to sleep at night and would awaken to a dark room. He kept his IPad on his night stand in case any thoughts occurred in the middle of the night or if he just felt like writing. He used it for the latter most nights. He just wrote. His words didn't make sense to him, but he could not stop writing. It wasn't a journal, as he felt journals were just glorified diaries, it was more so a collection of thoughts, and a timeline of actions he may have done throughout the week, the month or perhaps earlier that day.

"I can't sleep," Bryan muttered as he rolled over on his back. He stared at the dark ceiling tracing the patterns the streetlights drew there through the gaped blinds. He sighed roughly and flipped the switch on his lamp. Rubbing his eyes, he reached for his IPad and tapped the screen. He clicked on a file labeled "Untitled" and scrolled all the way to the end. He never reread any of his previous writings until his books were finished and ready to be edited. Instead of writing in his book tonight, he decided to jot down a memo.

He simply wrote, "I need to see Hailey. How can I feel pain and love at the same time? Before I see her, I'm going to see a specialist. At least I will be able to confront her and handle anything she may say to me."

Bryan rested his head back against the pillow. He closed the memo, did a search for specialists in the area and selected the first name listed in Google.

"Hmm, she seems to be highly accredited. Where is her office?"

Bryan continued searching the screen with his eyes.

"Okay, she's in D.C. I'll call and make an appointment with her tomorrow. This can't continue."

He lifted up and sat on the edge of the bed. He tossed the IPad on top of his comforter and made his way to his master bathroom. He sloshed the minty wash in and around his mouth and made a gurgling sound before dispelling it into the sink. He looked up at his rugged reflection in the mirror and stroked his beard gently.

"Let's see if you can help me Dr. Chase Billingsley."

*   *   *   *

While Donovan spooned Tamar as they rested in bed, his arm was thrown sloppily across her waist. He squirmed some, as if he were having a bad dream, which caused Tamar to slightly stir in her sleep. Donovan gripped her tight and kicked his feet slightly.

"Noooo!" Donovan yelled.

Tamar snapped to attention and threw Donovan's arm off of her. "Donovan? Wake up!"

"What? What?"

"You were dreaming," she looked down at him as he gathered himself and looked around the dark room with confusion, "and you yelled."

"I did? Oh I'm sorry baby."

"Donovan, you know I have to give a summation in the morning, baby!"

"I know, I'm sorry. Well I have to give a closing argument tomorrow too. I guess I'm just frustrated with the whole thing." He rubbed her back and gently tried to pull her down beside him. Once on her back, she turned to face him and he stroked her face tenderly.

"It must be difficult squaring off against Celeste, huh?" Tamar asked him with a sigh.

"Not really. She's gotten in a few digs during the case that's for sure."

"I hope the judge checked her smug ass."

"Baby . . ."

"Sorry. It hasn't exactly been all roses working for her. She has her moments, but you would be so proud of me baby. It's been all business with me. But I think she hates that everyone else in the office just loves Tamar!"

Donovan gave her a kiss on her lips as his hand moved under the covers to caress her other lips.

"I'm sure they do," he signified.

"Ooo."

"Since we're up . . ."

"Mm, yeah?" Tamar asked through a soft moan.

"You want to put each other back to sleep?" Before waiting for a response, he coddled her breasts and took one into his mouth. Circling and teasing its raised mound caused Tamar to clench her teeth and suck in the night air. She looked down at her man and enjoyed the view of how his tongue flicked her nipple. They both slept in the nude, so there wasn't any clothing to prohibit their flesh from becoming one at any time during a late night or early morning.

After two years of being together, Donovan could still turn Tamar on with a delicate touch and sometimes even with just a suggestive glance. She loved the amount of sex appeal he had. She enjoyed his intimate caress before she drifted off to sleep at night, which usually resulted in erotic dreams. Even still, Tamar continued to excite Donovan. The way she would lean in to his body to reach for something, her fragrance and a slight touch on his chest when she spoke to him. They were clearly in love with one another and the sex was more than amazing. Tamar had taken up "hot yoga" to improve on her flexibility. Hot yoga was still yoga, but done in a heated room. Her flexibility increased, which came in handy in the bedroom as well as other areas of the house.

Donovan ended up renting his home and moved in with Tamar about seven months ago. Her home was slightly bigger than Donovan's and was situated much closer to the city. Since they both worked on and near 15th and L streets, her place was the more logical choice. They weren't engaged yet and Tamar did not press the issue with him at all. She figured when Donovan was ready, he would propose. However, she secretly had a timeline set for him that he knew nothing about. Her rationale was that after a year of living together, he should be making preparations to pop the question. If he didn't, she was prepared to fan the fire under his ass just a touch. In her heart of hearts, she knew that it would take work, but ultimately that they would have a great life together. They communicated well, they both enjoyed each other physically and they both were great with their finances. Not to mention, they looked incredible together. It was a complete match.

But . . . Tamar had some doubts and she guessed that deep down, Donovan may have had some of his own.

"Mmm baby, you know that is my spot," Tamar whispered in Donovan's ear.

He turned his head and gave her a quick peck on the neck.

"Come on, ride this," he commanded as he popped her bottom firmly and pulled her up on him by her waist. Tamar straddled his midsection and leaned over to kiss him deeply on his soft lips. He welcomed her incoming kiss and rubbed her back tenderly as he met her part of the way. Her full bottom filled his hands as her wetness slathered his pelvis.

Gingerly, his fingertips teased the trench of her spine at the base of her back and then upward toward her neck. He wrapped his mouth over one of her plump breasts as the other filled his hand. Tamar's head fell backward as she enjoyed the sensation of rubbing her clitoris across the shaft of his hardened penis. Donovan gripped her ass firmly and lifted her up and down on him, simulating the movements of what would soon occur once he entered her. She teased him as she hula-hooped her hips around on top of him. He looked down at her lips that she had waxed clean last week. Just above that he smiled at her silliness, because she had her pelvic hair waxed in the shape of an arrow pointing toward her pussy. Her narrow waist wiggled from side to side as her hips continued to move around on him. His eyes followed her body upward toward her mouth, which held a wry smile across them. She rested both of her hands on his chest and Donovan couldn't help but wonder what her thoughts were behind that devilish grin of hers.

He gripped her ass and scooted both of them toward the edge of the bed. Tamar crossed her ankles around his lower back as he prepared to stand. He lifted her and turned her around so Tamar's back was toward the bed. He held her there for a moment, long enough for her to cease her kissing and for them to lock eyes with one another.

"Yes?" she asked seductively.

Just then, Donovan took one hand and unlocked her ankles from his back. He gripped her under her armpits, gave her a quick peck and threw her back roughly on the bed. His aggression often pleased her. She smiled after lightly bouncing on the king sized bed then lifted her head to look at him. He stroked his member with one hand and parted her legs with the other.

"Hmm, you look sexy doing that baby," she said to him.

He gripped her legs and gave her a single tug toward the edge of the bed so he could align their pelvises one to the other. He continued stroking his member and reached for a condom. Tamar spread her silk across her clit with her fingertips. The more she saw his hands stroke his hard penis, the creamier she became. She couldn't wait to feel him inside of her. Each time felt like a new experience between them. Carefully, she watched him as he unwrapped the rubber and rolled it onto his penis. Afterward, he looked up at her and smiled. His pectorals flexed slightly as he reached for her legs.

Strange, she thought.

Tamar parted her legs wide in a split as she prepared for him to enter her without restriction.

"Beautiful," he said as he got stiffer.

However, he closed her legs. With her feet pointed straight to the ceiling, he crossed her ankles and rested them on the right side of his head. He gripped her hips and slowly entered her. He closed his eyes at the tightened sensation and pumped ferociously inside of her. Tamar could barely contain herself during his powerful thrusts. She closed her eyes to prepare for the sonic boom that was about to cause her entire body to have an orgasmic quake.

"Yes, give it to me," Donovan murmured as he watched Tamar's breasts bounce with his strokes.

Her mind was somewhere else. While Donovan's bedroom voice could make Denzel Washington jealous, it snapped her out of her trance.

Tamar remembered him.

She often thought about him and he still called her from time to time. When he entered her mind she tried to distract herself. The more they met, the harder it was to push him out of her memory. Every once in a while they would link up to enjoy one another. No love, no strings, no life altering decisions were ever going to occur, just sex. That was their agreement. Even with this agreement intact, she never forgot their first encounter.

It was at a law conference that Celeste insisted Tamar attend in San Antonio, Texas. Tamar clearly did not have the time to go, but it was an opportunity for her to be educated, which she never refused. Tamar always enjoyed men who were articulate, clever, well dressed and witty. That was what initially drew her to Mr. Hedley a few years ago. Unfortunately for her, she had just gotten involved with Donovan, so a fling with Mr. Hedley was out of the question.

This particular speaker at the law conference in San Antonio had totally captivated Tamar. He was Arabic-American, well spoken, well dressed and extremely attractive. He gave new meaning to the phrase tall, dark and handsome. She entered his break-out session late because she had to make an important phone call back to the firm. She quickly read his bio before entering. An accompanying picture of him was not included in the program booklet, but his topic was interesting; Cyber Law in Thriving Corporations.

"Taj Morcos," Tamar quietly said to herself on the outside of the conference room. As she skimmed his bio, she noted that he was born and raised in New York, attended Harvard Law School and studied Cyber Security and Forensics. Sir Morcos owned his own law firm in New York for ten years and according to his own words, was highly successful.

Tamar tried to enter the conference room quietly, but the door was stuck. After several yanks and rattles the handle she was able to pry the door open. Upon entering, everyone's attention turned to her. Somewhat startled, she stopped in her tracks, looked at everyone intentionally, and then focused on the lecturer who brandished a gleaming white smile.

"Taj Morcos," Tamar started, "Harvard Law graduate who also studied Cyber Security and Forensics."

Taj smiled even wider and nodded his head gently.

"You even own a law firm and this crappy hotel couldn't find you a conference room with working doors?"

Taj chuckled, while some of the women clicked their teeth at her dry joke. As always, the men stared at Tamar, and she knew what those stares usually meant. What was her favorite position and what type of underwear was she donning?

"You know you are right," Taj responded to Tamar. "What's your name?"

"Tamar Woodruff."

"Please, have a seat, Ms. Woodruff," he suggested.

When Tamar found a seat in the rear of the conference room, Taj immediately objected.

"There's a seat right up front here. An unobstructed view," he said.

By now some of the women were huffing and shifting uneasily in their seats at the amount of attention Taj showed Tamar.

"Oh sure!" she agreed and sat down.

Taj tried not to stare at her legs when she crossed them, but he did spend a hefty amount of his lecture on her side of the room. Tamar couldn't take her eyes off of him. Dark wavy hair, chiseled jaw line, brown eyes, shadow beard and goatee, hazel complexion, tall lean frame. He looked more like a well paid model than a lawyer.

"Damn baby, you cumming again?" Donovan asked Tamar as he long-stroked her out of her nostalgic state.

"Donovan," she moaned.

"Yeah, baby?" he lifted her up and kissed her mouth and neck. "Hmm."

She wanted to be up front with him and tell her of her indiscretions just to clear her guilty conscience. The more it tormented her, the more it made no sense to hurt him with this information. The last time she saw Taj was two months ago and she didn't love him – nor was she going to leave Donovan for Taj. Not at all. She loved Donovan and knew that he was the man for her. They were a team equipped to conquer the legal world together. Even though it had been a few months since she last saw Taj, they spoke on the phone just two days ago. It was a lengthy conversation, reminiscing and giggling like dating teens attending rival high schools. She lacked nothing with Donovan and it nagged her that she stepped out on him with Taj. It was unnecessary but not without intention. Taj and Tamar had instant chemistry from the moment she stepped into the conference hall.

Donovan was about to blow inside of Tamar. He stroked harder and more ferociously. He gripped her body tighter into his, she tenderly kissed his earlobe and that sent Donovan over the edge.

"Damn girl . . . Hmmm," he grunted.

Tamar lay back on the bed and looked up at Donovan who was weakening from his orgasm. He laid his body partially over Tamar's and breathed his hot breath toward her neck. He swallowed hard and kissed her shoulder – his bedroom eyes fixated upon hers.

"I'm drained," he said to her. He closed his eyes and rested his hand on her stomach.

"Me too. I'll get you a towel," she said to him and wobbled her way to the bathroom. She ran the fluffy wash cloth under the warm running water.

As she reached for the soap and begin lathering the cloth, she gazed at herself in the mirror. She observed her naked body head to toe. As she stared, she recalled the various areas of her body where Taj's lips had been – where he nibbled and licked. She loved the way his long fingers felt all over her body. It was the way that he took the time to caress her, which was an appreciative touch. Taj didn't grope at her, he adored her body and that feeling stayed with her for months.

Donovan stood at the bathroom threshold as he stared at Tamar for a moment. He noticed her far away glare and peered over her shoulder. The wash cloth was completely covered in soap and the water had almost reached the brim of the sink's basin. He watched her for a moment longer, noticing her eyes boring a hole into the ceramic floor. It wasn't until the faintest of smiles crossed her lips that he decided to snap her out of her trance.

"You okay?" he asked her.

"Oh shit!" she looked at Donovan's reflection in the mirror and stumbled slightly. He lifted his hands to catch her in case she fell, but she didn't. "You scared me baby."

"You think you got enough soap?" He looked down at the sudsy glob in her hands.

"Oh!" she turned the knobs off for the faucet, leaving bubbles all over the handles. "I guess so."

She left the cloth in the basin and left Donovan standing in the bathroom. Turning to stare at her strange gesture, Donovan watched her climb into bed. He looked back at the suds, lifted the cloth and gently cleaned himself. Tamar lay on her back staring straight up at the ceiling while Donovan rinsed himself and the cloth. When he was done, he flung the cloth in the sunken tub as if he were making a line drive to a base runner for the Nationals. His fingertips roughly raked the light switch off and he violently threw his body into bed next to her. Without looking at him and ignoring his antagonistic entry, she lightly rubbed his leg.

Donovan wasn't the least bit moved by her poor attempt at affection. He was more concerned about what she was thinking at that particular moment. This wasn't the first time Tamar had taken a mental vacation in the middle of doing something. She once burned his eggs one morning and didn't apologize, just tossed them in the trash. What was on his woman's mind, he wondered and intended to find out.

Tamar continued to stroke Donovan's leg hoping the constant motion would lullaby her back to sleep. Thoughts of Taj were sudden and strong during sex with Donovan. She was unsure why exactly. Maybe it was the comment he made to her before he hung up during their last phone conversation.

"I'm coming to DC to see you real soon," Taj's hypnotic voice told her over the phone. "You thought the last time we were together was incredible, well that's nothing . . . *nothing* compared to what I'm going to do to you when I see you."

4

Hailey opened the door wide enough for Steve to bring in their sleeping toddler that was resting comfortably in his arms. Alex was the spitting image of Steve, just given to the world in a smaller package . . . at the moment. Steve had just returned from having his little munchkin paint, sing, play with clay, problem solve and story tell all day at Gymboree. It was the one structured father and son activity on Saturday for Steve and Alex each week. Steve also kept Alex two other nights during the week, one of which included time with his other son, Gabe. It was hard work, but he loved his boys. Today's task at Gymboree for Steve was convincing Alex why eating clay would not be a good idea. After about the fourth explanation, Steve finally got through to him. Alex's final thought on how clay tasted was, "It's nassy!" which in toddler terms meant it was nasty. Steve's joy came from watching his son's development and physical growth. Even though his other son Gabe favored Camilla, he definitely had Steve's eyes.

Hailey rubbed her sleeping son's back and smiled to herself when she saw that he had a yellow sun painted on his cheek and stickers on the back of his hands.

"He had fun today," Steve replied as he carried Alex up to his bedroom.

While Steve was upstairs tucking Alex in bed, Hailey tossed a few toys of his into his toy bin that was next to the sofa. Peering up the steps to make sure Steve was not returning Hailey quickly ran into the powder room to make sure she still looked as presentable as she did earlier that day. Bending over at the waist, she lifted each boob further up in her bra so they looked plump and perky as the tops peeked above her V-neck shirt. She found some clear lip gloss in the medicine cabinet and quickly smeared a light coat on her lips. Wiggling her hips, she pulled her low rise jeans down so they settled more on the curvature of her hips. She twisted slightly to get a good look at her rump, which looked great in her favorite jeans, and fled the bathroom before Steve returned.

She wandered around the living room doing nothing, but wanted to appear to be busy. Because she didn't want to readjust anything, she refused to sit down before he came back into the living room. Hailey wanted Steve to see the desirable, sexy side of Hailey, not just his son's mother. She could hear Steve's footsteps upstairs preparing to descend. Getting at the ready for Steve's initial view, she got on all fours with her ass in plain sight while she pretended she'd lost something behind the couch.

"He's all tucked in," he said as he trotted downstairs. When he got to the living room, he stopped for a moment and watched Hailey's arched back and round bottom move around as she fished for whatever disappeared behind the couch. He waited before saying anything to her, as he was admiring the scenery.

Hailey heard the hesitation in his footsteps and noticed that he abruptly stopped speaking. The fact that she knew he was staring at her made her smile to herself. She only needed to get him to approach her and decided to arch her back more and stick her behind further up.

"Uh oh, help!" she said.

Steve rushed over, "You okay?"

"I think I'm stuck!"

Steve placed his hand on the curve of her back and tried to peer over her to see what held her arm hostage. Without a clear view of what was happening, he managed to get a sneak peek of her cleavage. He was awarded an even better view when Hailey threw her head back to look up at Steve. He wanted to kiss her moist looking lips so bad, but knew he couldn't.

"Am I going to be like this forever?" she said and then smiled up at Steve.

"What? Stuck?" he asked.

"No," she started as she yanked her arm gently. She looked up in his eyes again, licked her lips slowly and said, "at your mercy."

Steve chuckled and stood up slowly, "That's a new one. Get up Hailey."

"Seriously, I'm stuck."

Steve stepped back and continued to be in awe of her rear end. He smiled and shook his head at her antics. Last year, Steve had almost fallen prey to her advances. Hailey made coffee for them and she clumsily spilled it all over the front of her t-shirt. The coffee was so hot, that she immediately took it off. She had on a lacey black bra and her breasts had gotten sizably larger since Alex was born. Steve had always been a breast man and Hailey knew this was his weakness. They ended up rolling around on the sofa in each other's arms kissing passionately. He stopped her when she had begun to undo his pants, quickly grabbed his car keys and left her there.

Tonight Steve was unsure what was going on with her and why the sudden attraction to him again, but he knew where all roads to Hailey led. It would lead to a severely broken heart and additional therapy. The only two good things that emerged from their split were Alex, and his therapist Chase. Steve wanted to keep it that way – indefinitely. However, Hailey didn't know his intentions. What she did know was that Steve would and could fall in love with her again. The time they spent together, the child they created together and the love he once had for her wasn't going to vanish. She intended to reignite that flame and keep it burning until her last breath.

"Uh," she grunted, "finally free! Thanks for nothing, Steve!"

"You need help getting up?" he chuckled.

"What's so funny?"

"You, Hailey," Steve told her blatantly. "Look, what's going on?"

Hailey held up her mangled bracelet and a Thor figurine. She brandished a chastising look as she sneered at Steve.

"I'm sorry, Hailey!" he reached for the figurine and tossed it in Alex's toy bin. He began caressing her wrist.

"I told you I was stuck!" She patted Steve's arm and sat back on the couch.

"I'm sorry. I thought it was an attempt at seduction gone bad."

Hailey frowned at him when he said that. Steve dropped his shoulders after realizing that it was a bit harsh. He lowered his head and then looked back at Hailey with his eyes.

"Steve, don't get it twisted okay? We have to be cordial for the sake of Alex and it's been going very well. But I know our ship has sailed . . ."

"Correction, it wrecked and sunk," Steve said.

Hailey shot him another damning look. "Uhm, is something wrong?"

"No."

"I mean, is this '*shit on Hailey*' night?"

"No. Our m.o. is to discuss Alex. That's it."

"Wait a minute," Hailey stood to her feet, "what is with the cold shoulder? We can't chit chat? Chill for a minute."

"A quick minute," Steve cautioned her. He sat at the opposite end of the couch and watched Hailey get more comfortable at the other end. She smoothed her hair back into her ponytail and tried to ignore his abruptness.

"So what did my baby do today?" She sat forward to get the details.

Steve gave an exhaustive sigh before he spoke, "Finger painted, sang, tried to eat clay and jumped."

Hailey, expecting him to elaborate more, slouched back on the couch and shook her head in disbelief. "Really, Steve? Am I keeping you from something? Do you have to be somewhere else at the moment?"

"Not right now, no."

"Your whole demeanor is like I'm worrying you or something," Hailey barked.

Steve rubbed the back of his head and tried to choose his words carefully before he spoke. "Sorry Hailey. Yes, we had a great time. Alex is worn out, I'm worn out. I just want to relax."

"I mean, okay. That was all you had to say. You can take your shoes off," she stood and headed toward the kitchen. "You want a beer?"

Steve stood to his feet and stretched. "No, I'm gonna go. I will talk to you on Tuesday."

Hailey stopped in her tracks as she watched Steve head for the door to leave. When he failed to look back to bid a courteous farewell, her mouth and shoulders dropped the moment the door closed behind him.

"Well, what the hell was that?" she muttered to herself just before she sucked her teeth. For a moment she stared at her cell phone, contemplating making a call to her most trusted confidante. Josephine knew just about all of the details of her relationship and Hailey valued her advice. She knew that after they survived the lies that Steve told on Josephine about sleeping with him, she could trust Josephine with anything.

"Hello?" Josephine asked.

"Hey girl, Steve just left. And he left in a hurry. What was that all about?"

"I haven't the slightest, Hailey. Didn't he have my little man today?"

"Yes," Hailey said.

"He's probably just bushed. Try not to think too far into it," Josephine tried to settle Hailey's thoughts before they ran amuck. "Are we still doing dinner tomorrow? Camilla may come too."

"I'm still good for dinner, but on the real, you and I need to talk . . . without Camilla," Hailey admitted.

"Um okay . . . I already mentioned it to her."

"Make something up," Hailey suggested to her. "Look, I gotta go. I will talk to you tomorrow at dinner."

Hailey abruptly hung up with Josephine and thought to herself for a moment. She needed a game plan in place and needed to act on it as swiftly as possible. After a few moments of concentrated effort, she had it all figured out and would put it into motion as soon as possible. Something so simple – yet effective. Hailey was upset that she hadn't thought of it much sooner. Game on.

5

Donovan swirled his Jack and Coke in his glass as he flaunted a sly grin. He chuckled softly to himself as he sat at the bar of the Jefferson Hotel on 16th street. His cell phone rested beside the soaked bar napkin that his drink held. After his compelling closing argument, the jury took all of an hour to deliberate. They sided with Donovan. He'd won.

The bartender set another Jack and Coke in front of Donovan.

"There you go," he said.

"Thanks, but I didn't order another. I'm not quite finished with this one," Donovan told him as he slightly pushed the glass back in his direction.

"It's from the lady," the bartender nodded in her direction.

Donovan grinned again to himself and didn't even turn to acknowledge who the woman was. He already knew. He gulped the rest of his drink down and nudged the empty glass toward the bartender. She knew that this was Donovan's place to grab himself a celebratory drink after a win in court. After today's win, his actions would not vary. She knew that he liked Jack and Cokes with very little ice and a wedge of lime. Why wouldn't she?

"Can you please get her a Vodka martini," Donovan asked the bartender. "And make sure there are three olives. That's how she likes it. Dirty."

"Sure thing," the bartender told him. "Would you like me to send it over?"

"No. Leave it here so she can come and get it."

"Sure thing."

After the drink was perfectly made and set next to Donovan at the bar, she made her way over to him.

"You know these are on me," Celeste told him as she approached. She placed a tender hand on his shoulder blade and peered at her drink to ensure it was correctly made. After she placed two bills on the bar, she carefully lifted her drink to prevent too much from spilling over the rim.

"Congratulations," she told him. "So . . . that's three drinks . . . 35 dollars. Not too bad. Have a good one, Donovan."

"Thank you, Celeste."

Celeste retreated with her drink. Donovan peered up at the television monitor that was set to CNN. He peered at his phone, noted that he had no messages, and then checked the time. He had about an hour and a half before traffic would start to get a little hectic. Luckily he didn't live too far so it wouldn't be that bad. But just in case, he wanted to allow himself enough time to make it home to his beloved Tamar. He gulped down his drink, which left him slightly inebriated. He walked to the lobby and pressed the call button for the elevator. The effects of the alcohol jabbed his senses.

The doors to the elevator opened. Once inside, he leaned against the wall as the elevator made its ascent. When it reached the proper floor, he started down the corridor and carefully checked the numbers to the rooms.

Donovan muttered to himself, "331, 333, ahh, here it is, 335."

The door was left open and he walked inside. Celeste turned to face him. Her blouse was balled up at her feet as she began pulling her skirt past her full hips and bottom. Her rich dark skin was electrifying against the royal blue lingerie. Donovan slammed the door shut and tore out of his clothes. It felt familiar to be with Celeste. For several months after the incident at the restaurant when Tamar hauled off and slapped them both, the two ceased communication. Donovan never called her to apologize on behalf of Tamar. Celeste felt needlessly neglected and when Donovan didn't check on her, she quietly decided to move on and let things be. She buried herself in her work and cringed every time she heard Tamar's voice, the mention of her name or whenever she saw her in the office. Celeste really couldn't stand how nice everyone was to Tamar and how well liked she was. To Celeste, she would always be the one who stole her man from her. Celeste just wanted the bitch gone, but Tamar was stubborn and refused to go, no matter how bad the cases were that she was assigned. Celeste figured the only reason Tamar stayed was to just keep an eye on her.

A while ago, Celeste was meeting with a client at a local restaurant when she saw Donovan. He grabbed himself a drink and noticed Celeste just before he was about to leave. After eight months of not speaking, he finally apologized. Donovan provided his number to her again, but Celeste never deleted it from her phone. She kept it because she knew in her heart that they would one day speak again. However, what she did not anticipate was that they would be fucking again. Donovan was supposed to be *her* husband. Celeste was going to stop at nothing to make sure that this destiny be fulfilled.

"You look incredible," Donovan told her. "You know I like my chocolate thick."

"Ooo," Celeste said with a smile, "I know. Which makes me wonder just why you are still with that scrawny Tamar. Yuck."

Donovan stopped, his libido deflated. "Don't do that."

Celeste exhaled sharply, "Whatever." She lifted her foot to cue Donovan to take her five inch heels off.

"Whatever? We talked about this. No mention of her at all," Donovan blindly tossed her shoes to the floor and then finished undressing.

"Yes, whatever," Celeste confirmed. She stretched her body out across the bed, legs bent at the knee with her moist pussy being offered up to him. "Just get over here and fuck my brains out."

"Oh, I plan to."

Donovan massaged her calves on up to her thighs. He nuzzled her crotch and basked in the aroma of her femininity. He roughly pulled her hips down toward him causing the bed spread to bunch up around her buttocks. He slapped the full part of her hip and gripped it tightly between his fingers. Celeste wriggled around in delight and anticipation. Donovan firmly gripped her waist with both hands and licked her navel with the tip of his tongue.

"Ooo," Celeste moaned.

Donovan took his fingertips and traced the band of her panties. He looked into her eyes and gave her a slight grin before he ripped them ferociously from her body.

"Yes!" she affirmed.

Donovan buried his face deep into her crotch, flicking his tongue rapidly across her clitoris. Celeste arched her back as the sensation made her eyes roll around in her head. Donovan rested his hand in the trench created by her hips and legs to keep her from inching away from him.

The mutely lit room quickly smelled of perfume, cologne and sex as Celeste's back writhed around.

"Hmm," Donovan uttered, sharing his appreciation for her reaction to his oral act.

"Donnie!"

He continued feasting on her as he reached up and squeezed her ample breasts. Donovan loved how Celeste's full but firm body felt in his hands when he squeezed her. Her chocolate skin was sweet to the taste and pleasing to his eye. Celeste was a gorgeous woman and Donovan could not deny himself of her any longer. Her wetness was unlike any other woman's that he had been with, as did the way her body received him. Her walls laminated his full member.

"Donnie, fuck me now!"

He lifted his body and looked up at her, aroused by her demand.

"Naa, you gonna get on your knees and suck on this dick first. Can you do that for me?"

"But Donnie…"

"Get on your knees now, bitch and suck this dick!"

"Okay . . ."

Celeste hopped up quickly and took her position in front of Donovan. She softly kissed his sac and lapped his tip with her tongue, teasing him. She slowly eased him into her mouth. Donovan pulled the air of the room into his parted mouth through closed teeth. He placed one hand on her head and rubbed it to show his pleasure. Celeste looked up at him to see his reaction as she continued to draw him deeper and deeper into her mouth. She slowly pulled his thick penis further into her mouth until her bottom lip grazed his sac.

"Ah shit!" Donovan exclaimed.

Celeste deep throated him and used her tongue to tickle his sac.

"Shit! Shit girl!" Donovan said. "Ah!"

Celeste's head bobbed up, down, back and forth, determined to have Donovan submit to her sexually. Celeste was going to gain this man's proposal and steal him back from Tamar. If that meant subjecting herself to any sexual fantasy he had, she was going to do so. She loved meeting up with him every week and especially loved making him too weak to perform for Tamar for the next day or so.

"Damn that feels good."

Celeste stopped just long enough to ask him, "You like that huh?" She rubbed her lips around his tip as she held it like a microphone.

"Yes."

"Does she do it like that?"

Donovan looked down at Celeste as she smiled, his penis wrapped by her delicate fingers.

"Get up!"

He lifted her by her shoulders and pulled her toward him, chest to chest he squeezed her tightly against his body.

"Ow."

"You just don't learn do you?"

"Donnie, I..."

"No, you *want* me to punish you. Is that it? Huh?"

"Donovan..."

"Shut up!" He threw her back on the bed. Celeste tried to collect herself on the bed as her eyes filled with excitement. She scooted back slightly to prepare herself for Donovan's strike against her body. "Come here my dirty whore. You gonna learn today!"

"Donnie, please!"

Donovan flipped Celeste's body over wildly. He mounted her from behind, wrapped one arm around her waist and lifted her up on all fours. Celeste arched her back and put her ass high in the air for Donovan to enter her. Donovan placed both hands on her shoulders and entered her deeply.

"Oh! My God!" Celeste managed to say.

"You like that rough shit, huh?"

"Yes baby!"

"Well if you like it rough, that's how you gonna get it, bitch."

Donovan deep stroked her for several minutes, his speed varying between strokes. His midsection pounded roughly against her soft round ass. Gripping her shoulders made him go deeper inside of her. The sensation made him want to erupt, but he wasn't ready to orgasm just yet.

"Oh Donnie, I'm . . . I'm cumming!"

He stroked even faster as her walls tightened around him. Shockwaves from her orgasm rippled from her pelvis through her entire body.

"Yes," Donovan managed to say.

Celeste gyrated to meet his strokes.

"Ooo, yeah," Donovan affirmed. "You know I like that."

This continued for quite some time before Donovan was compelled to have Celeste ride him for the finale.

"Get on this," he demanded as he lay feet pointed upward, his hard penis following suit. Celeste slowly and carefully climbed into the saddle and settled her buttocks on his midsection. She put one hand on Donovan's chest and the other on the headboard. She rocked forward and backward, up and down squeezing herself tighter around him with each compression.

"Yes," she said, the word passing through barely parted lips.

"Let me know when you are getting ready to cum," he ordered.

She didn't acknowledge his request. Instead, she concentrated on her strokes, clenched her muscles, circled his penis and tickled his sac. She felt a monster of an orgasm about to blow inside of her. Donovan watched his midsection, enjoying the sight of how he went in and out of her. He felt her moving up and down more rapidly, expecting to feel her ooze all over him. Donovan held his orgasm for as long as he could, he wanted to cum with her.

"Oh . . .," Celeste moaned, "Oh God, here it comes baby . . . here it comes!"

Donovan looked up at Celeste to see her prepare for orgasm. The moment she squeezed her eyes tight and her eyebrows bowed in ecstasy, he reached up with both hands, placed them on her throat and began to choke her.

Her entire body tensed up, her insides completely holding Donovan's penis hostage, which made him cum harder than he had before with her. She tried to gasp for air as a single tear trailed from her eyes down her cheek. Donovan grunted as he released himself and waited for the follow on orgasmic sensations. He released her throat and his hands slowly glided gently down the front of her body. Past her collar bone, her tender plump breasts down to the slope of her stomach until he rested them on her thighs. He laid his head to one side, still basking in the hard and fast orgasm. He could still feel Celeste's moist entry pulsating around his softening rod. She still coughed to recapture air to her lungs. She took one deep breath and rolled off of Donovan to collapse on the bed next to him.

"Oh my God, that was great," she told him while she lightly teased his nipple.

"I hate doing that shit, Celeste. I only do that because you like it."

"Bullshit, Donnie. You love that shit. You like calling me a bitch and a whore while we fuck. I never heard your ass grunt like that while you were cumming before! Never! Hell, if we weren't in this hotel, you probably would've screamed."

Donovan chuckled to himself, because he did in fact feel like yelling his head off at that apex of sheer bliss.

"How much time do we have?"

Donovan peered over at the alarm clock on the nightstand. "About half an hour. Oh, kudos on providing the room number."

"You like that, huh?"

"Three drinks at $35. Clever."

Celeste looked upward at the ceiling and lightly sighed. She told herself that she wouldn't bring up the subject of their rendezvous, but these meetings could almost be set by a clock. She knew eventually that she would want more, even though she tried to shake the desire after each encounter. This time was different. She knew that she wanted to be with this man for life. Despite being a sharp attorney who had a long history with him, she could not find the words to address the subject properly. She rustled next to him and sighed audibly. Her body was tired and she wanted to sleep for a few hours. Instead of basking in the sexual afterglow, she forced herself up and sat on the edge of the bed. She mentally willed herself to go take a quick shower. Her eyes scanned his tailored pants that were neatly covering the back of the desk chair with both shoes paired asymmetrically side by side. Just beside the shoes, was a tiny blue velvet box. With widened eyes, her heart raced. Just then, she felt his fingertips outline her shoulder blades and the channel of her spine. It was a loving touch that he did not often give. Perhaps all of her hard sexual work, being silent, and providing unlimited satisfaction to him finally paid off.

He stirred next to her before he got up to go to the bathroom. He looked at her and gave her a sexy toothed smile when he passed.

"My Celeste," he said before disappearing.

Her heart thumped gleefully with that affirmation. When she heard the water from the showerhead dance against the tub, she dashed for the box and opened it. Her mouth dropped.

"Holy shit!" She peered at it while it remained nestled inside, turning the box at different angles to get a better view. The light bounced off of the diamond like a symphony. It had to be two, maybe three carats. Cushion cut. She wanted to try it on, but did not want to smudge it in any way. She placed a tender hand on her chest, her mouth agape. The ring was beautiful and just what she had always wanted. Tears began to stand in her eyes, but she quickly told herself to suck it up before they fell. She wasn't supposed to know. *How would he ask her*, she wondered. She heard the water cease and immediately closed the box. She placed it sort of haphazardly in his shoe as if it clumsily fell from somewhere. She took her position back on the bed to give the impression that she hadn't moved an inch.

Donovan cracked the door to the bathroom as the steam freed itself.

"Your turn!" he called to her.

"I just want to sleep!" Celeste whined with an airy seductive voice.

"Okay, suit yourself, but I have to go," he called back using an airy seductive voice that mimicked hers. She chuckled at his silliness. "Oh Celeste?"

"Yes?"

"Can you get away for a few days?"

Celeste's eyes widened and she sat up. *Be cool*, she told herself. "Uhh, I guess. What did you have in mind?"

"Hmm, the beach. You know how we did in school."

"How could I forget?"

Wanting to read his eyes, she decided to go in the bathroom.

"We had some wild times, didn't we?" he asked.

"Of course. So what beach and when?"

Donovan smoothed his eye brows and hung the towel on the rack exposing his naked body to Celeste again. She smiled at his package as her eyes danced up his fit body and into his smiling eyes.

"Well, I want to see my feet on the ocean floor, so it's gotta be a nice beach. And I want to go soon. I need to get away. I'm having nightmares and shit, work is hectic. I just want some time with you. Not this sneaking around shit. You know?"

"I love that idea. I can get away with no problem. But you? How are you going to manage it?"

"Leave that to me, okay?" he rapped her lightly on her bare behind.

"Should I pack anything special? Like a formal gown or anything?" she probed.

Donovan reared his head back as his eyes narrowed. He shook his head and chuckled at her question. "No, just bring your fine chocolate self. Go 'head get showered, I gotta run."

"Okay Donnie."

Celeste turned on the shower and tested the water before she stepped inside the tub. Secretly, she gave Donovan a week to firm up the details on their trip. If not, she would just have to nudge things along by sending Tamar away to another conference. Maybe some place on the west coast. Several months ago, Celeste sent her to some cyber law conference. The entire time she was away, Donovan stayed with Celeste. She stocked up on groceries as they cooked, watched old movies and fucked. For that moment, he was hers and she loved every bit of it. She was amazed that Tamar barely called to check up on him.

Donovan was the one doing most of the calling – first thing in the morning and again in the evening. Their conversations were brief, which surprised Celeste. She wondered exactly what types of conversations they had when they were alone together. It was typically Tamar who ended the conversations first, she noted. In Celeste's opinion, they had a one dimensional relationship. Donovan never gave Celeste too many details about Tamar and how their relationship was. It didn't matter; Celeste had eyes of her own. Not to mention, he was screwing Celeste regularly. No man who was content at home would be going to such lengths with another woman. His relationship was absolutely almost over and Celeste knew it; otherwise he wouldn't be here.

As the soapy water glided down her body, she knew in her heart that the diamond ring she just saw was hers. It was about time.

Donovan, now fully dressed, sat on the edge of the bed and reached for his shoes. The tiny velvet box toppled out and onto the floor.

"How did this get here?" Donovan opened the box and looked inside to see if its contents remained. He exhaled noisily, rubbed his chin and said, "I hope Celeste didn't see this."

6

I sat at the wooden pub table waiting for Camilla to show up. I wanted to meet with her before I met with Hailey. I couldn't think of a good excuse to exclude Camilla from the three of us having dinner, so I just told her the truth. Hailey wanted to meet with me and talk in private. Surprisingly, Camilla didn't seem too terribly offended by that. I peered out of the large floor to ceiling window and watched the passersby trot on the bricked sidewalk. A few tripped here and there, but oh well. Everyone seemed to have bad motor skills when a bricked sidewalk is laid unevenly.

During my favorite pastime of people watching, it almost always never failed and today was no different. I would always see a woman pulling along a toddler by his tiny hand with an infant nuzzled closely to her bosom in one of those sling things. The husband is always a few feet behind, bringing up the rear. His job was to grab the toddler if he strayed because his attention was drawn away by a seemingly drunken butterfly or a passing puppy. Coincidentally, the mother would never just walk by, it was as if she would purposely stop in my direct line of vision, do something motherly and then move on. Like she *had* to be seen by me.

I want a baby!

"Sorry I'm late, the train had a slight delay," Camilla said, popping up from nowhere and scaring the hell out of me.

"Where is Gabby Gabe?" I asked her. I gave Gabe that nickname because he never stops talking and he asks a gazillion questions. I love his curiosity and unbridled boldness to ask. Oddly enough, I think because of his querying skills, he has an uncanny sense for spotting bullshit when he hears it. I love that kid!

"Steve has him."

"How is that going?"

Camilla sighed and put her bag down before she answered, "Going fine."

"You okay?" I asked.

"Not really. I had another date with a damned loser. Talk about someone being five-star dining on paper, but the kitchen is full of roaches."

"What?"

"This guy makes over three hundred thousand a year, owns three night clubs, is handsome, single, has a huge house and a huge breasted friend to match!"

"What?"

"Yes. Now he's threatening me on voicemail."

"What?"

"Josephine, stop saying *what*, would you?" Camilla pleaded as she pulled out her phone. She tapped and swiped the face of the device until the computerized voice boomed from the speaker.

"FIRST SAVED MESSAGE!"

"Camilla, you better give me back my sculpture! You have no idea how much that thing is worth!" Felix's voice grew increasingly louder and more ferocious. "I will find you Camilla! I want it back! I swear to God. Do you hear me!? I will choke the life out of . . ."

"That's enough, you get the idea," Camilla turned the device off and tossed the phone into her purse. She fished around in her bag until she retrieved a stick of gum. Casually, she popped it in her mouth, her jaws rotating carefully like a cow's.

As I watched her every move, mouth slightly parted, eye brows raised, Camilla didn't even break a sweat. She seemed to not be the least bit moved by the guy's threat, nor the fact that she had stolen something he claimed to be of value.

"Okay, back up," I demanded, "What is going on? What sculpture? Why are there roaches and someone with huge breasts?"

"What's going on is I've had it with this dating scene. I'm done. The next man that steps to me will get me quirking out on him. Plain and simple. He will get the verbal tongue lashing of the century. I don't care what he does, what he says, I'm unleashing the fury on him! I can't believe it is this difficult to snag a hubby in this town."

I carefully folded my hands on the table top and tried to figure out some encouraging words to say to my friend.

"Camilla, you have to give it some time."

"I have!" She raised her voice slightly. "What is the problem here?!"

A few patrons turned and looked in our direction. Camilla tried to come off as cool when she let me hear the threatening voice mail, but something else was clearly bothering her. Whenever she brought up dating, it was always a sore topic. I tried to avoid talking about it with her as much as possible because I knew of her frustrations with the men she had encountered here in D.C. The truth of the matter was I was out of explanations for her.

About three months or so ago, Ian and I tried to fix her up on a blind date. The guy was single, loved kids although he didn't have any of his own, he had a decent job, loved his mother, was attractive . . . the list goes on and on. But for whatever reason, it wasn't a match. I'm usually pretty good at fixing people up – well, when I do fix people up. If I recall correctly it was something very trivial.

Ironically, it wasn't Camilla who was being picky, it was the guy! He didn't mind that she had a son. Camilla did not have the dreaded "baby daddy" drama because Steve and Camilla were not in a relationship beyond that one night. Camilla looked great, she made her own money, had her own place, she is an excellent cook, she is intelligent, presents herself well . . . what was it that he didn't like exactly? He told Ian and of course Ian told me.

After the date, Camilla called me and said that it went very well! That the guy had restored her faith in dating and thought that he had potential to go the distance. He didn't have the proverbial wandering eye. He wasn't rude to her by taking phone calls during dinner or felt compelled to conduct incessant texting. Camilla offered to pay for the meal, but he declined and said that it wasn't her place to do so. He sounded like a great catch! She said he was a phenomenal conversationalist, was highly intellectual, but not boring, and he had a great sense of humor to boot. He was the perfect gentleman. Camilla was convinced he was the one for her.

She called him a day or so after the date just to say thanks again and wondered if they could see each other again soon. The silence was too loud. Homeboy did not respond to that message or any of her texts that following week. After her fourth text which yielded no response from him, she ceased further contact.

But what was the problem again?

Oh! I remember now.

He preferred women who were ethnically mixed.

"I don't know what the problem is, Camilla," I explained, "but it can't be as bad as you are making it out to be."

She stared at me briefly, scoffed and hooked her purse on her shoulder. Obviously frustrated by my comment, she stormed out of the pub. I pushed away from the table and awkwardly walked out behind her. She was almost to the corner about to cross the grounds of the National Mall when I caught up to her.

"Something the matter?" I asked her.

"That was a shitty thing to say to me," Camilla pounded her heels in the concrete across the crosswalk.

I followed closely behind her. "Excuse me?"

Camilla finally ran out of steam in the large grassy area and turned toward me. With her face twisted in anger and teeth slightly gnashed, she addressed me.

"How dare you tell me that I'm making up how fucked up dating is in this area? You think I'm purposely pushing men away because I *want* to grow old alone?"

"That's not how I meant it," I tried to explain.

"Then what did you mean? Because I have been out with every ass-stain in D.C.! No one wants me! Do you understand what I'm saying? Do you even give a shit about how I feel about it?"

"Of course I do! Otherwise I wouldn't have set you up with someone who I thought was a great catch!"

"A great catch? Who? Oh yeah, the brother who has an affinity to be Mr. Right for a black woman except she can only have 50% or less of black flowing through her bloodstream. You mean that guy? How could you guys not know something like *that* about him? But, no . . . I thought that guy was the last straw for me until Felix from this weekend. I'm done!"

"Okay, you're done. So why are you fussing at me?"

"Because you just don't get it! Dating is not as bad as I'm making it out to be? Really Josephine? You don't have to worry about dating, do you? You have the perfect guy, right? Mr. Ian!" Camilla exaggerated. Then she started imitating me, making my voice sound like some over acting movie star from the 40s. "Oh Ian does all the cooking, Ian never gets bored with sex, Ian and I went house hunting, Ian will be the perfect father, Ian loves my stinky feet, Ian worships the dirty, trash encrusted ground my stinky feet walk on!! I'm so sick of you two!"

"Now you wait a minute! Just hold on. I have never said any of that bullshit to you!" I defended. "And you leave Ian out of this! Do you remember before I met him I was in the same situation as you? I went on the crappy dates, I spent holidays alone, I cried with your ass as a matter of fact, while you flaunted dating someone who played for the Redskins! You forgot all of that huh?"

Camilla placed her hand on her hip and looked downward. Her shoulders lifted and fell as she exhaled sharply. She looked back up at me eyes narrowed.

"No, Josephine. I didn't forget that! I just thought that you'd be a little sympathetic since you *should* be familiar with what I'm going through. But you clearly don't care! I never thought in a million years that I'd be single with a son. I wanted the marriage first! Don't get me wrong I love Gabe, I do, but I wasn't ready for him yet! And certainly not with someone I slept with once! I just didn't want things to be this way. You know how hard it is out here and you just shouldn't have said that. And have the decency to not throw your perfect two year marriage to Mr. Wonderful in my face every chance you get!"

"You know I don't do that, Camilla!"

I was beyond upset with Camilla at this point. She was way out of line. She had this notion made up in her mind that I paraded Ian around to all of my single friends. Like I put him on a pedestal for all to see, admire, and pray to God for Him to grant them Ian's clone from another dimension. How dare she ride this pity train, and then get upset with me because I backed away and left her standing on the platform four years ago. I'm not going to apologize for my blessing! And

I will not put him down just to make another woman feel like she has a teammate during her sport of male bashing.

"Keep talking, Camilla . . .," I encouraged her, "get it all out – especially since you are so sick of me and Ian."

Camilla took a moment to calm down by taking a few deep breaths and paced back and forth for a moment. I wanted to say more to her, but I realized that this wasn't about me. Camilla lashing out at me was her way of wanting to be heard about another issue. Granted it wasn't a stellar method, but I understood.

"Look, I'm sorry I said that. It's not you I'm mad at Josephine. I'm just tired. You understand? I'm stuck in dating hell!" She turned to face the monument and took a moment to slow her thoughts down some more. "You know, everyone says that each individual is unique. I tried to think of what made me unique from the average woman. I got it. I finally got it. I didn't realize my uniqueness until just now. I'm unique in the fact that no one, not another living soul cares about me, or wonders how I'm doing, or just flat out gives a shit about little ol' me. That's pretty unique."

With an exaggerated motion, I started clapping slowly. With tears in her eyes, she slowly turned to face me with disbelief. She lifted her brows slightly and then sneered. Needing an explanation to my patronizing, she then glared at me as if she were preparing to pounce and scratch my eyes from my skull. I know she was hurting, but I wasn't going to give her the satisfaction. Not this time.

"End the pity party, Camilla. I've seen you go through and conquer worse, so spare me. Not another living soul, huh? No one cares? Do you think I'd be here, my heels sinking into this dirt if I didn't care? Ian and I know it's gotta be hard for you to raise Gabe by yourself, but Ian and I care so much that we are babysitting him as often as we can. We love Gabe! Not only for the kid he is, but we also love him because we love you!" Camilla finally seemed to simmer down a bit. Her shoulders dropped and the intensity in her face fled.

"Camilla, let me tell you something that I haven't told anyone, not even Hailey." I took a deep breath before I continued.

I certainly didn't want to tell anyone for fear that they would use this information against me later. Despite my fears, this seemed to be the appropriate time to share this with her.

"For the past year, Ian and I have been trying to have a baby and whatever is going on, it's just not happening. Honestly, I'm . . . I'm afraid that if this doesn't happen, Ian will leave me. He wants children so badly, Camilla. And I've been able to give him everything except that. So while you want the life we have, we are sitting back wanting what you have already. That's not fair for you to tell me I'm not sympathetic or that I don't care. Do *you*? Do you care? Do you think about anyone other than yourself? Everything is always about you! All the athletes, the red carpets, the after parties, that . . . that goddamned Bryan Bryant fiasco. You didn't even care that Steve already had a girlfriend, did you? Because it was what *you* wanted, right? Right?"

Camilla took a minute to regroup and quickly whisked away a tear that trailed her cheek. She sniffled and rubbed her palms together and then looked out again at the traffic, staring at nothing in particular. As if she reaffirmed something spoken to her by a voice in her head, she gave a slight nod.

"Yeah," she whispered, "you're right. I didn't know you and Ian were going through that. I'm so sorry."

"I didn't say it for an apology. I just wanted you to know that you aren't the only person going through stuff. We just deal with it and manage. That's what you have to do Camilla. I'm sorry for the comment. I am. Your guy is out there. I know he is."

"He'd better not be dead, that's for sure," she chuckled a bit.

"I love you," I told her with my arms outstretched.

"I love you too, girl," she leaned in and gave me a hug.

"And for your information my feet don't stink!"

We both laughed and headed toward the sidewalk.

*   *   *   *

By the time I got to Hailey, I was emotionally exhausted – not to mention famished. I could understand Camilla's frustrations whole heartedly because I had been there before. Ian and I were in the right mental and emotional place at the right time when we met and things worked out for the two of us. However now, he desires something that feels almost impossible at the moment. I checked with my OB/GYN and I wasn't having any physical complications that would prohibit me from becoming pregnant, nor was Ian. His doctor told him that everything was fine. I guess for the first or maybe second time in our relationship, we were out of sync and facing yet another challenge to overcome.

Ian is not pressuring me to have kids, but actions are so much louder than words. When we babysit Gabe or Alex, he goes into full father mode. I've heard him tell them when he preps them for bed that he hopes to have kids just as cool as them. Those boys absolutely love Ian. Although Ian isn't pressuring me, his mother sure is. And subtle is not a word that is in her vocabulary. I just have a strong feeling that she has been in his ear feeding him non-sense. As far as Ian leaving me, of course he hasn't said it, but sometimes he has a far off stare or a hint of disappointment overcomes him. Sometimes when he's watching me, I noticed that he studies my body, perhaps imagining what I would look like pregnant. I just wish I knew exactly what he was thinking in those moments.

Hailey was sitting in the waiting area of the restaurant playing with her cell phone. She didn't even notice when I walked inside. It wasn't until I lingered near her personal space longer than what may be deemed necessary that she looked up at me. She smiled and put her phone away while she stood to greet me.

"Josephine! Hey girl," she leaned in for a hug. "You look great!"

"So do you. Were you waiting long?"

"Not really, they should be seating us in a minute. How is everything?"

My lips fluttered as the air I pushed from my mouth passed them. My head throbbed for a moment, like sound traversing a live wire. I closed my eyes, trying to erase the conversation I had with Camilla just moments ago.

"Uh oh," she muttered.

"I just left Camilla and boy was she pissed off at me."

"What the hell for?" Hailey said as she reared back slightly, going into protective mode.

"Apparently, I was being a bit insensitive to her dating situation. And I often rub my marriage with Ian in her face."

"What? You do not! That's ridiculous!"

"She is upset, Hailey. We talked some more and her not being in a relationship is the issue. She was just projecting. I've been in her position before and I guess I could've been a bit more sensitive. But I'm not going to apologize for being married."

"And you shouldn't," Hailey cosigned my statement. "You need a drink?"

"I need something!"

As the host showed us to our booth, I filled Hailey in on the key points of the conversation Camilla and I had. I didn't want to belabor the topic, especially since she and I made up right after.

"So what are you going to do about the Camilla situation?" Hailey tinkered with a few items on the table. She always had to keep her hands busy. She twirled the salt shaker on the table top as if she were playing spin the bottle. Then, she gathered the spilled salt crystals with a sugar packet like a dustpan and pushed it away to a designated corner of the table.

"Nothing, it's over as far as I am concerned," I exhaled sharply. "So what's going on with you? You don't get too many evenings off. I'm so flattered you chose to spend it with little ol' me!"

"Tell me about it," she wiped her hands together to free them from any loose salt and locked her fingers before she spoke. It seemed like she had something important to discuss. "I need to come up with a plan."

"Okay. A plan for what?"

"You ready?" she asked me. I nodded. "I want Steve back."

"You *what?*"

"Yes, I realized that I want him and I have to get him back. So I need to devise a plan — a foolproof one. What do you think?"

"...k?" I asked her, "I think it's a horrible idea!"

"...xpression turned to one of bewilderment. Her back pressed ...her seating as a response escaped her.

"...rrible, Hailey. Why now anyway?"

"Why not now? Alex needs him in his life full time," Hailey blurted out.

"Okay, so what does that have to do with you? If Alex needs Steve in his life full time, give him custody. Don't use Alex as an excuse for you. So, why do you want Steve back and why right now? Can you please answer that first?" I asked her straight.

"I made a mistake," she admitted. "Steve has been a great father. But lately whenever he comes by to pick him up or drop him off, those butterflies that I had when we first met start fluttering again. He turns me on so much, Josephine! It's evident that I need him, but I really really want him back too."

"So how are you going to go about doing that?"

"I'm not sure yet. Honestly, I was going to use Alex," she said. I immediately gasped and leaned all the way back in my seat and gave her a look of conviction.

Hailey rolled her eyes upward. "Right right, I know. So since you said what you just said, I can't do that now. So . . . I need your help."

"I don't know about that one, Hailey," I told her. "Has Steve been giving you any kind of vibes or anything?"

"Not exactly, but I know he still loves me."

"How? If there have been no vibes, how in the world do you know he still loves you?"

"We almost did it that time . . .," she admitted.

"Wasn't that like months and months ago?"

"Maybe, but the passion that arose, the way he touched me and the way we kissed," she released a fanciful moan. "He *had* to stop himself. I have to come up with something and fast. I feel like I have a very small window here."

"Can I make a suggestion to you about that window?"

Hailey drummed her nails upon the table top, sucked her teeth and stared at me signifying that I may answer my own question.

"Slam it shut!" I laughed. Just as my laughter died down a deep voice hovered over our table.

"Hello, Hailey."

Hailey couldn't believe her eyes that were now locked onto the face that spoke those two words that sent shivers through her body like 20,000 volts. She gasped and I could tell that her heart had just skipped a single beat. Her mouth gaped slightly and her eyes widened. She studied his face intently. A smile slowly crept on his lips as her reaction fed his ego. I could barely believe what I saw myself. My eyes darted from him to Hailey and back up to him.

"And how are you, Jacqueline?" Bryan Bryant had still forgotten my name. I just didn't care anymore and wasn't going to correct him.

"Hi," I flatly responded.

"Bryan?" Hailey asked with a bit of uncertainty.

"Yes," he responded. "I've missed you so much. I didn't expect to see you here, but I'm glad I did."

"Wow, um, this is incredible."

With outstretched arms, his smile widened. "Can I get a hug?"

"Oh, uh . . . sure." Hailey slowly rose to her feet, wobbling slightly, her legs as rigid as melted ice cream. As she hugged his neck, he kissed her cheek before he pulled her in to his body tightly.

"It's so good to finally see you," Bryan leaned back to look into her eyes, still holding on to her waist and caressing it gently.

"You look so different, the facial hair . . .," she said through seductive breaths.

"I know," he bashfully admitted. "Look, I'm meeting my doctor here. Let me give you my card. Please call me, I'd love to catch up with you, it's been such a long time. Is that alright?"

Hailey was still mesmerized when she responded faintly, "Sure . . . yeah."

Bryan took a business card from his wallet and placed it in Hailey's hand, wrapping her fingers around it to secure it in place.

"I've missed you. Call me," he said. He waved at me and walked away.

Hailey stood there watching to see where he was sitting, which was in the rear of the restaurant. She poured herself into her seat and gazed at the pile of salt she made earlier. I smiled to myself and decided to pick with her.

"So um, that plan to get Steve back," I prompted.

"Who?"

"Steve. Steve! You want him back, remember?"

"Oh, that. I will think of something," she waved her hand in the air to shoo the notion off into the universe. "Wow Bryan looked great, huh?"

"He looked *better* and he was much less of a douche than normal," I told her with a giggle.

Just then, a lady walked sprightly past our table and headed for Bryan Bryant. I had a better vantage point and observed the couple closely so I could report my findings back to Hailey. Her long hair met the center of her back; she was small framed, but curvy. I noticed the red bottoms of her shoes as she stomped by. She extended her hand when she reached Bryan's table. He rose to his feet about half way and shook her hand and extended the other to gesture for her to have a seat. She tossed her hair and smiled, setting her large leather bag next to her. She pulled out a notepad, pen and a micro recorder.

"I hope you don't mind if I record this initial session," Chase told Bryan.

"You're the doctor, I don't mind at all," he affirmed.

"Why did you want to meet in a restaurant rather than my office?"

"To me, it's friendlier than being stretched out on a couch. But I'm wondering if this was a good idea after all."

"Oh? Why is that?"

"Yes. See . . . the reason, well part of the reason I'm meeting with you is sitting in that booth right over there." Bryan used his eyes to indicate to Chase the direction of the culprit. Chase slowly pivoted her head in that direction and noticed Josephine.

"Really?"

"Not her, that's her friend. You can't see her. Her back is to us. I loved her very much, but she broke my heart. I hadn't seen her in almost two years and seeing her tonight . . . all of those old feelings came back. I gave her my card and asked her to call me so we could catch up."

"Are you expecting her to call?"

"I hope so, Dr. Billingsley."

"If she does call you, are you hoping to catch up? Expecting closure to move on? Or are you looking to rekindle that love you had for her? I mean, what would make you happy?"

"Oddly enough, all three."

7

After I left Hailey, I stopped by the drug store and picked up two more pregnancy tests. I wasn't about to test myself again, since I had just done so, these tests were for the next time my cycle was late or I gagged at the smell of something from my daily routine like . . . like, soap. I just knew it wouldn't be long now. By the time I got home, Ian had dimmed all of the lights and lit a few candles here and there. He was ready for a night of love making and quite frankly, so was I. I could feel it! This was going to be the night of conception. Bulls eye, Bingo, Jackpot!

I walked in and tossed my keys on the counter. Ian was standing in the living room, shirtless, wearing black silk pajama pants. The light from the candle shadowed the areas hidden by his muscles. Noticing his manhood was partially hardened through in the PJs, my body was ready. He held a single long stemmed red rose and smiled wide when he saw me enter. Ian always turned me on – mentally and physically. Little did he know that I was going to fuck him senseless.

"Welcome home, baby," he said.

"Well well well, what have we here?" I walked closer to him, wondering what he was going to do to me first.

"You have your husband here, ready to satisfy his wife sexually until she begs him to stop."

"Oh yeah? Well, you know I'm usually not one for begging," I said coyly.

"Hmm," he licked his lips as he handed me the rose. I accepted the partially bloomed flower and sniffed it instinctively. I traced my lips with the velvety petals as if they were his fingertips. The silkiness of the flower glided down my chin, around the front of my neck – to indicate where his mouth and kisses should go. Like a lecturer with a pointer, I circled my breasts with the rose then down the center of my stomach to the creases of my pelvis and around the permanent residence for Ian's man-toy. My body's hidden treasure throbbed and moistened even more when he smiled and looked deeply into my eyes. After he approached me, he gently removed the rose from my fingers and tossed it on a nearby table. It tumbled to the floor as if to get a better view of what was about to go down.

Ian wrapped his arm around me and swiftly pulled me tight against his chiseled body. His rod pressed into my thigh and I could feel how hard he had gotten in just that matter of moments. My warmed body was exposed to his inviting eyes as he began to unzip the front of my dress.

"You little devil," he said as he feasted his eyes upon my red satin bra and panties. Slowly, he peeled the dress off of my body, which was now fully ready to feel him enter and please. My breaths quivered, my chest heaved up and down quickly, my pelvis continued to pulsate while my nipples perked. He grabbed my hips and lifted me onto him as I locked my legs behind his lower back. Our sturdy Amish made dining table that sat ten, would be the prop that would host our love making as he carefully laid my body upon it. With my knees bent, he tugged me toward him until my buttocks were at the edge. He knelt down, placing one leg after the other over his respective shoulders.

"Don't you move," he instructed.

Ian knew that this was going to be an impossible request. The way his mouth made love to my pussy warranted my body to writhe around like an unmanned fire hose. He planted his face deep and went straight for the key that unlocked a flurry of orgasms.

"Oh!" I moaned. "Ian . . ."

Instantly my back arched as he held me in place by my hips. I felt as if I needed to hold on to something during this wild ride, but there was nothing within reach – except his head and shoulders. I lifted my head up to watch him completely eat me out. I pushed his head further and deeper into my pussy, hoping to God I wouldn't suffocate him, but his tongue was driving my body insane like never before. The lovely view of his muscular shoulders and his strong hands as they pressed my lower abs, sent me into overdrive. He wouldn't stop circling and flicking his hot tongue. He lapped and sucked as I could feel the wetness trickle down to my buttocks.

"Oh Ian! Baby . . . damn!"

As his head shook from side to side and up and down he refused to let go of my hips - moaning while he was nuzzled securely in my femininity. My waist was being roughly combed by his fingertips before his hands moved upward to grope my breasts. He rested his hands on my rib cage as my body convulsed in response to the orgasms. Our eyes locked for a moment when he lifted his head; he took a deep breath and dove back in.

"Oh lord have mercy!" I managed to squeak out between faint breaths, my back bending to reveal the arousal felt from being orally pleasured. "I can't take it!"

Ian stopped for a moment and uttered, "Are you begging me to stop?"

Before I could answer, his tongue flipped my clit quickly. I unleashed the most powerful oral orgasm known to man . . . or woman, right on that Amish table. My body fell limp, but Ian refused to stop.

"Give me one more, come on," he ordered before his mouth disappeared between my thighs again.

"Oh Ian . . .," I moaned cheerfully. He wedged one hand on the small of my back and lifted me slightly. The other pressed firmly on my stomach, the central part of my body now sandwiched front and back between his hands felt so indescribably erotic. With his hands holding me in place like a vise and his tongue wildly tossing my clit, my vaginal walls detonated causing my eyes to slam shut and my breath to cease temporarily.

"Hmm, thank you," he said. "Good girl."

He rose to his feet and walked to the powder room. I heard some water running from the faucet as my brain took a moment to settle back in its rightful quadrants. As I breathed deeply, I remained stretched out on the table top. I wanted to move. I wanted to please him just as he had pleased me. I wanted to ride him. But knowing Ian, tonight was the night he wanted to reign as sex champion.

Ian approached me and caressed my body tenderly. I never got a chance to remove the satin bra and don't recall when or how he removed my panties. He looked down at various areas of my body, touching what he wanted to at that moment while his other hand stroked his thickness through his silk pajama pants. The vision of him needed to be framed and sold in stores everywhere.

"Ready?" he asked with a sly grin.

"I'm still tingling," I told him.

Ignoring my statement, he gripped underneath my knees and spun me on the table top 180 degrees. He giggled to himself at the surprised expression on my face. Carefully, he leaned over slightly as his hard penis grazed the top of my head, and reached for my brassiere.

"Let's take this off," he said.

Ian gave my boobs a gentle squeeze. My back bowed to allow him to unfasten the bra's clasp. When it became undone, he lifted the bra off of me and flung it away. We would find it later. He bent over and carefully kissed my forehead. He spun me another 180 degrees and our genitals now faced one another. The wood from the table top slid up my back as I was scooted down. My midsection was yanked a bit further down toward him just before his hands massaged my breasts. Ian took a brief moment to pull his silk pants down and step out of them.

"Hmm," he muttered quietly. He gripped my hips firmly and entered me delicately. He filled me completely as my walls squeezed around him, sealing the fit sweetly.

"Oh," I softly moaned. My body was enjoying the lavish massage from his member.

Ian stroked me long and slow; enjoying every sensation our bodies created for each other. We both loved to fuck one another, but when we made love, it was as if we were creating a symphonic score to a fairy tale. His fingers oozed into the flesh of my hips and waist while those long deep strokes from his penis fawned my inner walls.

When I looked up at Ian, his face looked solemn as he was concentrating on making me orgasm. His eyelids were low, his mouth parted slightly as his chest flexed with each inward stroke. When my eyes met his, he smiled faintly before he spoke.

"You feel so good, baby."

My body tingled and the sensation of a looming orgasm fluttered in my lower abdomen. I closed my eyes and released a hard orgasm. I tightened around him as he stroked faster to take advantage of my pussy hugging his shaft. My voice swelled as I expressed my pleasure with his steady slow rhythmic strokes. His strong hand gently caressed my breast down to my stomach and caused me to orgasm again.

"Oh . . . Oh Ian!" The supreme moment caused my eyes to shut so tightly that I saw stars. "Oh baby, you feel so good!"

I slightly choked on my words as my eyes began to get moist. Thirty straight minutes of passionate stroking was driving me to an emotional state. His steady rhythm allowed me to feel every wonderful inch of him. I couldn't thwart off the tears. He felt so good inside of me that I couldn't help but weep. I covered my eyes with my forearm. Ian knew I was crying. My husband stroked a bit faster now. I was unsure if it was to bring me out of the sheer ecstasy that I felt, or if he was being turned on himself. I removed my forearm revealing the smeared tears on my cheeks. As his hands caressed my body, then my cheek, his thumb slowly dried the tears. The gesture made me cum again.

"Oh Ian, you feel soo . . ."

"I'm about to feel even better," he told me. "Put your ankles up here." He patted one shoulder. I placed one shaky leg on his shoulder, followed by the other. He gripped my hips tightly and went to work on my pussy. I could barely contain my orgasms at that point. One by one by one after another, they were being released from my sugar walls like bullets through an automatic weapon. Ian didn't stop his pounding. I could tell that he was climaxing as his eyes closed and he gripped me tighter. His body was losing control as his hands spread further apart on my hips. He squeezed them tighter before he reached for my breasts. He grunted while he pumped ferociously.

"Mmmm!" he mumbled as he released himself into me.

I answered his sounds of bliss with one final climax.

"Oh shit!" he said when he felt it. "Josephine . . ."

He slowly made his way to the floor where he stretched out to catch his breath. All out of orgasms, I remained on the table top and would probably stay there for a better portion of the night.

"You alright my baby?" I asked Ian.

In a faint whisper he replied, "That was great. I just need a minute."

My body was devoid of energy, but I felt fantastic. I drifted off into a light sleep, but before doing so, I just knew that we had conceived. Everything about this evening was perfect. A few moments later, Ian got up and kissed my thigh. I could hear him stumble toward the powder room again and then heard the faucet. After several minutes, he returned. He rubbed my leg and I could feel the warm cloth on my nether region. After Ian freshened me up, he lifted me and carried me like a baby upstairs to bed.

"Thank you honey," I uttered.

The bed rocked and I teetered as he climbed inside to find a comfortable position next to me. One he was settled, I cuddled up beside him.

"I love you," he said.

"I love you too," I responded. "Baby, I'm pretty sure you just got me pregnant."

Ian pulled me in close to him, sighed heavily, kissed me on the forehead and said, "that would really be something, baby."

*   *   *   *

Last night after I fired off 20 or so orgasms, my body felt like there were no bones in it. Even though it hadn't even been 24 hours, a woman knows when her body's chemistry has shifted. In a few days I was going to check to see if I was pregnant. I already didn't feel the urge for the routine cup of coffee this morning.

Tamar called me shortly after I got in to work. She sounded like it may be a bit urgent, but assured me it could wait. She wanted to meet up for lunch, which I was always in the mood to get out of the office for a few.

Instead of working on that marketing campaign, I spent most of the morning looking at cribs, bassinettes and baby clothes. The expression on Ian's face was going to be priceless. I had to plan something special for him when I gave him the news.

I was so engrossed in baby websites that I almost missed leaving the office to catch Tamar. Thankfully, we worked in close proximity of each other and I was only five minutes late.

"Hey girl!" I greeted her with a hug when I arrived.

"What's up!" she smiled and sat back down. "You look so professional! And you're even glowing! Married life is still good to you I see."

"I'm loving it! We are still trying to get pregnant though. But I'm enjoying making this baby! What's going on with you? You sounded a bit annoyed this morning. Did I hear that, right?"

"Oh yeah, you heard that right. I don't like that Celeste keeps sending me away to these bullshit conferences. Don't get me wrong, you know I take my profession very seriously, but this is the fourth one in like seven months."

"Is anyone else going?"

"No. Just me." Tamar took a labored breath. "I don't think I should be away from Donovan this much. But oh well. I'm making the best of it while I'm gone."

"So where are you headed now?"

"Manhattan."

"Okay! That's not too bad. For how long?"

"No, it's not bad at all actually. It's just for a week. You gonna miss me?" she smiled.

"It depends. Is my friend going to bring me back some shoes?"

"I will think about it," Tamar chuckled. "Well, I won't be alone. At least I have a few friends up there to keep me company."

"Well, that sounds like a good deal. When are you leaving?"

"Sunday." Tamar shook her head at the thought of having to leave so soon.

"Well, I hope to have some news for you when you return! I have a follow up doctor's appointment scheduled for Monday. I had to go last week to make sure everything was . . . working."

"And I'm sure it was! Did Ian go with you? You know you two are inseparable."

"No, umm . . . I went on my own."

"Whaaatt?" Tamar stretched the word out as she said it. "Okay then. Well I will be eagerly awaiting this excellent news!"

After the girls ate their fill of sushi, Tamar returned to her office to finalize her itinerary for the trip. Even though she was flying out first thing Sunday morning, she could hardly wait to get there. Even though Taj had mentioned coming to D.C. in a few weeks, it was music to his ears when Tamar told him that she would be heading in his direction. Taj already made the necessary preparations. He wanted Tamar to stay with him in his penthouse, but she declined. In case the trip was audited later by human resources or the finance department at the firm, everything would be accounted for. Tamar hadn't planned at all to go to any of the lectures that week. They were topics that didn't necessarily relate to corporate law, none that really warranted her attendance anyway. However, she was going to sign in on Monday and show her face for a few at Friday's final session. She wasn't scheduled to be home until late Saturday night.

Tamar's office phone rang.

"This is Ms. Woodruff," she answered.

"I have a pair of navy blue lace thongs that will look so good on your honey colored skin," Taj told her.

Tamar mustered up one of her most seductive voices, "Well hello there, you."

"I can't wait to see you."

"Ditto. And just what are we going to do when I get there?" she asked.

"Well, I'm going to meet you at your hotel, fuck your brains out there and then take you to lunch. I may eat you for lunch while we are there, then we can do some sightseeing, and I'll have you . . . for dinner."

At that moment Celeste's assistant walked in to deliver some papers to Tamar. The young lady stood in front of her desk, so Tamar guessed it was something that required her attention right then. Tamar's sexy demeanor went from hot and spicy to an ice cold professional all in an instant.

"Okay," she began in her professional legal voice, "that's excellent news."

"Someone in your office?" Taj gathered.

"Yes of course. I will have that information emailed over to you on Monday. I will try to rush it to you this Sunday though, sir."

"I'm going to pour honey all over your body and suck it off of you," Taj told her.

"Fantastic," Tamar replied. Taj laughed. "I'm sure that action will gain a positive response from all parties involved."

"I love your sense of humor. Bye lovely lady. Travel safe to me."

"I will, sir and thank you."

Tamar hung up the phone and stared up at the assistant with a blank, but innocent expression.

"Yes?"

"I'm sorry to bother you, Ms. Woodruff but I wanted to leave Celeste's itinerary for next week with you. Her door is closed and I didn't know what to do."

"I'm not following," Tamar looked at the file folder in the girl's hand, then back up to her.

"I wanted to ask her if I should give you her travel plans because she will be unreachable. And well, you both will be out next week. If any of your client's call, should we assist them as best we can, or just forward calls to you in New York? I'm sorry, but I'm just at a loss."

Tamar's hand extended to beckon the girl to give her the paper work. The assistant handed them over to her. Tamar eyed the destination and the date. *This Sunday. Barbados.*

"Oh okay, it looks like she is just taking a vacation," Tamar said as she flipped through a few pages. "That's fine. I'm not surprised she didn't tell me. Yes just forward her clients to my cell phone if necessary and I will take care of it."

The assistant breathed a sigh of relief, "Thank you Ms. Woodruff. You have been such a breath of fresh air around here." With that comment, the assistant walked out of Tamar's office. Tamar closed the file folder and tossed it on her desktop. She had to calm her body down from Taj's voice and what he said he would do to her on Sunday. Tamar liked Taj for his freakiness and didn't have any inhibitions with him. Not that she had any with Donovan, but Taj was different. She didn't love him and knew that after all was said and done, they would not be together. By keeping things in the proper perspective, she could detach herself from Taj at a moment's notice if need be and it also prevented her from being emotionally adjoined. In a perverse sort of way, the emotional dispassion also allowed her to enjoy the sex more with Taj. Tamar was looking forward to next week and couldn't wait to sink her teeth into him.

Before Tamar went home, she stopped by her favorite lingerie store and purchased a few items that she was taking to New York with her. Tamar was a bit surprised to see Donovan's car there when she arrived home because he's had late nights recently. Often times, she would beat him home by at least an hour. When she entered, there was no immediate sign of Donovan.

"Babe!" she called out to him. No response.

Tamar trotted upstairs to see if he was tucked away somewhere. Although there was still no sign of him, she noticed a shopping bag. It was a paper bag, crumpled from perhaps being tossed around in the back seat or trunk, with its handles upright at attention. The neat letters were printed on the side of the bag "J. Crew". Tamar stood over the bag and peered inside without bending over. Nothing too shocking appeared to be inside. It looked like a shirt, shorts and flip flops. She trotted downstairs to check the backyard. She saw him sitting in the wooden lawn chair, his glass of Jack and Coke half empty or maybe it was half full, it was hard to determine. Apparently he was deep in thought because he was staring out at nothing in particular. With a tinge of wonder, she watched his catatonic frame for a moment before she opened the sliding glass door. He turned toward her when he heard the slight commotion.

"Hey baby," he greeted.

"Hey. I just got home. I was looking for you," Tamar leaned down to kiss his puckered lips. "You okay?"

"Yeah. Just relaxing," Donovan reached for Tamar's hand and ushered her onto his lap. She climbed on him and found a comfortable position, her shoulder nestled in the pit of his arm, her legs bent as they rested on his thigh. She lightly rubbed his chest over his dress shirt that had been unbuttoned just past his collar bone.

"So my love," Tamar started, "what are you going to do all next week while I'm in New York?"

"Nothing," Donovan replied without hesitation. "Sitting here, missing my baby."

Tamar shifted a little, "Yeah, right."

"You know you have me sprung girl. How did you do that to me?" Donovan said with a chuckle.

"Whatever, don't even try it," Tamar kissed the part of his neck that was exposed. "Donovan, I'm excited about New York, but I'm also concerned."

"Why?"

"I like traveling, but why does Celeste keep sending me away? I'm not feeling that honey. You know I don't trust her."

"What are you saying?"

"I'm saying I don't trust her. I know her well enough to know that she is up to something. I just hate that I have to triple check everything I do. I'm not trying to give her any excuses to get rid of me, you know? And she's tried before."

"I know, babe. I got your back. I won't let her hurt you."

"I know honey, I know."

"So will you have time for me if I take a road trip up there?" Donovan asked.

"Yeah, but it's not even worth the price in tolls, gas and what not. It's only a week. I will be back late Saturday. Like close to 11 at night. I took a late flight so I could do some last minute shopping. You want something?"

"Just you."

"Awww!" Tamar said revealing the softness in her eyes. She planted a deep kiss on his lips.

Donovan's cell phone rang. He peered at the number before answering.

"This is Donovan," he said.

"Sir, we have been unsuccessful, but rest assured we are still searching. There are quite a few frauds out there, so we are exercising a heightened level of scrutiny you understand?"

"Totally understandable. Keep me posted."

"Indeed, sir."

Donovan ended the call and tapped the corner of it on his bottom lip while he thought for a moment.

"You okay?"

"Oh yeah, baby. Just trying to do the right thing for once."

"Oh uhm, okay." Tamar wasn't completely satisfied with the response, but she didn't want to pry. She just logged it in her mental file and remembered how much she hated being interrogated herself. Tamar was not a saint, despite all of the "missionary" positions she planned to do with Taj next week.

8

Hailey stared at Bryan's card while her thoughts ran rampant. She tried to envision what the future would bring if she dialed the number on the card. She also wondered what would happen if she failed to call. The fingertip of her thumb grazed the raised ink on his card, practicing perhaps for the moment her hands would reunite with Bryan's flesh. Hailey had so many questions for him. Even though her son Alex didn't belong to Bryan, Hailey never wanted to end things with him. By Bryan's abrupt departure, she could only deduce that he did not want to have any further dealings with Hailey.

After she gave birth to Alex, Hailey suffered from a mild depression for several months. She tried to lean on Josephine for moral support, but it would only last for that initial moment. Her heart had craved Bryan, but he disappeared. After seeing him in the restaurant, she could barely think straight for the rest of the evening. Josephine had to repeat herself several times during the night and would try to change the subject to keep her mind off of him, but it didn't work. Despite Josephine's efforts, Hailey would steer the conversation back toward the topic of Bryan Bryant. Josephine did not give her the nod to pursue Bryan. So despite Josephine's objections, Hailey was going to contact Bryan; she just did not know exactly when. Too soon would come off as desperate, too late would appear that she was involved with someone else. Three days? One week?

"He *did* ask me to call so we could catch up," Hailey said aloud to herself as she stared at the phone.

Hailey wanted to throw all caution to the wind and contact him right then and there, but silently talked herself out of doing so.

"Mommy?" Alex said while he tugged at Hailey's skirt hem.

"Hi there, Munchkin!" Hailey snapped out of her trance and turned her attention to her chubby cheeked offspring.

"I have to go pow wow."

"Alright Stinky, let's go!" Hailey tugged him quickly to the bathroom.

She settled him on his personal potty and stepped away to give him a little privacy. Hailey leaned against the door frame, her back to him. Alex began singing softly and increased volume the more vocally confident he became – even though he destroyed the song.

"If you happy and you know clap your hands! If you happy and you know, then you betta betta show, if you happy and you KNOW CLAP YOUR HANDS!!"

Hailey giggled to herself and her child's willingness to sing while he was relieving himself.

"I'm done Mommy!"

"That was fast Alex, are you sure you're done?"

"Oh yes, Mommy. I don't mess around in here."

"What? Alex, where did you hear that? Mess around?" Hailey asked him as she cleaned his bottom.

"From Daddy. He said not to mess around in the bathroom, so I don't mess around, Mommy."

"Okay big boy!"

"Mommy? You look so happy. Are you happy?"

Hailey smiled at his observation, but was a bit taken aback. "Yes baby. Why did you ask me that?"

"You look happy. Did someone make you happy?"

"You do, my love! Every day!"

Alex looked at Hailey and touched her cheek with his tiny hand. "I love you, Mommy."

"Mommy loves you too!"

Hailey had an idea why she may have seemed happier to Alex. Hailey felt more optimistic regarding her future since she saw Bryan. She decided that she was going to definitely call Bryan, but not right now. Not today.

*   *   *   *

"So when you left, you didn't tell anyone? You just left?" Chase asked.

"Yes," Bryan told her. "I had to go. I didn't know what else to do."

"Why didn't you tell Hailey at least? I thought you loved her. You were going to propose to her that same year, right?"

"I know that, Chase. I was embarrassed and I fled. I was like Forrest Gump after Jenny left him. I just felt like running." Bryan chuckled at himself. Chase smiled and then scribbled something on her notepad.

"So now you are back. What is your first move?"

"Well, I gave her my number. I just have to wait."

"You shouldn't wait too long. Seek her out. Be aggressive. Let her know how you really feel. Whether you are hurt, angry, in love with her still . . . you will feel better once you get everything off of your chest."

Bryan rubbed his beard and stared out of Chase's office window, contemplating his next move with Hailey. He didn't want to come off as pushy or impetuous, but he sincerely loved Hailey. While he lived on the islands he thought about her every day. There were women who wanted to be with him and Bryan tried to move on by entertaining a few. It wasn't as if the selections weren't beautiful, he just didn't have any feelings for them. One Jamaican woman tried so hard to be with Bryan that she had become maniacal when he refused her suggestion for monogamy. She resorted to stalking him, as it wasn't hard with the island being so small. That was when the Dominican Republic became a place of refuge for him.

"I will make sure I let her know exactly how I feel," he told Chase.

"That's great news, Bryan."

"Can I ask you a question?"

Chase nodded.

"How is it that you are such a popular psychologist?"

Chase grinned and set her tablet down on the desk behind her. She tapped her temple with the tip of her pen.

"It's a lot of work, but I enjoy helping people get to the root of their concerns. The joy comes when I see that look of relief on their face that says '*I got it now*'. I live for that."

"Right. So how do you know so much about relationships? Are you married?"

"No."

"Anyone special?"

"Not at all."

"I hope you don't take this the wrong way, but you are a beautiful woman. I find it a little hard to believe that there isn't anyone special in your life."

"Well," Chase began with a labored sigh, "there aren't too many guys who want to tell their friends, my girlfriend is a shrink, ya know?"

"I understand," Bryan told her with a chuckle.

"Well, time's up. I will see you next week?"

"Sure. Hopefully I will have a positive report for you then."

"Good luck with that," Chase encouraged him. "If you need to talk to me between that time, by all means, feel free to contact me."

Bryan nodded and stood up to leave. Chase gave him a smile as her eyes gave him a once over from head to toe. Chase couldn't help but get a little sexually heated when she saw how broad his shoulders were and how powerful the curve of his lower back appeared under his loose fitting shirt. Chase was quite skilled at undressing men with her eyes. She noticed how muscular his thighs were and the promise of power they presented.

Chase was instantly attracted to him when she met up with Bryan in the restaurant. When she heard how hypnotically regal his voice was on the phone, she couldn't wait to meet him. At first sight, his voice fit him perfectly. The beard aided in his rugged good looks, but she could tell that the beard was something new for him. He stroked it too much. Chase wondered how his hands would feel stroking her. It was improbable because this man was in love with a woman that broke his heart. Some woman named Hailey. Secretly, Chase was curious about Hailey's looks. She only saw her from behind and it wasn't a full view, just the top of her head really. Chase had a picture of her in her mind, but wondered just what type of hold Hailey had over Bryan.

Bryan gave Chase a final glance and a wide grin that accompanied a slight flinch upward of his eyebrows.

"Until next time, Chase," he said.

She waved and smiled. Bryan closed her door and stepped into the waiting room. When he saw Steve sitting in the foyer, he stopped in his tracks. His stomach felt sour and his mouth became cold and dry. His smile faded and shoulders sank slightly. Bryan had no idea if Steve was going to start any shit with him or if he had been following him, which would be flat out ridiculous.

Despite the extra hair on Bryan, Steve immediately recognized him and stood up with his shoulders squared and feet planted. Bryan straightened his posture and prepared himself for anything Steve may attempt. The Rastafarians taught him a few moves that he was willing to use if need be.

"Bryan Bryant," Steve said humorlessly.

"Steven."

"What the hell are you doing here?"

"Minding my own business. Why are you here?"

"That's none of your damn business. But if you must know, I'm here to take my lady to dinner."

Bryan pointed to the closed door where Chase sat on the other side. "You mean that lady in there?"

Steve took a few non-confrontational steps toward Bryan. "Of course. She fine, ain't she?"

"Interesting. Talk about two versions of the same story," Bryan told him with a chuckle. Steve cocked his head, confused by his comment. Bryan realized that Steve had no clue why he said that and dare not tell him what it meant. He stared at Steve while he walked toward him. "Now, if you'll excuse me, Steven," he scoffed and promptly left.

Steve watched Bryan's departure and headed toward Chase's office. He shook his head and muttered, "Bitch ass."

Just then, Chase opened the door and jumped slightly when she saw Steve standing there. She giggled with embarrassment and placed a soothing hand on Steve's chest.

"Steve! You startled me," she explained her reaction.

He leaned in and kissed her soft lips, "You ready?"

"Ready? Oh! Yes. Dinner. Give me ten minutes." Chase turned to go back into her office, but Steve placed his hand on her forearm hindering her retreat. She turned to hear what he was about to say.

"Babe? What was that guy doing here?"

"Now now, you know I can't discuss the details of my patients."

"Oh! So he's a patient?"

"Steve? What's the matter, hon?"

"I know him is all. Just surprised to see him around. I thought he left the area."

Chase folded her arms in front of her. "Why would you think that?"

"Just hadn't seen his puss ass in a few years. I sure hope this isn't a case of déjà vu with him. I may have to stretch him out if it is."

"What? You lost me. I'm not sure I follow."

"Nothing baby, let's just go. Get yourself together."

Steve sat down, dismissing Chase. She stared at him for a moment before withdrawing back into her office. Once there, she opened her file drawer and pulled Steve's case file. She coupled it with Bryan's file and tossed them into her briefcase. She headed back out of her office to rejoin Steve.

"Okay, let's go."

On the drive to the restaurant, Chase had given herself time to process Steve's sessions and her new patient Bryan. Mentally, she began comparing notes of both men. The fact that they know each other, the time frame that Bryan left and Steve mentioning not seeing him for years was coincidental. What gave Chase pause was Steve mentioning something about déjà vu. She wasn't exactly sure what that meant. Her intention was to comb through Steve's notes and pray that there were some clues. She didn't want to be in the middle of feuding rivals.

"Hey, you are quiet over there. You okay?" Steve asked her.

"I'm okay."

"You sure? Look, I'm sorry about that shit back at your office. I'll be cool baby. I don't want to do anything to jeopardize your practice. And I don't want to jeopardize our thing either. You are special to me. You know that?"

"I do!" she smiled at him and rubbed his thigh. "Hey, listen . . . how 'bout we skip dinner and do something else?"

Steve smiled in her direction and licked his lips. "What'd you have in mind?"

"I say we go to your place and christen a few rooms. Maybe order up a pizza afterward."

"Ooo, that sounds good to me," Steve told her. He did a wild U-turn in the middle of the street and sped in the direction of his house.

Once there, Steve quickly unlocked the door and Chase kissed her way inside, pushing Steve with her body.

It was her first time at his apartment so she quickly surveyed the room. There in the corner next to the window sat a sturdy loveseat. The street lights from outside shone in through the partially opened blinds. Graciously, she pushed him and he toppled onto the couch. Steve smiled in between the wild tongue kisses while she unhooked his belt from a straddled position and unfastened his jeans. Steve lifted her skirt and smiled when he realized she didn't have on any underwear. Wanting to rip off her blouse, he opted to nuzzle her full breasts instead. They continued kissing and groping one another. Quickly, she undid her blouse and then flung it away to give Steve access. He lifted her bra and immediately began feasting on her tits as she swirled her hips. Chase's feminine dew could be felt on Steve's leg and he knew that she was ready. He gripped her hips and rubbed the length of his shaft on her moistness. As he did that, Chase fished for her purse that was next to them and ripped open a condom. With haste, Steve rolled it on him, lifted and dropped Chase on his dick and went to work. Up and down she went, but Steve aided her by placing his hands on her hips. Chase was small framed, but shapely. He could easily lift her as she probably only weighed in at 120 or so. Her long hair draped over her face and into Steve's. It fluttered every time they breathed heavily with his strokes. She flipped it back with her hand, but it fell again anyway.

Steve could barely contain himself. Because of Chase's background, every time they had sex, he felt like he was fucking a Kardashian. Easily she could fit into their family tree with her long dark hair and olive complexion. After she rode him for more than half an hour, Steve wanted to finish this session off in a different position. He settled his buttocks on the edge of the loveseat and instructed her to lean back on her hands. With her moist passage aligned perfectly to his stiffness, Steve's strokes became more rapid as he squeezed her hips and waist fast on him.

"Yes! Yes! Yes!" Chase shouted.

"I'm cumming baby!" Steve announced loudly.

Chase waited patiently for Steve to come down from his climax. When he got himself together, she suggested that they go to his bedroom to take a nap. Feeling spent from the orgasm, Steve was too willing to accommodate. They rested and Steve drifted off to sleep. But not Chase.

While Steve was asleep, Chase conducted reconnaissance to gather some additional information about Steve. She was interested in how he and Bryan were linked more than anything else. Steve was snoring rather loudly, so he would be out for a while as long as she kept the noise to a minimum.

Chase searched a few drawers in the kitchen and came across several papers and photos. She began rifling through them. Most of the photos were of him and his son. Steve talked about him all the time to her, but this was her first time seeing exactly what he looked like. Chase's heart melted.

"He's so cute," she whispered as she smiled at the photo. Chase came across another photo of a woman. She looked seductively at the camera, in her dark blue off the shoulder shirt. Her hand rested on her temple, causing her eyebrow to lift slightly, and her fingertips were laced by her hair. Immediately, Chase knew exactly who this was. This had to be the woman that broke Steve's heart and sent him to therapy – or sent him in the arms of Chase. She was pretty, Chase thought. Chase did not know her, but instantly disliked her. It was probably because of the pain that she caused Steve, or perhaps it was because she was still present in Steve's life. Unequivocally, her dislike for her was because Steve still had this picture and he should have moved on destroying it the minute he began dating Chase. This was the face that Chase could now associate with Steve's pain. She wondered what her name was. Maybe Chase didn't need to know her name. The face was enough to digest for the moment. Against her better judgment, she turned the photo over and there it was, written in Steve's handwriting . . . Hailey.

"Oh my God," Chase whispered.

9

I fed Gabe and read a story to him for the evening. He was curled up with Ian watching a baseball game when I decided to give Camilla a call just to see what time she would be headed over to get him.

"How is my baby?" Camilla asked me.

"He is doing fine. Watching baseball with Uncle Ian."

"Thanks so much for watching him again. You know we are gearing up for this tax season. A lot of new regulations were just published and my boss can be a bit anal."

"No problem, girl."

There was an uncomfortable silence between the two of us.

"Josephine? Are you there?" Camilla asked.

"Yeah, I'm sorry. Just debating sharing some information with you. But now that I've said that, I may as well, huh?"

"Hit it."

"Bryan Bryant is back in town. I saw him yesterday at a restaurant when I met up with Hailey."

Silence.

"Are you there, Camilla?"

"Yes, I'm here. For a moment there I thought you said that Bryan Bryant was back in town." She chuckled a bit.

"That's exactly what I said. And he looks totally different," I added remembering his scruffy beard mostly.

"Really?" Camilla voice had a bit of surprise. "I mean, oh well good for him. So did he stop to talk to you guys?"

"Actually, he did. We barely recognized him. His crazy ass still called me Jacqueline though," I chuckled.

"How did your girl act?"

"She was a bit thrown," I started and then cleared my throat before continuing, "kinda like you . . . just now."

"What? No! I'm not thrown. Just surprised. I mean, if you recall, he hated me."

"Hate is a strong word, Camilla."

"Well Josephine, it wasn't love."

Just then Camilla's cell phone beeped to indicate she had an additional call. She peered down at the screen to see the read out on the display. It was Felix again.

"Oh lord, this guy Felix is calling me again."

"Do you need to go?"

"No, I'm not talking to him right now. Or ever."

Camilla looked at the display again before she made a left turn. She turned the car a bit too sharply and it caused her phone to slide off of the armrest and clear across the floor of the passenger's side. For a split second, Camilla took her eyes off of the road to see the destination of the phone so she could retrieve it later. By the time she looked back up, it was too late.

Even I could hear the crunch of metal from Camilla's vehicle as it slammed into another car.

"Oh my God!" Camilla screamed.

"Oh no! Camilla? Are you okay!?" I immediately stood up, my eyes widened as they darted from side to side while I awaited confirmation from Camilla.

Hearing the urgency in my voice, Ian sat up and looked at his panicked wife with concern.

"Babe?" Ian asked. "What's wrong?"

"Camilla?" I asked again when she didn't respond quickly enough. I could hear what sounded like tussling during the periods of time that weren't muted.

"Hello?" Camilla responded as she tried to catch her breath.

"Oh my God, are you okay? What happened?"

"I just ran into the back of a Bentley. Fucking great! Let me call you back, Josephine."

"Are you okay?" I asked with my hand to my heart to keep it calm.

"I'm fine. I'm sure it sounded worse on your end. I'm fine. I'm going to have to curse this person out though. He just dammit stopped for no reason! I'll call you back."

The line went dead.

"Is Camilla okay?" Ian asked me.

"Yes, baby. She had a fender bender. She is going to call me back." I sighed with relief and plumped back down in the chair.

Camilla hopped out of her car to assess the wreckage. She placed her open palm to her forehead and tallied up the damage in her head. Her heart pounded quickly causing a nasty silvery taste in her mouth. The man in the other vehicle stepped out and headed toward the rear of his car.

"Are you alright?"

"No!" Camilla boomed. "Why did you stop? There wasn't anything in front of you! Where did you learn how to drive? Stevie Wonder High School or Ray Charles University?"

"Hey, hold on. I'm sorry, but there were some kids playing and I could've sworn one was about to run out in front of my car. Please don't be upset."

"And on top of that you are driving a Bentley. I may as well rip up my insurance card and burn my license. I can't afford to fix a Bentley."

The gentleman took a closer look at his damage, which was technically minor compared to the damage to her car.

"Don't panic. It's not that bad."

Camilla paced back and forth slightly beside the front fender of her vehicle.

"No . . .," she muttered. Camilla could feel a lump swelling in her throat. She didn't want to cry, but felt like she was at the end of her rope and would explode if she didn't.

"Oh no, don't do that," the gentleman told her. "Please don't. It's not that bad. Don't cry. Please."

Camilla doubled over and buried her face in her hands. The man came over to console her by rubbing her back.

"It's not that bad," he reassured her.

Camilla could not see his face, but was immediately comforted by his soothing voice. She wanted so desperately to believe that it *wasn't* bad, but Camilla felt as though she was about to have a nervous breakdown. The only thing that kept her partially sane was her beautiful son, Gabe. She pressed on for him and everything that she did was strictly done for his sake. Camilla did not have any intentions of letting this stranger see her cry, but she just could not contain her frustration, hurt and displeasure with life any longer.

"Hey," the man said to her. "Come on." He tried to lift Camilla upright. When she stood up, the man hugged her. He knew that there was something else going on with this young lady. Since her immediate response to the situation was to cry, he didn't think it would be appropriate to reprimand her. She was clearly overwhelmed.

Camilla buried her face in the valley of his underarm and shoulder and let loose round two of her tears. He held her tightly and rubbed her back up and down to soothe her. For a moment, it felt to him as if this were his woman and instead of a car accident, she actually needed him – wanted him to be there for her.

Camilla carefully released herself from him by taking a step backward. Realizing the awkwardness of the situation, she gathered herself. She wiped her tears from her reddened eyes and chuckled slightly with embarrassment.

"I'm so sorry," she told him. "I ruined your suit."

"It's okay."

"I wrecked your car."

"I told you it's not that bad."

"I'm sorry. I don't know what came over me. I guess a good cry was long overdue." She rubbed his suit where she cried and tried to smooth out the rest of his clothing. She smiled nervously and unsuccessfully tried not to make eye contact with the man. He was attractive, obviously a gentleman and very well dressed.

He smiled at her nervousness and held her arms gently.

"You okay? It's going to be okay."

"You must think I'm a freak now. Let me get you my insurance information."

"Hold on a minute. You sure you are okay?"

"Oh gosh, don't tell me you are a shrink," she chuckled again. "That would just top off this day perfectly."

He laughed a bit, "No. I'm not. What's your name?"

"Camilla Anderson."

"Hi Camilla. I'm Jameson Hedley. Now are you sure you are okay?"

"I'll be fine. I'm sorry. It's just been a trying year, Jameson."

"Camilla, I tell you what. Forget about the car. Let's have dinner instead. I'd love to turn that frown upside down, beautiful." He smiled and it warmed Camilla's heart completely.

"I don't want to impose." Camilla secretly looked at his hands for a ring. The last thing she needed was yet another love triangle. She didn't see anything, but it didn't necessarily mean he wasn't married.

"You wouldn't be. Please join me."

"Well, I have to pick up my two year old. My friend is watching him."

"Okay. This is what I'll do, I'll give you my number but I'm also going to get your license plate number too. If you don't call me, I'm going to chase you down and beg for a date." He smiled that warm charming smile again that was infectious. Camilla smiled and rubbed his arm.

"You must be an angel, Jameson."

He smiled and shook his head. While he held Camilla's hands, he couldn't help but get lost in her eyes. They stood there for a moment, both taking the other into them. Jameson appreciated how she trusted him enough to release her emotions with him along the side of the road – it certainly helped that she was attractive.

"Call me when you make it home. Please." He reached in his jacket pocket and handed Camilla his card. Whipping out his cell phone right after, he snapped a photo of her license plate and winked at her. Gallantly, he crossed to the door of her vehicle and held it open for her to climb inside. She blushed as she hadn't had this treatment in quite a while. Humbly and sweetly, she gazed up at him from her seated position. Jameson leaned against her door frame and smiled down at her.

"Seriously, Camilla. I want to make sure you are at home safely. Call me."

"I will . . . Jameson Hedley."

He closed the door and smiled at her through the glass. His kindness had finally given her hope. Camilla didn't want to get overly excited, but there was a calmness that came with Jameson. The way he held her while her emotions were unleashed made her feel protected and safe. She wanted to feel more of that with him and hoped to just enjoy him for however long she was meant to.

Despite the dent in the front of her car, Camilla smiled all the way to Josephine's house. She remembered that Felix called her and left a message. She wasn't going to check his message until after the weekend was over. Camilla was not going to allow any negativity to destroy the long awaited euphoric feeling of a man giving her butterflies.

Camilla knocked on Josephine's door. She could hear Gabe's muffled yelling in the background.

"Mommy! Mommy! Mommy!"

"Hold on sweetie," I instructed Gabe so I could unlock and open the door.

"Hey girl," Camilla said as she entered. Gabe hugged her legs and Camilla bent down to scoop him up in her arms. She smothered his face with kisses. Gabe smiled and giggled as she tickled him. "Hi Creepy! How is mama's baby boy?"

"I'm fine, Mommy! Where were you?"

"I had a little fender bender, sweetie. I'm so sorry I'm late. I missed you!"

"What's a fender bender, Mommy?"

"I hit another car with mine, sweetheart."

"Are you okay, Mommy?" Gabe asked as he played with her earring.

I rubbed Gabe's back as he continued to inspect his mother to ensure she was indeed okay. His concern was precious to me.

"Mommy is fine."

Ian approached Camilla to better hear what exactly had happened.

"You okay, Camilla?" he asked.

"Thanks, Ian. I am. You guys are the best."

"Okay." Ian reached for Gabe and tossed him over his shoulder as if he were an overcoat. "Come on partner, let's get your stuff together."

"Do we have to get a new car? I can drive. Mommy is not a good driver Uncle *In*."

Camilla looked at Gabe and shook her head.

"I know, come on," Ian agreed and carted Gabe off to the rear of the house.

"My heart was pounding so hard," I admitted. "What happened?"

"So I rear ended this Bentley and this handsome gentleman steps out. And Josephine, I don't know what happened. I think everything that was built up just came rushing out. I was prepared to curse him from here to southeast D.C. and I just broke down and cried."

"Are you serious? What did he do?"

"Girl, he held me and rubbed my back. It was beautiful. I never felt so protected and loved."

"Loved? By a stranger?"

"I know. It was so . . . so . . ."

"Strange?"

"Whatever. Anyway, he wants to go out on a date and said not to worry about the damage. Come on Gabe!!"

Gabe came barreling toward the ladies with a smile on his face. He reached for Camilla's hand and then disappeared around a corner.

"Did I say something wrong again?" Josephine asked her.

"Not at all. I told him I would call him when I got home. He wanted to make sure that I made it home safely."

"Wow. And he wants a date? Well, this guy sounds like Mr. Prince Charming."

"He is quite charming. Well, so far he is. I'm not trying to get all geeked up about him just yet. But I have a good feeling about him. Gabe!"

Just then Gabe popped up by his mother's side and looked up at her.

"Come on, Creepy!" Camilla smiled and leaned toward me for a hug. I hugged her and then squatted to give Gabe a hug and kiss.

"I love you, my Pumpkin!" I told him.

"I love you too Auntie *Joe-feen*. Bye Uncle *In*! I love you."

"Alright little man! I love you too, partner. See you next time."

Camilla winked at me and tugged Gabe along. Camilla mouthed the words "*I'll call you*". I smiled and closed the door behind her.

Camilla carted Gabe to the car and strapped him in his car seat securely. She kissed him on his forehead and tucked his favorite stuffed animal in the seat with him. Soon after, Gabe would be asleep, his little chin pressed into his chest, and drool leaking from his partially opened mouth.

On her careful drive home, she couldn't help but to think about Jameson. He was older than she, but attractive. His smile was irresistible. She was definitely going to call him the moment she got Gabe settled. Camilla wasn't one to believe in love at first sight, but Jameson had such a commanding presence and strength which intrigued Camilla.

She parked her car, grabbed her purse and diaper bag on one arm, and then scooped up Gabe with the other. Her keychain dangled from her finger as she fished around for the one to unlock the front door. With two years of practice, she had this technique down and always managed never to disturb Gabe from his nap. She kicked the door open, which the bottom of it was riddled with scuff marks from doing so, and set the bags down first. Carefully, she set Gabe down on his favorite Superman *Chill-ax* chair, which was just a fancy name for "beanbag". Gabe waddled and wriggled around until he found a comfortable position.

Camilla started on dinner and decided to call Jameson while she was doing so. She loved to multi-task.

"Well hello," he greeted her.

"Hi," she smiled. "As promised, I'm calling you to let you know that I made it safely."

"That's great news!"

"Jameson, can I ask you a question?"

"Of course, Camilla."

"What made you do that? I mean, you hugged me like we were . . . I mean, I don't want to frighten you off with this statement, it's just an observation, but you hugged me like we were . . . a couple. Why did you do that?"

"Did it make you uncomfortable?"

"Not at all. I was just curious. It was actually one of the nicest things anyone has done for me in a while."

"You're kidding?"

"No."

"Well stick with me, Camilla. I can be notorious for spoiling someone I'm quite interested in. But to answer your question, we all have bad days. It's the choices that we make that can either perpetuate the bad or make the bad a positive. I knew you were upset and it would've been pointless to make you feel worse. So I decided to just be there for you."

Camilla quietly exhaled and smiled to herself. "Wow. I guess you have a point there."

She continued preparing food. Jameson could hear a slight commotion and inquired as to what she was preoccupied with at the moment.

"Are you cooking?"

"Yes. I'm going to wake up Gabe in a bit and feed him, read to him some, get him bathed and then put little Creepy to bed. Oh, sorry. My nickname for him is Creepy. Which he is anything but."

Jameson laughed, "Don't apologize, I think it's adorable. Your friend wasn't upset that you were late were they?"

"Oh no! Josephine . . . that's my friend, she loves Gabe."

"Josephine?"

Camilla stopped prepping dinner for a moment and then responded, "Mm hmm."

"I met someone named Josephine a while ago. That's not a common name these days, you know?"

"Oh really? Well, the one I know does marketing and is somewhat popular in this town. I know she loves to go out to eat because she can't cook," Camilla chuckled. "Where did you meet the other Josephine?"

"Oh, I actually met her through an attorney who was working on my case. I played a trick on her. But she was cool with it."

"An attorney?" Camilla gulped a bit.

"Yes. It was about two years ago."

"By chance was the attorney's name Tamar? Woodruff?"

Jameson paused a bit before he spoke, then let out a light scoff, "Why yes, it was."

"Oh wow. I uh . . . I know all of them."

"How fortuitous," he concluded.

"Quite."

"Well lovely lovely Camilla. I have a web meeting to chair. I would love to see you again soon."

"I would too. It just depends on when I can get a babysitter again. I've been leaving him with Josephine a lot lately," Camilla admitted with a sigh.

"Well, I tell you what. If you'd like, we can make it a family friendly date. Bring him along. A walk around the Harbor and some ice cream. No pressure, but it's up to you. I'd love to meet this "Creepy"," he laughed at his own joke.

"Uh, let me think about that and I will let you know," she told him.

"That's fair. I hope to see you soon. I have to run, Camilla."

"Okay."

Camilla finished up her dinner and peeked in at Gabe. He was awake now, but lying comfortably. It almost seemed as if he were in deep thought. She watched him for a moment, unnoticed. Gabe sighed and then reached down and pulled out his Superman figurine that was buried under this leg. He held it up and pretended to make him fly. He then looked at it for a moment.

"I'm going to be Superman for mommy."

Camilla smiled and almost broke down in tears just then but restrained herself. She wanted nothing but the best for Gabe and it sounded as if he wanted nothing but the best for his mother. She was tired of the same bad results and decided to do something different for a change. Different tactics should yield different results. What harm could it be to have a family date with Jameson? He seemed like a very nice man and the possibilities of where this could lead to were endless. Worst case scenario, they wouldn't hit it off, which would be no different than where she was currently. Camilla made up in her mind at that moment to go all in, feet first and let the chips fall where they may.

But still, a small part of her had a sinking feeling about exploring the unknown.

10

Tamar checked in to her hotel room and began unpacking. She opened the curtains wide to allow the sunlight to spill into the large room. Her chest rose and fell as she took a deep breath before peering down at the street and at the other buildings in the vicinity. After kicking off her heels, she dug her stocking feet deep into the plush rug and nibbled on a few grapes that were in the fruit basket sent to her suite. The basket had to have been from Taj even though there wasn't a note that indicated so. Desperately she wanted nothing more than to wash off the residue from the airport and plane from her body. Before turning on the shower, Tamar tossed one of her lingerie sets on the bed. Eagerly, she anticipated Taj's arrival.

When the water was hot enough, she climbed in and let it caress every inch of her body. She lathered up and rubbed her soapy hands over her shoulders, arms, breasts and stomach while she pretended her hands were Taj's. The suds were being massaged into her butt, hips and thighs. Before she put the soap down, she lathered up again and her right hand disappeared into the crevice of her vagina. Her fingertips glided gently across her femininity. Eyes closed, she extended her neck backward and gasped with enchantment.

Carefully, quietly and very nude, Taj entered the shower behind her. He slowly placed his hands on her hips and slid them around her thighs. Tamar smiled to herself as her eyes remained closed. Taj's hands found her bosoms from behind as his mouth kissed her moist neck. The water bounced off of her shoulder and splashed his face gently. Tamar ducked underneath the stream of the water and placed both palms against the marble in front of her. The water from the showerhead now pounded against Taj's chest and stomach as it trickled down Tamar's back. To keep his caressing motion constant, he lathered his hands.

Tamar wasn't expecting him quite this early, but because of the welcome he gave her, she didn't mind at all. He teased her back with his fingertips while he watched the suds roll off of her bottom and onto his feet. Deeply, he penetrated her while he held her shoulder with one hand like he was riding a wild bronco. Although Tamar's moans were soft, he could still hear them over the streaming water.

"Louder!" he instructed in his voice that unsuccessfully masked his native dialect. As he gave his instruction, he thrust himself deeper.

Tamar moaned again when his single hard thrust teased her G-spot.

"Louder!" he demanded again with another single hard thrust.

Tamar obliged, her body preparing for an orgasm.

"I said louder!" he demanded again. Instead of the singular thrust, he pounded rapidly, barbarically into her. His hammering caused Tamar's back to bow as she released her first orgasm. Taj pressed his hands in the center of her back trying to get her to stick her rear end back out, but Tamar's orgasm was stubborn to his touch. It only made her have another. Taj popped her on the rear to get her to obey him and stick it back out.

"Oh God . . .," she mustered. He popped her on the fleshy part of her ass again. "Oh!"

Taj chuckled, "That's what happens when you don't do what I tell you. Now are you gonna stick it out for me? You sexy girl." Then he whispered seductively, "Stick it out."

Tamar was trying to control herself as his take charge attitude and dialect just did something to her. It was an erotic combination. Still unable to "stick it out" for him, he turned her gently with his hands. He held up a single finger and shook it naughtily at her with a smile. He knelt down in front of her in the tub and patted her legs and then patted his shoulders. Tamar looked down at him in awe as he smiled. Tamar thought the worse place to do "stunts" would be in the shower. Dispelling the idea, she shook her head slightly.

"Trust me, I got you," he reassured her.

With some hesitation, Tamar did as instructed, pressing her back hard against the steamed marble. Lifting her slowly, he gripped her hips firmly.

"Hold on to the showerhead," he told her. Tamar lifted her hands and gripped the pipe of the showerhead tightly. By now, Taj's thick, curly hair was wet and laid like icing on a sheet cake. He lifted her carefully and buried his face between her legs.

"Oh lord!!" Tamar whimpered.

After several minutes of fun in the shower, they both decided to make their way to a dry area of the hotel room. Their pruned fingertips caressed one another as the scent of soap mixed with the flow of steam filled the room. Taj wanted nothing more than to make Tamar's clean body dirty all over again. He couldn't keep his hands off of her and wanted to be sure that he made up for lost time. Just about every position he tried was sure to make Tamar cum – quickly and repeatedly. After almost two hours of fooling around, Tamar was spent. Her body was empty and weak. Taj collapsed next to her on the bed and they both fell asleep.

Almost three hours had passed and the sun was about to rest for the night. The glow from the orange and red sky awakened Tamar. Her eyes rolled about lazily as she focused on the sunset. Taj was at the foot of the bed watching her being lulled out of her rest by the sun.

"Hey sexy," he said.

"What . . . what time is it?"

"A little after six. Are you hungry?"

"I'm starved."

"You looked so gorgeous lying there. That sunlight is hitting you in all of the right areas."

Tamar smiled and reached for his hand. He took it, lifted it to his mouth and softly kissed it.

"This is going to be a great week. Come on, let's get you dressed and get some food, 'eh?"

When Taj said *get you dressed*, he meant in the literal sense. When they were first together and Tamar was preparing to leave, Taj dressed her. It took longer than her standard ten minutes, but they both enjoyed it nonetheless. His hands would glide with the clothes, his lips touched whatever appealed to him at that moment, and he would squeeze her tight against his body in between putting on her articles. Tamar had never experienced anything quite like it. Even Donovan didn't do anything as intimate as that.

Donovan!

She forgot to give him a call when she arrived to New York. *He must be worried sick*, she thought.

"Oh no!" Tamar reached for her cell phone.

"What's the matter?"

Tamar ignored his question and began tapping her phone. She noticed that there weren't any calls or texts from Donovan even wondering if she had made it safely. She called his phone and put a finger to her mouth to indicate to Taj to remain quiet. He sighed and flopped on the bed with his back to her. Donovan's phone went straight to voice mail.

"Hey baby, it's me. I'm in New York. I came in and wanted to rest my eyes for a minute and fell asleep. I hope you weren't worried. Well, let me run. I'll talk to you soon. Love you, bye."

"You left a message?"

"Yeah. What's wrong with that?"

"If you were my woman, I'd answer every one of your calls."

Tamar smiled and swung her legs around to prepare to stand, "yeah right."

"Okay, I guess I just have to prove it to you one day."

"What? No. There will be no *one day*. I already told you what was up. Let's not discuss this right now."

"Okay, keep fighting it. I'm not gonna let your man come between us. I want you twenty four seven," he said with a smile.

"Taj? Please," Tamar stood to get herself ready.

"Let me ask you something, what if you guys broke up? What if he didn't want to be with you anymore? Would you be with me then?" Taj pulled up his pants.

"What?" she scoffed, "We are *not* breaking up."

"How can you be so sure?"

"Because I know. We are compatible. In all areas."

"So are you and me."

Tamar ignored him and walked to the bathroom. The water ran for several minutes. After he could no longer wait, Taj walked toward the door and spoke to her from the other side.

"I won't pressure you about it now, but I have a feeling we will be together. Then we can run this town. We will take New York by storm, baby. Just think about it."

Tamar continued brushing her teeth and flipped her eyes upward quickly. She kept what was happening between her and Taj in the proper perspective. It was just sex! If he continued to discuss a future with her, she would be forced to cut off all communication with him permanently. A future with Taj was not what she wanted.

"No pressure. Let's just enjoy this week," Tamar told him.

*   *   *   *

Meanwhile, at that exact moment, in a southern part of the east, Donovan's flight landed in Barbados. Even though he and Celeste were on the same flight, they didn't sit together. Celeste was seated at least eight rows back and on the opposite side of the plane. Communication between them was terminated when they both stepped foot into Reagan National airport. The two of them maintained the façade for the duration of the travel, but knew that those walls would be torn down the minute they made it to the resort. The sneaking around was exciting and adventurous, but certainly not needed on the island.

Celeste maintained her composure on the flight. She wanted to stop by his row and give him a knowing glance and subtle smirk, but remained in her seat. As she stared out at the fluffy cumulus clouds that hovered at 30,000 feet, she wondered if this was going to be the moment that Donovan would declare exclusivity with her. Celeste seeing the ring certainly wasn't a coincidence. She just wondered why he didn't ask her right there in the hotel room. Perhaps it wasn't romantic enough and not as symbolic. Stealing away to meet someone who is in a stalled relationship, may not have been the proper back drop to a proposal. One thing Celeste had been was patient. Determined to enjoy this week with the man of her dreams, she was confident that at its conclusion, she would wear that beautiful ring proudly on the flight home. She would stare lovingly at her man as he asked to be seated next to his fiancé. But until then, it would be a week of excursions, booze cruises, beach combing and non-stop love making.

When they arrived at the resort, Donovan dropped his bags and stretched out on the bed. Shortly after, Celeste entered the room, saw him on the bed and smiled. She climbed in beside him and snuggled.

"You want to head to the beach?" she asked.

"I just need to rest. We probably should've flown down tomorrow, but it's okay, we are here now. Let's nap first honey. I'm tired as hell."

"Okay. I have some very nice bathing suits that I can't wait to wear for you."

"I can't wait to see them."

By the time they awoke, the sun had set, but it was still warm. As promised Celeste donned a bejeweled bikini and matching sarong. Donovan was relaxed in linen shorts and a V-neck t-shirt. As they strolled the beach hand and hand, Celeste felt an overwhelming sensation of being in love. It was reminiscent of the feeling she had when they were in law school together. She smiled to herself as she looked upon the dark waves, lit only by the moon as they crashed before kissing their ankles. She wanted this feeling to last forever.

Donovan on the other hand was trying to locate a nice secluded area of the beach so they could fuck undisturbed. He was sure that some other couples may stumble upon them, but that would probably be because they were looking to do the same thing. Donovan didn't turn his phone on after the flight and was a little concerned about Tamar calling and possibly worrying about him. It didn't bother him too much because he knew how secure she was despite his sneaking around. Tamar didn't question his whereabouts unless something absolutely didn't make any sense to her. Even then, she chose her battles carefully and wouldn't badger Donovan with guessing games and 50 questions. Tamar only acted when she had proof and Donovan never gave her any, nor did he give her reason to suspect anything was happening. There was no question that Donovan was good at the game. However, the games were getting old to him and he wanted to hand in his player's card for good.

"Let's go over here," he tugged Celeste along.

The sand was sprinkled with moonlight as it peaked through the leaves of the tree. The trunk of it was big enough for Celeste to grip comfortably from the front or to lean her back against. Ironically enough, there was a slight "hump" in the tree where he could maneuver a few additional positions with her. It was as if nature knew this tree was going to be used for screwing.

"You have a great eye," Celeste told him.

"I know, now get your fine ass up against this tree!" Donovan ordered, turning on his maniacal sex-craved aggressive man routine that Celeste loved. This time, she stopped him.

"No Donnie," she placed her hand on his chest. He looked into her sincere eyes as she slightly smiled. "Not here. Let's just . . ."

"Let's just what?"

"I want to say it, but . . .," she stopped herself.

"Say it."

"Let's just make love," she gently told him. She cast her eyes down immediately regretting saying that. Her heart beat quickened as she anticipated some sort of backlash. But she calmed herself as she remembered that they once were in love a long time ago.

Donovan paused and took a moment to gather himself. Even though her request took him off guard, it was sincere. In every way imaginable, he certainly was going to oblige her because he wanted this to be a special trip for the both of them. As she read his eyes to gather a reaction, Celeste waited patiently for his response.

"Of course baby," he told her.

He pulled her in with a soft embrace. Celeste rubbed his back tenderly and kissed him deeply. It's true – the tree offered much for the couple.

By the time they were finished, they heard a party at a nearby resort get well underway. The steel drums drew them toward where it originated. Celeste was feeling excessively close to Donovan and instead of the hand holding, she hooked her arm with his.

"I'm hungry, you?" he asked her.

"Not really. I could use a drink though."

"Rum punch?"

"No doubt."

The two of them walked up to the bar and ordered up some drinks. Celeste stared at Donovan, taking in his full essence as if it were for the first time. Donovan was watching the folks on the wooden plank laid dance floor. Several women were whining their bodies to the reggae music while their dance partners were enjoying the view or the feeling of their backsides brushing against their midsections.

"Can you whine?" Donovan asked Celeste as he watched one talented woman in particular.

"What?" she asked with a smile.

He looked at her, "can you whine your body?"

"I'm sure I could if I tried. Maybe not like the natives here, but you *know* I know how to grind my hips," she chuckled.

"That I do know," Donovan smiled as he directed his attention back to the dancers. One guy was across the dance floor just opposite the bar with his camera just snapping away. *There were plenty of sights to record as memories*, Donovan thought. He almost wished he had brought along his camera. The man who was taking the photos was being overly bold. For some of the women, he would place the lens extremely close to their bottoms or their cleavage. No one chastised him for his photographic aggressiveness – some even stopped so he could do so.

Celeste gulped down her drink. "Come dance with me, Donnie."

She stood and tugged Donovan along. Donovan shook his head and held his position in his seat for a moment. His reluctance was dissipated by Celeste's smile. He couldn't resist her so he slid off of the barstool as she tugged him onto the dance floor.

"You know I'm not a dancer," he forewarned.

"I got this," she assured him.

They danced the entire night away. Celeste grinded against him and just like the other men with their partners, he enjoyed each moment and did very little in return. The rum punch was doing the dancing for her, as she had no control of her lower body. She hugged Donovan close, stole kisses and told herself that she was back in love with this man. Before they flew back to D.C. that Friday, she knew he would be hers again.

11

The next day Steve went to Chase's office for lunch. He took a much needed day off to rest because he was going to have both boys this weekend. Even though he craved the break, he couldn't help but etch out an hour or so to see Chase. He didn't love her, but he cared for her very deeply. Steve felt this woman saved his life during a tumultuous time. He would always love Hailey because she was the mother of his child, but the flame that once was, had burnt out completely. Steve looked forward to moving on and was optimistic about his future with Chase. He understood fully that he would fall second to Chase's practice, but he was now emotionally equipped to handle it, thanks to her.

Chase was going over Bryan's file some more when Steve rapped on her door. He opened it slightly and peered inside.

"Ready baby?"

"Oh, right," she flatly told him. "Can we eat here in the office? I have so much to do. Not to mention, one of my patients will be here in a few."

"Who? Bryan Bryant?" he said with a smirk.

Chase paused and gave him a scolding glare. The air from her slapping the file closed stirred her hair slightly. Before slamming the desk closed, she tossed his file in the drawer.

"Actually yes. But you know better than to ask me about my patients."

"I'm sorry, but I really hate that guy." Steve collapsed on the leather couch and sucked his teeth.

Chase stared at him for a moment, grinned to herself and asked, "Really? So why exactly do you hate him? Well actually, how do you two know each other? You never really told me."

"And I won't."

Chase reared her head back slightly and raised a single brow.

"Is that right?" she asked.

"Right that is."

"I thought we talked about being emotionally open and honest."

"No disrespect Chase, but that was when I was paying to sit on this couch."

"Oh? So were you acting then or something?"

Steve scoffed, "Come on baby, no. Let's not do this. You know I hate arguing."

"I hate it too, but you started it. You were fine until Bryan's name was mentioned," Chase instigated. "And to be honest, you haven't really been yourself since you saw him leaving my office."

"Stop psycho-analyzing me."

"Uhh, you're deflecting."

"I said stop!" Steve huffed. "You know what? Forget lunch. I'll talk to you later. Enjoy meeting with your *patient*."

"Oh, I plan to," Chase said with a chuckle.

Steve glared at her for a moment to which Chase was unfazed. He stood up and quickly left. He stomped to his car and sat inside for a moment deciding what to do and where he should go. After a few minutes of contemplation he called Hailey at her office.

"Hello?"

"It's Steve."

"Hi!"

"You want to have lunch with me?"

"Oh Steve how thoughtful, but I can't. I already have lunch plans."

"With who?"

"I beg your pardon?"

"I said with whom?"

"Since when have you been that interested in who I'm having lunch with?" she laughed at his false concern.

"Never mind. I'll see you tonight."

"For what?"

"I need a reason to see my kid and kid's mother?"

"I'm sorry, Steve. No, you don't need a reason. It's just that last week, you were giving me the cold shoulder, now you want to be . . . well . . . more involved."

"Okay, and you were throwing your panties at me last week and now you are turning on the ice. What's up with that?"

"Why are you being so sensitive?" Hailey abruptly concluded.

"Okay, I'm hanging up. I will call you later to stop by and if you are free, then let me know. Is that cool?"

"Sure, no problem," she hung up the phone.

Steve was now irritated and hungry, but wanted some sort of verbal or non-verbal affection from someone. He debated calling Camilla and it wouldn't do him any good anyway because they never had a real relationship. It was strictly cordial and that was for the sake of Gabe. Outside of issues or news with Gabe, they never spoke. Steve knew that he was solely to blame for that and never considered Camilla's feelings in the grand scheme of things. He never asked her what she wanted from him or if she ever considered forging a relationship with him. He just didn't care and he certainly didn't care enough to ask. Because he was feeling dejected, he regretted doing that. Despite that, Steve was going to call her anyway.

"Camilla?"

"Hi, who's this?"

He chuckled, "It's me, Steve."

"Oh. Hi. Is Gabe okay?"

"He's fine."

"Oh well, you are still getting him Saturday, right?"

"Of course."

"Great. Well . . . okay then." Camilla tried to rush him off of the phone.

"So . . . how is your day going?"

"*What*?"

"Are you having a good day?"

"I'm busy."

"Oh. Well, okay. I will uh . . . I'll see you Saturday."

Silence.

Steve paused and lightly jeered, "Well, I'll let you get back to work. Have a good day."

Camilla hung up the phone – aggressively. Steve pulled his phone from his ear due to how loudly she slammed the receiver down. *She must really hate my guts*, Steve thought. Like a rookie league player, he struck out three times at the plate and felt he wouldn't swing again until next season. Chase didn't deserve Steve's attitude or the argument he started. Agitated by the mention of Bryan, he took it out on her. He wanted to – no, he knew he needed to apologize to her for his behavior.

Steve crept out of the car and headed back to her office to do just that.

When he arrived at her door, he lightly tapped on it and pushed it open slightly. Chase looked up from her paperwork and noticed Steve's apologetic and woeful eyes. *He could be so cute when he wanted*, she thought.

"Back so soon?" she smiled.

Steve smiled and then dropped his head. "I needed to come back and apologize. Baby, I'm sorry. You didn't deserve that."

"No I didn't. You snapped at me."

"I snapped at you, yes. I wanted to spend some time with you and it felt like I was being put off."

"Put off? I'm working, sweetheart. You know that."

"I know. It was just that I felt like I was being put off for another man. A man who I dammit hate."

"Come on Steve, you don't hate him."

"Well, I don't love him."

"Well, whatever. I forgive you. And I'm glad you came back. It turns out we can have lunch after all, he cancelled."

"Good! Now I have you all to myself."

Chase rose to kiss him, "Yes you do."

*   *   *   *

Bryan stood in the lobby while he waited for Hailey to come down to meet him. He smiled at everyone that passed by to include men. Some returned the smile while others wondered what sort of illness he may have had. He didn't care what they thought, he was about to be reunited with his love Hailey and have that much needed conversation with her.

Hailey glanced at her wristwatch as she stood impatiently in front of the elevator. She hoped that she wasn't too late and prayed that he didn't leave. She knew that Bryan was a stickler for promptness. The elevator doors opened and Hailey rushed inside without allowing the riders off first. She grazed one man and slightly knocked him off balance. He muttered some obscenity to which Hailey ignored. She pressed the door close button several times as if it would make them close faster. Once shut, she depressed the "L" button for the lobby and impatiently bounced around. As her chest pounded rapidly, she had no idea whether to greet him with a hug, a double hand shake, or a hug accompanied with a quick peck on the cheek or lips. Frankly she wanted to touch him and to feel his heartbeat next to her body. Bryan looked more mature and relaxed now and she could hardly wait to find out everything that had been going on with him.

The doors opened and Bryan was brandishing a smile as if some game show host told him his grand prize was in that particular elevator. Hailey returned the smile and headed in his direction. Bryan's arms instinctively widened, inviting her in for a hug. Without question or hesitation, Hailey reached for him and pressed her body next to his. Bryan squeezed her close and kissed her gently on the forehead.

"Hi there," Hailey sung out.

"Hailey," Bryan exhaled and stroked her back while his eyes were closed. He dreamt of this moment ever since he left to go to Jamaica. Even though the lobby was bustling with people coming and going during the busy lunch hour, it felt as if they were in the lobby all alone. After an extended amount of time hugging one another, Bryan released her to get a long look at her. After all, it was almost two years since he'd seen her.

"You're here," Hailey said.

"Of course," Bryan held her hand. "Let's go grab some lunch."

They decided to go to a nearby deli and sit in a booth toward the rear of the restaurant. It was secluded and they wouldn't be interrupted. They entertained each other with small talk until they were able to sit down and look eye to eye.

Bryan sat across from her. His eyes gleamed while he looked at Hailey and watched her every movement. He loved her little subtleties like how she positioned her food in a perfect square formation. Drinking glass at the upper right, utensils lower, entrée in the center and side items along the left edge with the napkin in her lap. After fixing her table setting and nibbling on her salad, she looked up and noticed that he hadn't even unwrapped his food to eat. She smiled at him and then looked at his untouched meal.

"Are you okay?" she asked with a giggle.

"Just watching you," he admitted, still in awe.

"Oh," she chuckled nervously and sipped her tea. "So . . . it's been a long time Bryan. I tried to reach you a few times, but your number wasn't working. Where were you?"

"You wouldn't believe me if I told you."

"Try me."

"I was living in Jamaica and the Dominican Republic."

Hailey's eyes widened as she stared at him in disbelief. For a moment, the thought crossed her mind that he must not have wanted to be found – at least not by her.

"Why so far, Bryan?"

"I had to go. I was heartbroken, embarrassed, just flat out broken, Hailey."

"I'm sorry. I guess I'm to blame."

"Not totally. I could've handled the situation differently. I shouldn't have run away. Especially since I loved you so much."

Hailey looked down away from Bryan as his words seeped into her heart like a garden being watered on a summer day. Being with Bryan felt like being at home to Hailey, despite the fact that they were apart for nearly two years. She wanted desperately to pick up where they left off, but she knew that they would have to go through a brief period of getting to know one another again. After all, he wasn't the same man that left D.C. His outward appearance changed, so there was no telling what else had changed, better or worse, with his character. Admittedly, Hailey wasn't the same either. Because of Alex, she knew she had the capacity to give more love than she'd imagined. She realized how selfish she was when she was with Steve and how toxic that relationship had become over time. Hailey just wanted to be in love again and it seemed that Steve was the only logical option last week. But here was Bryan, coming back into her life, or so she'd hoped.

"I loved you too," Hailey admitted. "Truth is I never really stopped."

Bryan bore a stifled smile as he looked at Hailey. Perhaps that was the confirmation he needed to make sure his return to D.C. was the right decision. It wasn't the job, the money or his continuity of book sales. It was Hailey's love. He wanted to make love to her so bad, but he knew that things had probably changed for her. Bryan always thought that Hailey was an amazing woman and he knew that amazing women didn't stay unattached for long.

"So are you in love with anyone?" Bryan asked her.

"Just Alex," Hailey said with a smile while she recalled his adorable face. "What about you? No Jamaican princess or Dominican goddess?"

Bryan chuckled, "No. I couldn't stop thinking about you. There were a few women who were interested, but I was trying to focus on myself and my tourism business there."

"That's amazing that you were successful in another country," Hailey looked deeply into his eyes, "you are such a leader. You have smarts, the charm, it doesn't surprise me."

Bryan was flattered. Hailey was always good at stroking his ego without appearing to be ostentatious.

"So your son, Alex. Do I get to meet him?"

"I would like for you to, but I don't want to confuse him. Steve has been pretty prominent in his life. He really is a great father. Meeting him depends on if we plan to move forward or if we are just going to be really great friends," Hailey gave a labored sigh. "Not that I don't want you in both of our lives, I just don't want to be presumptuous."

"I understand," Bryan told her. There was a brief moment of silence between them as they both ate a portion of their food. The truth was Hailey had enough butterflies in her stomach because of Bryan that it left no room for lunch. She just wanted to cuddle with him, play with his new facial hair, swap stories and be intimate. Bryan sipped his drink and gave her an obvious seductive look. When she recognized what he was doing, he smiled bashfully and averted his eyes away to mask the undeniable attraction that still lingered from years before.

"What?" Hailey asked him with a knowing smile.

"Nothing. You look good – like you are glowing. You sure you aren't in love?"

"It's all because of my son, I told you that."

"Would you travel with me?" he asked. "To Jamaica? There is this place that I want to show you. I found this place when I was really missing you. I call it my place of healing."

"Are you serious?"

"Very."

"Um, sure I suppose," Hailey replied, "I mean, I'd have to coordinate something first though."

"Well, not right away at least. I tell you what, if things go well, then I will take you there."

"That sounds fair. So you seem really calm . . . and don't take this the wrong way, but not as uptight as I remembered."

"No, I understand. Being on an island where life is much slower tends to have that affect," he told her. "And seeing a therapist."

"A therapist? There?"

"No here. I've only had a few sessions with her, but she gave me some sound advice and so-called homework. The homework was you."

"Me? You discussed me?"

"Yes. Hailey, for a while I was stuck. So with me moving back to the area, I needed to speak with someone. At least before I awkwardly bumped into you. I'm glad I did."

"Was she the woman Josephine saw at the restaurant when we were there?"

Bryan took a moment to think about it as his eyes narrowed and mouth curled up slightly. When he realized the event Hailey described, he relaxed the tension in his face and nodded.

"Yes."

"Okay, I didn't see her so . . .," Hailey cleared her throat at her white lie. Although undetected, Hailey's curiosity didn't allow her not to sneak a peek at the attractive therapist that night.

"I actually had an appointment with her now, but when you agreed to lunch I immediately cancelled."

"Really!?" Hailey was surprised. Bryan reached for her hand and caressed it. Hailey blushed and gave a faint smile accompanied with a nervous chuckle.

At that instant, Steve and Chase walked in and stood in line. They both were looking at the menu board deciding on what to order. Steve was beyond famished, but he couldn't rush Chase out of her office. She had to finalize a few emails and return a few calls so she wouldn't feel guilty for indulging in a brief lunch with her lover.

"You know what you want?" Steve prompted her to have her mind made up so they could get their food quickly.

"I haven't the slightest, but it will be something with melted cheese. Today is my cheat day," Chase informed him as she rubbed her flat stomach.

"You could cheat with food for the rest of your life and you'd still look awesome."

"Oh, how sweet!" she rubbed his arm and leaned in to kiss his cheek. Steve looked over her shoulder and spotted Hailey and Bryan. They did not see him, but Steve saw that they were holding hands, smiling and gazing into each other's eyes. The space between Steve's eyebrows crinkled in response to his slight twinge of anger as his blood pressure rose. He clenched his jaws when his earlier affirmation rang out in his subconscious, *"I hate that guy"*. Steve composed himself just long enough to give Chase some instructions.

"Uh babe, order me whatever you are having. I have to hit the head. I'll be right back."

He patted her lightly on her bottom. Before she could comply or refuse, Steve was headed toward Hailey's table. He meandered around a few people who were in his way and stood at attention when he reached them.

Hailey looked up at Steve, obviously surprised, but not annoyed. Bryan on the other hand was upset that he couldn't shake this guy at all.

"Steve! Hey! What are you doing here?"

"What are you doing here?"

"Oh! Bryan and I are catching up and having lunch," she said with a smile.

"Why is it your concern?" Bryan asked Steve.

"Excuse me?" Steve clenched his fists as well as his teeth.

"Um, what a minute," Hailey interjected, "Steve what's wrong? Are you okay?" Hailey looked down at his fists that were balled and prepared to strike.

Chase looked around the deli and noticed Steve hovering by someone's table. When she recognized Hailey from her photo, she sensed Steve may be trying to reconnect with her and wasn't about to encourage that. For Chase, Hailey had her chance and Steve made his choice, so there was no need for them to be speaking. She immediately got out of line to stand by Steve's side. Quickly she approached and sensed his anger. She tried to steer Steve away by his shoulders, but he was unfazed by her delicate hands. Bryan coolly sipped his drink and silently refused to engage in the cliché of fighting over a woman publicly.

"Steve, we have to order, come on let's go," Chase prompted.

"Hi there, Chase," Bryan smiled and waved at her. She gave him a quick smile, followed by a scolding look for taunting Steve.

"You don't talk to *her* either!" Steve demanded.

"Steve? Calm down!" Hailey quietly yelled. "Will someone tell me what is going on?"

"Right, calm down and let's go. I'm sorry," Chase finally steered Steve away from the table. Steve continued to look back in their direction until his neck prohibited him from doing so. Chase pulled him toward the exit instead of back in line.

"Who was that?" Hailey asked Bryan.

"That was Dr. Billingsley, my therapist. Apparently, that is also Steve's girlfriend. I saw him in her office one day while I was leaving and he made it very clear who she was to him."

"What?"

"Yeah," Bryan said with a labored sigh followed by a chuckle. He remembered that Chase told him she wasn't involved with anyone.

A bit disturbed, Hailey slightly pushed her food away from her. She didn't know what to think or how to feel. Seeing Steve with someone else explained a few questions she had about why he was so cold to her. But the bitter truth was seeing her with Chase, or someone as attractive as Chase, made her feel cast aside and unloved by Steve. Clearly she was hurt. Trying to mask her pain from Bryan, she looked toward the exit of the restaurant. They were long gone. Shaking the anguish and rebuking the visual of them having sex, she gave Bryan a reassuring smile.

"Oh well, good for them," Hailey said. She sipped some of her drink to swallow the lump of rejection and continued her reunion with Bryan. "So where were we?"

Not too far from the restaurant, perhaps about a block, were Chase and Steve. Steve was still clearly shaken by the fact that Bryan and Hailey had successfully reconnected, along with their rude exchange. Chase was slightly jogging behind Steve because he was walking away so quickly in his rage.

"Wait!" she called out to him.

Steve stomped toward the corner, his hunger overcome now by his anger.

"Steve!"

He stopped at the corner and turned to face her.

"What's the matter?"

"I don't know," he told her.

"Why did you get so upset? Were you going to fight him?"

"I don't know, Chase."

"So that's her, huh?" she asked, her shoulders dropping. "That's Hailey."

"Yes, that's her."

"You still love her."

"I don't."

"Oh come on, Steve! I've never seen you react that way over anyone."

Steve looked down and then up into Chase's eyes. He was bereft of utterances and waited to hear her summation about the entire incident.

"Nothing to say?" Chase asked. "Okay. I understand."

"You understand what, Chase?"

"So all the therapy, all the homework, the sex on the ninth hole, in your apartment and mine," Chase exhaled, ". . . was nothing?"

"It's not like that, Chase. You know I care about you."

Chase held his hand with both of hers and chewed on her bottom lip as she bowed her head deeply for a moment. She took a deep breath and fought back her tears. Rocking on her heels, she tried to find the right words to say to him. Steve knew what was coming. He just didn't know how Chase was going to say it and how he was supposed to react. After what felt like several minutes, Chase finally looked into Steve's eyes. Hers were welling up, but there were no tears.

"I'm not going to compete with your past."

"Chase . . .," he interrupted.

"No," she continued. "I just wish that my work helped you. Goodbye, Steve."

She reached for both sides of his face with her hands and pulled his lips gently to hers. She planted a hard closed mouth kiss on him, forced a smile and walked away.

12

It was only Tuesday, the second day of a weeklong seminar, and Tamar was already tired of Taj. The love making was phenomenal, but he smothered her and she couldn't take it for four more days. During the lectures, her mind wandered immensely. She thought about Donovan of course, but more importantly she wondered how to let Taj down easy. She didn't think he would take it hard because of his social dexterity, his attractiveness and his prestige. Taj would probably have some blonde bombshell cleaning the crusts between his toes in the nude by next week. Although Tamar assumed this to be true, his clingy, bedroom-eyed expressions made her have her doubts about how he would react. Of course she would be tactful, but firm; she wanted to express her appreciation, but not come across as if it were meaningless.

After the day's seminar, Tamar and Taj met up in the Four Season's lounge called "The Bar" for cocktails and hors d'oeuvres. Tamar had heard that their 100-Mile cocktail and the New York Gin Cream, was the most popular drink served there. She ordered one while she waited for Taj. Tamar checked her phone and saw a text from Donovan that said "I'm missing you, will call you tomorrow." She smiled and responded, "I can't wait."

Taj arrived about ten minutes after Tamar, which was enough time for her to get about a third of the way through her drink. It was tasty and she wanted to savor it for the moment.

"I see you started without me," Taj said as he approached Tamar. He leaned over and planted a lingering and sloppy tongue kiss on her. It was thoughtful, but Tamar was embarrassed by it.

"Wow," was all she could say. She dabbed her lips with her fingertips to sop up the moisture.

"I've been waiting to do that all day," he told her and took his seat across from her. "You look ravishing my future wife."

Tamar scoffed and allowed the comment to roll off her like rain on a tent. "Why thank you, Taj. Did you want something?" she held up the menu.

"What I want isn't on that menu."

Tamar smiled at his verbal innuendo regarding his sexual vivaciousness. She shook her head and set the menu down on the table.

"I thought *I* had a healthy sexual appetite," she told him.

"Are you saying that you've finally met your match?"

"Yes, clearly I have."

He stared longingly into her eyes.

"Taj, I've never been one to beat around the bush, so here goes. I'm leaving in the morning."

Confused, Taj tilted his head slightly and leaned forward so he didn't miss anything else that she was about to say. His hand covered his forehead for a moment while he shook it in disbelief. His eyes rolled up to look at Tamar for validation.

"Yes, I'm going back to D.C. I don't belong here."

"What do you mean?"

"I can't be any plainer than that. Don't get me wrong, I've enjoyed our time together tremendously, but my heart isn't with you. It's with Donovan and I miss him. I love him."

"Now I know you don't mean that."

"Excuse me?"

"You would've never come up here to see me if you loved him."

"Well, let's just have a moment of preciseness shall we? I came up here to attend a seminar. While I was attending said seminar, I wanted to see you after the daily sessions concluded *at* the seminar. After the seminar, I was going to go back home to D.C. to then discuss the seminar with my legal team. So you see honey, I came up here for a seminar. I didn't come up especially for you."

"That was cute," he said and then stressed his words to mimic her. "The *seminar* and at the *seminar* and after the *seminar*. Cute."

"You like that?"

"Tamar, what do you really think you will have with Donovan that you can't have with me and more?"

"Love, Taj. Love."

"Love? Really?"

"Yes."

"You haven't talked to him the whole time you've been here. Do you even know where he is? Sure he is in D.C., but do you know where he is specifically at this moment? How many times has he called you? He's sent sporadic texts. I've seen you glancing at your phone every hour and looking defeated. You call him, it goes straight to voice mail. That's the love you are missing? If that's love I don't want it."

"Taj, I can't focus on where he is at every possible moment. That's not me. We trust each other. And if spying on him or getting uptight every time I can't reach him, or going insane because I don't know where he is at every minute of the day *is* love, then I don't want *that*!"

Taj smiled slightly and gave a single nod. "There's no right or wrong with love, Tamar and I don't want to debate it with you. I guess I just care about you a little more than you do me."

"And that's why I have to leave, Taj," Tamar held his hand. "I had no intentions of making this permanent. It was a fling."

She paused for a moment and looked away slightly ashamed. Tamar reminisced about what Taj did to her body just last night and smiled to herself. She caressed the back of her neck and her hand trailed around delicately to the front of it. She closed her eyes and lazily reopened them.

"An incredible, extremely sexually satisfying fling," she confirmed.

Taj grinned to himself. "You didn't know your body could do that, huh?" He squeezed her hand gently to snap her out of her trance.

"No, I knew it could, I just didn't think it would!"

They laughed together and it slowly faded. She smiled and patted Taj's hand sympathetically.

"I'm so sorry, Taj. If I met you two years ago, we would not be having this conversation at all and would be planning our extremely freaky honeymoon on some Greek island."

"It's not too late," he told her.

"Sadly sweetie, it is."

Tamar stood to her feet and waited for Taj to join her. He reluctantly stood and placed his hand on the small of her back. He pulled her toward him and kissed her neck softly.

"Can we have sex one more time?" he whispered to her. Tamar giggled and shoved him slightly. Taj was smiling waiting for her response.

"No Taj," she told him as she stroked his chest. "I've done enough dirt to feel guilty about."

They began walking out of the bar and into the lobby of the Four Seasons. He stood in front of her and held both of her hands down by his side.

"I've never met a woman like you, Tamar. I do care for you and I'm not going to give up on us. I will wait."

"Taj, please," she told him, "you are too fine to wait. You will be loving another woman in a week."

He laughed at her comment.

"No. I'm saving my love for you. Not trying to quote Whitney, but you get it right?" they laughed.

"I will miss your silliness, Taj," Tamar looked down a bit saddened. "I will miss *you*."

"So, what if you discover he isn't the man you think he is?"

"I don't think that I will. But, I will deal with that if the time comes."

Taj wrapped his arms around her and hugged her close to his body with a gentle tightness. He rubbed her back up and down and wanted to remember the feel of her body for the moment. Taj wanted to remember every curve of Tamar. He looked deep into her eyes for a second before he planted a soft kiss on her lips.

"Goodbye, Taj," she told him.

"See you later, Tamar."

She backed away from him slowly, their hands still connected with their fingers intertwined until just the tips touched. She smiled, blew him a kiss, turned and walked away. Taj watched as her curvy hips swayed back and forth until she disappeared from view. Taj knew in his heart that he would see Tamar again. He was going to make sure of that. Wanting nothing more than to be with her, he would stop at nothing to have her. He reached for his cell phone inside his jacket pocket and tapped the face of it to dial a number.

"Yes, it's Taj," he breathed deeply and exhaled. "Send it."

13

Camilla had dropped off Gabe with Hailey. They had a civil relationship and felt no need to be nasty to one another. Camilla didn't want Steve, she had wanted Bryan. Unfortunately for her, those feelings were not and would not ever be reciprocated. Camilla had finally gotten over him, but when Josephine mentioned his name to her last week, it was as if someone punched her in her gut right after shooting her in it. She tried not to let those feelings swell up inside of her and by crashing into Jameson, odd as it may seem, helped to keep those feelings at bay.

She wasn't sure what to expect with Jameson, but remembered to keep her heart open and be positive. He said that he had a really exciting date planned and asked her to meet him at the marina off of Maine Ave. Camilla thought to herself and hoped that they were not going to go to the Channel Inn. The Channel Inn was the last surviving restaurant slash bedraggled night club for people over 70. Not to put the Inn down because she was sure that the patrons enjoyed it and surprisingly it managed to survive the hey-days of the FoxTrap, Zanzibar and H2O. She found a parking space and Jameson asked her to head toward the pier where the Odyssey docked.

Jameson held a single yellow long stemmed rose and was dressed in navy nautical attire. Camilla looked at Jameson and thought to herself, "*damn*". He held the rose out for her to accept it.

"Thank you, how sweet," she told him as she greeted him with a hug. He kissed her cheek and held out his hand for her to take. They walked toward the edge of the pier and Camilla wondered exactly where they were going.

"Did you have a good day, Camilla?"

"It was too slow. I couldn't wait to get here."

"Good answer! I hope you are hungry. I have my chef preparing several dishes for us tonight."

"Your chef? As in, personal chef?"

"Yes," he said with a giggle.

"And just where is he going to do this?"

"On my yacht."

They stopped in front of a white and navy tri deck yacht. It had to have been a ninety footer. Its name was Beleza Natural.

"Beleza Natural?" Camilla asked as she leaned in closer to him and gave his arm a gentle stroke.

"It's Portuguese for Natural Beauty," he said, "I think it fits you."

The chef was almost done preparing their meal as they boarded. They began to set sail as Jameson poured her a glass of champagne. He led her up the staircase to the upper deck so they could see the sun setting. The colors danced around in the sky, the blends of orange, gold and blue bathed Camilla's smiling face. Jameson admired her and took in the silence of the moment. He sipped his champagne and escorted her to the L shaped seating area just opposite the wet bar.

"This is spectacular," Camilla told him.

"I will give you the tour after dinner, which should be ready for us soon."

"Okay, so first the Bentley, now a yacht," Camilla sighed, "it's nice to see how the other side lives."

"You think?"

"Yes. What is it like to be able to do what you want, whenever you want?"

"I wish it were that way, but it's not totally true," he admitted. "I'm constantly checking behind everyone, there is always some employee issue, I'm always fighting a law suit or settling out of court. This is just a perk. I'm considering selling the business and exploring a new venture."

"Really? Like what? You've had such success with Beefy Burger."

"I know, but the restaurant industry can be tricky sometimes."

Camilla considered what may possibly be some ongoing issues dealing with food and the public. She nodded as she was empathetic to his concerns while she sipped her champagne.

"If I stay in this area, I'm considering opening a supper club," Jameson smiled. "I think D.C. could use something classy, but with variety, great food, great music, dancing. If advertised right, it would be for upper echelon residents of the area. It would be the "it" spot for celebrities when they come to D.C. The must visit spot. You know?"

"Sounds like it could be fun! Upscale is always good."

"For all ethnicities. So I've been working on a business plan and running the numbers, so we will see. It's looking like a go so far, but I want to make sure no stone is left unturned."

"You are fascinating, Jameson," Camilla told him. He beamed at her comment. Camilla was great at stroking a man's ego. Even though Jameson was powerful and successful, she knew he still needed that encouragement. After all, he was a bachelor.

"Thank you," he smiled. "So Camilla, I have a question for you."

"Sure," she set down her glass so she wouldn't miss a word.

"Before we have dinner, I have something I want you to take a look at."

Camilla was a bit confused, but open-minded nonetheless. "Okay . . .," she responded.

Jameson pulled a folded document from a hidden drawer beneath the cushion of where he was seated. Camilla raised an eyebrow as she was curious to what the document could be.

"Would you mind signing this?"

Camilla chuckled lightly, "What is it?" She took the document and began reading as Jameson told her what it was.

"It's an agreement actually. Even though we are dating, it states that if it gets serious to the point of marriage this will serve as a pre-nuptial agreement that would entitle you to none of my assets nor sue me for emotional damages, etcetera etcetera."

Camilla skimmed through the document and chuckled.

"Um," she started, "this is interesting. It's like a *pre*-pre-nup."

Jameson studied her reaction intently. It was difficult for him to read her reaction right away, but Camilla brandished a slight smile as she read its contents. She chuckled lightly again.

"You know what? Life is a crazy thing," she started. "Sure, what the hell? Do you have a pen?"

"You read everything?" he asked her.

"I read enough," she accepted the pen and signed the paper. Camilla handed the paper back to him and sipped her champagne. "So what is the chef making?"

Jameson was silent as he set the document on the table top just in front of them. He placed his pen on top so the paper wouldn't blow away with the breeze. He was at a loss for words for a brief minute and then stared deeply into Camilla's eyes. He had never met anyone like her. She seemed unfazed by the document and signed it rather quickly which baffled him.

"Grilled salmon and artichoke with jasmine rice."

"That sounds great. I so rarely get an opportunity to have grilled artichoke. It's one of my favorite vegetables. You know I'm a great cook too."

"Camilla," Jameson began, "help me understand something."

"Sure, what's that?"

"I'm a bit taken aback by your actions."

"My actions?"

"I'm actually shocked that you signed this so quickly," Jameson pointed to the document and leaned forward to ingest Camilla's response.

"Why? You are a millionaire who just wants to protect yourself. I get it and I'm not offended. The old Camilla would've been, but my concern is my son and our happiness. Not your money."

Jameson, who was at a loss for words was about to address Camilla's statement. At that very moment, one of the staff appeared and announced that dinner was ready.

"Shall we?" Jameson stood and helped Camilla up to her feet. "You can follow them, I need to grab a bottle of wine."

"Okay," she smiled and left Jameson behind.

He took a deep breath and exhaled. He took the document that Camilla signed, tore it up twice and tossed it overboard. Jameson decided not to tell her anything about destroying the document until about the fourth date or so. He wanted to see if her interest would still remain or would it slowly wane. Impressed by her no questions asked gesture, and the explanation that she gave, it emitted trust to Jameson. He certainly needed a woman and potential wife whom he could trust. This was really the reason why Jameson remained single for so long. So many women said that they were attracted to him, but were enjoying his lifestyle more than they were enjoying him. Jameson craved the love of a woman who genuinely cared for him and Camilla's act gave him hope. He swore to himself that if he ever found someone who he could trust with his heart that he would move swiftly to make them his and lavish them with nothing but the finest.

He joined her in the dining area and sat beside her.

"There you are!" she said with a smile.

"Hi gorgeous," he kissed her cheek and rubbed her back.

"This is beautiful, thank you so much for having me here."

Jameson smiled and stared at her as she watched the chef prepare their plates. He couldn't believe his ears as he watched her in secret. She seemed happy with the moment and had no unrealistic expectations. During their numerous conversations, she never asked about his money. All of her questions were about him and that meant so much.

"Hey?" he rubbed her arm.

"Yes?"

"Can I have some sugar?" Jameson smiled and puckered his lips. Camilla giggled and answered his request with a deep sensual kiss. Jameson knew a kiss like that wasn't fake. Certainly if she were secretly upset about signing a hands-off my finances document, she would not have kissed him with such passion.

"Wow you have great lips," she told him. "I could kiss you all day."

"And I would let you."

Jameson was astonished. He'd heard of this type of thing from his father when he told him about his mother. Jameson's parents had been married for forty two years and counting. He never thought in a million years that he would experience the same feeling that his father described to him. However, here he was in this moment feeling a sense of calm with this woman. He wasn't about to deny or question the feeling. It was obvious.

Jameson knew that Camilla was the one.

14

Hailey decided to meet up with me at the mall. I told Hailey that I just felt like walking and looking, but that if I saw something that sparked my interest, like maternity clothes or onesies, I just may be inclined to buy it. Hailey thought that I was being preposterous, but I've always heard that you should speak things into existence. I've already spoken it, so I'm walking into my destiny. If Hailey didn't want to join me, or anyone for that matter, well then I will go it alone.

I noticed that Hailey wasn't her usually perky self when we met up in front of the makeup counter at the MAC store.

"Hi there," she said flatly joined by a weak hug.

"What's up, Hailey? You are looking a bit gloomy."

"I don't feel gloomy, I'm a little confused though."

"About what?"

We slowly strolled down the wide and long corridors of the mall. The faster patrons rudely dipped in front and around us, some clearly annoyed by our slothfulness.

"So I had lunch with Bryan," she started.

"Really? How did that go?"

"It was fine, until . . .," she stopped herself.

"Until what?"

"Until Steve showed up."

"What?" I stopped in my tracks and stared at her while she kept walking. "What do you mean Steve *showed* up? Did he know you guys were there? Was he following you?"

Hailey turned back toward me. She hooked her arm in mine and moved me in the direction we were originally headed.

"No no! Nothing like that. He just happened to walk into the deli. I didn't even see him come inside. But he was with some woman named Chase."

"Chase? Interesting name for a woman."

"Well you know that is Bryan's therapist."

I stopped again, but Hailey tugged me along. "What do you mean therapist? Wait . . . is she Steve's therapist too?"

"I'm not sure, but I think so. He told me he was seeing a professional."

"Wait, and they were together at the deli?"

Hailey nodded.

"He's boning his shrink?" I asked in slight disbelief.

"Who doesn't?" Hailey said with a chuckle, "I'm kidding. Anyway, I don't know all of that. But she was really grabby and tried to soothe him."

"Soothe him?" I was puzzled. Listening to Hailey tell a story sometimes was like watching a bad soap opera with multiple cliff hangers. Sometimes I just wished she got to the point. The suspense is past annoying.

"Yes. Soothe him. Girl, Steve was about to fight Bryan."

"For what?"

"Jealous perhaps?" she shrugged and stopped at a gold jewelry kiosk.

"Hailey!? What happened? Spit it out already!"

"The bottom line is . . . Steve still has feelings for me! I'm a bit confused."

"That's true."

Hailey stared and waited for me to elaborate. I'm guessing that she didn't want to miss anything because she found a vacant bench in the middle of the corridor and sat down. I gave a labored sigh and sat beside her. Unlike with Camilla, I didn't have to choose my words carefully with Hailey. Hailey instantly got the point and never took it personally. I admired that in her. She was always willing to listen.

"Hailey, last week you were plotting to get Steve back. I mean, you were clearly on the Steve Bus! You see a bearded Bryan and now you have shifted focus. What is it that you want? You realize the rest of your life can't be a love triangle. So because Steve shows up with some grabby soothing woman named Chase of all things, what? Let me guess. You want Steve again?"

Hailey was silent, so I took that to be a yes. I grunted at her quietness and nudged her. She chuckled and shook her head then looked over at me, somewhat ashamed.

"Don't say it," I pleaded.

"Okay, I won't," she laughed. "What's wrong with me?"

"There's nothing *wrong* per se. You are just attracted to two men. I get it. One is a great father who you've known since God said "Let there be light". The other is intriguing and helped fill a void. Ahem, *filled a void . . .*," I ribbed her for emphasis. "I guess what you should ask yourself is who is the guy that you love? Who can't you live without?"

"I understand, but I'm not sure it's that simple," she admitted. "Not anymore."

Just then my cell phone rang.

"Hold on I have to take this. Hello? Yes. Right now? It did!? Okay, I'm on my way. Thank you!" I hung up, tossed the phone in my purse and stood up quickly. "I gotta go. I'm sorry. I will call you tonight okay? Bye!"

I don't even remember if Hailey said goodbye or even if she stood before I left. I had to get to the doctor's office.

                    *   *   *   *

After being in the doctor's office for almost two hours, my anxiousness subsided and I started to feel a little more at ease with each passing minute. It was hard to describe how elated, nervous, and nauseous I felt all at once.

The doctor returned into my waiting room. He was a short man from Trinidad with a slight accent that hinted to his heritage. He wore circular rimless glasses that were similar to Gandhi's. He set my medical folder down on the workstation closest to him and smiled.

"Okay, I received your blood tests back from the lab," he took a long pause before he said, "Congratulations, you are now pregnant!"

"Are you absolutely sure, doctor?"

"I'm absolutely sure."

I reached for both of his hands and gave them a gentle squeeze. I tried to contain myself, but the tears emerged and couldn't be contained at that point.

"Oh Dr. Ramai! I'm so happy!"

"Yes, yes, congratulations! Let's do a quick ultrasound just to see what is going on in there, shall we?"

Just as he said that, his assistant came in to oversee the process and make any notes if need be. I leaned back into a flat position on the examination table. He opened the gown to expose my stomach. It felt like I was a little pudgy there, but that could've been my imagination. The assistant rubbed the cool gel over my stomach while the doctor set up the ultrasound device. He put his rubber gloves on and was humming some tune that I couldn't identify.

"Okay, let's see," he rubbed the thick wand across the lower part of my stomach with just a bit of pressure. "Okay . . .," he said again.

I stared up at the ceiling, a bit nervous and fearful. I slowly turned my head toward the ultrasound monitor and tried to make out the blur that emanated on the display.

"Okay . . .," he repeated while he rubbed the device around more. "Ah. There we go. Come on, child."

I continued to look at the display and tried to make sense of the image.

"See there?" he pointed. "There he is. And oh! Wait . . ." He moved the device around a bit more and squinted through his lenses at the monitor.

"What?" I asked. I could see the nurse in my peripheral and she started to smile.

"You rolled doubles."

"What?!"

"Yep," he coolly said as he continued moving the device around while peering at the monitor. "Let's get a snapshot of this."

The nurse hurried over and depressed a button on the device. Seconds later a slip of paper shot out and she set it on the workstation. The nurse handed me some large paper towels to clean myself off with.

"Great news!" the doctor affirmed while he ripped his gloves off and tossed them into the trash bin. "I will see you back here over the next several weeks just to monitor everything and we will continue to do some more blood work.

Continue your prenatal medicines, no seafood for now and we will see you next week. We will do another ultrasound as well. Do you have any questions?"

"Oh well, there goes the sushi! I'm too happy to ask questions right now. Oh! I'm just ready to tell someone! Can I tell my husband?"

"If you'd like, although we aren't completely out of the woods yet."

My smile faded slightly.

"Everything will be fine. Don't worry," he reassured me and patted me on the shoulder. "I'll let you get dressed."

He and the assistant left the room.

I wanted to tell Ian so bad, but I didn't want to build his hopes up only to have complications later and the pregnancy fail. I'll be carrying two babies! I'm so excited. I don't want to keep this from him. I need his love and support. I have to tell him when I get home. But how? I wanted to make the news cute. I wonder if he would cry when I told him. We will have to keep it under wraps for a while, but I can't keep this news a secret a day longer.

As I headed home from the doctor's office I started thinking of names. I was secretly hoping for a boy and a girl. We could name the boy Ian, Jr. of course and the girl India. How sweet. Knowing Ian, he would want them to have names beginning with the letter J. Joshua and hmm, what is a good girl's name that begins with a J? I chuckled to myself as Bryan Bryant's voice popped into my subconscious – *Jacqueline*. I giggled to myself and shook my head rebuking the thought completely. Without even realizing it, I ended up at a local department store that had a wide selection of baby clothes and accessories. I proudly parked in the "Expecting Mother" parking space, even though I was nowhere near showing and hopped out of my vehicle.

The best way to spring the news on Ian was to keep it simple. After I found what I was looking for, I zipped through the check-out line and headed home. Ian should be there by now, but I wanted to call and make sure.

"Hey baby," he answered.

"Good you're home!"

"Yeah, I was on my way out in a few to shoot some hoops with Steve. You okay?"

"Yeah. Can you wait for me before you leave? I will keep it short, I promise," I pleaded.

"Of course baby. I will see you when you get here."

When I walked in, Ian was dressed for ball. He had gotten a tad more muscular over the years, but not overly so. He still drove me wild whenever I saw him in his workout gear.

"Hey you!" I went to go kiss him and he hugged me tightly. He was about to get me started when he began nibbling on my neck, but I remembered why I asked him to wait for me. "Easy, Ian. You know you will get something started and I know you have to meet Steve, so have a seat and I'll tell you."

"Tell me what babe?"

I turned my back to him and then looked seductively over my shoulder. I tossed the onesie at him. He clumsily caught it, and situated it to get a good look at it. It took him a minute to hold it up the correct way because he had no idea what it was at first.

"This is for a baby." He shrugged a bit and continued inspecting it.

I smiled and nodded.

"Wait, this is for a baby!" he said again with more enthusiasm. I tossed the other onesie at him.

"And that's for two."

"What?!" I could see his knees shaking as he sat. "Are you serious baby?"

"Yes!"

Ian stood to his feet and hugged me. He lifted me slightly and then put me down.

"I'm sorry are you okay?"

"Yes, silly!" I laughed. "You're going to be a father!"

"Oh wow," he said as he caught his breath. "That's great I don't know what to say."

"Well, don't say anything to anyone yet. I want to make sure it's officially official. You know the first trimester is hard. Anything can happen. So mum's the word. Okay baby?"

"Uh, yeah, you got it!"

I planted a firm but loving kiss on him and shoved him.

"Go. Go play ball and beat that crazy ass Steve."

"Okay baby."

"I love you," I rubbed his back as he headed toward the door.

"Love you too!"

I locked the door behind him and rested against it with a smile. I think that went well. He seemed excited about the idea of being a father. This actually could work and the icing on the cake was having twins. Finally, we would be parents.

After Ian fastened his seat belt, he stared blankly at the dashboard before cranking the car. Motionless, he sat there as he pondered the news his wife just shared with him. He placed his hands on the steering wheel and bowed his head deeply. He tapped the steering wheel lightly with both hands and then in a crescendo his blows to the steering wheel became harder and faster.

He lifted his head, teeth gnashed as he began pounding his fist in the cushion of the empty seat next to him. Ian beat the seat with his right hand for several blows. He pummeled the seat and grunted in anger while doing so.

"I gotta get outta here."

Ian turned the ignition and sped away from his house to meet up with Steve at the court. Ian's mind was racing just as fast as he was whizzing in and out of traffic. He thought he handled the news well, but was in complete disbelief. Not one, but two babies. How could that be? Ian had no idea how to handle this situation. A situation that was going to be stickier and more challenging than anything he had ever faced in life. He loved his wife and he certainly wanted to be there for her, but on the drive to the basketball court, he made up in his mind that he would walk away if need be. Without question, he would leave her all alone to take care of the babies if he had to.

Steve leapt from the curb when he saw Ian's car barreling toward him.

"What the fuck?" Steve murmured.

When Steve realized that Ian was taking longer than normal to get out of the car, he crept cautiously to the passenger side window and tapped it lightly. Ian looked over at him with a woeful expression. Steve reached for the door handle and yanked on it, but it was locked.

"Unlock the door man!" Steve ordered.

In a daze, Ian failed to immediately comply to which Steve pounded his fist against the window.

"Come on man!"

Ian unlocked the door and Steve hopped in slamming it behind him, apparently perturbed by almost being run over and somewhat frazzled by the excessive wait.

"What the hell man? You almost ran over my ankles!"

"I can't do this man," Ian told him.

"You can't do what? Play ball? Well hell, I know that already!"

"No man!" Ian sighed before he was about to deny Josephine's request to keep the news quiet. "It's Josephine."

"Okay, what about her? She okay?"

"She's pregnant."

"Oh! That's what's up! Good for you man!" Steve punched Ian's arm to show his congratulations. However, Ian did not share the same enthusiasm.

"With twins."

"Oh shit!" Steve jostled, "Someone needs a part time job at Outback!"

"Will you shut up man!?"

Concerned by how serious Ian had been, Steve simmered down to understand just what the issue was.

"I swear man. I love my wife, but I will choke her ass man."

"What?!" Steve could barely believe his ears.

"She is pregnant with twins man, she came in celebrating, tossing baby clothes at me . . ."

"Okay . . ."

"How man?" Ian looked at Steve, his jaws tightened.

"What the hell? Y'all are having sex. If it's unprotected, then she just *may* get pregnant!"

"Naa man."

"What do you mean 'naa'? Y'all are having sex, right? I mean, that is an activity that you partake in with your wife right?"

Ian nodded.

"I'm not following," Steve told him.

"Josephine is pregnant, but they can't be mine."

"What the hell you mean?"

Ian took a labored sigh and looked forward to avoid eye contact with Steve. "My sperm are dead man. There's no way those are my babies."

15

Celeste could not have been having a better time with Donovan. Donovan suggested they go to Harrison's Caves and nearby waterfall and then grab some lunch afterward. He wanted to squeeze in a quickie before they ate, but it would be strictly up to Celeste. He knew that she would be more than willing to oblige. The caves would be a nice change of scenery and would add another physical activity to this trip. Donovan needed the exercise even though all of the sex that he was getting from Celeste was an ample enough work out for him. Celeste had a vigorous sexual appetite, but she couldn't hold a candle to Tamar in that department. Outside of Celeste enjoying being choked, there really wasn't too much sexual intrigue left with her. Donovan didn't want to end this vacation, but he had to go back to reality.

Donovan waited beside the van for Celeste to come out to meet him. He went down early to see if he could call Tamar and check up on her. He just needed some brief alone time because Celeste had gotten overly clingy during this trip. He still didn't have a decent signal there. He was however able to send her a text and told her that his phone was acting up and he was going to get a new one. That would buy him a few days and a few missed calls; by then he would be back in the states.

When Donovan saw Celeste he almost erupted through his khaki Bermuda shorts. Celeste donned a white string bikini that looked awesome against her skin. She had a short white sarong and sported her beach shoes so she wouldn't slip on the large rocks at the falls. She carried a large shoulder bag with her that had other essentials for their excursion.

"Damn," Donovan said to her as he looked at her up and down. He licked his lips and peered around her to check out her rear.

"You like?"

"I love!" Donovan responded. "Hurry up and get on this van before I drag you back upstairs and fuck the shit out of you. Go on."

She grinned at his remark and was tempted to disobey his request so he could follow through with his threat. She was about to pull herself onto the van when she felt a sharp slap on her behind.

"Easy," she told him as she turned to look at his sly grin. "Just help me up."

"Got it." Donovan used both hands to palm her bottom and helped her into the van. Celeste just giggled at his silliness.

The van dipped and dodged in and out of traffic on its way to the falls; the horn honking intermittently along the way. It was a frightening ride, but Donovan tried not to think about it too much. He was focusing on what to do with Tamar when he returned. Oddly, being in Barbados with the woman he used to care for made him consider solidifying a future. He and Celeste had fun there and he knew he and Tamar would've had a great time too. He loved Tamar's fearless nature and sophisticated social skills. He tried not to compare the two; they both were brilliant in their own right.

"Hey you . . ." Celeste interrupted his thoughts.

"Yes?"

"Why are you so quiet?"

"Just enjoying the moment."

"Okay," Celeste responded and left him to his thoughts.

When they arrived at the waterfall, there were crowds of people waiting for their turn to be guided up the layers of rock and rushing waters just to dive from the cliff. She was enjoying having him all to herself for a whole week no less, but the suspense was killing her. Every night before they went to bed there, she thought about that ring. There were only a few days left. Celeste knew they would be together, but her patience was quickly dwindling.

"You ready baby?" he asked her.

"Let's do it."

After a refreshing dip at the mouth of the falls and cave exploration, they were both soaked and headed back to the van and finished toweling each other dry. The driver let them inside while they waited on the rest of the group to arrive.

"Dis be ya' 'oneymoon?" the driver asked them with a thick Jamaican accent.

Donovan looked at Celeste and smiled. Celeste rubbed his shoulder and responded, "Why yes it is, how did you know?"

"I can always spot da newlyweds."

Celeste laughed, "He was a bit reluctant about the idea of marriage, but he realized what a wonderful woman I was and came around."

Donovan smiled, shook his head and peered out of the window at several soaked climbers.

"Him ah man o' few words," the driver said with a chuckle.

"I'm just ready to get my lady back to the hotel."

"Everyting cook an' curry," the driver replied with a wide smile. Celeste gave Donovan a puzzled expression to which he shrugged.

The two of them agreed to get a bite to eat after the cave, but Donovan just wanted to have sex with Celeste. Her white bikini drove him wild and he was keeping his feelings at bay all day. They arrived at their resort and Donovan commenced to rushing Celeste while walking briskly to their room.

"Come on!" he demanded.

"Okay, I'm coming!" she called behind him.

He put his key card in the door and left the door wide open for Celeste who was about ten paces behind him. When she entered, she closed the door gently behind her and kicked the flip flops that she changed into at the falls off near the door. She turned to put her bag in the closet. When she turned back around Donovan was in front of her, the lust rippling deeply in his eyes. Startled, she gasped a bit and before she could say a word, Donovan pulled her closely to her in a single tug. His hands were tightly gripping her waist while he planted a deep kiss on her.

He turned her around forcefully so her back would face him. He reached around and unbuttoned the front of her shorts which fell to her ankles; she stepped out of them while Donovan kissed the back of her neck and shoulders.

When he saw her white bikini bottoms, he popped her rump before he ripped them off of her.

"Oh!" she said with surprise.

He tilted her pelvis into position and entered her from behind. He knew that this was going to be a quick session for them as he needed to satisfy his primitive urge immediately. Donovan was silent with the exception of a few grunts and moans. He forced her into him so deeply that she had never felt this sensation before. He gripped her waist and hips so tight that they began to get sore. She wanted to tell him to stop, but the pain felt so pleasurable.

Celeste's palms slid up and down the wall as she braced herself for his powerful strokes. She looked down at his hands that made their way to her breasts. He moved his hands up to her shoulders which allowed him to go deeper. Celeste felt as though her back was going to break at any moment. Donovan was so deep inside of her that she could not muster any dirty talk for him. His strokes were faster and Celeste squeezed out a few tears because it felt so wonderful.

"Donnie . . ." she whimpered.

Just at that moment he released himself and wrapped both arms around her midsection as he rested his head on her back.

"Ooo wee!" Donovan said softly. "I was holding that one since this morning. You looked so fucking good in that bikini. Damn."

"You've seen me naked, what was it about the bikini?" she asked while she tried to catch her breath.

"It just looked good on you. Come on," he said as he gently tugged her toward the bed. "I need a nap real quick."

"Go ahead," she instructed. "I'm hopping in the shower."

She left his side and turned on the water for the shower. Celeste was a bit curious to see if Donovan had tried to contact Tamar. He didn't mention her at all. It was over, she had won. Celeste got her man back. He was in a secluded tropical paradise with her, not Tamar. This was sweet satisfaction. She waited for a moment longer and peered out of the bathroom to check on Donovan. His chest rose and fell gingerly. Donovan looked peaceful and content as his head rested to one side exposing his kissable neck and collar bone. Celeste could definitely get used to seeing this vision every day for the rest of their lives.

Celeste scouted the room with her eyes as she tried to locate his cell phone. It was on the dresser. She tiptoed over to take a quick peek at it. She tapped the face of the phone expecting to have instant access, but it asked for a code to unlock it. Celeste took a wild guess and tapped the numbers for his birthday. Celeste smirked, her face overcome with defeat as she knew the code wouldn't be something so simple. Her eyes beamed as the phone granted her access. She quickly tapped the icon for text messages and saw Tamar's name. The last message was from Tamar earlier today that read, "*Call me later.*"

Celeste's lips curled upward as she took a moment to think. She tapped the menu button for the message and deleted it. She saw another message from an unknown number in D.C. Curious, Celeste tapped that message and it read, "*Success! Call us.*"

Celeste turned when she heard Donovan stir a bit in the bed behind her. She returned the phone to the home screen and set it down on the dresser. She quickly tip toed to the bathroom and started showering the water from the falls and Donovan's love sweat off of her body. She smiled to herself as she wondered what went through his mind as she wore that bikini. All she packed were bikinis, however, that one apparently drove him into an animalistic frenzy. She didn't regret deleting Tamar's text, but the other text made her wonder exactly what that meant.

*   *   *   *

When Tamar returned, it was to an empty home. All of the lights were out and when she illuminated the residence, it looked as if no one had been there for several days. After putting her bags down near the entrance, she walked around the house to inspect it briefly. She wanted to ensure nothing looked out of the ordinary. Tamar always believed that the energy of a dwelling changed if an unwelcomed or unfamiliar person to the residence had visited. Fortunately, she did not get the sense of either.

She continued upstairs into the master bedroom. The bed was still made and didn't appear to have been slept in at all. Tamar walked into the bathroom and looked in the shower – it still looked clean. Seldom did Donovan do anything domestic in the way of cleaning, especially the bathrooms. Tamar went to the toilet, took a deep breath and hoped for the best. She kept a blue Ty-D-Bol tablet in the tank of the toilet. If it hadn't been flushed for a while, the water would be a deep blue color. She bit her bottom lip gently and flushed the toilet. The water was dark blue.

Okay, she thought to herself, *keep cool.*

She trotted downstairs to retrieve her luggage. Her heart raced as she tried not to let her imagination run wild.

The main thought that she couldn't keep at bay was that she hoped that he was okay and hadn't been in an accident or worse while she was having her rendezvous in New York. Tamar's gut feeling was that Donovan was fine – wherever he was.

She lugged her suitcase upstairs and began to unpack. With the ease of an NBA star, she tossed her dirty clothes into the hamper for tomorrow's wash. After she unloaded her suitcase, she walked to the closet to set it back in its rightful place. After unfastening her pants, she let them fall to her ankles and then stepped out of them. Her arms were folded behind her as she began to undo her brassiere, but she stopped herself abruptly. She turned her head and looked in the direction of the closet. She thought to herself for a moment as she stared at the entrance before she slowly looked away toward the bedroom threshold.

Carefully, with each step more deliberate than the first, she headed toward the walk in closet. She leaned her body against the door jam and looked around the area where she just placed her luggage. She noticed that Donovan's bag was missing. She gave a labored sigh and shook her head.

"Son of a bitch," she whispered to herself. She rolled her eyes upward in disgust, shook her head and plunked down on the bed. She sat for a moment and wondered where in the world her man was.

After a night alone and no word from Donovan, not even a text, she made her way into the law office. Restless, she tossed and turned all night and barely slept a wink. Tamar tried to convince herself that there was a logical explanation, but no matter how she pulled the pieces apart and put them back together, something didn't fit quite right. She didn't panic because she knew that something would be revealed to her sooner rather than later.

Before she bedded down last night, she called Josephine to see if Ian was at home. Tamar figured maybe they planned a boy's night or something. It was a far-fetched idea, but she wanted to leave no stone unturned.

Tamar was in a daze as she thought of nothing but Donovan. She didn't remember parking her car or walking into the building – but she ended up on the elevator about to return to work early from her seminar. She passed several co-workers in the hall, all of which greeted her with the standard *Good Morning*. Tamar was unaware if she even responded back to them or not. Briskly, she passed her assistant's desk. She was surprised to see Tamar.

"Ms. Woodruff?" she asked with an astounded tone.

Tamar kept walking and unlocked her office to let herself inside. Puzzled, the assistant shook her head slightly, because it wasn't like Tamar to ignore her. The assistant leapt from her seat and made Tamar a cup of coffee, just the way she liked it with lots of cream and no sugar. After she heard Tamar get a bit settled, she knocked on her office door lightly.

"Ms. Woodruff?"

"Yes?"

"I'm sorry if I seemed surprised, but I wasn't expecting you until Monday." She set the steamy coffee on Tamar's desk.

"I know, the seminar wasn't too beneficial," Tamar spoke, but did not look at her assistant right away.

"Are you alright, Ms. Woodruff?"

Tamar finally looked up at her from her seat and tried to muster a smile. "Why yes? Why do you ask?"

"I'm sorry, you just seem preoccupied with something."

Tamar chuckled and realized how zombie-like she must have been. She shuffled a few papers on her desk and tried to muster up a light conversation.

"Oh, well I kinda am. I just can't believe how useless that conference was. I'm sorry. Can you check Celeste's availability today? I want to get on her calendar for an hour."

"She is still out, remember? She will be back Monday morning though. Would you like me to schedule you for that day?"

Tamar closed her eyes briefly at her faux pas and smiled as she shook her head a bit.

"That's right. Scratch that. Monday afternoon is fine. Thanks for the coffee."

"My pleasure," the assistant said with a smile. She stepped out of Tamar's office and returned to her desk.

Tamar stared at her phone. She hated feeling like a detective and she wanted to trust Donovan as he trusted her. However, she couldn't escape feeling that something was terribly wrong with this picture.

She lifted the receiver and called his office. There was no answer and it went to his voicemail. She felt like an idiot for calling the receptionist, but she needed to. She hoped it was still Andrew from when she used to work there.

"Hi, is Donovan in today?"

"No, he is out of town," the male receptionist replied.

"Oh? I didn't realize that."

"It was last minute."

"Okay, can you tell me where he went?" she asked. "I'm sorry. Is this still Andrew?"

"Yes."

"It's Tamar."

"Oh, hi there! We sure miss you! Umm, let me see." It sounded as if the receptionist was flipping through some papers while Tamar waited. "Okay, it says here that he went to Virginia Beach. I guess there is a client down there."

"Virginia Beach, huh?" Tamar asked him. "Okay, thanks."

She hung up the phone and instantly didn't buy the explanation Andrew provided. Tamar decided to suspend her investigation for the moment. At least she knew that he was unharmed. However, it certainly wasn't like Donovan to just take off and not tell her anything. Tamar by no means kept a tight hold on Donovan, but they respected one another. She decided to dig in to her case load and table her thoughts of Donovan until later.

After what seemed to be an extensively long day of work, Tamar gathered her items to leave. Her trusty assistant always left after her, just to make sure she didn't require anything else. Tamar hooked her purse on her arm and locked her office door behind her.

"Good night!" Tamar told her assistant.

"See you tomorrow," she replied, "Oh! I have something for you. It was delivered today with the rest of your mail." The assistant handed her a few envelopes. Tamar smiled and looked them over quickly before stacking them under her arm.

"Okay, thanks."

By the time Tamar made it to her car, she was curious about one envelope in particular. The red envelope was unmarked except for Tamar's name scribbled on the front of it in magic marker. She loaded herself into her car and opened the envelope before she started her vehicle. The ripping noise from the glued paper sounded louder than usual in the quieted garage. Her heart pounded, although she wasn't sure why. Instinctively she looked up and around to see if anyone was around her vehicle, but there was no one. Confused, she creased her brows, opened the flap and slowly removed the heavy stock paper. When it was free from the envelope, she flipped it over and gasped. She placed a hand to her chest and couldn't believe her eyes.

It was a photo of Donovan and Celeste dancing outside. He was smiling and had his hand placed on the crease of her hip and thigh. She had her back to him smiling as she peered over her shoulder at him. Tamar had no idea where this photo was taken or when. Because she had so many questions that would have to wait to get answered, she had to calm herself down before she drove. Her heart felt as though it were trying to free itself from being prisoner in her chest. She took several deep breaths to console herself.

"Okay, Tamar, get it together. I don't know when this picture was taken. It's probably someone playing a cruel joke. Get it together. Ask him and no one else. Come on girl."

She took more deep breaths and closed her eyes as she exhaled. Her fingers gripped the keys as she fired on the ignition to the car. Carefully and slowly she wheeled her car out of its designated space and headed home. She needed to get a better look at the photo before she jumped to any conclusions. Tamar prayed that nothing ridiculous was going on between Celeste and Donovan. She didn't want to answer their behavior with bad behavior as well because Tamar was not a turn the other cheek type of woman. She believed that if the person was bold enough to behave a certain way, they should be just as fearless when they are facing the consequences.

The only caveat is that Tamar would be dishing out consequences for two.

16

Bryan was finally invited over by Hailey. She felt it was only right considering their lunch date was interrupted by Steve's craziness and his shrink. It seemed like old times. She prepared something for him to eat and he brought over some wine. Her son Alex was spending the evening with Camilla and Gabe because she wasn't ready for Bryan to meet him just yet. Hailey still had some thinking to do about her situation because she was not the type of person who chose to be alone. Before her lengthy relationship with Steve, she was with another guy very long term. Their break up happened so long ago that she had forgotten exactly why. All through high school she had a boyfriend, despite her father's grumblings. The past two years Hailey had not been in a relationship and focused on her son. It was difficult for her to not have someone to share that intimacy and adult affection with. In the past weeks, she wanted to stir things back up with Steve, but seeing Bryan caused a new influx of emotions to stir inside of her. Seeing Bryan while she was contemplating getting back together with Steve was like fate. All of a sudden Bryan appeared to her like a stop sign on a dangerous road to a land called "Steve". She needed to explore how and if Bryan had changed, if her feelings were the same and if he wanted to continue where they left off.

Bryan entered her house with a bottle of wine under his arm. He still donned his beard and wild hair which Hailey loved on him. Their conversation was cut a bit short due to Steve and Chase. After Steve's performance in the deli and seeing his probable love interest, Hailey could barely concentrate on her conversation with Bryan that day. Now she had him all to herself and knew that while the dialogue would be easy, it was going to include some tough questions and uncomfortable discussions.

"Hi."

"Hey. Come on in."

Bryan walked inside and visually inspected her home. He looked around to see what had changed and what stayed the same. She had painted and gotten rid of some furniture which as a result, gave it the appearance of looking larger. He noticed that her child had his own personal corner of the living room, equipped with an activity table and miniature chalkboard. Bryan smiled and wondered who he looked like. He stopped at his photo and picked up the frame. His eyes traced every line of Alex's little face. To him, he looked like Hailey. Bryan so wished that he were his son. Hailey and he were going to be married and they would've moved to a different residence in another part of town for sure. It would've been a great life. But he would not have had the experiences in Jamaica and the Dominican. Even though he wasn't romantically involved with anyone, he wouldn't trade those moments for anything.

"Are you hungry?"

"I'm fine for now," Bryan told her. He lifted the bottle of wine and extended it to her. "I brought some wine. You may want to let that breathe for an hour before serving."

"You still have such exquisite taste."

Bryan looked at her seductively, "Some things I never lose my appetite for."

Hailey blushed and gave a soft smile. Not knowing how to respond, she chuckled nervously and went into the kitchen to open the wine.

"So, I'm sorry about the other day," she called back to him. "I feel like we really didn't get a chance to talk explicitly."

"No need for an apology," he continued to look around.

"Oh! Where are my manners? Have a seat, please."

"Hailey, we are past that. I'm not a visitor at least I hope I'm not." Bryan sat down and got comfortable on the couch.

"Of course not," she came in and sat next to him.

Hailey tried not to relive the night in her mind, but the last time they sat on that couch was the same night she broke up with Steve. As she recalled, they were seriously about to fist fight. Instead, Bryan retreated in a hurry and left

Hailey to deal with Steve alone. It was for the best, but by then her romantic feelings for Steve were squandered. She wanted Bryan to stay and for Steve to go. Even though it was a while ago, it felt like yesterday.

"So here we are," Bryan said with a sigh.

"Bryan, I've missed you so much. I didn't understand. After the paternity test you just abandoned me. I didn't know what to think or what to say. I was a wreck for eight months. Then when I didn't hear from you, I tried to move on and just focused on my son."

"I understand Hailey. Please know that I never stopped loving you. I didn't know what else to do except run."

He reached for her hand and patted it gently. He let out a sigh and looked into her eyes deeply.

"Hailey, you are a wonderful woman but I have to know . . . are you seeing anyone now?"

Hailey gulped, "Why no. Why do you ask?"

"Well, I don't know if you noticed, but Steve was ready to fight me the other day. I just assumed that with that sort of primitive behavior on his mind, you and he had rekindled something."

"No," Hailey nervously chuckled. "Um, honestly Bryan, he doesn't want to have too much to do with me. I'm not too sure why he got so upset."

"You know why."

"No really," she told him. Bryan looked at her with a smirk as he blinked at her slowly as if he were fighting sleep. "What? I don't."

"He still loves you. Do you still love him?"

"He's the father of my child."

"That's not what I asked."

"Bryan, I . . .," she began, "as the father of my child I love him, but romantically he has made it clear that that ship has sailed. I believe his words were *wrecked and sunk*."

"How did you feel about that?"

"It is what it is."

"Hailey, you never give me a straight answer."

"Bryan . . ."

"Do you still love me? Did you ever love me?"

"Of course I did and yes I do!"

"Prove it."

"What?"

"Prove it to me right now."

"What do you mean?"

"Make love to me, right here, and right now."

"Bryan!"

Bryan sat back on the couch with his arms spread open on the back of the chair. He looked at Hailey, with a serious thirst for her that she was dared to quench. Hailey's gaze was still fixed upon him, her mouth still agape with disbelief as she figured out how to respond to him. She needed to act quickly because if Bryan was the same type of man she remembered from two years ago, he wanted what he wanted, when he wanted it.

"Bryan?"

Analyzing her reaction, he didn't speak. Bryan continued to sit and stare at her wondering if she was up to the challenge or if she would withdraw. Remaining in her space, she sat back a bit and lightly cleared her throat. She tilted her head to the side slightly and gave a soft sigh. Bryan wished he was a fly on the walls of her mind. He could see her imagination stirring and ramping up into gear as she looked longingly at his mouth, the base of his neck and his shoulders. Bryan changed so much, but it was in a good way. He looked so much more rugged and masculine.

"Okay," she told him. "Take your clothes off."

"No," he responded.

"What?"

"*You* show me not, me show you."

Hailey sucked her teeth slightly, her shoulders perched.

"If you want my clothes off," Bryan said with a smile, "you take them off."

Hailey didn't remember him being so unyielding, but if that was what he wanted, she was going to oblige him and oblige him well. Hailey unbuttoned her shirt slowly but stopped at her sternum. Her breasts had gotten fuller over the past two years. Bryan looked at their plumpness under her cream colored laced bra and immediately wondered if she had on a thong. It didn't matter to him because he had planned to yank them off of her the moment she undressed.

She reached for Bryan's shoulders and caressed them before moving her hands toward the base of his neck. Lovingly her hands trailed down the center of his torso and looped around his waist and back. She tugged the tail of his shirt upward and away from his waist. He felt her fingertips graze his stomach and rib cage as she slid his shirt up his body. His penis hardened with her delicate touch. He couldn't wait to become one with her again. Bryan helped out her efforts by removing his shirt for her. She kissed his nipples and circled them with her tongue. Bryan sucked air into his mouth through clenched teeth making a slurping sound. He had forgotten how good that felt when she did that to him. She lightly bit down on his fully exposed neck and licked it from its base up to his earlobe. She sucked and nibbled on it gently and felt his thickness stiffen. Not long after, his pants were unfastened by her, unleashing his rod that was nestled in his boxer briefs.

"Can I taste that?" she asked him in her airy seductive voice that sent tingles up his shaft.

Bryan's eyes rolled upward as he leaned his head back. He was fully hard and couldn't wait to feel her wet mouth wrapped around his hardness. He pulled his pants down to his ankles and kicked the linen shackles free from them. While he was tussling to get his pants from around his ankles without using his hands, she finished unbuttoning her shirt, took it off and tossed it across the room.

Bryan gripped the waistband of her jeans just above the zipper and pulled her midsection toward him in a single tug.

"Mmm," she said. She massaged him and licked her lips. His penis was free and being stroked gently by her hand. Intentionally she stared at it, wondering where she should kiss or lick it first. The tip or the shaft, she pondered. It had been over a year since she'd given a guy head but just like riding a bike, she knew that once she found her rhythm, he would be putty in her hands all over again.

"Come on," he whispered, rushing her to do something to him.

She smiled and looked into his hungry eyes, enjoying the fact that she was teasing him. She continued stroking him with her hands while admiring his manhood. In one single movement she swallowed his entire penis and released it. Bryan couldn't contain himself. He squeezed his eyes tight and wanted to scream like a woman because it felt so good to him. He gripped the cushion and felt like ripping the fabric off of it.

"You like that huh?" she asked.

"Hell yes!"

Without further adieu, Hailey deep throated him for several minutes and treated it as she would a Popsicle. Bryan rested a hand on the back of her head as he watched her perform the art of fellatio. Truth be told, this was one of the many things that made him fall so hard for her. He loved her spirit, independence and her intelligence without a doubt. This skill that she possessed was the whipped cream on the banana split.

Hailey remembered how much of a traditional lover Bryan was; specifically meaning that he always had sex in bed. She made the offer to him as she needed to hurry up and get things with him started.

"Quick! Let's go upstairs," she told him.

"We don't have to," he responded. "Let's do it right here." He began to undo her jeans and Hailey, a bit stunned by his suggestion, obliged. He stood up and twisted her around in one quick motion allowing her back to press against his chest. He leaned over her shoulder and kissed her neck. His hand was shoved down the front of her pants as he tickled her love button. Hailey almost fell limp in his arms. He spun her back around to face him and planted a deep kiss on her. Bryan craved this woman. He thought of her day and night while he was on the islands. Several nights he could barely sleep even though the sound of the waves and the clang of the buoys in the distance would lull anyone else to sleep. He told himself then that if he had the chance to be with her again that he would do whatever it took to keep her in his life forever. He loved her. Bryan had never been in love with anyone before.

"Do you have a condom?" Hailey asked.

"No, but do I need one?"

"Hell yes, Bryan," she smiled, "You were living on two islands for almost two years. Come on. I heard about how they roll in the islands. Yes baby, you need a condom."

"I don't have one. I didn't want to assume we would . . ."

"Okay, I have one."

Hailey went to the kitchen of all places, and grabbed a few condoms.

"I bought them last week when I saw you at the restaurant. I haven't been with anyone in a year," she admitted while she handed him three of them.

Bryan took them and smiled.

"You don't have to explain," he said. "Uh, I have to go to the bathroom first. Keep it wet for me."

"Oh, I plan to. Don't be too long!"

Bryan smiled and made his way to her powder room. Hailey dimmed a few lights and then looked at her watch nervously. Pacing slightly, she impatiently patted her bare thigh before she checked her watch again. Her near sweaty palms didn't make a sound as she rubbed them together while she anxiously awaited his return.

Bryan looked around in her medicine cabinet and quietly moved a few items out of his way to look for something specific. Baby lotion, Q-tips, Vaseline . . . *hurry, she's waiting*, he told himself. He moved some prescription creams for Alex out of his way before he saw what he was fishing for – a single safety pin. He smiled when he saw it and grabbed it. Quickly, he opened it and poked four holes in two of the three condoms she handed him. The only way that would ensure Hailey would be in his life forever was if she had his child. Bryan thought long and hard on this while he was away and decided to carry out his plan tonight.

17

Donovan and Celeste were enjoying a lovely breakfast under a cabana before their flight back to the states. The breeze lightly kissed the both of them as the sun had not yet begun to bathe the island with its heat. They certainly turned Barbados on its end while they were there. They partied every night, fucked at least three times a day – once five times that day. Donovan had so much sex with Celeste that the muscles in his lower back were sore and he felt completely drained. He had planned to make an appointment for a full body massage and was going to enjoy a round of golf with Jameson. Donovan and Celeste ate the first portion of their breakfast in silence. Donovan guessed that Celeste may have been reflecting on the week they were together. She had certainly gazed lovingly at him quite a bit this week and grew overly clingy. He noticed that for a moment she had stopped eating and was just looking out at the ocean. Her designer shades shielded her eyes.

"What's up baby?"

"Just thinking," she said.

"About?"

She shrugged and sighed lightly, "This was a wonderful trip. Probably the best I've ever had."

"Oh, that's a good thing. I'm glad you enjoyed my company."

"I would enjoy your company forever," she said as she caressed his hand.

"Forever?"

"Yes baby," she stroked his hand a bit more forcefully.

"Wow. I totally understand. Well, I guess I'd better get this done. Celeste," he began, "this week has been one of the best weeks of my life."

Celeste arched her back slightly to sit up in her seat. All she could think about was the ring that he had at the hotel. It looked great on her finger and now it would have a home there for the rest of her life.

"You always have a place in my heart, you know that right?"

"Of course!"

"It was great to reconnect. I know the fiasco at the restaurant a few years back drove us apart and I didn't know how to say I was sorry to you without feeling like I would be betraying Tamar."

"I was just happy you finally did."

"Baby, I'm so sorry. I wanted us to have a great time this week, I wanted us to create a new memory you know?"

"Yes yes," she rushed.

"I'm sorry, Celeste."

She frowned and slouched down a bit in her seat. She released his hand and sat back. "Sorry? Sorry for what?"

"I can't do this anymore. I love Tamar and I brought you here to have a good time, but I also needed to say goodbye to you."

"*What??*"

"I can't speak to you anymore and we can't see each other anymore."

Celeste scoffed and shook her head quickly as if to rid it of the bad news she'd just been handed. Her jaw was slacked as she stared at him, speechless with tears welling up in her eyes.

"There was no nice way to say it, so I just said it. I'm sorry."

"Wait. Wait!" She took a deep breath to calm herself, "You had a ring! I saw it! I saw it when we were at the hotel! What the fuck was that?"

"What? You saw a ring?"

"Yes motherfucker!"

Donovan gave her a stern look and clenched his jaws together tightly. "Someone lost that ring. I've been coordinating with the hotel to find the owner. It's not even mine!"

"What??"

"Yeah."

"Donovan!"

Celeste usually called him "Donnie" and he knew that when she referred to him as Donovan that she was extremely upset. Donovan tried to think of a way to let her down easily, but there wasn't one. He couldn't even respond to her and thought it best to remain silent. When Celeste became irritated with his stillness, she called him again.

"Donovan!?"

"Yes?"

"Why the hell would you bring me down here to do *this*!? Are you out of your mind, boy? Why would you have me spend my money to come down here to get dumped? Who does that?!"

Donovan looked down in his lap and then away toward the ocean. He didn't know how to explain it to her, besides he just told her it was to create a good memory out of a bad experience.

"Look at me!!" she yelled.

Vacationers looked in their direction right on queue with Celeste's demand. A few whispered amongst themselves while some continued to stare undetected to see what the ruckus was about. Irritated, Donovan turned to look at her after performing an eye roll.

"Don't roll your damn eyes at me! You know this is wrong! You are so dirty Donovan! You have no soul at all!! You care about nothing but yourself! I hope you rot in fucking hell. I hate you!"

Celeste stood to her feet, grabbed her glass of juice and emptied its contents right in Donovan's face. He reacted by cringing, his eyes shut tightly, maybe a bit too late as they stung a little. He blindly reached for the linen napkin and wiped his eyes. By the time he refocused, Celeste was gone, but not before dumping her unfinished breakfast in his lap. He tried to locate her with his eyes and saw her stomping through the lobby of the resort. Thankfully for him, he had the wait staff pack his luggage and hold it in a separate room. Anticipating her reaction, he figured that she would destroy all of his belongings and he would have nothing to change into for the flight home. He was thankful that for the flight back, his seat was in first class while she would remain in economy. He tried to schedule a later flight, but it was booked solid.

He took a deep breath and slowly stood. Partially eaten fruit and bread fell from his lap onto the ground. He shook his hands away from his body in an attempt to rid the dripping liquid from him.

"Shit," he muttered to himself.

He headed toward the lobby to go to the changing quarters to get out of his soaked attire. After he got changed, he just decided to head to the airport on his own. It was several hours before his flight, but he knew he couldn't stay at the resort. The sooner he left, the sooner he could move on with his life. He was anxious to get back to see Tamar.

*   *   *   *

Tamar sat at her desk, unable to focus on anything other than the photos she received. She studied them as if it were material she needed to know to pass the D.C. Bar exam all over again. The major issue that Tamar had was that she wasn't sure if it was a photo from the past or from the present. She desperately looked for clues. Sometimes it could be the smallest detail. Maybe she was looking at the photos too hard and was missing the obvious. If it was a photo from the past, it would be hard to tell because neither of them aged that much. Besides the past, at a minimum, would only be two to four years ago. Prior to losing her job to him at her previous firm, she didn't know Donovan. Tamar stared at the photo and swiveled her chair away from the desk toward the window. When she turned a stack of papers fell off of her desk and onto the floor.

Tamar sucked her teeth at her blunder. She wheeled the chair back slightly in order to pick up the items. She stared at one paper in particularly long. Still holding the paper, she sat back in her seat and studied the context. It was Celeste's itinerary that her assistant gave to Tamar the week before.

Barbados.

Tamar looked at the photo again but instead of looking at Donovan and Celeste, she looked at the background a bit more closely. She narrowed her eyes and leaned forward into the picture. There was a marquis in the photo that was slightly cut out of the picture. W-E-R and then the word "ISLE". Tamar looked at the itinerary again. It was somewhere in Barbados. She did a search on her computer to see what, if anything would come up. After about a minute or so of investigative maneuvering, "Couples Tower Isle" was listed in the search results. She saw a number listed and picked up her desk phone. She waited for a moment and returned the phone back in its cradle.

"What am I doing?" she said to herself.

Tamar hated spying and did not like digging around for answers behind someone else's back. That was not her at all. She would ask him about the photos and leave it at that. However, she couldn't resist being a little put off by Andrew telling her that he was in Virginia Beach this week. She was having such a hard time reaching him. There had been a few texts here and there and maybe an email, but they hadn't *spoken* to each other in almost a week. That was odd behavior for Donovan. Tamar took a moment to regroup to gather her thoughts. If Donovan was working in Virginia Beach this week, he would drive. Celeste however, since she was in Barbados, she would be flying back. *Spying on Celeste wouldn't be the same as spying on Donovan*, Tamar thought. That would be Tamar's plan of action. She was going to have herself at the airport exit by the time Celeste's flight landed. If Celeste spotted her, Tamar would have to make up some story as to why she was there. She would figure it out. She had until 7:20 p.m. to think of a plausible excuse.

18

Jameson had been in several meetings every day to discuss the sale of Beefy Burger to another restaurateur. He wanted to make sure that he received a fair amount for this chain and would be free and clear of any residual building or electrical repairs once the sale was final. Camilla stayed away from his business affairs, as was her choice. Jameson was surprised by how hands off Camilla remained when it came to his money or financial affairs. The extent of Camilla's concern was asking if he was satisfied with how his deals were going. That was all. Besides she had already signed a document that would entitle her to nothing, so there was no sense in her asking too many questions anyway. Jameson thought that her lackadaisical demeanor toward his finances may have been because she was an auditor for the IRS. She looked at numbers all day and may have just enjoyed having the break when she was with him. He wanted to do something special for Camilla. Just to show his appreciation for her. They were dating very heavily and were always communicating throughout the day, be it emails, texts or phone calls. Jameson couldn't get enough of Camilla. Without being prompted, Camilla would often rub his back after a long day and showed him affection in ways that Jameson hadn't experienced.

He had arranged to have flowers sent to her job today. For their first date, he gave her a single yellow rose, today he was going to send her a small simple bouquet of ½ a dozen yellow roses. Jameson didn't want to overdo it right away because he had the tendency of falling hard rather quickly. He wanted to gauge her appreciation for the small things before spoiling her immensely.

Jameson was sitting with an attorney discussing one particular Beefy Burger on U St. when his phone rang.

"Excuse me," he told the attorney. "Hello? Hi my darling."

"Thank you so much for the lovely roses!"

"You are welcome. Will you I see you this evening?"

"Of course you will! Listen, I know you are probably busy, but I just wanted to call and thank you!"

"It's no problem. I will see you later then."

*   *   *   *

After Camilla hung up with Jameson, she contacted her babysitter to see if she could watch Gabe. Camilla didn't always want to rely on Hailey because she knew she had her hands full with Alex. Camilla felt that she exhausted her requests with Josephine for the moment and did not want to inundate her too much more. Camilla needed that one on one time with Jameson and even though they hadn't been seeing each other for long, everything came easily with them. Camilla didn't feel the need to mask anything about her with him. She confided in him about her one night stand with Steve that resulted in her pregnancy. She told Jameson that Gabe was the best thing that had ever happened to her. Even though he didn't arrive in the manner that she had hoped, she was glad that he was here. Camilla made it very clear to Jameson that nothing would come before Gabe, not even him. Jameson completely agreed and understood.

Camilla felt such a connection with Jameson. He seemed genuine and she constantly wanted to be around him. He pampered her endlessly and was ready to feel that oneness with him right away.

After Camilla spent some time with Gabe and got him prepped for bed, the babysitter arrived. Camilla had used her a few times before and she came highly recommended, however, she reiterated a few things with her anyway.

"Don't forget to read him Dr. Seuss before bed. He loves Green Eggs and Ham for some reason."

The babysitter nodded frantically.

"You have my cell phone in case there is an emergency."

She nodded again.

"No sweets, no matter how hard he begs!"

She slathered her son with kisses, hugged him tight and told him to be good. Jameson had sent a car for Camilla and the driver was there promptly. After their fender bender, Jameson didn't like for Camilla to be out on the road at night and felt safer knowing that she wouldn't have the stress of driving. Even though they spent a lot of time together, they went out quite a bit so this was her first visit to his home. Camilla's jaw dropped when the car drove up the estate in Potomac, Maryland. Although it was dark, she could see that the bushes and yard were perfectly manicured.

The driver opened the car door for Camilla, while the butler opened the front door for her.

"Good evening, madam," he greeted.

"Thank you, sir."

Camilla stood in the immaculate foyer and looked around and upward. She felt as though she was in the Sistine Chapel for the first time. The large staircase wound around the curved wall and ascended to the second floor. The décor of the house was very crisp, as the color white was the overlying scheme. There was marble everywhere, oil paintings, sculptures and very few photos of him or his family. There was one exception; a portrait of his father was over the fireplace in a navy blue painted room. Despite the gray hair, the resemblance was striking.

Jameson appeared from the rear somewhere almost startling Camilla.

"Hi baby," he greeted as he hugged and kissed her softly on her lips.

The butler smiled and excused himself quietly.

"Would you like a tour or would you like to eat first?"

"Oh goodness, this is incredible," she said as her head pivoted from left to right.

"I'll take that to mean you want the tour first," he said with a smile.

"Sure."

"Let's start from the top then work our way down, eh?"

They ascended the long staircase with its wide steps. The dark wood was covered with a black runner. When they reached the top of the stairs, there was a large opening in the hallway that overlooked the foyer. There was a leather loveseat flanked by plants; Camilla guessed the love seat was there in case someone needed to rest after walking up the stairs.

The long hallway led to five large bedrooms, of which only two shared a bathroom. Each room was decorated sophisticatedly but still had a warm inviting feel. Jameson stopped for a moment, pointed in one room and smiled.

"What?" Camilla asked.

"Gabe's room?"

Camilla blushed and rubbed his arm lovingly.

"Let me show you where I reside."

They headed back down the hallway and opened the double doors to his room. Camilla was wonderstruck. She immediately noticed the fireplace and California King sized bed. The warm rich color and multiple pillows made it look inviting and comfortable. Camilla just wanted to jump in and be swallowed whole by its fluffiness.

"That's a huge bed!" Camilla commented with a chuckle.

"It's even bigger when I'm in there alone."

"Oh yeah? And how often is that?"

"Every night."

Her saddened eyes aimed at the floor then over to the window. Hypnotically, she walked over as if she were afraid at what may be on the outside. Jameson followed her movements with his eyes.

"Why is that?" she asked as she parted the sheer curtain with her fingertips to take a peek.

He walked up behind her and gripped her gently from behind. Camilla gasped softly at his touch and leaned backward into his frame.

"I suppose it has been waiting for you." He kissed the back of her neck tenderly. She turned around to kiss him as she reached up to wrap her arms around his neck. He kissed her passionately, more passionately than their first kiss on his yacht. Camilla could not control the rush of emotions that she felt for this man. They spoke so frequently that it felt as if they were old friends who had known each other since grade school. She loved the way his fingers spread wide across her back and caressed it as they kissed. She loved his masculinity and how sexy he was for his age. She never thought that she could feel this way about anyone after having her heartbroken from a man that she thought she loved very deeply.

"We can eat later," Camilla whispered softly in his ear.

While still holding her, Jameson leaned back to get a full view. His expression wasn't one of surprise, but instead he wanted to make sure that this was what she wanted.

"Are you sure?" he asked.

"Yes."

"Why do you want to do this?"

"You're asking why?" she gave a light chuckle.

Jameson pulled her body toward his and held her close. He wanted to make love to Camilla so bad, that his loins were churning the minute she walked inside his home. But he needed to know from her – he wanted to be sure.

"Yes, I'm asking why."

Cradled in his arms, she spoke softly into his chest. "Because I can't stop thinking about you. And the only way to be closer to you than we are in my dreams is to . . . have you in reality. I know it's mushy, but I haven't felt this way about anyone. I guess when it's right, it's right."

She looked downward, vulnerable and bashful for bearing her heart to him so early, but it was how she felt. She had lied to herself for so long and didn't feel the need to subject him to the same.

He lifted her head by her chin and kissed her softly on her lips. He pampered her back as his hands found the hem of her dress before he raised it. His fingertips glided delicately across the base of her back feeling the softness of her skin. Camilla melted from his soft and loving touch. He reached behind her and started to unzip the dress that hugged her curves securely. Camilla peeled herself out of her dress and let it fall to her ankles. As she helped Jameson unbutton his shirt, he stopped to shimmy out of his pants. Her body looked good with her clothes on, but outside of that dress, he couldn't believe her figure. Supple breasts, narrow waist and curvaceous hips, the best parts of course, were hidden under her deep purple satin bra and panties. It looked regal against her caramel colored skin.

"Camilla . . .," he moaned softly.

Camilla tried not to stare at the massive erection looming behind his brick red satin boxers. His body would put any man her age to shame. She knew that he worked out and maintained a healthy lifestyle despite the food his restaurant served, but his body was phenomenal. Squared shoulders, defined pectorals, trim waistline, muscular legs and back. She couldn't wait to feel this man's naked body pressed against hers.

As he kissed her with his arm wrapped around her back, he guided her to his enormous bed by backing up into it. Camilla following his lead trusted him as she was blindly moving backward. When she felt that the bed was behind her, she stopped and turned her head toward it awkwardly.

"It's so big."

Jameson smiled at her for a moment.

"The bed I mean!" She blushed and then looked down at his crotch, "Well, that too."

He smiled again and gently held her face in his hands while he softly kissed her lips. Camilla lay down on the bed and scooted backward on it – one leg was propped up as if she were shooting an ad for lingerie. Jameson took in the visual for a moment as he stroked his manhood that was still nestled in his boxers. Camilla could barely contain herself. She was still equipped with the knowledge of Kama Sutra and remained flexible enough to perform them. The Kama Sutra images flipped through her mind in a sexual montage. She would get to use them on someone finally. She didn't want to overwhelm him right away, so she allowed him to take the lead – this time.

"Turn over on your stomach," he instructed.

Camilla rolled over slowly and looked back at him over her shoulder.

"I wished I had a camera for this view," he told her. "When was the last time you had a massage?"

"It's been a while," she admitted.

"I'm going to massage every inch of your body," he told her. "Inside and out."

"I like the sound of that."

He began to stroke her back, allowing every inch of her body to move smoothly across his fingertips. Certain areas deserved a kiss or a lick when he felt the need. Camilla's walls responded in kind with a quick ripple that sent shockwaves to her clitoris. She was enjoying the way his hands felt all over her body, but she really wanted to feel him inside of her. Camilla was unsure if she would be able to handle his tool judging by the way it looked in his boxers, but she was going to try.

"Turn over," he commanded in a milky voice.

As if being hypnotized by a Svengali, she followed his command and slowly turned over. He removed her underwear and commenced to feasting on her sexual nectar. Jameson performed this as if he were being graded for extra credit. Camilla arched her back in what felt like a 90 degree angle because it felt so good to her. She could barely control her body's movements as she twisted, turned and bent in several directions as he pleasured her. His firm grip on her hips kept the star of the show in place so he could explore it all with is hot tongue. Camilla continued to moan and writhe about which put her on the opposite side of the bed. Jameson followed her squirming midsection like a puppy, refusing to let her get away.

He lifted his mouth from her and rose to his knees as he stared down at her with his rod in his hands. His jovial expression that was brandished earlier was replaced with one of lust and sexual hunger. He gulped hard with anticipation. Unbeknownst to Camilla, Jameson had tossed a few condoms on the bed while he took off his pants earlier. He reached over to retrieve one as he came out of his boxers. Camilla sat up to get a look at his goods. Her eyes widened as she lifted up more to be sure of what she saw.

"Oh my God," she muttered.

Jameson stroked her thighs and ignored her comment. He was going to have sex with this woman. He would be gentle as he wanted to please her.

"Umm . . .," Camilla started.

"Relax," he told her as he gently stroked her.

Camilla had been with maybe one guy since Steve. Steve was average sized, but nice. The last guy that she was with wasn't working with much at all.

Bryan's tool wasn't anything to sneeze at. She didn't know why she was doing a schlong comparison at that precise moment, but she was trying to measure if she could handle Jameson or not. It was the trunk of a baby elephant!

He got on top of her and Camilla gulped as her heart rate seemed to double. Nervous about the penetration, she began to break out in a light sweat. He kissed the side of her neck affectionately and whispered for her to relax again. The tip of his penis teased her lower lips and she gasped. He massaged her breasts and continued to kiss her mouth and neck. He eased more of himself inside of her.

"Oh!" Camilla said as she inhaled sharply.

"Come on baby," he eased more of it inside of her as Camilla closed her eyes tightly. She felt like a virgin. He eased a bit more and rested himself inside of her. He throbbed and filled her completely.

"It's all the way in baby," he informed her in a soothing tone.

Camilla took a deep breath and exhaled. "Oh, okay. Okay. Okay," she told him.

Jameson held himself inside her for a moment as she settled down completely. Shortly thereafter, he began stroking her, slowly and gently.

"Oh God!" Camilla squealed. "You're big!"

"It's okay, I'm going to make you my fit," he said as he continued stroking her gently. Camilla threw her attempts of any sort of Kama Sutra out of her mind. She wouldn't be able to do any of that until she was completely accustomed to his member. For now, all she could do was lie there with her legs spread as far apart as she could and concentrate on her breathing. He continued stroking slowly and deeply until Camilla was completely relaxed. He tried to increase the rhythm of his stroke just a bit.

"Oh! Oh! Oh!" Camilla blurted with each stroke.

Jameson buried his face over her shoulder and continued.

"Oh! Oh God! Jameson!"

Deeper strokes.

"Jameson!"

Camilla dug her nails into his back as her body reacted to his deep but gentle thrusts. She arched her back and squeezed her eyes together tightly. Jameson moaned as her walls tightened around him as it aroused him even more. He stroked a bit faster and Camilla did not object. Her response was a low bellow that came from her pelvis and travelled up her torso out of her mouth.

"Yes!"

From the base of the stairs in the foyer, the butler peered upward in the direction of Mr. Hedley's bedroom. He smiled to himself when he heard the moans of Camilla and grunts of Mr. Hedley. After he strolled into the kitchen, he gave a "thumbs up" to the chef, who ceased cooking for the time being. He knew that it would be a minute before they even made it down to dinner and he wanted everything to be hot for them.

After several minutes, Jameson wrapped both arms around Camilla and squeezed her tight as he came. His body jerked to release every last bit. Camilla was frozen, astonished by how good Jameson made the experience given the size of his Johnson. Camilla was hooked. Jameson rolled over to catch his breath while Camilla stretched. Thinking of herself as a rubber band, she elongated her body as much as she could to realign anything that may have been jarred. Jameson threw his hand over her stomach as he panted.

"I knew you were special," he told her.

"Is that right?"

"Yes," he tenderly touched her body as he spoke with his eyes closed. "I believe everything happens for a reason, Camilla. I'm not sure what was going on with you that day we crashed and I never asked. I'm just glad that I was that shoulder for you at that moment. I hope you will always allow me to be that for you."

"What are you saying?"

"Camilla, I'm almost done with the sale of all of the Beefy Burgers. The final one is in D.C. I was actually speaking with the attorney when you called to thank me for the flowers. After that, I was going to take some time off and get away."

"Get away? You're going somewhere?"

"Yes. I had planned to do that before we met anyway. I'm traveling Europe and my first stop is the Netherlands."

"Oh," the tone of her voice dropped a bit. "That sounds exciting. When did you plan to leave?"

"Well the arrangements were made a while back, but I'm leaving next month."

"Next month?" Camilla sat up to look at him. She felt like bawling, but restrained herself. At that moment, she couldn't understand why he waited until they made love to tell her something so drastic. However, her eyes still welled up with tears. "Jameson . . .," she muttered.

"Camilla, I need you with me. Since we met, I've thought a lot about this. I want you and Gabe with me. I've already talked to some top notch tutors and nannies for him."

"What?" She said softly through a light breath. Camilla could barely believe her ears.

"Yes."

"My job . . .," she began.

"I hope you don't mind, but I talked to your supervisor and she assured me that you will have a spot when or if you decided to return. She said you were one of her best auditors. She'd be sad to lose you, but understood that this is a great opportunity for you."

"You did?"

"I'm sorry for going behind your back. I swore her to secrecy."

"Jameson, I don't know what to say. I want to, but . . .,"

He reached for her hand and kissed her fingertips, "But what?"

"I don't know if I can take Gabe away from Steve. I mean, granted he and I aren't together, have had no sort of relationship outside of that one night, but he is a good father."

"Do you want to be with me?"

"Of course, I do, I just . . .,"

"Just talk to him, Camilla. If he objects, then we will figure something else out. But, I want you in my life. Just think about it, he will have some great experiences that he won't get in the classroom. So will you."

Camilla stared up at the ceiling, her mind darting in and out of thought while her heart raced. The light touch of Jameson's fingers across her body was making her decision an easier one. Who wouldn't want to travel the world with a millionaire? To experience a life that she may not ever know otherwise.

"Just think about it, Camilla," he told her. He got up and stood next to the bed while he peered down at her. He stared at her curves with lowered eyelids. He wanted to make love to her again.

"Okay, I will."

"Are you hungry?"

"Starved."

"Let's get cleaned up and get some food. The chef is making one of his specialties. Leg of lamb. It's very good."

"It sounds good."

Camilla stood up on wobbly legs. She couldn't believe that she took all of him on the first try. When she saw the length and width of his penis, she knew for sure that he would split her in half. She tiptoed to the bathroom where Jameson was already in the shower. Circular in shape, it was actually a shower and steam shower combo. There were multiple shower heads and two tiled seating areas on either side. If everyone stood, you could probably fit 12 people comfortably inside. She had never seen anything quite like it before. He turned his lathered body to face her. Camilla smiled while she stepped inside.

"You need a shower cap?" he asked.

Camilla had her hair bunned when she came over, but unfastened it just before they had sex. She didn't care if it got wet she just wanted to be near him.

"No, I'm good."

She stepped in and stood next to him. He pulled her close with a hug and kissed her deeply. The warmth of the shower covered her body from several angles, his arms wrapped around her and gave her insurmountable pleasurable that made her body want him again.

"Tell me," she said.

"Tell you what?" he asked.

"Why do you want me and Gabe to go with you?"

"It's simple. I don't want to run the risk of losing you. I want us to keep building what we have started here. I care for you very much, more than you could possibly imagine."

Camilla thought on his words and replied with a gentle kiss, the water from the shower danced around them.

"How long is this voyage?" she asked.

"At least six months, but I've planned for a year maximum."

"A year. Wow."

"Exactly. A lot can happen in a year. Hell a lot can happen in a week, Camilla. I would be remiss if I left you only for you to meet someone else. And it wouldn't be fair to ask you to wait. The only other logical choice is to have you come with me."

"Well, am I going as a friend?"

"Initially, yes. But you would return as my wife."

19

Tamar arrived at the airport at seven and was prepared for her amateur stakeout. As she was nibbling on some Twizzlers, she felt terrible for spying but just needed to be sure. Some things weren't adding up. The main issue was not being able to get in contact with Donovan all week. He never complained about his phone before last week. But, today she wasn't spying on Donovan, she was spying on that damned Celeste. Tamar just wanted to know how her Barbados trip went. Or at least that was the excuse she was using.

Defiant to the laws of the airport roads, Tamar was blatantly parked in a no parking and no loading zone. She tried to keep a low profile, but there were a few airport security officers asking her to move along. There was plenty of time before the flight landed and Celeste grabbed her bags from the claim area, so Tamar obliged them for the moment. She circled around and returned to the area that was noted on Celeste's itinerary. Tamar eased up to the curb and depressed the button for her hazard lights. Shortly thereafter, she saw Celeste being unruly with her bags. She was yanking them along behind her and had a brutal scowl on her face. Tamar stepped out of her car and planned to casually bump into her.

Tamar walked through the automatic doors and headed for Celeste, but pretended that she didn't see her. Celeste on the other hand, didn't even see her at all. Darting past, Celeste's lips were tightly pressed together – her bags wobbling unsteadily behind her.

"Celeste?" Tamar called to her.

"Tamar?" She looked at her up and down with a raised brow. "What are you doing here?"

Tamar just smiled at her. She practiced her explanation at least three times in the car, but it escaped her at that very moment. She was supposed to tell

Celeste that she saw her itinerary and came to meet her because there was an urgent matter at the firm that couldn't wait until Monday. Or was it that she was picking her up to discuss the urgent matter at the firm but it *could've waited* until Monday? Awkwardly, Tamar continued to smile. Celeste gave her a pressed look by tilting her head slightly to prompt Tamar to speak.

"Oh, let me guess," Celeste started, "you're here to pick up Donovan? Isn't that poetic? Well, he's getting his bags. You win. He's all yours, sweetie."

Puzzled Tamar looked at Celeste speechless; her brows frowning as her blood slowly began to boil.

"You know," Celeste continued, "this is twice that he has made it clear that I have no place in his life. I get it. You are the one he wants. Just tell him to stay the hell away from me. And you better steer clear too. I'm sick of both of you!"

"Wait. Wait. Hold on, Celeste," Tamar interrupted her rant. "What are you talking about?"

"What I'm talking about is you don't drag someone to Barbados to break up with them after sexing their brains out all week. Hell, all year! He could've saved me the time *and* money and just broke it off here."

"Break up? What the hell are you saying, Celeste?"

"I'm tired of being played is what I'm saying, *Tamar!*" Celeste emphasized her name to mock her. Celeste noticed that Tamar still looked clueless. "Oh. You didn't know, huh? You really are slipping sweetheart. Before you find out incorrectly and want to haul off and hit me again, which will not go unanswered if you try that by the way, I may as well get some pleasure from this whole messed up situation and inform you."

Tamar shifted her weight from one leg to the next and put her hands on her hips. "Tell me what, exactly?"

Celeste smiled. "Now *this* is going to be worth the money spent going to Barbados."

Tamar folded her arms now and was awaiting Celeste's news. Celeste took the time to set her bags upright and adjust her clothing while she rubbed her hands together greedily.

"Donnie and I have been seeing each other for the past seven months. Right here in D.C. We switch hotels and give each other code words for which room we will be in that day. The last seminar that you went to, oh honey . . . he spent the whole week with me at my house. Actually we've done that quite a few times while you were gone. I put it on him so good girl that he was talking about leaving you. He had a ring and everything. When I told him 'no' was when he decided to pull this travel stunt. So now you know that your relationship was and is one big lie!"

Tamar looked into Celeste's eyes and kept her tears at bay. She swallowed that hard lump in her throat and took a deep breath. She knew how conniving Celeste could be and Celeste offering all of the details of their so called affair was probably a lie anyway. Tamar decided to do the unthinkable; she wasn't going to punch Celeste in her mouth that spewed all of this detriment about her relationship. She was going to screw Celeste's mind. She thought briefly.

"Oh yeah, he told me all about that. You didn't seriously think he was going to *be* with you, did you? He was fucking you to get you to quit the firm so he could join *me* there. Ipso facto, he *never* wanted you! Walk away empty handed. Again. Anyway, I don't have any more time for you right now, but believe me, I will deal with you."

"Is that so?"

Tamar nodded.

"You fuckers. You won't have time, sweetie," Celeste told her. "I always have a backup plan. Believe that. Your days are numbered, bitch."

Puzzled by her comment, she stared at Celeste and watched her calmly turn and walk away to the exit.

Tamar looked around for a moment, expecting to see Donovan rounding some corner. Even though she didn't see Donovan, she thought that maybe Donovan saw them talking and thought it best to stay far away. Tamar was going to also deal with "Donnie" when he got home.

When Tamar got to her car, she saw an airport security person walking around her car about to call someone on the radio.

"Ma'am?"

Tamar ignored him as she approached her car.

The security guard repeated it louder, "Ma'am?!"

"*WHAT??*" Tamar hollered. The guard was shocked by how rotund her voice was because it didn't match her physical make up. She stood facing him with her fists balled and teeth gritted. The security guard backed away slightly, his hands were slightly raised by his sides.

"Nothing."

Tamar sped home, cursing Donovan out during the entire journey.

"Ooo, you wait until I get home! How dare that bastard cheat on me with that trick!"

Tamar turned wildly onto their street and slammed on brakes in front of their double garage door. Donovan was already there.

"Oh yeah, it's on baby!" Tamar said to herself when she saw his car parked. She leapt out of her car and slammed the door shut. Ready to have it out with Donovan, she nearly stumbled up the walk way because she was in such a hurry to get inside.

She entered the house and slammed the door. Throwing her keys hard on the table, she called out to him.

"Donovan! Bring your ass!"

Donovan came from around the corner to confront her. It was as if he knew what was about to happen. He had his hands at the ready preparing to grab Tamar to calm her down. She raced toward him, squealing, her arms flailing wildly, but Donovan calmly and coolly reached for them and wrapped them around her body. He gripped her tightly against him as he forced her to face the opposite direction.

"Stop," he calmly said.

"You bastard!" Tamar was jumping around trying to free herself from his grasp.

"I said stop, baby."

"I can't believe you lied to me! You went to Barbados with that piece of trash! How dare you! We're done! I can't believe you did that! Let me go!"

"Who is Taj?"

Tamar stopped jumping after she heard Taj's name. Her chest heaved up and down rapidly as she tried to catch her breath from her workout with Donovan.

"What?" she muttered quietly.

"I said who is Taj?"

"Taj? Taj who?"

Donovan loosened his grip, but didn't let her go. He turned her around and pressed her tighter to him, her arms crossed over her chest. Although his voice was calm, his eyes didn't reflect the same sentiment. They were burning with rage and pierced Tamar's soul.

"You heard me."

"Taj is a lawyer. A New York colleague. Why?"

"Did you fuck this New York colleague?"

Tamar looked stunned by the line of questioning and struggled to get free. "Let me go!"

Donovan shook her hard once to get her to behave. Tamar's head bobbled just before her body stiffened. "Did you fuck this New York colleague? I'm not asking a third time!"

"Of course not!"

"Wow. Really?"

"Get off of me, Donovan."

"A liar *and* a cheat," he muttered.

"What?"

He tugged her toward the coffee table and showed her the pictures of Taj and Tamar cuddled in a restaurant, of them sharing kisses and intimate touches. Tamar could barely believe what she was seeing. After all of the rendezvous' with Taj, she thought that the distance would assure she would not get caught, but she was wrong. Apparently so was Donovan because he had traveled even further than she. Tamar's stomach felt twisted and her mouth tasted as though her insides were rotting. She could not lie any longer because the truth was spread across the coffee table. So she did what Donovan did earlier – deflected.

"Oh and how long was your affair with Celeste? Seven months! I said let me go! You took that slut to Barbados? All hugged up grinding on her fat ass near the beach! Fuck away from me!"

Donovan released Tamar from his grasp. She pushed his upper body away from her and walked a few paces to distance herself. She turned slightly as her eyes began to fill with tears.

"How could you do that?" she asked him. "You went on vacation with *her*?"

"You cheated too! Why?!" Donovan yelled.

"Because you were seeing her!" Tamar covered her eyes and lowered her head. "You think I didn't know, Donovan? I knew already. That's why I chose to do what I did! You think I care about Taj? You think I have feelings for him? Well I don't! I did it just to get back at you until you came to your damn senses! I mean, are you back yet?"

"Don't talk to me right now."

"Excuse me?"

"Do *not* talk to me right now! You gave that man something that belonged to me!"

"And you had that trick parading herself in front of me every day like fucking you was just business as usual! No wonder she kept smiling in my face! You gave her attention that was supposed to be for me!" Tamar cried out in a soft low moan at the humiliation. "I just hate you right now."

She turned to walk away from Donovan, but he reached for her hand which stopped her. She looked up at him. He was at a loss for words, but his eyes told her that he was sorry for hurting her. Tamar's eyes echoed the same sentiments as she gripped his hand slightly before releasing it. She didn't hate him; she still loved him, but the hurt was too much for her to bear. Her only resolve was to retaliate by cutting him with her words. She ran upstairs and Donovan heard her door slam.

Tamar dropped herself on the edge of the bed and sobbed uncontrollably. She reached for her tissues and buried her face in them while the tears were collected there. She told herself to get it out now because she refused to cry anymore about this after tonight. After tonight, she was going to plan on how to repay Celeste for making her look like a fool. Tamar gave her a pass a few years ago and let her off easy for her slight infraction, but she swore that if she tried to wedge herself between her and Donovan again that she would destroy her. Tamar didn't know what to do about the situation with Donovan at the moment. Things were different now. They were living together now. There were no other residences to run to and no other place to be banished to. They would have to work this out amongst themselves. The only thing is that she was unsure if he would be willing to work it out with her or if he would be able to get pass her act of infidelity. It was different from before. Before, he was the one asking for her forgiveness, but Tamar purposely reacted to his indiscretion by committing one of her own. She did not have to respond in that fashion, and although they both were at fault, she would have to carry a larger portion of the blame this time.

She sniffled and blew her nose until she could breathe again. Staring at her hands that rested limp in her lap, she began reviewing certain aspects of their relationship. *Was there something that she missed that hinted to her that she and Donovan should not be together*, she wondered. During this instant the only red flag had been Celeste.

Tamar had a feeling that at some point Celeste would make another play for Donovan. When Tamar slapped her in the restaurant, she knew then that Celeste would be plotting for the right moment to strike. Tamar had to give it to Celeste because that bitch could be cold-hearted and ruthless when she wanted to be. This brilliant heifer waited until Tamar got comfortable with Donovan and then resurfaced. She waited until their relationship was on the risk of getting stale. Even though it wasn't, Tamar knew the type of relationship he had with Celeste before they met. It always seemed to her that those two had unfinished business. Perhaps now since they reconnected, it was over. Tamar recalled the rage in Celeste's eyes when she said Donovan had ended it.

Tamar just needed a moment to think quietly. She just needed to be left alone so she could sort things out for her own peace of mind. Tamar was a sensible woman who knew the power of sex and the hunger that it craved. Like a puzzle, she needed to make sure all of the pieces fit and made sense before she made any decisions. The conclusion that she arrived at was that their relationship was over, just as was her relationship with Taj. Tamar certainly wasn't going to excuse Donovan's behavior because he should not have done it in the first place, but he ended it with Celeste and he was still here with her.

Donovan leaned against the door just opposite the entrance to their bedroom. He had come up right after her, but wanted to give her some space. He knew how Tamar worked. She needed a moment to process things, but so did he. While she closed herself in the room, Donovan thought about some things that Tamar said. Being lawyers, they both were good at recalling certain aspects of a conversation that others may miss. One thing was that Tamar said she already knew that he was having an affair. The other was that she said he was hugging and grinding on Celeste in Barbados. There was no way she would've known that unless she was there herself. Donovan knew that Tamar would not have even allowed it to continue had she been there, so how did she know this? Since he and Celeste continued their trip uninterrupted, this one stumped Donovan.

His emotions teeter tottered like two kids on a see-saw. He wanted to comfort her and choke her all in the same vein. He was hurt. The thought of his woman rolling in bed with another man made him want to vomit. It was one thing to attach this experience to a faceless male, but Donovan couldn't do that. The photos didn't lie. It wasn't as if he were some common guy from down the block; this man was self-made, rich, and looked like a movie star who women killed to be with. Donovan didn't feel inadequate in any of those departments, but the fact that this man has the tools all men desire that could potentially take his woman, made him want his blood. The bitter pill to him was that she chose to be with him after all he had done for her. He gave up his independence and freedom to make things work with her. Celeste meant nothing to him and it was easy to hurt her. But Tamar damaged his heart. He truly loved that woman and knew that if Celeste meant nothing, there should be nothing. That was why he ended it – for the love of Tamar. Again, he had given up things for her and the pay back was she gave herself to another man.

Donovan tried to simmer down, but he really wanted a more solid explanation from Tamar. He was careful and he knew that there was virtually no way that she could've known about his affair. He wanted to kick the door down and shake her wildly to demand answers, but he couldn't do that. He was wrong and he forced her into Taj's arms.

The door opened and Tamar released it and walked back toward the bed as if she knew that he was standing outside of it. Donovan took it as an invitation to come inside, but he was still cautious to enter. He saw her as she sat back on the edge of the bed and stared ahead blankly, not acknowledging him at all. He crept forward slowly, but stopped at the threshold. He saw her close her eyes and take a deep breath. When she exhaled, she opened them but still did not look his way.

"Babe," Donovan whispered to her, "I'm so sorry."

Tamar continued staring blankly and did not respond to his broken apology. Donovan didn't repeat himself. He finally mustered up the courage to enter the room and sat down near her, but not right beside her. He dare not try to touch her as this was enough for now. He just wanted to be in her presence and maybe so did she. They sat there for what felt like hours, but it had only been ten minutes. He wondered what she was thinking as he looked at her on a few instances. Her tears fell silently down her cheek and she remained still. She could not look at him right now because she knew the power that Donovan's handsomeness had over her. His single-dimpled smile made her melt every time. Even though she knew he wouldn't be smiling at this particular moment, his eyes would still mesmerize her. She didn't have the emotional strength to look at him right now.

She inhaled and exhaled again.

Tamar didn't know what to say. She knew she messed up as well, and yet he apologized first. She needed to swallow that rotten chunk of pride and be a big girl. After another five minutes or so, Tamar wiped her tears, but still didn't look in his direction.

"I'm sorry," she said.

"You don't owe me an apology babe," he told her, "it was my fault. If I didn't step out, I know you wouldn't have. I just need some time to deal with it. I'm not going to lie."

"Same."

"I still love you, I just fucked up," he admitted.

"Same."

"You don't want to look at me?"

She shook her head and then turned her head even further away.

"I have a question," he said. "You said something about me dancing and grinding on her at the beach. What made you say that?"

Tamar reached under her side of the bed and pulled out the pack of photos. She placed it between them and sighed audibly. Donovan looked at the red envelope, unsure of what he may see. He opened it slowly and marveled at its contents. Several pictures of Donovan and Celeste were taken during their Barbados trip. There were other photos of them in D.C. He was flabbergasted as he rubbed his chin nervously.

"Well . . .," he began, "there it is. So you knew all this time because of these?"

"No. I just got those this week."

"You said you knew I was having an affair."

"I just knew Donovan. I'm not about to tell your ass how. But I knew. You think if I had those photos from when you first started that I would've let it go on for this long? Hell no. But I knew you were doing someone. I just didn't think it was that skank."

"Pictures," he scoffed and shook his head. "I got yours tonight. It was like the delivery person was waiting on me. As soon as I closed the door, he was knocking on it."

Tamar looked at him for the first time since he entered the room, surprised at this bit of information.

"You just found out tonight?"

"Yeah."

Tamar thought for a moment and shook her head. She laughed a bit and clapped a few times to give a sick applause.

"That bitch is brilliant."

"What?"

"She sent these to us."

"How babe? I'm not following."

"Think about it, the photos of you guys was to rub it in my face. She probably thought that you two were committed. I mean travelling together is serious. You end it with her, so she sends photos of me to keep you from staying with me. Either way, we end up apart. Oh, she's good."

"No! You think she would do something like that?"

"She's evil and miserable. Yes."

"Wow, I guess I never thought of it like that."

"Why would I send you pictures and why would you send yours to me? It was her. I'm going to get her. I told her a while ago to stay out of our relationship. I told her!"

"What are you going to do?"

"I'll think of something."

20

Several weeks and several treatments had passed which affirmed that I was in fact pregnant with twins. I had no idea in my wildest dreams that I would be blessed twice. My stomach began to show slightly and despite having numerous cravings, I had no appetite. What amazed me was that the foods that I typically loved, the stench of them unequivocally revolted me now. Every moment I had my nose in the infamous book "What to Expect When You're Expecting." Needless to say, it was a precise guide regarding the effects of pregnancy that was freakishly accurate. Even though I was enjoying some of the new experiences of pregnancy, I couldn't help but feel as if I were in this alone. Lately, I noticed that Ian had little to say to me, so I tried not to bother him too much. I'd guessed that he was still letting the news sink in while trying to make preparations for the new additions to the family.

It was after 8 p.m. and I was beginning to wonder where Ian was. Typically he was home by four in the afternoon and sometimes no later than five. For the past three weeks, he has been home no earlier than seven. I wanted to keep the peace, but this would be a trying time for both of us and I needed my husband by my side.

The door opened and closed gingerly. I came from the rear to greet Ian. He gave me an unemotional smile, an almost air kiss on the lips and side hug.

"How is everything?" I asked.

"Great. I'm going to take a shower."

"Before you do that, have a seat," I suggested.

"I really do stink, babe."

"As long as it's not perfume, I'm sure I can tolerate it," I joked – sort of.

He sighed audibly as if I annoyed him. At about six feet or so away from me, he sat down, rested his elbows on his knees and waited for me to speak.

"Okay, what is this, Ian?"

He shrugged, "What is what?"

"You have a problem, so what we do is discuss it, not block it by shutting the other person out. We are a team, so let's communicate."

He sat back in his chair and folded his arms in front of him. His eye brows arched in reaction to something I just said. His face revealed an expression as if he were taken aback by my suggestion.

"So that," I pointed, "what the hell is that? Why are you behaving so strangely toward me?"

He took a deep breath and shook his head lightly after he scoffed. "It just occurred to me a few weeks ago that I don't have to tell you anything."

"Excuse me?"

"I think you heard me just fine. I said I don't have to tell you anything about what I do when I'm not in your presence. So *Wifey*, I'm going to go upstairs to wash my ass."

Ian stood up, but I stood in front of him.

"Hold on! What do you mean you don't have to tell me anything? And yes, I am your wife so I deserve for you to tell me everything you do when I'm not in your presence. But do I ask? No, because I trust you. And for the record, I didn't ask what you were doing, I asked why you were acting so strange to me, like you're doing now. What is the problem? I'm asking how are you feeling, not what are you doing?"

"Josephine, please get outta my way. I don't want to talk to you right now."

"Ian!" I held my hands up to his chest to keep him in place.

"WHAT? Don't touch me! Get your hands off of me!"

I jumped, startled by the tone and anger in his voice. Ian had never yelled at me before. It wasn't anger in his eyes, it was hatred and it terrified me to the core. My only response was to cry. I felt so silly for doing that, but I loved this man so. I had done so much for him to keep us both happy and now, it seemed like none of that mattered to him anymore. I just wanted him to tell me what was wrong with him.

"Move, Josephine!"

My shoulders flinched out of fear from the volume in his voice before I stepped out of his way. He zipped by me and headed upstairs. I tried to catch my breath between my heavy sobs. My knees were beginning to buckle so I just crumbled to the floor with my face in my hands. What was happening in our home? It just seemed clear to me that Ian in all probability was having an affair. Why else would he be so cold toward me and unconcerned. Normally, he would be devastated if I cried about anything. Today, he was the one who caused me the pain and did nothing to rectify it.

I heard the shower starting as he banged items around loudly, clearly still upset with our exchange. Although, my heart was hurting, I needed to find out what was going on with him. We were not going to continue this beyond tonight. I had to reach deep down to rekindle my inner strength to confront him about what just happened. I didn't want to make him even more upset than he already was, but I wanted to make it clear that I didn't appreciate the tone he took with me.

By the time he finished his shower, I had just enough time to get my emotions together. I left the television off and sat back in the recliner with my legs raised. I could hear him walking slowly down the stairs, his feet purposely clunking on each step. Making his way to his favorite spot on the couch, he reached for the remote. He kept depressing the buttons, but nothing was happening.

"I took the batteries out."

"Why did you do that?"

"Because we need to discuss what just happened in here. Ian, you've never raised your voice at me. Just tell me what's going on."

Ian rubbed the back of his neck and looked up toward the ceiling for a few, collecting his thoughts, I'd gathered.

"I'm sorry I raised my voice at you Josephine," he began. "How far along are you now?"

"I'm almost three months."

"Great great," his voice trailed off. "Have you told anyone yet?"

"My mom and I think Hailey has an idea. Other than that no one knows. You?"

"Steve."

"Just Steve? You haven't told your family?"

Ian looked at me, his eyes seemed to darken before he said, "For what?"

I sat up, mouth gaped, "are you kidding me right now?"

"No. Josephine, when do you *think* I got you pregnant?"

"If I had to guess it was the night we made love on the dining room table."

Ian scoffed and nodded. He laughed a bit and shook his head. "Oh yeah. I remember now. You said something like 'you probably got me pregnant' or something like that after I busted my nut, right?"

"I guess, I'm not sure."

"Good set up."

"What?"

"How'd you get pregnant, Josephine?"

"What? By you, how else?"

Ian stared at me, his jaws tightened before he rose to his feet. He stood up, his fists balled and chest protruded.

"Baby, I'm giving you the chance to tell me the truth before I walk out of that door forever. Who the fuck got you pregnant because it wasn't me!? Tell me!"

I froze. I didn't understand what he was saying. I certainly knew the truth of what I had done, but how was it that Ian was so positive that he couldn't have impregnated me? I didn't want to lie anymore to him and decided not to. It was going to be the only way for me to get some sort of information from him.

"Ian, baby. I'm sorry . . . ,"

"Josephine . . .," he interrupted as if he did not want to hear that I had cheated on him.

"Ian wait! I did not sleep with anyone else. I wouldn't do that to you. But I did lie to you and I'm sorry, baby."

"Lied about what?"

"Seeing a specialist. For about five months I've been getting IVF treatments. The first two didn't take, but the last one did. I'm sorry and I know I should've waited, but I just couldn't stand it any longer. I didn't understand why we weren't conceiving so I took matters into my own hands."

"You did what?!"

"I'm sorry, Ian. I felt like I was in the best shape, and that this would be a good time for my body to handle something like this. As far as I'm concerned, these will be your children."

Ian thought for a moment. He was relieved that his wife did not lay with another man, but he was furious that someone other than he would be secretly credited with providing life to children that he would raise. Steve was the only one who knew about Ian's problem, but Steve's lips had the tendency to get a little loose. The closest person to Steve other than Ian was Hailey – and Ian certainly didn't want Hailey informing Josephine. Ian needed to contact Steve to make sure he kept it quiet. Ian wasn't about to tell Josephine that his sperm was dead. She would no doubt take the children and leave him for good. He wanted to milk her apology for all it was worth. She deserved it after the way she made him feel. In his opinion, she committed a marital crime – pawning off someone else's kids as his. Ian felt that Josephine was doing this just to keep up with her girlfriends who had children already. It wasn't enough to have one child like her friends had, she had to do it bigger and better and have twins. Ian felt a bit differently about Josephine after finally discovering the secret she undoubtedly was going to keep until one of them passed away. For that, she needed to suffer a bit with his bitterness before he would even consider telling her about his problem. In fact, he may never tell her the truth about that. It would serve her right.

21

Camilla had just about finalized her packing and her bulk furniture was nestled gently at Jameson's home. He had plenty of space to store her items in the interim. This relationship was beginning to look as if it would be long term. Not long after Jameson asked Camilla to leave with him, he met and had spent a lot of time with Gabe. Gabe absolutely loved Jameson and Jameson was a natural with him. Camilla couldn't believe how well they got along. She was afraid that Jameson would get tired of Gabe's endless questions, but he entertained him until Gabe was satisfied. When Camilla asked him how could he do it without being annoyed, Jameson just told her that he was usually curious as to what Gabe would ask next. To Jameson, Gabe's inquisitiveness and the way his mind worked were amazing to him because he did not have any children of his own.

"Knock knock!" Jameson said while he entered Camilla's front door.

"Come on in honey!"

"It looks pretty bare in here, you're almost done, huh?"

"Yes." Camilla wiped her forehead with the back of her hand and put her hands on her hips as she looked around.

"I had movers who could've done this for you."

"I know, but I need to do this myself."

"Can you take a break?"

"For you? Of course!"

"What's this? Your shirt looks a little tight on you," Jameson put his hands under the hem of her t-shirt and teased the sides of her waist with his fingertips. "Here, let me help you with that." He smiled and lifted her t-shirt up and over her head.

Camilla smiled and shook her head at him while she raised her hands up to help him. She knew that her t-shirt was anything but tight. His touch was a gateway to ecstasy and she immediately began to moisten at the thought of what he was going to do to her body. His massiveness no longer intimidated her as she had since gotten adjusted to how he felt and welcomed it as often as she could. It was the perfect opportunity for sex right now with Gabe still being at day care. What made this moment even sweeter was that Steve was picking him up and bringing him home to her.

Jameson pulled her close to him and began kissing her on her neck and earlobe.

"You sure you can take a break? This kind of break?" he asked while he nuzzled his mouth next to her skin and placed her hand on his tool.

"Yes." She said as she caressed his inflexible member. She gasped at how quickly he had become so hard. "Oh yes!"

Jameson couldn't wait to have her. He frantically looked around her near-empty space. Almost all of the furniture was at his house and the only thing sturdy enough to hold them was the granite on the kitchen counter. Camilla must've read his mind because when she kissed him, she began pulling him toward the kitchen. She blindly removed his shirt tail from his trousers and undid his belt buckle. He reached down to palm her ass and lifted her up with ease to straddle his hips. Camilla crossed her ankles behind his lower back and continued to kiss him. He pressed her back against the wall and Jameson pulled her midsection out toward his. Gripping her waist with both hands, he leaned forward and nibbled on her breasts through her brassiere. Camilla stroked the base of his neck and breathed inward making a slurping sound through her clenched teeth. Jameson finished undoing his pants and they dropped to his ankles quickly, like a stone in a pond.

He pressed his chest firmly against hers as they became one. Camilla moaned at the sensation and wanted to weep because he felt so good. Jameson took his time as he savored the mood and sensuality of her and how she responded to him. Almost instantly she came whenever he first filled her and today was no different. Jameson loved how Camilla's body instantly reacted to his. It did insurmountable measures for his ego. He could get used to that for several years to come.

Camilla firmly kissed Jameson's mouth as he stroked her deeply. She leaned backward after having stolen a kiss. Her upper back was being massaged from the lip of the granite that introduced the bar on the opposite side of the counter. The sweat from Jameson's forehead trailed to the base of his neck as a single drop landed on her stomach. Instinctively, he took his thumb and massaged it into her skin.

"Jameson . . .," she muttered.

"You like that?"

"I love it."

For several minutes the friction caused Camilla to have an uncontrollable amount of orgasms. Jameson had stroked her so well that she felt as if she had no backbone. Her body responded to his fluid movements, she casted all care aside and hollered upon reaching the apex of her orgasm. Jameson smiled as he soon felt his orgasm being stirred in his loins. He watched Camilla's face contort into a thing of beauty as she basked in her orgasm. Her temporary loss of breath, eyes squeezed together tightly and her femininity tightening around his rod made him stiffer. His thrusts became more uncontrollable, his strokes were accompanied by his own soundtrack of grunts and moans that would preface his own explosive climax.

"Oh Jameson, I never came like that before," Camilla said in a soft voice that lingered in the air. With that harmonious admission, Jameson also had come like he never came before.

"Oh God!"

He gripped Camilla tightly around her midsection as he rose up on his tiptoes. Camilla felt helpless as her body was being compressed gently in his arms. His muscular wrap-around squeezed a mini orgasm from her. After which she caressed his forehead. Jameson's eyes opened slowly and he looked up into Camilla's.

"Wow," he said. "I need a nap."

She smiled and traced his lips with the fingertip of her index finger. He pecked it and carefully released her body from his grasp. He quietly made his way to the bathroom while Camilla gathered herself to go to the powder room to freshen up. She looked at the time; Steve would be dropping off Gabe in another hour or so.

Camilla didn't know why, but she didn't want Steve to know about Jameson. The only thing she wanted to let him know was that she would be leaving with his son. She expected that he wouldn't take the news too terribly and would welcome the freedom. However, she knew from Hailey that Steve could be stubborn and unyielding at times so she would have to handle this delicately.

When Camilla came out from the bathroom, she could hear her phone vibrating on the counter as it rattled around. By now, Jameson came out and glanced at the face of her phone.

"Felix. Who's Felix?"

"Nobody."

"Are you sure?"

"Yeah. He's a nuisance nobody. I'm just keeping his number so I know not to answer it."

Jameson gave her a puzzled expression and then scoffed, "Okay."

"Uh, my son's father will be here in about an hour and I need to talk to him about this trip. This will be his first time seeing the boxes and no furniture. I'm sure he will ask questions, especially if Gabe has told him anything . . . and I'll bet he has."

"Okay."

Camilla nodded and gave a faint smile in an attempt to prompt Jameson to prepare to leave.

"Oh! You want me to go?" he asked.

"If you don't mind. I'm sorry, but he needs to know and I'm not sure if this will be sensitive to him or not. So it may be best if you weren't here. No offense though."

Jameson began buttoning his shirt and stuffed it into his pants. He smiled and shook his head lightly as he reflected on Camilla's timidity on the subject.

"None taken. Sweetheart, you can talk to me about anything. I want you to. And you know that I won't come between you and Steve as far as Gabe is concerned. You know that."

Camilla nodded and gave a sigh of relief.

"I'll be at the house. Come on by when you are done talking to him, okay?"

"Sure."

Jameson gave her a peck on the lips and showed himself out of the house.

Just like clockwork, Steve arrived with Gabe a little less than an hour later. Before they arrived, she had a few more moments to pack away a few stray items as well as throw some in the garbage. She wiped down the sex counter with soap and Lysol and lit a scented candle.

When Camilla heard Gabe's voice getting louder as he got closer to home, she opened the door.

"Hi Creepy!" she said as she reached down to hug him.

"Hi Mommy! Daddy got me Spiderman!" Gabe held it up just millimeters from Camilla's nose. "See!"

"Yes, I see! Let's put you and Spiderman in the tub, okay? Mommy needs to talk to your Daddy."

Steve looked around a bit baffled by all of the boxes.

"Um, you want me to put him in the tub? It looks like you are pretty busy."

"Could you? I'd appreciate it."

"Something you need to tell me?" Steve asked.

"If you could throw him in the tub, we can talk while he's bathing. Okay?"

Steve slowly nodded and gave Camilla an apprehensive glare. He stumbled around the boxes to get to the bathroom and took one last look at Camilla before disappearing. She sighed heavily and flipped her eyes upward as she silently prayed for strength to have this discussion.

About fifteen minutes later, Steve reemerged from the rear and found a sturdy box to sit down on across from the wall where Camilla was leaning.

"Are you moving?"

She bowed her head, gave a labored breath and rubbed her palms together nervously, "Yeah."

"To where? I mean, when were you gonna to tell me?"

"I was going to tell you today and I'll be traveling to several places. So there won't be one address."

"What?"

"Yeah."

"Wait, what are you talking about?"

"I'm leaving this area indefinitely."

"Indefinitely?"

Camilla nodded and then sighed as to prepare for the slew of questions.

"I mean like, where are you going?"

"Europe for starters. And um, Gabe is coming with me."

Steve stood up as his eyes narrowed and his head tilted slightly to hear her better.

"Wait. You were going to leave the country with my son and not discuss it with me? You were just planning to leave?"

Camilla nodded and then quickly shook her head to correct her blunder. "Well, I'm discussing it with you *now*. But yes, I had already planned to leave."

"You can't just up and do that, Camilla!"

Camilla stood erect and put her hands on her hips. "You're joking right?"

"No I'm not joking! He's my son!"

"I understand that, but there was a time when you didn't want to have too much to do with him either."

"That was the past and it was well before . . .," Steve stopped himself and lowered his voice, ". . . it was well before I knew he was mine. But once that was settled, I stepped up and I've been in his life ever since. Now you just want to take my son and leave like I'm some fucking deadbeat?"

Camilla bit her bottom lip and looked down searching for some delicate words. It was true that Steve was a good dad, but he was nothing to Camilla and even though there hadn't been the opportunity for many feelings to develop with her and Steve, she resented the fact that they were just co-parenting.

"Steve, no one said you were a deadbeat. You are great. The only tie we have is Gabe. You do not care about me and you never have."

"Oh, so you are doing this to spite me? Because we never had anything meaningful you want to take away someone I love, is that it?"

"No, that's not it."

"Bullshit! You are so vindictive and you always want what you want. You never give a damn about anyone else but yourself!"

"Hold on! Hold on! First of all you don't even know me well enough to even draw that conclusion, so you need to back it up. Secondly, it's not about you! It's not about me taking someone that you love away. It's about me finding the love that you and no one else was willing to give to me. I found it, I'm smothering myself all in it and I'm going! I'm going . . . and Gabe is coming with me, end of story."

"You can't do this."

"Steve, please. I know about you and your therapist friend. Think of all of the time you will have to spend with her. We will be back and you will have plenty of opportunities to talk to him on the phone, Skype, all of that. But the decision has been made."

"So it's another dude? Who is this guy anyway? Who do you have around *my* son?"

"He's a great guy and Gabe adores him. I'm begging you, Steve. Don't fight this because you won't win. At least this way you will still have a chance to be in his life in some form. If you fight it, you will lose and you may not see him again. I'm not trying to put you or Gabe through that, okay? We are coming back in maybe six months. At the longest, it could possibly be a year. Just don't, okay? We *will* be back."

"I can't fucking believe this. I can't believe you would do this."

"Believe it! I'm done talking about it. You never even cared about me. Do you realize that this is the most we've talked in two years and you can't even be happy for me. You are so damned selfish. Just go. I'm not dealing with this right now. Go. Get out."

"Camilla . . .," he started.

"What?"

Steve reached for her hand and caressed the back of it with his thumb. Camilla looked up at him. Steve looked as if he were about to break down, but Camilla knew he dare not show that side to her. She didn't want to hurt him at all by taking Gabe from him, but Camilla felt as though she had given so much of herself and her time to everyone else. She was not about to turn down a chance of meaningful love because someone was whining. Those days for her were long over. She looked deeper into Steve's eyes and saw the man from the coffee shop reading his paper. Drawn to his innocent eyes, that was the day she chose to be daring and reckless. It was a bittersweet memory. It was the day that served as a catalyst to her pain, but also the day that would show her what real love between a mother and son was.

"Camilla, I *do* want you to be happy. I'm sorry I couldn't do it for you. You knew where I was when we met."

"I'm not blaming you at all for that," she told him. "I'm just not denying myself this experience of having real love. Not for anyone. I hope that you will understand that in time."

"I guess, Camilla. I'm sorry. It's just so much is slipping away from me lately and I just wasn't expecting that. I need a day or so to think about it."

"Steve, I'm sorry, but we are leaving like in a week and some change."

"*Camilla?*"

"Look, I'm sorry."

He released her hand and gave her a damning look.

"I gotta go, Steve."

"What about his brother? Did you tell Hailey and Alex?"

"Not yet. I'm just trying to finalize some loose ends first before I go. That has been taking up a lot of my time. But I will."

"Can I at least meet this guy?"

"That's not a good idea."

"What? You don't think I need to know who my son is around."

Camilla sucked her teeth and put her hand to her head. "Okay, fine. I will talk to him. If he says no, don't push it. That's it."

"Bullshit, Camilla. You better make it work."

"Okay, bye. I gotta go." Camilla walked toward the door to show him out.

"Make it work."

"Okay!"

22

"Yes, it's positive. You are pregnant. Congratulations!"

Hailey's heart pounded heavy in her chest and she tried to muster a smile for the sake of the doctor and nurse.

"Thank you," she weakly managed.

"You're about five weeks . . .," the doctor told her. She was a small framed woman who had Middle-Eastern roots, perhaps India or Persia. She wore her hair pulled back into a bun and spectacles low on her nose. She looked over the rims of her glasses to speak to Hailey, but through them when she needed to recall something from her notes.

"Five?"

"About."

Hailey had been hot and heavy with Bryan lately. They full out rekindled their relationship after they had gotten together for the first time in years. Oddly, it was about five weeks ago. But Hailey had been extremely careful and used her condoms religiously. She wasn't prepared for another child. Steve was the only consideration to father the second one if she chose to have it.

"We will step out and you can get dressed. I will get some prenatal vitamins for you to start and some literature."

Hailey eased off of the examination table. She nodded and began to gather her clothes. The nurse gave a confused look to the doctor before they both headed out of the room.

Hailey didn't even remove the exam robe; she just pulled her clothes on over it and slipped into her shoes. It's not that she didn't love and care for Bryan, she just thought this was a bit premature. The two of them hadn't even discussed getting married and certainly hadn't discussed being solely exclusive.

She tried to figure out how to tell him she was pregnant. She wasn't even sure how he would feel about being a father. Her main concern was if Bryan was going to be in it for the long haul. After all, he fled when he didn't get his way the last time. Hailey needed to be certain that he was going to be there through the good and the bad times.

Hailey made her way to the front desk to check out, get the paperwork and sample vitamins the doctor mentioned.

"Okay, here you are," the receptionist handed her some documents. Hailey instinctively but blindly stuffed them in her purse. She looked at some of the other pamphlets behind the receptionist's desk and saw one that stood out to her.

"May I have that one?" Hailey pointed to the pamphlet.

The receptionist looked a bit stunned and shook her head slightly to regain her senses.

"Are you sure you want that?"

For the first time since Hailey approached the desk, she looked directly in the receptionist's eyes and gave a stern nod.

"Oh. Okay." The receptionist handed her the pamphlet and went back to typing on her screen, dismissing Hailey. Hailey held the pamphlet and keys in her hand and left.

Hailey couldn't even remember how she made it home. The turns, traffic signals and other cars were all a blur to her. She could not stop thinking about how miserable she felt when she was pregnant before. She had no desire to go through any of that again. It's not as if Alex didn't have a sibling, thanks to Steve's cheating ways. Alex loved his brother Gabe and they got along great. It was a little awkward celebrating their birthdays together, but the kids loved it.

When Hailey pulled into her driveway, Bryan's car was already there with him inside, head bowed. Despite his retreat to Jamaica, she knew that he hadn't become a religious man, so he wasn't praying. More than likely he was checking his IPad or texting. He looked up and smiled at her when she pulled up beside him. Hailey looked over at him and forced a smile.

He hopped out of his car and ran to open her door. Unconsciously, she left the pamphlet from the doctor's office in the passenger seat of her car. She stepped out and gave Bryan a kiss.

"How was your day?" he asked.

"Interesting."

"I hope in a good way."

"Meh," she muttered.

Once inside, she tossed her purse on the couch and it slumped over in its side. She went into the kitchen to wash her hands to prepare a salad for them and have something ready for Alex when Steve dropped him off later. She marinated steaks the night before so Bryan could grill them.

Bryan stepped in the kitchen and cuddled up behind her to kiss her neck and hugged her from behind. Hailey loved the affection shown in that manner and smiled.

"You can get the grill started," she instructed him.

Bryan gave her a final peck on the neck and headed for the grill. He was at the sliding door when he realized that he didn't have the grill brush. He snapped his fingers when he remembered and doubled back to the kitchen. The brightly colored leaflet caught his attention from Hailey's purse. He peered back to ensure she wouldn't pop out to find him pilfering through her bag. When the coast seemed to be clear, he reached in, retrieved the papers and took a look at the contents.

Congratulations! You are pregnant! What to expect when you are expecting. The ABC's of being a mother.

Bryan read the first few lines. He looked at a second piece of paper, which was a follow up exam date scheduled in two weeks. He saw a prescription for pre-natal vitamins and also saw a few samples.

Bryan smiled wide to himself and threw his head back with a grin. He was going to be a father. *This is how it should've been from the beginning,* he thought to himself. He jumped up and down in place like a toddler meeting a pseudo-Superman for the first time. After calming himself, he stuffed the papers back in her purse. Bryan didn't think in a million years that poking holes in a condom would actually yield the result of him having a child. It was just a theory that he tested. He thought the odds were stacked against him, but it worked!

Now the challenge for him would be playing it cool until she told him about it. He walked back into the kitchen and watched Hailey while she sliced some tomatoes. He gave her a loving glare. She felt as though she was being watched and turned to look at him. Bryan bore a wide closed-mouth grin on his face.

"What's your problem?" She asked with a chuckle. He looked so funny with the beard and mustache while he grinned.

"Baby, you've made me happy!"

"What?"

"I was trying to wait, but I can't. You're pregnant!" He rushed to her and hugged her while rocking her back and forth.

Hailey was completely stunned, she had no idea how Bryan even found out and how he had managed to do so that quickly.

"What? How did you . . .?"

"I saw the papers in your bag. I know. I wasn't looking. I just saw it."

"Oh well . . . I guess congratulations are in order!" Hailey faked her excitement.

"It is mine this time, right?"

"What? Yes!"

Bryan hugged her again. Behind his back, Hailey's face contorted to one of frustration while she waited for Bryan to finish his personal celebration. When he released her and looked into her eyes, she smiled and patted his chest lightly.

"This is so great!"

"I know! But we still can't make a formal announcement for another month or so."

Bryan stepped back to get a good look at her. He brandished a puzzled expression and then asked, "Why?"

"Well, you know anything can happen in the first trimester. So we need to be sure before we start telling our friends and family."

Bryan nodded. "I understand, but I *know* that this is it. We were meant to be together and this now solidifies it."

Hailey smiled and rubbed his chest again. "Great. Okay baby, *now* can you get the grill ready?"

Bryan skipped out of the kitchen toward the grill. Hailey watched him as he left and then reached for the cucumber she rinsed just moments ago. She picked up the chopping knife and began whacking the cucumber on the cutting board, unconcerned with how wide or small the pieces may have been. After about seven or eight whacks at the defenseless cuke, she stopped and bowed her head.

After the steaks were done, the doorbell rang. Hailey managed to finish preparing what she needed by the time Steve showed up with Alex. Hailey knew Steve was coming by and poorly assumed that Bryan knew this as well. After they saw each other in the deli, Hailey figured that everyone knew what was going on with one another. Even still, she silently prayed they would behave themselves before the eyes of her son and not cause a scene.

She opened the door and Alex latched on to Hailey's leg.

"Mommy!"

"Hi my love, how are you?" Hailey knelt down to give him a big hug and a kiss. "How was your day?"

"Busy mommy."

Alex rubbed his mother's cheek and walked inside to go to his room. Hailey puzzled by his grown up response, smirked and tried to stifle her laughter. Steve shook his head and gave Hailey a hug.

"Don't ask," he told her. "How are you?"

"I'm good. We were about to eat if you care to join us."

"Sounds good! I smell that barbeque!"

Just then Bryan emerged from the kitchen and stood by Hailey's side. He put his arm around her and kissed her cheek. Steve's smile faded and his teeth were slightly gnashed.

"Hopefully we have enough," Bryan interjected.

"Hailey, what the hell?"

"Steve, please. It's time we all sat down and just . . . talked. I can't do this back and forth with the both of you. So for the sake of my son . . ."

"*Our* son," Steve interposed. Bryan smirked at him knowingly.

"Let's have a civil affair, shall we?"

"Anything for you my darling, Hailey!" Bryan told her.

Dinner was extremely quiet with the exception of the noise of food being chewed, drinks slurped and utensils clanking amongst the plates. Even though Alex seemed to be the only one making small talk, he was still unusually quiet. His precious eyes darted to and fro the adults while he played with his pasta and took small nibbles on his chicken bites.

"Alex, did you tell Mommy what you found today?"

"No Daddy."

"What'd you find sweetie?"

"A frog. He was small like a baby."

"And what did you do with the frog?" Bryan asked. Steve narrowed his eyes at him and glared at Hailey. He huffed audibly and took a swig of his drink to keep his mouth from spewing numerous expletives. Hailey noticed Steve's reaction and shifted in her seat. She shook her head quickly at Steve to get him to calm down. Steve's jaws tightened anyway.

Alex looked down in his plate, not sure how to answer Bryan or even if he should respond to him. He bashfully looked up at Hailey.

"Alex, Mr. Bryan asked you a question, sweetie."

"No mommy."

"No what?" she said.

"It was bad."

"Come on, man," Steve asked, "what did you do? Tell them what you told Daddy."

"I squished him with a rock. He wouldn't stop jumping."

Bryan's eyes widened as he wasn't expecting that response. Hailey looked a bit disappointed. Steve was trying not to laugh.

"And you made him stop jumping?" Hailey asked.

"Yes."

"That wasn't nice, sweetie. Frogs like to jump. You stopped him from doing something he likes honey."

Alex lowered his head even more, "I told him I was sorry."

"Aww, come here," she reached for him. Alex climbed from his booster seat with Steve's help and went into his mother's arms. "I'm sure he accepted your apology."

"Babe, he's dead." Steve said with a smile. "I squished frogs all the time. Killed bugs too. It's part of being a boy."

"I certainly didn't do that," Bryan interjected.

"Well uh . . . girls typically don't," Steve responded without missing a beat.

"Okay!" Hailey jumped in to cease the spat. "Alex, it's okay. I'm sure Mr. Frog forgives you. Mommy forgives you. Come on, let's go put in your favorite DVD to cheer you up. Mommy has to talk to Mr. Bryan and Daddy okay?"

"Okay Mommy."

Hailey scooped up Alex and carted him off to the bedroom. Steve followed her with his eyes and waited until she was out of sight before he turned his attention to Bryan.

"You will never be his father, you got that?"

"Not *his* father maybe, but a father soon enough. I'm just practicing."

"Well you can take your beard wearing ass and practice with someone else."

"Hailey loves my beard wearing ass. I believe I'll be the one in her bed tonight. Where will you be? Cuddled up telling your dark secrets to that shrink?"

Steve stood up with his fist balled. Bryan stood up as well. Just then Hailey rushed in and stood between the two, her arms outstretched with her hands pressed on both of their chests.

"Okay, okay. Sit down!"

"Someone should smash him with a rock to keep him from jumping!" Bryan said as he shuffled to the sofa.

"Bryan!"

"Here I am bitch," Steve retorted, "You don't have a rock that's big enough."

"I said sit down!" Hailey told them. "We can't do this anymore."

"You're right, we can't," Bryan told her.

"My baby is in the other room and I will not have him growing up with people constantly fighting around him all the time."

"Our baby," Steve corrected. Bryan scoffed at his comment and shifted in his seat.

"Well, you and I have a lot to discuss anyway," Bryan announced.

Hailey's eyes became woeful as she looked at Bryan and softly shook her head to indicate for him to cease. Bryan interlocked his fingers and placed his hands in his lap. His grin was wide and intentional as Steve looked at him befuddled.

"No Bryan," Hailey warned.

"So what? Discuss it," Steve dared him. Hailey shook her head as she remembered the last few times they were together and how the situation had turned from bad to worse.

"Oh lord," Hailey muttered. She moved out of the way of the two men. Hailey was tired to being their referee. Maybe they should just fight and get it over with, she always thought.

"Well, Hailey and I are pregnant."

Hailey closed her eyes tight and held her head with her hands. She could only imagine Steve's look of disbelief at the repeat of betrayal while her eyes remained shut.

"What? When? What are you talking about? Hailey what is this fool talking about?"

Bryan nodded and stroked his beard as he smiled at Steve.

"Hailey!" Steve called to her. She opened her eyes to look at Steve. His eyes looked as if they had gotten red from a vessel bursting.

"Bryan, I asked you not to say anything. I swear!" Hailey stood and approached Steve. He backed away from her slightly. "I *just* found out today. I'm five weeks so it's not even really official until we get through this trimester."

"You told me you didn't want any more kids!" Steve told her. Bryan's smile evaporated and his jaw slacked. He stared at Hailey as he tried to read her facial expression to what Steve had just said.

"I said I didn't *know* if I wanted more kids."

"No, you sat right there on that chair last year when we discussed having another one and you said I don't want any more!"

"What? You were trying to have another child with Steve? And decided you didn't want any more?" Bryan quietly interjected. He wanted to just leave and let them hash out whatever disagreement this was between them, but Bryan was tired of running. He was exhausted from being left out of Hailey's life and constantly working his way back into her heart.

"No, she doesn't!"

"Steve I can speak for myself! You know, I'm so sick of you two always going at each other like this. What happened between the three of us was two years ago. Can't you guys let it go? I mean, really, what is the deal here?"

"Well Hailey, I will tell you what my deal is," Bryan began. "Ever since I found out Alex wasn't mine, things with us have been abnormal to say the least. We had a great relationship before Jacqueline brought Camilla over to my house that day. I've questioned our relationship almost every single day since I left. Trying to understand where I went wrong with us. And honestly, I can't think of a single thing that I could've done differently."

"Oh having an affair with me and Camilla was okay?"

"Was having an affair with me and Steve okay?"

Hailey sighed and looked down in her lap then over at Steve. Steve returned a damning glare at Hailey as the wound of her infidelity was reopened. Hailey decided not to interrupt Bryan anymore.

"I've loved you for so long and have nothing to show for it. I don't even have you. What is it that you want from me? Why am I here?"

"Bryan you know I care about you!"

"Do you love me?"

Hailey looked at Steve and then back to Bryan. She bit her bottom lip and her eyes began to swell with water.

"What are you looking at Steve for? I asked you the question!" Bryan said.

"Don't do that crying shit either, Hailey," Steve said.

Almost immediately Hailey sucked up her emotions by squaring her shoulders and looking Bryan head on before she spoke. She took a deep breath and exhaled sharply.

"Yes."

Bryan smiled and nodded his head gently. He felt somewhat victorious that she had finally admitted her feelings and in front of Steve no less. Maybe his days of kicking down the door to her heart were over for good this time.

"That's bullshit," Steve said. "Hailey, you called me over here a few months ago with your ass in the air. Trying to get me to stay and smash that."

"Steve please. It didn't even go down that way. You are always rewinding and fast forwarding reality to only see what you want to see."

"What?"

"You heard me," Hailey said.

"Well bust this, do you love *me*?" he asked her.

"Oh come on!" Bryan said.

"You stay out of this. You got to throw your mush in this, it's my turn to get some shit answered."

"Steve, you know that I do."

"What?!" Bryan's voice went up two octaves.

"Ha! In your face Bumbaclot!" Steve teased while he laughed.

"Steve, will you shut up?" Hailey ordered him. Steve's laughter died down as he instantly got serious in response to Hailey's request. "The truth is I love both of you. I can't even lie about this anymore. You both do something for me emotionally that the other doesn't. Bryan I didn't mean to fall in love with you. Initially I was using you to pass the time with Steve some two years ago and maybe even make him jealous. But then I started to really like you and eventually I fell for you. And Steve, in a way, you pushed me closer to Bryan with that crazy lie that you told on Josephine."

"I apologized for that," Steve noted.

"I know, but the damage was done. And Bryan when you left the way that you did, you left a lot of room for me to reconsider getting back with Steve. We tried early on, but it wasn't working. I hadn't been with anyone else."

Bryan was somewhat relieved to hear this from her. He always thought that at some point during his sabbatical that Hailey had gotten married and he lost her forever. He didn't regret sabotaging the condom and impregnating her, he wanted to be tied to her in some way. Hailey was his drug and he was going to make up for lost time.

"What are you saying, Hailey?" Bryan asked.

"I'm saying that I have feelings for both of you."

"That's not good enough for me," Bryan told her.

Steve nodded, "Me either."

Bryan gave a surprised glance in Steve's direction. He felt as though Steve was riding on his verbal coat tails and was confusing the situation by agreeing with or disagreeing with everything that he said to Hailey.

"What are you talking about?" he asked Steve.

"I mean, I'm just sick of this back and forth, spoiled brat behavior. I'm doing the father thing and doing it well, and no one appreciates it worth a damn. So I need some answers too. Loving us or liking us both isn't going to cut it with me. Not anymore. If you have a kid with this clown, I'm going to sue for full custody of Alex. You're unfit."

"What?! No. You can't live in a separate household, and then demand full custody because I choose to see and have a child with someone else. Get real, Steve."

"I mean it. I'm tired of y'all acting like I don't mean a damn. I love my sons and y'all just shit on me every chance you get!"

"Y'all. What *y'all* are you talking about?"

"I'm talking about you and that motherfuckin' Camilla. Even Josephine is wacked out. I'm sick of y'all."

Bryan's ears perked up when he heard Camilla. He hadn't seen her since he'd been back from Jamaica. Not that he was trying to catch up with her, he was just a bit curious as to how she had been. Even though he never loved Camilla, he *did* like her.

"Don't talk to me about no damn Camilla, Steve! I don't have anything to do with whatever is going on with you two. Keep me out of it."

"Well, whatever. It affects you too."

"Can we please?" Bryan interjected. They both ceased their bickering and looked in his direction. "Hailey and I were about to have a discussion about this pregnancy before you showed up and joined us for dinner. If you've said all you needed to say, you can go."

"What?" Steve pointed to Bryan and looked at Hailey, "Is this fool for real?"

"Well, we *do* need to talk," she affirmed.

"No, I've actually said all that I need to say. You are having my baby. I want Steve out of our lives so we can move forward." Bryan told Hailey.

"And if she makes a bone head decision like that, I'm taking my son."

"Are you both crazy?" Hailey fidgeted and jumped in place, hoping that her movements would get them to come to their senses.

"Naa, that's it. So you guys talk. But you need to let me know something in a week," Steve petitioned. "In the meantime I will be making some arrangements to get my son full time."

Steve gathered himself to leave. He went to Alex's room and was there for a short while. Hailey assumed it was to tuck him in bed. Minutes later, he resurrected from the rear.

"I mean it, Hailey."

"Whatever, Steve."

"Good bye, Steven," Bryan mimicked.

"Shut up, bitch." Steve replied and slammed the door behind him.

Hailey turned to Bryan, "He's not taking my child."

"He won't, but I will leave . . . for good this time if he doesn't keep away from us."

23

Tamar had reached the end of her rope with Celeste. After Tamar had a good cry the night she ran into Celeste at the airport, the next morning she and Donovan had an incredible two and a half hours of makeup sex. They stayed in bed all day and only got up to shower and nibble on snacks. Every time Donovan made her cum, which was over 50 times during that morning alone, they both apologized and gave each other a passionate kiss.

While they were in the shower, Donovan washed her body tenderly as he kissed her sincerely. Tamar stared deep into his eyes as he massaged her body all over with soap. He slid his finger inside of her causing her eyes to softly close. He bent down to kiss her stomach as she arched her back from the sensation. Their hot bodies were being rained on by the lukewarm water from the shower head.

"Are you hungry?" Tamar asked.

"I stay hungry."

"Well, let's feed you."

Donovan knelt down in the shower and began to kiss her moistness. Tamar lifted one leg and threw it over his shoulder so he could bury his face deeper into her crevice. His hands gripped her hips firmly to keep her balanced and in place. Tamar's body jerked slightly every time he caressed her clitoris just so with his hot tongue. Her body was definitely weak from the several orgasms earlier and while she continued to crave him, she didn't think she would be able to muster anymore. Donovan wanted to try though as he circled and teased it which caused her to shriek with satisfaction. Not long after, Tamar squeezed her pelvis and came again. Tamar felt as if her sexually soaked body had been wrung dry. Truly spent and needing to drift off into a coma, Tamar's body fell limp over

Donovan's shoulder. Smiling at his sexual handy work, he turned off the shower and then helped her stay on her feet while he toweled off her curves. Before carrying her to the bed, he quickly toweled off, missing several pertinent areas of his body. After he stretched her body across the bed, he kissed any mounding parts of flesh and covered her with their chenille throw. By the time he tucked her in, Tamar found a comfortable position and was out like a light.

Donovan walked downstairs with a towel wrapped around his waist to see what food or drink he could grab to replenish himself. While he had his head stuffed inside the fridge, his cell phone chimed to indicate that he had text messages. One was from the hotel, which he remembered he had to return the ring, another was from an unknown number, and the last was surprisingly from Celeste. He opened Celeste's message and it read *"We aren't over."* Donovan scoffed and deleted it. The message from the unknown number read, *"We should meet soon."* He tilted his head puzzled by the text and even more so by the number because he didn't recognize the 646 area code. He shrugged and disregarded it as an incorrect number. At that precise moment, Tamar's phone rang. He peered over to see who was calling her. The name was J. Hedley. Since Donovan and Jameson spoke on occasion and forged a friendship, he answered her phone on her behalf.

"Big J, this is Donovan. Tamar is sleeping. How's it going?"

"Not so good," Jameson told him.

"Is there anything we can do?"

"Actually there is, I need to speak with Tamar as soon as she gets up. I've sold my chain of restaurants and . . ."

"Yes, I heard about that in the news."

". . . and my accountant has been going through my books. It's important that she call me."

"You want me to wake her?"

"No no, that's not necessary, just make sure she contacts me."

"You got it."

"Sorry to disturb you on a Saturday."

"Not a problem, Big J. I'll make sure she calls you."

"Thanks, we all will have to do dinner next week okay?"

"Sure."

They hung up and Donovan immediately became concerned. He wanted to wake her to find out what was the matter, but he knew Tamar needed her rest because he was going to do all sorts of things to her later on that afternoon like cover her body with whipped cream. Donovan found a Red Bull in the rear of the fridge and began to gulp it. He piddled around in the kitchen for a few minutes more. As he slowly turned to leave he saw Tamar walking toward him – naked.

"Ooo," Donovan said as he almost dropped the half empty can of Bull. He distorted his face to symbolize that he was extremely pleased with how good she looked. Her eyes were low, no doubt from the orgasmic highs her body experienced that morning. Her breasts were perky and nipples were hardened. Her narrow waist sloped perfectly into her round hips.

"Hey baby," she said with an airiness in her voice.

"I thought you were sleeping."

"I just needed to rest my body for a moment. The shower helped to recharge me." She pressed her body firmly against his and kissed him. Donovan wrapped an arm around her and kissed her passionately. They both looked into each other's eyes. Donovan placed both hands on her waist and massaged it gently. He loved how small her waist felt between his hands and so did she.

"Hmm, you rested enough to get fucked again?" He quickly flicked his tongue over her partially opened mouth.

She kissed him and sucked on his bottom lip before she whispered, "Yes."

They began their trek back upstairs but Donovan pulled her back toward him.

"What?" she asked concerned about his abrupt halt.

"Damn, Jameson called you. He said it was urgent and needs you to call him back."

"Can we get it in first?"

"Aww baby, you know I want to, but he sounded bad. You need to call him while it's on your mind."

"Okay." Tamar reached for her phone and contacted Jameson.

"Tamar, thank you for calling me. Did you rest well?" Jameson asked her.

"Yes, I did. What's going on? Donovan said you sounded bad."

"Well, it is something that I need you to look into. You remember the case we settled out of court with the two young men who fought in my store and one slipped and fell?"

"Umm," Tamar thought for a moment, "yes. Yes."

"I need you to locate the billing charges, break out of billable hours, everything that you charged me for. I need that a.s.a.p."

"Okay, but what's going on?"

"My accountant found a major discrepancy in the books. I sold my restaurants and he decided to do an audit of my books for the past three years. Everything appeared to be fine except for some figures from your law office."

"More, less, what?"

"A substantial amount more. But I really need you to get on this for me. I don't have a lot of time. How soon can you do this?"

"Um, I'll get right on it."

"You're the best, beautiful."

"I got you covered. I'll call you the minute I have it all in order."

Donovan looked at her concerned, awaiting an explanation while Tamar disconnected the call. She looked a bit stumped by the call as she appeared to be in thought.

"He okay?"

"I hope so. Apparently there is a discrepancy with the billing. I know I recorded everything accurately. I mean, he didn't go into too much detail, but he said he needed it quick. I have to go to the office, babe."

"What? Now?"

"It's now or later and you know I like to get business out of the way before I handle my pleasure," she stroked his member when she told him that. He smiled and nodded. Donovan didn't want to let her go, but he knew how serious Tamar took her work.

"Can I help?"

"You know you aren't allowed. I got it."

"Well keep me posted. I'll try and have some food for us later and I'm keeping you hostage for the rest of the weekend. I have a lot planned for you and that body of yours."

"Alright then, well let me hurry and get these numbers for old boy."

Tamar got herself together and headed for the firm. Once there, she disarmed the security system and made her way to her office. She went through a few files on her computer and some paper files that were locked in her desk. She pulled her paper case files for Beefy Burger and began to read its contents. Everything appeared to be in order. She logged into the accounting system and tried to locate the billable files for his restaurant chain.

Tamar grew frustrated because she couldn't find them. She knew that they should have been in the accounting system because all of the attorneys were required to log their billable hours there.

For the next hour Tamar desperately searched the entire system for those Beefy Burger files. After several unsuccessful attempts, she checked a separate account file in a secure location on the network and was able to access that document. Once she opened it, she compared the figures to the paper file. They matched up correctly. She went back into the law firm's accounting system and tried to locate them once more.

"Ugh!" she grunted, "I don't even know what the hell I'm supposed to be looking for."

She sat back in her seat for a moment to take a light breather. After several minutes, Tamar sat up and decided to do a search for anything related to the case. She tried the names of the plaintiff and defendant and it yielded no results, she put in Jameson's name and there was still nothing. Tamar was at a loss because she knew that the file should be in the system. Even trying attorney's names associated with the case were nowhere to be found. She looked at the date on her paper file and decided to try that. After a moment, it populated to bring up the file.

"Finally!" she said with a sigh of relief.

She combed through her notes for the case and it appeared to be fine.

"Okay, what's the problem Jameson?" she muttered.

Tamar continued to scour through her notes along with the dates and times associated with them. She stopped at one entry and leaned closer to the computer screen.

"Uhm," she whispered, her eyes still narrowed. "Hold on."

Tamar scrolled further down to look at a few more entries.

"Wait a minute . . ."

She looked through even more and shook her head in disbelief. Tamar hit the print button and retrieved the files from the printer. She looked through them once again to make sure that what had printed was what was actually on the screen. She made copies of her paper files and the invoice that she drafted for Jameson a few years ago. When she was done printing everything she turned everything off and left the office.

Before Tamar reached the elevator she wondered if any of her other cases would be as difficult to find. Again she disarmed the security system and rebooted her computer. After about a half hour of scouring the database and cross referencing them with her own files, she discovered that none of the billable charges were congruent.

Tamar gave an exhaustive sigh and sat back in her chair. She tried to change the figures in the database to match the invoices she supplied to accounting. Unfortunately for her, the entries were static. She creased her eyebrows as she felt sick and became hot and clammy. Taking another deep breath and giving a weary sigh, she realized her fate with a verbal proclamation.

"Oh shit. I'm in trouble."

24

I had literally been walking around in a daze. Work was an extreme challenge and I was doing poorly at securing a few accounts for marketing. We needed this new account and I was dropping the ball. I had no idea what my life would be like without Ian and I didn't even want to think about it. I needed him, but I didn't regret doing what I did. He knew that I desperately wanted to be a mother and for him to be a father. I admit that it was selfish but something was hindering us. I just pray silently and diligently that it would not backfire on me or us down the road later. The evenings between Ian and I were still silent and uneventful. Slowly he was coming around, but it wasn't like it used to be. I just wished he would accept this new reality so we could move forward. I needed my girlfriends and our lives had been so busy that I barely knew what was going on with any of them.

I called Tamar and she sounded completely distraught. We only talked for a few moments, but I could tell that she was exhausted. There was no life in her voice at all. Maybe I will just go by to see her. I was convinced that Camilla, even though she didn't say it, was still upset with me about that comment I made some months ago about her being single. I don't even know how things were going with her and that guy she crashed into. She just stopped talking to me. Hailey and I were definitely closer friends so I wanted to reach out to her.

She met me for a late lunch, she was tied up with things at work and I was trying to regain my dignity for nearly losing an important account. Needless to say, we were both hungry and dragging along. I hadn't even told her about the pregnancy.

When we arrived at the restaurant, we were shown our seats and thanked the hostess. I sat down and placed my purse next to me and sighed. Hailey got situated and tried to smile. Suddenly she just started to silently cry.

"Hailey? Oh my God, what's wrong?" I tried to stand to go to her side of the table to console her, but she lifted a halting palm indicating that she would be okay. Surprised, I placed my hand to my heart as it ached for her. I was a walking emotional wreck with too many highs and an equal amount of lows and if I continued to watch her cry, I was going to break down myself.

"I'm sorry," Hailey apologized as she dabbed her eyes. The waitress stopped by the table, saw her trying to get herself together and quietly kept moving along.

"What's happening?"

"This Steve and Bryan mess. And I'm pregnant."

My eyes widened, somewhat in disbelief and also a little perturbed. I hate to be selfish, but I didn't want to share the spotlight as far as being pregnant. I wanted this moment for myself and now it looks as if Hailey and I will be celebrating together. After all, this is my first pregnancy and will be her second. Nevertheless, I was happy for her, but she didn't seem too thrilled about the news, similar to the first time she found out that she was carrying.

"Congratulations!" I tried to add some life to my voice.

"I don't want it."

"Hailey, please okay? You said this before and the love you have for little Alex is insurmountable. Why don't you want this one?"

"I know, but I don't. It's not that I don't want any more kids, I don't want any more fathers."

"Ohh! I understand. So wait, *this* one is Bryan's?"

"Yes! And I don't know how! Each time we used a condom!"

"Did it break?"

"No!"

"Well, was it . . . not to be crass, but was it full after he came?"

"It didn't really look like it, but does it ever though?"

"Yeah, it should!"

"Well, it didn't. Not to me."

"Have you told Bryan?"

"No, he found out! He saw the test results in my purse by accident."

"Was he excited?"

"Way too excited."

I thought for a moment, looked toward the front of the restaurant in reflection and then stared at Hailey. I debated giving her my theory, especially since it was just that, a theory. There is no way I could be absolutely sure, but I know how much Bryan loves this girl.

"What?" Hailey asked after she noticed I was staring at her for too long.

"I shouldn't."

"What?!"

"Is it possible that he sabotaged the condom?"

"Josephine! Come on! No. Who wants that responsibility without being married?" Hailey shook her head to rid her senses of the ridiculous notion.

"Well . . . someone who wants to make sure the other person remains in their life for a very long time," I drummed my nails on the tabletop.

"No." Hailey shook her head. She thought again about what I had said before she scoffed and said, "No. No way."

"Has he told anyone? You know how Bryan gets when it comes to you."

"Girl, he told Steve of all people. Steve went through the roof."

"He told Steve!? Oh my God, what did Steve do?"

"He threatened to file for full custody of Alex." Hailey tried to calm herself by placing her palm on her forehead.

"What?!"

"Then Bryan threatened to leave for good. It was nasty girl. But I don't want to talk about that anymore. It makes my head and my heart hurt. What's going on with you?"

I took a deep breath and sat back in my chair. I rocked for a moment as I tried to keep myself from erupting in tears. Of course I failed. I began to silently cry and reached for Hailey's hand. She gasped and held on with one hand and placed the other on her heart.

"Oh no!"

The waitress came back by again and noticed that it was me that was crying this time. When she briefly stopped, she glanced at us again, her eyes widened with confusion and then she kept moving.

"Ian . . ."

"What's happening with Ian?"

"He hates me girl."

"No! No! He does not! What happened?"

"I'm pregnant too."

Hailey beamed and smiled wide. "Congratulations! I know you guys have been trying for a while now! That's awesome!"

"With twins."

"What!? No way! That's double the fun! Do twins run in you guys' family?"

"No."

"Oh okay, so he's got that super sperm! Go Ian!" Hailey laughed as I wiped away my tears.

"No. He and I didn't conceive. I went to the doctor and had IVF treatments. They took, but somehow Ian found out. That is what baffles me. Now I fully admit that what I did was wrong. I tried to pass off this pregnancy as his, but he knew it wasn't. I don't understand it. He was pissed off and threatened to leave."

"What? That doesn't make any sense! I mean did he think you were cheating on him or something?"

"I think he may have, but it's impossible. I'm at work, the gym, home or with him. There is no time for me to cheat with some guy. And besides, I didn't cheat! So how was he so sure it wasn't his?"

I shook my head when I thought about how improbable it was for him to question my loyalty or the pregnancy. The waitress came back and brought us some water; she also set down an appetizer, winked at us to let us know it was on the house and rushed away. I guessed she was feeling our pain from afar. I was thankful that she stayed away for a moment until Hailey and I could talk, and even more thankful that she was gracious enough to bring us something to nibble on while we got ourselves together.

"Oh shit, Josephine."

"What?"

"Oh, it makes sense now! Steve was ranting about me, Camilla and you playing games or something. I could see him getting upset with me, but you and Camilla? I wasn't following that one. I guess I get it now. But check it out, the only way Ian could've known that he *didn't* get you pregnant was if he already knew he *couldn't* get you pregnant."

"What, Hailey? You lost me on that one."

"Think about it. Why would he get so upset and threaten to leave? Come on! He *knows* you wouldn't cheat on him, but he also knows *he* couldn't have gotten you pregnant. Come on, Josephine. You graduated from college, act like you got some smarts."

"Talk to me like I'm six years old, Hailey. 'Cause I'm not tracking."

"His soldiers aren't marching! No wonder you guys weren't getting pregnant. Then you get yourself pregnant and pass it off as his and he gets mad?? Come on. His ass should've just played it off and went with it."

"No . . .," Now it was my turn to wallow in disbelief. Hailey was blowing my mind right now, but what she was saying was making sense. I never understood why Ian was so upset. I tried to dissect what was going on, and wondered why he was giving me the cold shoulder and treating his wife so poorly. I understood now and he and I needed to have a difficult conversation when I got home.

*   *   *   *

When I arrived home that evening, Ian once again wasn't there. He did however arrive only about 40 minutes after me, so I was guessing that he was getting less and less upset with me. He came in, gave me a weak peck on the lips and went upstairs to shower. I was patient and milled around in the living room and kitchen until he resurfaced. I decided to dust while I waited for him. I seldom had the opportunity. We cleaned our home, but dusting was in another class by itself.

When he came downstairs, he had on his baggy knee length basketball shorts and black tank. He knew that I loved that look on him and it often aroused me, but today I needed to get down to some business with him.

"How was your day?" I asked him.

"Fine."

"So for the past month or so, you've been coming in late. Where are you going?"

Ian stared at me for a moment. He probably sensed that this was the prelude to a discussion and possibly an argument. He looked as if he didn't have the energy for either as he let out a low grunt.

"No where special. Mainly for a jog down GW parkway, extra time at the gym, sometimes to get a drink . . ."

"Are you finished being mad at me?"

"What? I'm not mad. I'm disappointed that you lied to me."

"But now that you know the truth, why are you still mad?"

"Josephine . . .," Ian shifted in his seat and rubbed the back of his head.

"You know, Ian. One thing is nagging me about how upset you were."

He shrugged and then lifted his hands up from his sides to prompt me to continue. He dropped them down against his thighs and they made a loud clap.

"How did you know for sure that these babies weren't yours?"

Ian stared for a moment. He took a long look at me and gulped hard before he spoke.

"I just know. The timing seemed off."

"Are you kidding?"

"No."

"Ian we have sex all the time. Even though the thought of me cheating would be probable, you know without a doubt that isn't true."

"Hey, I'm not with you 24/7. I don't know what you do when I'm not around you."

"Really, Ian? I mean, we talk all day."

"I'm just saying . . .," he finalized his comment with a deep sniff through his nostrils as if that was the end of the discussion.

"You were ashamed and didn't know how to handle the news. I get it."

"Ashamed of what?"

I went to sit beside him and patted his thigh before I gave it a delicate squeeze. He looked at me, his eyes shifted downward a bit and then our eyes met again. I covered my mouth, unsure if I wanted to come out to say it. My eyes watered a bit. I felt for him and this couldn't be an easy thing for him to accept or admit.

"I understand baby and I still love you," I told him.

"What are you talking about?"

"You have a low sperm count."

"*What?!*" Ian leaned all the way back in his seat as his eyes darted in my direction. His brows were low, nose flared and jaws clenched.

"Baby it's okay! I understand!"

Ian stood and walked away from me for a few paces. He turned to face me, his eyes appeared to be shadowed and darkened with anger and resentment. He shook his head and rubbed his hands together nervously.

"I can't do this," Ian told me.

My heart dropped and an odd taste filled my mouth. It was bitter and disgusting, I frowned in response. The pounding in my chest resonating against my eardrums, I was sure Ian could hear it. I tried to stand, but the most I could do was sit on the edge of the couch.

"Do what? You can't do what?"

"I can't be with you. You lied to me and tried to make me think I was going to be a father."

"You *are* going to be a father!"

"No! I'm not! I can't forgive that, Josephine."

I stood and walked toward him, I reached for his hand. I held it tightly, but his was limp. He turned his face away from me as he choked down his tears.

"Ian, come on! In all fairness, you lied to me as well! Let's just enjoy these gifts that will be *our* children. They will be here soon, so let's be grateful for that."

It seemed as though he simmered down a bit. I stroked the back of his hand with my thumb and then leaned in to give him a kiss. When my lips were just centimeters from his, he turned his head and pulled his hand away from me slightly. Shocked by his gesture, I reared back to get a good look at him. He stared at me for a moment with hurt in his eyes.

"I'll be at Steve's."

Ian began to walk away from me, but I gripped his hand to keep him next to me. He stopped in his tracks, but didn't look back at me. When I realized that he had no intention of doing so, I released his hand and he ascended upstairs.

25

Ever since the first text from the 646 number, Donovan had received quite a few more. He ignored them all except for the last one that was sent. Donovan only agreed to meet this mysterious person because Tamar's name was mentioned. He wanted a neutral, public location and since he would be dropping off the ring at the hotel where he fucked and choked Celeste, he decided to meet up with the person there. He had a mysterious feeling that it was probably Celeste. The irony would be too much to bear.

Donovan sat at the bar and decided to order himself a drink to calm his nerves a bit. He internally scolded himself for agreeing to do something so stupid, but he couldn't take the rogue texts anymore. Donovan checked the face of his watch. He had been there for about ten minutes. He took another sip of his drink and swiveled the bar stool around to face the entrance across the lobby. He noticed a man with shielded eyes sauntering toward him as if he were on the runway. His tan colored suit was a European cut, alligator shoes polished like mirrors. Donovan thought it couldn't be him. He shook the crazy notion and turned his attention back toward the bar, checked his watch again and started to get his bills together to pay for his drink before leaving. Before Donovan could prepare to stand, he felt a firm hand on his shoulder. Stunned slightly, Donovan turned, his brows dipping deeply downward with perturbation.

"Donovan?"

"Get your fucking hands off of me!" he told him as he rotated his shoulder to indicate to the man to keep his hands to himself. The guy smiled and lifted his hand in surrender before extending it for Donovan to shake.

"Sorry about that brother."

"I'm not your brother," Donovan told him as he rose. "You better keep back about five feet."

"Donovan, Donovan, relax," Taj told him in a cool tone, "I'm not here for that."

"Fuck you here for?"

"Take it outside, take it outside!" the bartender gently warned.

"To talk. Please have a seat."

Donovan stood his ground, feet planted firmly with his arms having enough distance to gain momentum if need be.

"Please, man." Taj extended his hand toward the seat. Donovan took a deep breath and clenched his jaws tightly. He balled his fist and crashed it against the top of the bar. He hoped that gesture would let Taj know that he was ready to stomp him in the ground on the word go.

"Why the hell are you texting me? I'm trying to get things straight with my woman and we don't need this extra bullshit."

"Donovan, I know it must be difficult to sit here, but I will make this worth your while and I mean it."

"Why the hell would you think I would want to meet the guy who was fucking my girl? Are you crazy?"

"Maybe I am, but I'm also a business man. Just listen for a second," Taj settled in his seat comfortably. Donovan thought that he was a little too at ease to meet the man whose woman he'd "borrowed" for months. Donovan followed Taj's eyes as they looked over Donovan's right and left shoulder.

Donovan turned and saw two overly husky hairy men who looked as if they had been stuffed into their black suits, no tie of course. Donovan wasn't sure, but it looked like one of them had brass knuckles wrapped around his fist. With that powerful image, and the thought of having his handsome face become unrecognizable, Donovan decided to calm down.

"They were here thirty minutes before you arrived so let me be brief. I have a confession."

"What?"

"I sent those pictures of me and Tamar to you. I wanted her to be with me and she declined. When she told me no, I had them delivered to you."

"So what? We are past that."

"Well, I have another confession to make," Taj started.

"What now?"

"I also sent the pictures of you and Celeste to Tamar."

Donovan's eyes bucked, "You did what?! That was you?"

"I told you I want Tamar."

"You can't have her and I'm fucking leaving. I'm gonna tell her about this."

"Donovan hold on! I told you I'm a business man." Taj unbuttoned his jacket and locked his fingers in front of him. "Do you know who I am?"

"Some bullshit New York attorney in a tight suit. I checked your shitty Linked In profile."

Taj laughed and pointed to Donovan, "That's funny! No, what's not on my Linked In profile is that my family controls 35% of the oil in the Middle East."

Donovan nonchalantly shrugged, "So why are you here, pretending to be a lawyer, banging my lady?"

"I'm not pretending to be a lawyer. I'm a good lawyer in fact. So is Tamar and I want her."

"I already know where you are going and the answer is no. She's not for sale."

"Everyone has a price and everyone can be bought."

"Not me and not her." Donovan stood, "so you can take your America's Next Top Model looking ass and go somewhere. *Tadge* is it?"

Taj chuckled, "The A is long. A lot like my . . . well never mind, but it's not Tadge it's Taj, like Taj Mahal. But anyway, here," Taj reached inside his jacket pocket and pulled out an envelope. He extended it to Donovan and waited for him to accept it. "Take this and you think about it."

"I don't need it."

Taj stood and leaned in toward Donovan. "Her pussy is worth this to me. Is it worth this much for you to let it go?"

Taj leaned back and snapped his fingers at his two henchmen. They came toward the gentlemen and looked strong, but uncomfortable. Taj patted Donovan hard on his chest to let him know that although he had guards, he could handle his own.

"You look at that and get back to me in a few days. And don't try anything stupid, you are still being watched." Taj gave Donovan a dark and frightening glare before he said, "You stupid motherfucker."

Taj turned and walked away. Donovan pushed the bar stool to the ground, stuffed the envelope in his pocket and stomped out of the hotel.

When he reached the street, he pounded the sidewalk so hard that he swore he left his footprints in the concrete. Once he got to his car it received no mercy either. He collapsed in the chair and then opened and slammed the door shut aggressively three times.

"Fuck! I want a piece of that motherfucker! Dammit!"

Donovan hit the gas and sped off to head home. He was trying to put the whole affair out of his mind, but meeting up with Taj to discuss Tamar just rubbed him raw. He was beginning to hate her all over again. With that exchange, he had doubts about if Tamar was even still seeing him. But she would have to be pretty crafty in doing so because she was home every night and was always at work when he called her. He knew in his heart that it was over and he wanted to believe that she had nothing to do with this, but Donovan's world was so topsy-turvy that he didn't know what was real anymore. Celeste still periodically texted him, but Donovan had turned the page on her. It was over. He wanted to stay with Tamar. He didn't even want to tell Tamar about what just happened. He felt that if he did, he would take out his anger and frustration on Tamar and she didn't deserve it anymore.

After battling one of the thickest traffic days, he finally made it home. He wished he had left the envelope on the bar.

Why did I grab it? he asked himself.

He slowly walked up the driveway to enter their home. Just as he thought, her car was there. He stood outside of the front door for a moment, head hung low as he tried to control his emotions before seeing her. *I love her*, he reminded himself. *I forgave her. I'm going to marry her.*

He took a deep breath and turned the knob.

Tamar was seated at their desk in the office and had a ton of papers sprawled out before her. She had a pen tucked in her mouth and was shuffling items around as Donovan entered. When she noticed him, she smiled, pen still in mouth and said, "Hey Baby!" in a distorted voice.

Donovan gave her a gentle smile because he loved those little things that she did. It made her unique. He was exhausted from the drive and disturbed by his meeting with Taj. At least he returned the ring to the man who was about to propose to his love in the very room that Donovan and Celeste slapped pelvises. Donovan felt as though he had done his good deed for the day. It seemed right, it was a beautiful ring and he knew that the woman probably deserved it.

"Hey. What are you doing?"

She removed the pen and stood up to greet him. "Just looking over some numbers. No big deal." She kissed him. "How was your day?"

"Full and long."

"Hmm, that sounds freaky!" she laughed as she kissed his neck and rubbed his back.

"I know. Baby, let me go upstairs and get myself together. It wasn't that great of a day. I will come back and tell you all about it."

"Oh. Okay babe. Anything I can do? You need a lap dance?"

He chuckled and hardened a bit at the thought of her swirling her hips around in front of him. "Maybe." Pressing her against him, he kissed her lightly and headed upstairs to the shower.

Donovan's mind ran wild. He couldn't get those photos of Taj and Tamar out of his mind. There was even one of them in front of the window of a hotel, her breast pressed against the glass as some man's hand was nestled between her legs. Tamar was an exhibitionist. She loved to fuck and loved to tastefully show off her body. She knew how to drive a man wild with her mystique and Donovan understood why Taj didn't want to be without her. But neither did he. Tamar had made her choice hadn't she? He contemplated that and more as he stood in the shower allowing the water to trail the nape of his neck down to his feet.

Tamar entered the room slowly and peered in the bathroom. Donovan was standing in the shower, appearing to be in deep thought. Tamar stared for a moment and then began to get undressed. To her, not only did Donovan look sexy as hell, but it seemed something was bothering him and she wanted to please him.

"Hey you," she said as she entered. She stood on the other side of the glass shower stall where Donovan let the water rain on him. He lifted his head, looked at her and instantly smiled.

He opened the stall door for her to come inside. She kissed him as he allowed her body to get wet. Continuing to kiss his neck and his chest, she licked the warm water off of his nipples as she got wetter. She stopped and looked up at him, with alluring yet innocent eyes. He closed his eyes tightly as if to take a mental snapshot of the image. Guiding him down to sit on the ledge in the stall, she knelt down in front of him with the water bouncing off of various parts of her body.

She opened his legs gently and Donovan leaned his head back preparing to be cared for orally. He let out an audible sigh of satisfaction.

"Ohhh," he moaned.

Tamar did every type of oral technique she could think of at the moment. One of which caused Donovan's right leg to shake. She tasted him and wanted to swallow him, but he was too big for that. After thirty minutes, Donovan couldn't contain himself anymore. Tamar flicked his tip with her tongue, looked up at him seductively and smiled. The minute she inserted him back into her mouth, Donovan had let it go.

The steam from the shower caused the glass from the stall to fog. He reached out with both arms and pressed outward. His hand print was made firm on the glass, but had trailed off as he began to gather himself from his orgasm.

Tamar smiled after keeping that and asked him, "You feel better now?"

Donovan breathed heavily as he kept his eyes closed for a moment. He smiled and chuckled lightly, "Oh yeah. Daddy's all better now."

Donovan toweled off and headed straight for the bed. In any other circumstance, Donovan would've made love to Tamar until she begged him to stop, but she reluctantly declined. Shortly after she pleasured him orally, Tamar trotted downstairs to finish up that paperwork for Jameson. She was just about done with getting together the required information. After going through several of her cases and the charges, Tamar realized that her invoices were not being reported properly to accounting. Someone was going through the accounting system and changing her entries and passing off those charges to the customer. Tamar figured that there was only one person with enough motivation and opportunity to even do something so detrimental to her career.

If enough clients came to the firm and asked about the inflated costs, it would have warranted an investigation. The only name that Tamar saw tied to each inflated invoice was hers. She thanked Jameson for bringing it to her attention which caused her to immediately spring into action. Otherwise, she may have possibly been investigated and subsequently disbarred. Tamar wanted to handle this piece of business first, and then she would deal with Celeste later. She had just about enough of her meddling. To Tamar, it was one thing to mess with her man, but a totally different game to tamper with her career, reputation and money.

By the time she made it back upstairs it was 11:45. She fell on the bed face down and didn't move. Donovan stirred just a bit and looked over at his exhausted woman. For a moment he watched her and she remained still. At about 12:15 when Donovan realized that she was fast asleep, he got up and headed for the walk in closet to retrieve the envelope. He peered over again at Tamar who was still lifeless. Creeping out of the room and tip-toeing downstairs, he headed to the kitchen.

He glanced back at the staircase to ensure Tamar had not followed him. Donovan took a deep breath and leaned over the stove top, bent at the waist and held the envelope with both hands. He mentally kicked himself for not leaving it on the bar where it belonged. Curiosity infected him and he needed to know what idiocy Taj was proposing. End over end, Donovan flipped the envelope in his hands. Finally he began to rip one side open carefully as to not make too much noise. Again, he looked over at the staircase – it was empty and dark.

Once opened, he took another deep breath and tried to see what was inside by closing one eye and looking in the arc the envelope's opening created. He slowly pulled out one slip of paper. It was a check. He looked at the name on the 'Payable To' line, which was his. Donovan's eyes scrolled to the right to see the amount. Eyes widened and mouth parted in shock, Donovan straightened his body slightly.

"What the . . .," he whispered. "Ah shit."

He couldn't believe what he was seeing. He shut his eyes tight and then reopened them to ensure the check hadn't evaporated like it was a prop in some sick magician's show.

"Two million." He shook his head as if it weren't true and muttered the amount again. "Two million dollars."

It was like someone handed him a winning lottery ticket. The check was legitimate as Donovan inspected it for various watermarks, original signatures and such. He placed the check on the stove top and stared at it blankly for several seconds. His mind instantly began to purchase items, tallying and subtracting all of the goods and services rendered until the funds dwindled down to zero. The things he could do with two million dollars. For Donovan the possibilities were endless. He could pay off the house, start his own firm, or travel the world, invest it, buy Tamar that . . . wait a minute. This was the price offered to *leave* Tamar. Donovan unwillingly revisited reality as the dollar signs that danced in his eyes decided to "take five" for the moment. The glee and joy evacuated as he began to grimace slightly. Donovan didn't even want to imagine life without her. That was his woman.

Before Donovan began to reminisce over all of the good times he and Tamar shared, he noticed that there were a few other items in the packet. One was a note to Donovan from Taj. Donovan carefully removed the paper from the envelope and read it.

"I hope this is enough for you. As you can see, Tamar means quite a lot to me. As I told you, I'm a business man and I'm fair. You won't be left alone. I've attached one of the most beautiful women that I could find for you. Her name is Kalila. Although she does sordid things, she is a virgin and she is yours. If you do this, you must leave Tamar cold. If you tell her anything about this, there is no deal."

"What?" Donovan said to himself. "This guy is nuts."

Donovan slammed the envelope down on the stove and paced around the kitchen a few times. His hand covered his mouth as if to restrict it from blurting expletives. He leaned over the counter and rocked back and forth as if his abdomen pained him and he was about to vomit. The thought of losing her churned his stomach.

He walked back over to the envelope and looked at the remainder of its contents. There were photos placed in clear jackets that were secured together.

He saw the first picture and became mesmerized by the woman that he saw. Just as Taj had mentioned, Kalila was in fact very beautiful. She was probably one of the most gorgeous women that Donovan had ever seen. Her shapely and supple glossed lips curled upward in a faint smile that previewed possibly the straightest white teeth. Kalila's eyes were the deepest shade of green imaginable cloaked with long dark eyelashes. Her high cheekbones and jaw line were chiseled but soft, her skin the color of buttermilk. The dark tresses framed her face, but Donovan couldn't tell how far they went because the head shot was tight. Donovan was mesmerized by her eyes and her stare that was captured at that moment. He wondered exactly what she was thinking about when the shutter clicked. He instantly wanted to know how her voice sounded – if she had an accent and if she spoke her native tongue or new other languages. Donovan instinctively traced her cheek to her chin with the tip of his finger. When he realized what he was doing exactly, he stopped himself by pulling his hand away as if he were burned by a flame. He flipped the page to look at the next picture.

"Oh my God," he whispered.

Kalila had taken the infamous "ass shot". She stood and looked over her shoulder, the same faint mysterious smile. Her tapered waist was double-chained by black jewelry with dark rhinestones. Her hips would make Kim Kardashian hate her and put simply, her ass was perfect. Her hair flowed to the tops of her buttocks, and stopped just centimeters from those two sexy dimples that were paired at the base of the spine. Her shoulders were squared and her eyes and ass drew him into the photo. He wanted to reach into that snapshot, grab her waist from behind and ferociously thrust himself into her doggie style.

Donovan flipped the page and when he saw the next photo he closed his eyes tightly and softly shook his head from side to side before opening them. There Kalila was – spread eagle. She was waxed clean with a pussy as gorgeous as she. Her belly and clitoris were pierced. Even though she was seated, her stomach did not fold at the waist. Dangling from her mouth was her slender index finger in a flirtatious pose along with that mysterious smile of hers. Donovan was already lusting after this woman. Her full pouty breasts had erect nipples that were begging to be sucked and licked. He pushed his stiffness down to get it to behave and settled. It was no use as it continued to get stiffer the more he stared at her photos.

When Donovan turned to the final picture, he almost dropped the entire packet along with himself to the ceramic floor.

"Holy fucking hell," he said. "No way."

Kalila was also a contortionist.

In her bejeweled golden two-piece, she held a hand stand position. Her legs were in a split, one leg being bent to touch the back of her head as her back was in a perfect U shape. Donovan grabbed his penis and massaged it. The things he wanted to do to this woman were beyond human understanding. He wanted to hear how she would sound when his dick was inside of her – if she moaned, squealed, or screamed. As beautiful as she was, he wondered what she looked like when she came and what he would have to do to get her there.

"Oh my God."

Donovan shoved the photos back into the envelope.

"She's a virgin," he said as he continued putting the items into the envelope.

Donovan grabbed the packet and walked stiff-legged back upstairs to the bedroom. He hid the envelope and looked over at Tamar who hadn't moved. He was so horny from seeing those photos that all he wanted to do was fuck. But his woman was asleep and he knew how tired she was. Donovan just had to.

He began sliding Tamar's underwear off of her. He was gentle at first, but he couldn't contain himself any longer. He began ripping them off of her. Tamar awakened a bit, her eyes lazily rolling around as she focused to see Donovan next to her. Tamar had on a button down silk sleeper with just a few buttons fastened. Donovan ripped it open and began eating her breasts aggressively. Tamar moaned and squirmed from the pain and pleasure of his feast.

"Ahh!" she softly said, which turned Donovan on even more. Tamar immediately began to melt between her thighs. Donovan did not have to do much to get her prepped for loving as she constantly craved him.

Donovan rose up on his knees with his lower legs tucked under him and lifted Tamar's hips up into position. Tamar threw her legs on either side of his waist and stared at him eyes widened, awaiting that first intense thrust. Donovan pulled her onto him as he gripped her hips firmly.

"Oh!" Tamar gasped.

Donovan delivered steady and deep strokes, he stared down at Tamar's bouncing breasts and then up into her eyes. He closed his eyes slowly and leaned his head back and he continued to move Tamar's lower body back and forth on him. When he closed his eyes he saw Kalila's face, the pouty lips, waxed pussy and her chained waist. He imagined that it was Kalila in his bed that he was fucking with the piercing on her clitoris sliding back on forth on his shaft. He wondered how it would be to feel her tight virginity wrapped around him.

Donovan pumped harder, eyes still closed.

He imagined Kalila moaning with pleasure and speaking some exotic language to him as she begged him not to stop. Donovan pumped faster, his mouth parted as it became cool and dry, his eyebrows raised but his eyes remained closed as his orgasm took control over his body and released into Tamar.

"Oh!" he grunted, "Oh God baby."

Tamar, somewhat satisfied, was a bit puzzled. Donovan had never come that quickly before not to mention he ripped her clothes off of her.

When Donovan's high from his climax began to subside, he opened his eyes and looked down at Tamar. He smiled slightly and then slumped over next to her on his chest.

"Oh my God. That was great," he mumbled.

"Where were you?"

"What?"

"I said where were you just now?"

"Inside of you, what do you mean?"

"Donovan, your mind was elsewhere. Is there something I need to know baby?"

Donovan lifted up to look at Tamar. He stroked her forehead with the tip of his index finger and then kissed her tenderly there.

"No honey. You just looked so good and I couldn't help myself. Sorry to wake you." He lay back down and exhaled heavily. "Wow that was good."

"Donovan, you keep forgetting that I know you. I know you weren't here and that's cool, but I don't want any more surprises out of your ass. You hear me?"

He rose again to look down at her face, which was twisted with mild anger. "What?"

"You heard me!" Tamar rolled over and huffed loudly, "With your cumming too quick tonight ass. No more surprises! Good night."

"Good night baby." He kissed her shoulder but she pulled it away.

Donovan could in no way tell Tamar that he was thinking about some young bendable virgin with perky breasts who had a belly and clit piercing. And according to Taj's instructions he wasn't supposed to even mention anything at all about the money, the proposition or Kalila to Tamar in the least. But that was only if he was considering taking the money, which he wasn't.

The things he could do with Kalila were also fresh on his mind. Donovan definitely wanted a go with her. Two million dollars was a lot of money and the

things he could do with it still danced around in his mind. He guessed that the
money would have to be used to keep her. But Donovan had other plans.

26

Steve had come to a decision about the entire Camilla situation. He knew that he was a good father to Gabe and he maintained a civil relationship with Camilla for the sake of him. He didn't want to appear selfish, but he understood Camilla's position and didn't want to stand in her way. She made a valid point about him choosing to see him sometimes or not at all. Steve just didn't have the fight in him to even start a battle with Camilla. He didn't love her, but as the mother of his child, he cared about her well being and wanted her to be happy. Steve made his way over to her place to wish them well.

"Wow, this place looks different from last week. Not a box in sight," he said to make small talk. Steve tried not to get too emotional, but he was going to miss his little soldier.

"I know," Camilla responded. "Thank you, Steve. I was praying that this didn't get ugly."

"No, I thought about what you said and you deserve to be happy."

"I do. I'm just glad that he helped me realize that before it was too late."

Camilla nodded and leaned against the bare wall. She didn't have too much to say to Steve at the moment; well, she never really did anyway.

"So," Steve cleared his throat to break the nervous tension in the air, "where are you guys headed first?"

"The Netherlands."

"I mean, so what are you guys doing this for?"

"Well, this is something he wanted to do. He will be opening up a new night club when he gets back and he wanted to make sure he had a different menu from anyone in D.C. So while he's vacationing, he's also working."

"What will you be doing?"

"Taking a break from auditing and raising our son," she smiled.

Steve nodded as he paced a bit in front of her. He sighed and continued to clear his throat as the silence was deafening and awkward. Camilla noticed his nervousness and smirked a bit.

"They should be here any minute."

Steve nodded and rolled his eyes upward, "I really hope I don't knock this guy on his ass when he gets here."

"You won't," Camilla said with a stern look. "On a side note, you may want to check that temper while we're gone. I don't want our son seeing you act like a thug. I'm just saying. Hailey told me about you and that punk Bryan at the deli."

Steve scoffed, "Everyone knows all of my business. That's how it's always been, I see."

"Yeah, well . . .,"

Just then, Jameson walked in carrying Gabe. Gabe looked at Steve and smiled wide.

"Daddy!" he reached for him. Steve's face lit up like the Vegas strip when he heard his son's enthusiasm and eagerness to see and hug him.

"Hey! How is Daddy's soldier?" Steve pulled him out of Jameson's grasp and hugged him tightly. "I've missed you, man. What have you been up to?"

"We are leaving! All of my toys are in a box, Daddy."

"I know, huh? All of them?"

Gabe nodded bashfully as Steve tried to tickle his tummy to lift his spirits.

"Hey man, not all of them." Steve pulled out an Iron Man figurine. "You remember when we went to go see him?"

"Yes! He was flying!"

"He was!" Steve looked at Camilla. "Can I get a moment alone with him?"

Camilla extended her hand to Jameson, "you don't want to meet Jameson first?"

"In a minute," Steve told her.

"But . . .," she started.

"Camilla? It's fine," Jameson smiled at Steve and reached for Camilla's hand as he escorted her to the rear of the apartment. Camilla looked at Steve and Gabe before following Jameson out of the room.

Steve took a deep breath and placed his forehead on Gabe's.

"Daddy."

"Gabe-Master G," he started. He tried to choke down his tears as he squatted on the floor with Gabe allowing Gabe to stand in front of him. "You know your Daddy loves you, right?"

"Yes."

"And we are going to be apart for a while. You know that?"

Gabe's voice lowered, "Yes."

"I'm always going to be your father and you will always be my son, you understand that?"

"I know."

"I'm going to miss you so much, but it's only going to be for a little while. You can call me whenever you want and we can talk on the computer like they do in those old Sci-Fi movies. Wouldn't that be fun?"

"I guess . . . ,"

"It won't be the same as us hanging out and I understand, but your mom has a new friend. Is he nice to you?"

"Yes."

"Good good." Steve gulped as he was hoping for some indication from Gabe that Jameson wasn't fit to be around his son and he'd have a reason to fight to keep him. "I love you."

"I love you too, Daddy."

"I'm going to miss you so much. But I mean it, whenever you want to talk to me, I'll be right there, you understand?"

"What if you are sleeping?"

"It doesn't matter man, anytime. I'm always there for you."

"If you say so, Daddy. You are a sleepy head sometimes."

Steve giggled and then choked on a few tears. "I know, but not for you, man. You are my little soldier and I'll stay wide awake for you."

They hugged each other and Gabe twirled around his Iron Man figure for a bit.

"Camilla!" Steve called out to her. She came from the back with Jameson close behind her.

"You take care of my son," he told her.

"*Our* son," she corrected him. "Steve this is Jameson. Jameson this is Gabe's father, Steve."

They shook hands.

"I've heard a lot about you, Steve," he told him. "I understand that this is probably hard for you to do, but I assure you that I will take care of Gabe as if he were my own. I'm not trying to replace your role so don't ever feel that way. Whenever you want to come and visit while we are away, I will make sure there is a place for you."

"I appreciate what you said and I will hold you to all of it."

Camilla smiled slightly. She was actually impressed by how cool Steve was behaving. She knew that Jameson was going to handle it like a man and not allow Steve to do otherwise. That was one of the things that she loved about Jameson. He was such a gentleman.

"Oh! Almost forgot," Jameson mentioned, "Gabe, did you give your dad his drawing?"

"Oh Daddy, I drew you a picture!"

Jameson handed the folded paper to Gabe so he could give it to Steve. Camilla looked at Jameson with a hint of surprise. Jameson winked at her and gave a single hard nod

"Here Daddy!"

Steve opened it and he smiled wide as his eyes watered. "You drew this for your old man?"

"Yes. It's you and me!"

Steve once again tried to maintain his composure. It was probably one of the greatest gifts that anyone had given him. Steve knew that the first thing he was going to do was to get a frame for it and hang it up in his house.

"This is cool, man. I'm going to frame this, okay? Is my head really that big though?"

"Yes Daddy!" Gabe giggled. Steve hugged him again and kissed his forehead.

"I'd better go before I . . .," Steve gulped hard and closed his eyes tightly. Camilla looked at him sympathetically as she had already begun to cry. "You guys contact me the minute you get to your first location. You got that Gabe-Diggity?"

"Yes!"

"Daddy loves you."

"I love you."

Steve knelt down and gave Gabe one more kiss and hug. He firmly shook Jameson's hand when he rose from Gabe. He hugged Camilla and gave her a kiss on the cheek.

"Take care of my son."

Steve, refusing to look back because he knew his heart would break if he did, walked out and headed for his car. Once inside he opened the picture again and set it in the seat next to him as if it were little Gabe. Skipping his normal routine of driving with his music blaring from the speakers, he cranked the car, sat for a moment and drove home in silence.

27

After Hailey bathed Alex, she tucked him in bed and read him a bedtime story. Alex soon drifted off to sleep when Hailey made it to about page five of the story. The story was about some grasshopper who wanted to jump as high as his other green friend the frog. Hailey had no inclination as to where or why Alex was so fascinated with frogs. As long as he didn't bring one in the house, Hailey was fine with his frog obsession.

Tired, Hailey sauntered to the living room and dropped herself on the couch. She was too exhausted to eat, but was a little hungry. It seemed as though the only meal that she was able to eat every day was lunch. She didn't complain too much about it because it kept her trim. Bryan saw how tired she appeared and he reached for her feet and put them in his lap. Leaning back on the couch as if she were at a spa, she enjoyed having her feet massaged. She moaned as Bryan's hands made love to her feet. He even pecked them gently with his lips.

"Oh honey, that feels so delicious."

"You like that?"

"I love that," she told him. "How was your day?"

"Boring until now. I love our time together and now that we will be having a child, I just don't know what I'm going to do with myself. You've made me so happy and I want to make you happy, love."

"Bryan, you do make me happy."

Bryan smiled wide and kissed her feet up to her ankles this time.

"Ooo," she moaned at the sensation.

"Come on, let me carry you upstairs. I'll bring you something to nibble on and some tea. Would you like that?"

Hailey smiled and rubbed the side of his face through his beard. She blew him a kiss and winked. "Yes honey, I would love that."

Bryan carefully moved her feet from her lap and stood up beside the couch. She sat up a bit as Bryan reached down to pick her up in a cradled position. Hailey noticed that Bryan loved picking her up and carting her off somewhere. This manly gesture made her feel so absolutely feminine.

Once they made it upstairs to the bedroom, Bryan carefully placed her on the bed – kissing her softly while she rubbed his shoulders and upper arms.

"How is the mommy-to-be?"

Hailey sighed a bit and then smiled, "She's exhausted, but it's to be expected.

"And the father-to-be is just fine!" he kissed her again. "Let me get you something and I'll be right back."

Bryan hustled out of the bedroom and Hailey could hear his footsteps going quickly downstairs. She smiled at his willingness to please her, but soon after the thought entered her mind, it quickly faded along with her smile. Closing her eyes tightly, she breathed heavily. Her personal thoughts caused her to shake her head. *What was Steve doing*, she thought.

When Bryan returned, he had a tray so Hailey could eat in bed. He borrowed one of her miniature porcelain vases and put two daisies in it, which was her favorite flower. Knowing that Hailey did not like to eat heavy meals after seven at night, he made her a tiny salad. He brought her a cup of piping hot orange spice tea with a little bit of vanilla flavor, just how she liked it. He tented a linen orange napkin, her favorite color, on the tray as well.

"My goodness, would you look at this?" Hailey beamed when she saw all of the goodies on the food tray. "You have all of my favorites here! You must be trying to get some tonight, huh?" She giggled after she said that.

"If you are hungry, I want to feed you. If you are sleepy, I want to put you to bed and if you want to be touched, I want to be the one that holds you."

Hailey gave Bryan a mushy expression and then smiled. "Aww! That's so sweet, B."

She reached for the linen napkin and opened it to put in her lap. Once she saw what was underneath, she froze. Bryan looked into Hailey's eyes so he could read her expression. Gulping hard and placing her hand on her chest, she swore that for a few seconds she stopped breathing.

"Umm," was all she managed to say.

Underneath the napkin was a small red velvet box, opened to reveal a round cut diamond, embedded in white platinum.

"You know that I love you and I've always loved you."

Hailey gazed into Bryan's eyes while he spoke.

"While I was in the Caribbean, there wasn't a day that passed that I didn't think about you. There was no one that I connected with and no one that I wanted. I just wanted you, you were all I ever wanted or needed. I know I needed to make my way back to you. I'm just sorry it took me so long. And now baby, that you are carrying my child, I know that this was meant to be and I want to make it official this time. I know we talked about it a few years ago, but let's get married. I love you."

"Oh my God! Bryan?" She sat up even more erect as her heart pounded rapidly and her eyes began to erupt with tears.

He smiled at her reaction and held her hand. "Is that a yes?"

Although Hailey was still speechless from her tears, she nodded. Bryan came around to hug her and kissed her several times. The ring was placed on her finger; it shone brilliantly despite the soft overhead lighting and looked perfect on her finger. Hailey hugged him and instead of the soft flow of joyful tears, Bryan noticed that she was actually bawling in his shoulder. He thought it was a bit strange at first, but shunned the notion and attributed it to her being overcome with happiness. He tried to release himself so he could get a look at her, but she continued to hold him tight as she unleashed her tears.

Unable to comprehend, Bryan's affection turned into consolation as he stroked her back up and down gently. He wanted to ask her what that was about, but decided to save that discussion for another day. He wanted to make sure they both enjoyed the proposal, that's if in fact it was a joyous one.

*   *   *   *

Chase was still a bit heartbroken by her and Steve's break up, but she was able to manage by diving deeply into her practice. She had new radio spots created which generated several new patients. One of whom was a young girl of 15. She had just happened to wander into Chase's office a few weeks ago and said she didn't know where else to go. Chase listened to her as she bore her soul and instantly was overwhelmed with compassion. Chase agreed to continue to see her and mentor her. Instead of wallowing in her anguish because she was rejected by Steve, Chase decided to focus her energy on letting this young girl know that she was valuable.

On that day that Rayne entered, Chase remembered that her face was covered in tears.

"May I help you? Are you okay?" Chase asked her.

"I'm sorry, but I don't know where else to go," Rayne pleaded.

Chase stood up and guided Rayne to the chaise lounge and got her a bottle of water.

"Take a deep breath and tell me what's going on," Chase instructed.

Rayne took a huge gulp of water, hoping it would contain the remainder of her tears and sorrow. She wiped her eyes with the back of her hand and sniffed so hard that she snorted.

"I can't go to the church because he's there."

"Who?"

"Uncle Milford. He helps collect the money."

"Your uncle is a deacon?"

"No, the other name, I can't think of it right now." Rayne lifted her shirt and used its hem to wipe her face. Her stomach was a bit puffy for her frame and the button to her jeans was undone.

"A trustee?" Chase handed her the box of tissues from her desk. Rayne took one and wiped her nose roughly.

"Yes! I couldn't tell anyone there. They love him too much."

"Tell them what?"

"Please . . .," she started. "I can't . . ."

"Okay, okay. It's okay. Let's just talk like two old friends. If you want to tell me, you can, if not, it's okay. You don't have to. My name is Chase. Do you want to tell me your name?"

"It's Rayne."

"Rayne. Such a beautiful name for a beautiful girl. Are you hungry or anything?"

"No ma'am."

Chase chuckled, "Please, call me Chase. I hope I don't look that old!"

"No, you're very pretty," Rayne told her.

"Thank you and so are you. Do you live around here?"

"Not too far, I just needed to go for a walk. I can't think straight. When I was walking I saw your sign."

"I walk too just to clear my head sometimes, it helps a lot. But something drew you to my office. I'd like to see you again, but since you are here now, I believe you walked in for a reason. I can try to help you if you'd like."

"He gave me some money that he took from the church," she admitted.

"Okay. Why did he do that?"

"He was trying to help me."

"Help you with what?"

"To get rid of the baby."

Chase breathed in and held it for a moment before she continued. "You're pregnant?"

"Yes."

"Do *you* want to get rid of the baby?"

"I have to."

"Why do you have to?"

"I just can't!" Rayne began to cry again, but silently. She reached for more tissues and wiped her tears as soon as they tried to trail her face. Chase couldn't muster any more questions; she just listened to Rayne and comforted her by rubbing her shoulder. Chase had experience with navigating through this type of scenario. She had treated many patients, some who were older men, who had relationships with girls in their family and they wanted to clear their conscience.

"Help me. Please." Rayne begged.

"Of course, what do you need me to help you with?"

"I have to get rid of it. I can't keep it."

"I will help you. I promise."

"Miss Chase you have to help me, but what I tell you, you can't say anything."

"I promise."

"My uncle . . . he raped me. Right in the church. I told him that I was pregnant and he stole money to help me get rid of it. I don't want to keep it. Please help me, Miss Chase. He hurt me! My mother doesn't know and she makes me go to church but I can't face him. I just can't. Please . . . please?"

Rayne's voice was garbled as she continued to spit out her confession as if they were nasty food particles that needed dispelling.

"Yes! Yes! I will help you. Oh my God." Chase hugged her close as Rayne continued to bawl uncontrollably.

Chase remained in contact with Rayne over those next few weeks and they scheduled the appointment to have the child aborted. Chase tried to talk her into giving the baby up for adoption, but she said that she couldn't even carry the child. She did not want her uncle exposed and she couldn't pawn off the pregnancy on a young man because she didn't even have a boyfriend. Her pregnancy would raise too many questions and would cause too many lies to be told. What Chase discovered from the time spent with Rayne, what that she was a special and gifted young lady. She was an honor roll student and wanted to be a forensic scientist. Her mother instilled in her the value of education at an early age and it resonated with Rayne when she began school. She told Chase that she didn't have many friends in middle school because she was so focused on her school work and community service. The uncle raping her had completely thrown her off kilter. For a straight A student to score a C minus on a test, she knew that the ordeal was negatively affecting her. Even still, she tried to put it out of her mind. She had no one to discuss it with who she felt would take her side. Rayne had been through a lot in the past month and Chase had to help her.

The following day Rayne arrived at Chase's office and was dressed comfortably in sweats and a large t-shirt.

"How are you feeling?" Chase asked her quietly as they settled into her car and secured their seat belts.

"I'm scared Miss Chase. I'm so scared."

"I know. I know. If you don't want to go through with it . . .," Chase began, but Rayne stopped her.

"I have to do this."

"Okay. I understand. But promise me something."

Rayne looked down in her lap and was about to unleash the water works. "What?"

"I think you are so brave, but when you are ready even if you think you may not be, you have got to tell your mother about this. It may not be soon but at some point, you have to let her know," Chase held her hand. "It will hurt her, but it's too much for you to carry on your own. Then you all can heal together. Okay?"

Rayne continued to look in her lap and didn't respond.

"Just think about it, okay?"

She nodded and then looked out of the window.

The drive to the clinic was extremely quiet. The tires could be heard as they rotated against the pavement. Every single bump in the road, from the smallest dip to the speed bumps, nudged them in their sits, but didn't cause them to speak. Chase had no idea what sort of emotions were running through Rayne's mind at the moment and she didn't want to disrupt her thought process either by asking. Chase wasn't feeling too comfortable with the decision, but she understood Rayne's position.

They arrived and signed in at the receptionist's desk. Rayne took the paperwork and headed to take the seat next to Chase. Rayne had begun crying again and her hands were shaking. Chase took the clipboard from her and filled in the portions of the paperwork that she could. For the questions she didn't know, she asked Rayne quietly and she responded. Rayne returned the paperwork to the receptionist, returned to her seat and waited to be called.

Chase quickly scanned the room and saw only about three other women there. Two of them had someone with them, while one woman was alone.

Rayne reached for Chase's hand and squeezed it tightly in hers.

"I know. Try to think of something that makes you feel better. I know it's rough. But you will be okay."

"You understand why I have to do this?"

"Yes, sweetheart I do."

"I'm not a bad person am I? I don't want anyone to know I was here."

"No doll, you aren't. And they won't. They only call you by your first name in the lobby area."

After a painstaking ten minutes later, the nurse opened the door that led to the rear of the facility. Chase leapt at the sound and Rayne squeezed her hand tighter. Rayne sat up in her seat anticipating to be called next.

"Hailey? You can come on back!"

28

Ian continued to divert their marital problems on Josephine going behind his back to get pregnant. Ian wondered who in the world those kids would look like if they didn't look like Josephine. By hanging out after work, avoiding going home, and spending a lot of time at the gym, it forced him not to concentrate too much on her pregnancy. The very thought of it made him angry. Josephine was too smart for him and she was chipping away at Ian's truth that was soon to be exposed. Technically, Josephine already knew the truth, Ian didn't know how else to handle this situation. Ian just wanted to be with Josephine and now that he was caught in a lie, he couldn't turn back now.

Although it was convenient, he hated living with Steve. Ian strongly considered heading back home today. Granted, Steve wasn't supposed to make it comfortable for him since it was temporary. Ian liked to cook, but he wasn't about to cook for him and another dude. He didn't intend to be away from his wife for this long and not to mention that Steve never had any food in his house – just tuna and noodles for some reason. It was as if he was stuck in freshman year.

They both were becoming grumpy men. Steve often complained to Ian about Camilla and Hailey while Ian was constantly reminding Steve how upset he was that Josephine betrayed him. Faithfully, Josephine called him every day and asked if he was coming home. Ian had been gone for five days and wanted to fill the warmth of her body next to his. He missed his wife and he knew deep down that pretty soon Josephine wasn't going to continue to tolerate his abandonment.

Howsoever, Ian knocked on the door to Steve's apartment. Steve opened it, and Ian shuffled his way inside, with his head down.

"What's up?" Steve asked. "You want to watch a movie? I got the bootleg of that Liam Neeson action flick. You know he kicks ass for a 60 year old."

"I gotta go, man," Ian confessed. "I miss Josephine and I gotta tell her the truth. She already knows anyway."

Steve snorted and walked away from Ian. Ian was puzzled by his reaction puzzled.

"Why are you acting like a bitch?" Ian asked.

"I'm just sick of these women."

"Well you brought your problems on yourself. And why do you give a shit about Camilla anyway? You never have before."

"She's got my son. That's all I care about."

Ian shrugged, "It's not like Camilla is a bad mother."

"And that punk ass Bryan and Hailey. Just tired of it."

"You love that girl, I get it, but she is with another dude. She was with his snobby ass two years ago and she is back with him again. Let it go. She is over you, man. Why'd you break up with Chase?"

Steve sat roughly down on the couch and shook his head because he really couldn't answer that question sensibly. Ian began to gather his stuff that he threw around Steve's place and shoved them in his duffle bag.

"I don't know. I thought there was still something left with Hailey."

"Why did you think that shit?"

Steve shrugged, "I don't know. The way she looked at me in the deli. Something was there. She still loves me."

"Are you kidding right now?" Ian asked him, "Steve, she is gone! Move on!"

"I tried to move on."

"Well, keep trying," Ian stuffed the last of his items in the bag and zipped it. He hooked the strap on his shoulder and stood near the door. "I'm not gonna keep sitting here with your ass eating noodles and tuna. Is it too late to get Chase back?"

"Probably. I liked her, but I didn't love her."

"Figure it out man. Hit me up. I gotta go see my wife. I miss her."

Ian walked toward the door to let himself out. Steve fanned him away with his hand and mouthed the word "Whatever." Steve contemplated the phone for a moment and scoffed. He shook his head to dismiss the thought of calling her. The sound from the television boomed when ESPN came on so he could catch the latest sports highlights. The announcers roared about the most recent athletic scandal, millions promised on upcoming contracts and who were the hot heads of the breakout rookies. Steve glared at his phone again. He reached over and snatched it off of the coffee table and tapped the numbers on its face.

"Hey baby," Steve said. He leaned back in his seat and rubbed his midsection as he smiled. When his salutation wasn't returned with the same enthusiasm, he sat up and immediately became concerned. "Are you okay, baby?"

Steve's eyes darted back and forth as he listened to the voice on the other end.

"Okay, bye." Steve locked his phone and set it down on the table. He covered his face with his hands.

*   *   *   *

When Ian arrived I was resting in our recliner with my feet up. I was reading and rubbing my belly which had gotten a tad bigger since last week.

"Hey baby," Ian quietly said as he entered. His head was down as he dropped his bag on the floor near the entry way. I did not acknowledge his presence and continued to read. Ian walked toward me and kissed my forehead. I smirked at the gesture and continued to ignore him.

"What are you reading?" he asked me. He looked at the cover of the book and then sat across from me. I pretended to keep reading even though my concentration was broken.

"Take your duffle bag upstairs please," I instructed.

"I'll get it in a few. I missed you."

I turned the page and huffed.

"Oh, so you just gonna ignore me?"

I closed the book and looked at him. "What do you want me to say? You walked out on me in this condition and I needed you. Are you planning to walk out again? What is going on with you, Ian? Do you not want to be with me anymore?"

"Are you crazy?" Ian asked.

"Are *you*?" I responded. "I can't believe that you left."

"Baby, I'm sorry. I just needed to clear my head, this is a lot."

"I don't know what else to do, Ian. The babies will be here in four months. I need your support but I mostly need your love, baby. Are you in or out?"

Ian rubbed the back of his neck and fidgeted. I sighed as I waited impatiently for his response. Ian wrestled with himself before he mustered a response. I tossed the book onto the table and it hit the floor. Ian was a bit startled by the noise and looked up at me.

"Are you in or out?" I asked again.

"Baby, I love you . . .,"

"Okay . . .,"

"You mean so much to me and I'm sorry that I didn't tell you about my problem. I was embarrassed."

"Oh so you admit that you couldn't help us conceive?"

Ian nodded.

"Why did you have me thinking it was me? Why didn't you just tell me?"

"Because I was ashamed and I knew how bad you wanted kids. And it was the one thing I knew I could never do for you. But you . . . you did the unthinkable baby. I'm trying to get past it, but I don't know if I can."

"Ian, I can't change things now. I've apologized and I know it's wrong, but what can I do now? Had you told me you couldn't help us conceive, I would've never done that without consulting you. I know I was wrong! I did it because I didn't want you to think something was wrong with me and then you'd leave me. I want to make it up to you, I do. But there's nothing that I can do about it now!"

Ian quietly rocked in his seat as he listened to my words settle on his ears. He looked at me and narrowed his eyes.

"What?" I asked.

"There *is* something that you can do."

"What?"

"Do you love me? Do you want to stay married?"

"Yes, Ian! I love you and you know I want us to stay together."

"I want us to be together too. I love you, but I need to know that you love me."

"Of course I do."

"You played me and there is only one thing that you can do to fix this mess. One thing that will make me feel better about what you did to me."

"Anything. What is it?" I pleaded.

"You have to give those babies up for adoption."

My eyes widened and I leaned forward to make sure I heard him correctly. I couldn't even gather my breath. It felt as though my heart stopped for a moment as I tried to read his face. Was Ian joking? His eyes didn't flinch and I've never seen his face look as stern than right now. I felt the babies move and I jerked a bit in response. Then I felt more subtle movements from my belly. Ian couldn't be serious.

"*What?!*"

Ian stood up and walked toward the door where he dropped his duffle bag. He picked it up and prepared to carry it upstairs. He faced me and shrugged slightly.

"Give them up for adoption. Those babies are *not* mine! It's either that or this marriage is over."

29

That morning when Donovan awoke, he rolled right on top of Tamar and started to caress her body. He wanted to please her and feel her wetness on him first thing in the morning. Tamar never disagreed with being awakened to Donovan's stiffness because she knew that he would totally satisfy her. Donovan didn't allow her to speak; he just kissed her deeply and penetrated her likewise. Tamar felt Donovan go so deep that it made her shed a tear. Not one from pain, but from pleasure. This morning, his love making was so intense and clearly meaningful. The other night when he accosted her while she was dog tired was different from this session.

Afterward, Donovan showered and went downstairs to make himself a cup of coffee and breakfast for the two of them. After Tamar prepped for work, she headed downstairs to join him.

"Hey baby," she greeted.

Gripping her body close to his, he smiled and kissed her. She sat across from him after she made her plate of food. Donovan was reading the paper. He watched Tamar eat and sip her juice. Thankfully for him she didn't have too much conversation this morning. She was still high from their love making.

Tamar noticed that Donovan wasn't in a rush to get to work so she asked him about it.

"Are you going in today?"

Donovan shook his head and smiled as he sipped his coffee.

"Okay, taking the day off," Tamar nodded and smiled, "Understood. I wish I could stay with you, but I've got some important business to handle."

Donovan nodded again and smiled at her. Tamar gave him an apprehensive look.

"You okay, baby? You haven't said too much this morning."

"Just enjoying your presence."

Although Tamar smiled, she was a bit confused. "Okay . . . well I will see you this evening then."

"Of course."

Tamar kissed Donovan, but he held her tighter and longer than she anticipated. He wanted to make love to her again, but he knew she had to leave. Before he walked her to the front door, he kissed her long and good. She gave him another peck on the lips.

"Bye Donovan, see you later."

When Tamar arrived at the law firm, her assistant had already placed the necessary paperwork on her desk. Tamar immediately took a look at it and compared it to what she was able to pull over the weekend. Sure enough, all of the client's invoices were inflated after someone else submitted them to accounting. Tamar had her assistant pull timestamps of the entries and the IP addresses of each to show that it was a different computer name, login and password than Tamar's that altered the information.

Tamar was ready to lower the boom on Celeste but there was a small problem. Even though it was her computer name and login details, there was no proof that she was actually the person inputting the erroneous information. The good thing however, is that it wasn't Tamar and she couldn't be connected to any wrongdoing. Tamar had provided the information to Jameson through email because he was out of town. He replied once he received it and gave his sincerest thanks for clearing it up for him and his accounting team. It was really up to him to pursue this matter, but as he told her he wanted to make sure that she was in the clear before doing so.

After the run in at the airport Celeste and Tamar didn't speak. Tamar preferred it that way. However, Tamar knew that if Celeste so much as breathed in her direction that she would unleash her fury in a matter of seconds. They would pass each other and act as if the other didn't exist. Celeste saw to it that she and Tamar never were put on the same cases. In fact, Celeste gave Tamar cases suited for a junior attorney. Tamar didn't care though, she had the skills to prep and check those cases quickly and it freed up her time to investigate these trumped up charges billed to her clients.

Tamar looked up from her paperwork and saw Celeste walk by her office.

"Celeste?" Tamar called out to her. Tamar peered in the direction of the door and wondered if Celeste heard her. She spoke loud enough and after several seconds had passed, Tamar figured Celeste flat out ignored her. After a few more seconds, Celeste slowly walked back by Tamar's door. She stopped at the threshold and took a deep breath that displayed her agitation of being summoned by her nemesis.

"Did you need something?" Celeste said flatly.

"Come in, please," Tamar said as she tossed the papers on her desk. "You can close the door."

"I'd prefer it stay open," Celeste said as she cautiously entered Tamar's office.

"Suit yourself. Celeste, whatever you are planning, I'm warning you now, not to do it. Normally, I would just let you hang yourself, but I know how hard you've worked on your career and I know you wouldn't throw it away because you are bitter about losing a dick, right?"

"Excuse me?"

"Whatever you are planning to do to me, don't. It's not going to work. That's all I have to say."

"Tamar, I'm sorry to disappoint you, but I *do* fill my days with other thoughts than those of you. In case you hadn't guessed, I've moved on. I'm no longer interested in the distasteful relationship that you and Donovan have. It's just not in the forefront. So, having said that, I have no idea what you are talking about and I'd appreciate it if you not bother me with personal issues or thoughts of vendettas during business hours. I am still your supervisor, so I'm warning *you*. You are treading a fine line here, darling. Watch yourself."

Celeste turned to walk out and Tamar added, "Ditto . . . darling."

Because Donovan acted a bit strangely this morning, she decided to call him to see how he was, but at the precise moment, her office phone rang.

"Hello?" she answered, "Jameson! Hi, how are you?"

"I'm great. I just wanted to say thanks again for the information. I think we are going to pursue this. Are you good on your end?"

"I believe I am."

Jameson chuckled as he sounded like he was far away.

"Where are you? You sound distant."

"Oh, I'm standing across from the Stonehenge. I just wanted to call you before I got too busy and forgot."

"Wow. I want to be like you when I grow up."

"You're on your way. How is Donovan?"

"He's good. I was just about to call him before you called. He took a much needed day off today."

"He's probably on the golf course. Let him have a day, Tamar. He works hard. Just make sure you let him know how much you've missed him when you see him later."

"Okay, I will let him be and I will surely have a welcome for him. Take care. Be safe and let me know when your team gets the ball rolling, okay?"

"You bet."

When Tamar arrived at home, she grabbed the mail from the box before she entered the house. She secured her purse further on her shoulder while she put the keys in the lock. Shuffling through some of the mail, she entered. For a moment, she looked at one piece of mail that she didn't recognize and then tossed her keys on the table in the mudroom. As she got further inside, she couldn't believe her eyes. Half of the furniture was missing, along with some paintings and other trinkets.

"What?"

Tamar sprinted to the kitchen. The cabinets were opened and some appliances and a few dishes had been removed. Wide eyed and baffled, Tamar looked around the kitchen and began peering through the open cabinets while closing a few. She opened some drawers, looked inside and then slammed them shut.

"Oh God."

She darted upstairs and stopped at the threshold of the bedroom.

"Oh God!"

The closets were open and it was clear that Donovan's items had been removed. There wasn't a trace of him having even lived there from what she could tell.

Tamar gradually screamed. "No. No! No!!"

She walked into the closet and only saw her things hanging there. Empty hangers were either on the floor or remained on the rack. Some of her clothing and shoes were also on the floor – items that undoubtedly got in the way during his retreat. She slumped down to the floor of the closet and grabbed her chest. She took deep breaths, heaving in and out as her chest rose and fell rapidly. Thinking she wasn't taking in enough air, she tried to breathe in and out deeply. She rested her head on her knees before throwing it back to scream.

"No!"

Her tears came quickly as her face became wet with them. Her nose ran, she gasped for more air as she closed her eyes tightly to unleash her deep emotional hurt.

"Why did you do this to me?" she asked out loud. She pounded her heart lightly as if to stop it from breaking. "No . . . no. Not my, Donovan."

Without even realizing, her body was curled in a fetal position as she rocked her body back and forth while she cried. He left her without explanation or reason.

It was sudden, like death.

She remembered his face from that morning. The way he smiled at her. How he held her a little bit longer. And the intensity with which he made love to her as if . . . as if it was for the last time.

Tamar had no idea how long she remained on the floor, but she apparently had cried herself to sleep. After what must've been hours, she got up and went to the bathroom. The lights hurt her eyes initially as she squinted to protect them. When she walked closer to the mirror, she couldn't believe how red and puffy they had gotten. With her fingers she dabbed them and inspected them a bit more. She stood there and looked at herself for a long time without emotional display. A few tears streaked her face as she silently cried again. Her mouth curled upward as she winced in pain. The tears burned and it felt like a thousand shards of glass were in her eyes. She sniffled and reached for a tissue to blow her nose. She felt like going back into the closet and just staying there for a week or more. Knowing that it wasn't a good solution, she now needed answers. She and Donovan were on the mend, or so she thought.

Why leave now? she asked herself.

It didn't make sense to her. They had been over the Celeste – Taj ordeal for at least five weeks. Tamar felt stupid for trusting him again. Her initial response when she got those pictures was to throw his stuff out and lock him out of her life as well as the house.

Now she wished that she followed her instincts, but it was too late. She needed answers. Like most women, the first reaction is to pick up the phone and call the heartbreaker. Tamar was the opposite. She refused to call. Make no mistake she wanted to, but she knew that it would be fruitless. He had already left, so what was he going to tell her when she called. Certainly he wasn't going to answer the phone to have an argument. It was clear that he was gone. She didn't need any affirmation for that. Tamar wanted closure, but it may not come in the typical manner she may want or need. All that she knew for now was that he left and the last thing that he said to her today was a lie. It was going to be hard, but Tamar needed to try to get some rest. She couldn't stay up all night crying. Two years of loving and sharing with this person she felt was for naught. It's over.

Now she needed to move forward, no matter how hard it was going to hurt her.

The next morning, Tamar was not about to go in to work. Her eyes were still a bit swollen and she knew that her mind would not be able to focus on nothing more than Donovan. As expected, she barely got any sleep. At 5:30 a.m., she showered and threw on a silk nightgown because she knew that she was going to wallow around the house all day. She tossed on her robe and went downstairs to the kitchen.

Her kitchen was in complete disarray as if it had been raped. Things were still gaped open and it was a mess left over after the scene. She rifled through the cabinet and got herself a wine glass. She poured herself a glass of expensive red wine. She had saved that bottle of wine for her wedding night with Donovan, which would never come now. She sniffed it realized she would probably drink all day anyway, so she let the wine breathe. She made herself a Mimosa instead and sat out on her porch. It was 7 a.m. and her neighbors were slowly sifting out to go to work.

They would wave on their way out and she just lifted her glass. Her eyes remained shielded with oversized shades. She felt the fresh air would help the swelling on her eyes but the truth was she couldn't stand to be in the house at the moment. The memories were too much to bear and erase all in one day.

"I thought you left."

Tamar heard a still voice from nearby. She looked around as she tried to find the body connected to it. She saw her neighbor, Mrs. Dunbar peering over at her with her hand raised to shield her eyes from the sun.

"Ma'am?" Tamar asked.

"Is that Mimosa?"

Tamar smiled slightly. "Yes ma'am it is."

"Well, I thought you left. I'm glad you didn't. Good neighbors are hard to find."

"No, I'm still here."

"I saw the moving truck yesterday and Donovan was yelling at the guys to hurry up."

Tamar set her glass down and stood up. She approached the edge of her porch closer to Mrs. Dunbar. Mrs. Dunbar ripped off her gardening gloves and stuffed them in her pocketed apron. Tamar fastened her robe more securely and waited for her to continue.

"It was about five or six guys. It looked like they were moving the entire house. I said to myself, how come Tamar didn't tell me she was leaving? Well, now that I know you are here, what happened? Why did he leave?"

Tamar sighed before she mustered up a lie.

"It just got old," she told her. Mrs. Dunbar was a sweet woman, but that did not give her carte blanche to know personal facets of Tamar's life.

"I understand. But he was mad. And those guys were speaking some language." Mrs. Dunbar tried to imitate it and sounded hilarious to Tamar, but she didn't want to laugh at the moment. She needed these details. And from what Mrs. Dunbar tried to emulate, it was Arabic.

"Arabic?

"I guess, who knows? They were probably cursing Donovan back out. Well, I'm glad you are still here. Now there was a rather handsome young man who also stopped by. If I was younger and wasn't married to Mr. Dunbar, I'd be interested!"

Tamar bowed her head and put her hand on her hip. She had no idea Mrs. Dunbar was the flirty type.

"He was handsome. Dark hair, tall . . . he didn't stay long. Exchanged words with Donovan and left. Donovan looked like he was cursing him out too. Everyone was cursing yesterday! Did you throw him out?"

Tamar walked back toward her front door and picked up her glass of Mimosa. She turned to Mrs. Dunbar and said, "Something like that. I will holler at you later Mrs. Dunbar. I need to make a phone call, honey."

Tamar slammed the door behind her and headed straight for her purse. She fished around in it, hoping his business card he gave her a while ago was still in there. She found the tattered card and called. His phone rang three times before he answered.

"Taj? This is Tamar. I took the day off, why don't we meet up somewhere? Now that he is gone, I have all the time I need to spend with you."

30

It had been over a week and Bryan realized that he and Hailey hadn't properly celebrated their engagement and pregnancy. He planned for a romantic lunch on the grounds near the monument. They had recently finished the renovations to the structure and all of the scaffolding had been removed. The weather was great for being outdoors and Bryan felt that Hailey needed it because she had been moping around for several days. Bryan wasn't exactly sure why.

He made sure he had all of her favorites and some of his too. The wine was chilled, the blanket was thick and he was ready to have this lasting memory with his soon to be wife. For the first time in two years, Bryan felt as though everything was back to where it was with his love and finally coming together for the long term. The joy he felt shielded his desire to do anything other than love this woman with all his heart.

"This is beautiful sweetheart," Hailey told him.

"I'm glad you like it. It seem like you needed some cheering up."

"Really?" she asked. "What makes you say that?"

"You seemed a bit well . . . depressed. Am I mistaken?"

"Uhm, yes, you are," she replied and then scoffed. "Depressed. What have I got to be depressed about?"

"I'm sure nothing, but just the same . . . it appeared that way." Bryan poured her a glass of wine. Hailey clanked her glass against his and sipped it. Bryan observed her and dropped his shoulders a bit. She looked at him and partially smiled.

"What?"

"I was going to toast," he told her.

"Oh! My manners. I'm sorry!" She held her glass up high and waited for his toast. He smirked and shook his head at her absentmindedness.

"To us. To our future, our unborn child, and our new life together as man and wife. Cheers!"

"Cheers!"

They both sipped their wine and nibbled on some fruit for a moment. Hailey stared at him for a few as he sipped the wine and looked out at the passersby and cyclists that flanked the area. She wondered what he was thinking, but did not bother to ask. She cared very deeply for him and wanted to be as happy as she could with him. Hailey had no idea what her future held with Bryan, but she knew he would be the more stable choice than Steve. Steve was all over the place in her opinion. He lived in the past and had a hard time letting go. In several ways, Hailey felt as though Steve had more growing to do. She didn't feel threatened by his relationship with his therapist because she knew that woman was just a band-aid that temporarily covered a larger wound.

When Steve called her up the other night, she wasn't sure why she confided in him. It was probably because to her she still considered him a friend and only at times wished she could have more. She trusted Steve with some of her deepest secrets and he held them close to him exceptionally well. It was other people's dirty laundry that he chose to air.

Bryan was different though. Even though he left, he returned with his heart in his hands. She respected and admired that about him. It made her want to explore how he had changed. Hailey knew in her heart that he loved her and that he would do anything for her. His love for her overshadowed her wrongdoings.

Hailey knew that time afforded them no guarantees. She wanted security more than anything else. One didn't love her enough to commit and the other loved her so much that all he wanted to do was be committed to her. She was torn, but she knew that Steve would forever be in her life because of Alex. Hailey felt Bryan needed reassurance that she would remain in his life before committing totally to her. Hence his marriage proposal *after* they conceived. Unfortunately for him, Hailey wanted to be married first. She always did, but she knew how Bryan operated. He was a business man, but Hailey was just as smart and calculating.

"So," she started, "I thought some more about your proposal." She twirled the rock around her finger.

"Yes?"

"I was so surprised when you asked me!"

"I know because you cried."

"I did, didn't I?" she rubbed his face with the palm of her hand. He smiled in response and kissed the inside of it.

"No, like . . . you *cried*."

Hailey wielded a confused expression and slowly took her hand from his face. She disagreed by shaking her head as she smiled, hoping to divert his statement.

"Yes. You were bawling. What was that about?"

Hailey thought quickly. She looked down in her lap for a moment and then gulped down the rest of her wine. Bryan's eyes followed the wine as it disappeared down her throat rapidly. To stall for time, she breathed in and rubbed his hand.

"Honestly?"

Bryan closed his eyes and then opened them to look deep into hers. He expected to hear some sort of bullshit from Hailey but tried to be open-minded.

"I really dislike when people say honestly before a statement," he said quietly as he sighed. "So please . . . let me hear it."

"I *did* cry."

"I know! Why?" he asked.

"Because I wanted the proposal *before* getting pregnant," Hailey told him. She tossed the glass into the basket and crossed her arms tightly across her body.

"Really?"

"Yes Bryan. You wanted to get married quickly a few years back, but it was only after you found out that I was pregnant with Alex."

"Who's not mine," Bryan said under his breath.

"Well, in all fairness you made that assumption. I told you right then that he may not have been yours. So I cried when you asked me again because it seems like you need to lock me in before you can marry me. Don't you love me?"

"Of course I do but that's not it. I just thought that if you were pregnant, we should get married before he or she is born."

"But you know that isn't the natural order of things. You are supposed to get married first."

"Supposed to?" Bryan asked her. "Says who?"

"Says me. That's what I want. Baby that is all I ever wanted – to be married to a great guy and have a great life. Make no mistake, I love Alex with all of my heart, but I didn't need children. I just needed a provider and a lover for life."

Bryan wasn't expecting to hear this and had put his own desires ahead of hers. He wanted to solidify their bond through a child before making that commitment to her, but never thought that Hailey would marry him if only he'd asked her.

"Wow," he told her. "I'm sorry. I had no idea."

"So . . . do you love me?"

"Yes Hailey, I love you."

"Then let's get married. I don't want to wait any more."

Bryan smiled, "What are you saying?"

"Let's go to the courthouse and get married." She leapt around on the blanket and gripped both of his hands. Joyously, she caressed him so he would give in to her whim.

"What?" Bryan could barely believe what he was hearing. "When?"

"This weekend!"

"Wait, wait . . .," he slowed her down by placing her hands in her lap and held up a single finger to stop her excitement. "I don't understand. For someone who is all about marriage . . . you don't want a big wedding?"

She sighed and rolled her eyes around. "No! It's not about the wedding. I never said anything about having a grand wedding. I said I want to be married. It's a difference."

"Hailey? You are unlike any woman I have ever known."

"Good enough to be Mrs. Bryan Bryant?"

"Perfect to be called Mrs. Bryan Bryant."

Hailey leapt into his arms and they fell backward on the blanket. She was on top of him and covered his face with kisses.

"Watch our baby!" Bryan scolded with a smile.

"Oh, sorry." Hailey slowly sat back up and rubbed her stomach. "You have made me so happy! I've got to tell the girls!"

After she and Bryan came home from their outing, Hailey immediately hopped on the phone. She tried Josephine first and got her voicemail. Hailey didn't want to leave a message of that magnitude on her phone, so she decided to call Camilla. Camilla's phone went straight to voicemail.

"Wow."

Hailey rarely called Tamar, but decided to share her good news with her anyway. Her phone also went to voicemail. Instantly, Hailey got offended. She wondered what everyone could be doing at the moment where they couldn't be available to share in her happiness. Since there was no one else that she cared to tell at the moment, she tossed her phone down and tried not to settle into the feeling of disgust. Being unsuccessful, she pouted.

"What's wrong?" Bryan said as he walked in and noticed that she was in a bad mood.

"I tried to contact the girls and no one was free to talk!"

He laughed, "It's okay baby. They will find out soon enough. Life gets in everyone's way sometimes. Don't take it personally."

"I know, but still."

"Well, I have to turn in some paperwork to the Post. I'm back to work next month and I've already secured a book tour for the month after that."

Hailey sat up in her chair, "Wow, really? You'll be on the road?"

"Yes."

Hailey dropped her shoulders and sulked.

"I know it's soon after the proposal, but we need this extra income."

He put on a lightweight jacket and headed toward the exit. The keys jangled as he grabbed them from the counter and opened the door. He gave her a wide smile and winked.

"We've got a baby on the way!" he blew a kiss and left.

*   *   *   *

When Bryan hopped in his car he made a phone call. He made sure that he was backed out of the driveway before he began speaking. The phone rang twice before she answered.

"I'm on my way now," he told her.

By the time Bryan got to D.C., the parking had somewhat subsided a bit. He was able to find something fairly close and only had to walk about a block. Bryan stepped with determination until he reached his destination. He turned the knob and walked right inside.

Chase looked up from her computer and smiled when she saw Bryan.

"Well hello there," Chase greeted.

"Thanks for seeing me again."

"Of course. I'm just glad that you kept your appointments for all of these weeks. I was afraid that after you connected with your long lost love that you would feel as though you didn't need to see me anymore."

"No, I was going to commit to my mental well being no matter how long it was going to take. So again, thank you. I know today wasn't scheduled, so I appreciate you being here," he told her.

"So," Chase began, "what's going on?"

"Well, I proposed to her the other day."

"First off, let me congratulate you. Why did you do that?"

"We need to be married. I should profess my love for her and I do love her."

"That's good. So you believe that the other man is no longer in the picture?"

Bryan took a deep breath and adjusted his shirt a bit before he answered. Chase looked over the rims of her fashionable glasses while she awaited his response. After a few moments, she removed them and placed them in front of her. As she leaned back in her chair she interlocked her fingers in front of her.

"I want to believe it, but I'm not totally sure. I mean, he will be in her life for a long time, so I have to get used to that idea."

"True."

"But on the other hand, we have one on the way as well."

Chase looked puzzled and rocked a bit in her seat. She waited for Bryan to continue. His smile lit up his entire face and she saw the thoughts of fatherhood fill his eyes. He transformed into another person right before her. Bryan was no longer the snobby guy who knew how to make money with his words; he was now the hopeless romantic who had shared his heart with the woman he loved. That love in turn created something special that they would share amongst themselves until the end of their lives.

He deserved better, Chase thought to herself. Chase knew nothing of his past; only what Bryan shared with her in confidence. However what she knew about him now made her feel sympathetic to his desire to be loved. This woman named Hailey, played with the hearts of too many men and destroyed her relationship with Steve.

To Chase, Steve had been happy with her until Bryan walked back into his life. Without Steve knowing about Bryan, the things Steve shared with Chase about Hailey in his sessions were attributable to some faceless entity. To Chase, seeing her photo in Steve's home and knowing that he couldn't disconnect from her sent shockwaves through her body. Chase thought that she was more than enough for Steve. Chase chose to put the photo out of her mind, but when she noticed how upset Steve was when he saw Hailey with Bryan, Chase knew that Steve could never love her the way he loved this manipulative and conniving excuse for a woman. Chase despised Hailey and had no allegiance to her at all and would never.

"You can congratulate my proposal, but not the future birth of my child?" Bryan scoffed a bit. His smile faded when Chase sat poker faced.

"Child?"

"Yes! I told you we're expecting."

Clearly bound, Chase rubbed her face with her hands. She shook her head and bit her bottom lip for emphasis.

"What? Why are you doing that?"

"Bryan, I'm so sorry."

"Sorry for what?"

"I don't think that you guys are having a baby," she rested her head in her hand.

"And just how in God's name would know that? Are you psychic? Is that part of your practice too? Should I leave a dollar in a copper bowl up front and burn incense when I get home?"

"Bryan, please. I'm being serious."

"Okay, would you mind then telling me what you are talking about?"

Chase gulped hard and then sighed. "She was at an abortion clinic last Friday."

Bryan was frozen, his eyes filled with concern and disbelief. He tried to muster up words to respond to Chase's allegations. He took a deep breath. When he couldn't think of a response, he laughed.

"No. I'm sure you are mistaken."

"It was her."

"I know you are making this up. In fact, what were you doing at an abortion clinic anyway?" Bryan narrowed his eyes and smirked as if he knew he had caught her in a lie.

"I was taking a young client of mine who didn't want her mother to know. I didn't really recognize her. But then the nurse called her name. It was her. I'm sorry."

"No."

"Maybe she had complications or something. I don't know, but she was definitely there. I have no reason to lie to you."

Bryan rubbed his temples with his finger tips and raked his face with his hand afterward. His expression went blank as he pressed his lips together. He grabbed a lock of his beard and twisted it between his fingers.

"Why did you tell me that?" he asked Chase with a solemn tone.

"You needed to know. She just strikes me as a very manipulative person. I've seen her type far too often. I don't want her making a fool out of you. You are a good person and I care about your feelings."

Bryan stopped twisting his beard in his fingers and stared into Chase's eyes deeply. She realized his hurt as his eyes looked glossed over as if he wanted to weep. He looked defeated and certainly broken. Chase came around from her desk and patted his shoulder to help comfort him.

"I am truly sorry," she told him.

Bryan placed his hand on hers as she continued to rub his shoulder. He held his head down and Chase studied the curve of the back of his neck. It looked so delectable that she wanted to kiss it, but she refrained. She stroked it lightly with her finger and noticed that Bryan did not move or stop her from doing so. She knelt beside his chair and kept massaging his shoulder and upper arm. He looked into her eyes and she stared longingly into his. She gazed at his lips for a moment and leaned forward to kiss him.

Bryan enjoyed the softness of her lips and the touch of her hand on his shoulder and now chest. She kissed him passionately as if she had been waiting to do that for a long time. Bryan indulged for a moment and then regained his senses. He gripped Chase by her shoulders and gently pushed her away. Chase looked startled as their lips disconnected.

"Wait wait . . .," Bryan told her softly.

"I couldn't help myself. Please forgive my unprofessionalism," Chase pleaded. Standing up, she looked down at him with woeful eyes, "Please?"

"I gotta go."

Chase backed away from him to allow him to stand. She pressed her fingers against her lips in embarrassment and cast her eyes downward.

"I'm terribly sorry."

"Goodbye, Chase."

Bryan walked out of her office and slowly sauntered to his car. Bryan felt like his life had just drifted into slow motion. He had no idea what to do or how to even ask Hailey about what Chase told him. He needed to ask her, but he wasn't going to ask her right away. After the kiss, Chase could have been lying.

For him, this new revelation regarding his child being terminated by the woman he loved yielded some personal changes. Bryan wheeled his car in the direction of the closest barber shop. It was time for the beard and overgrown hair to go. He needed to get back to his old self. Business minded, professional, strong and debonair.

When he returned, he would look like the old Bryan and have a long heart to heart with his beloved Hailey.

31

Taj declined Tamar's offer to meet up with her the day after Donovan left. Instead he thought it would be more strategic to make her wait an additional day. Taj knew that Tamar was a smart woman and even though her calm demeanor on the phone made her appear to be okay with Donovan's retreat, Taj figured that Tamar was probably devastated. Who wouldn't be? He agreed to meet her that weekend. Initially, Tamar wanted Taj to come to her house so he could get a full view of the devastation he had caused. However, after she had a day to think about it, she decided against it. They were going to meet at a neutral location, preferably outdoors in case Tamar felt the need to get loud with him. She found a nice secluded trail at Anacostia Park.

Taj approached her as only he could – stealthily and as if he was back on the runway for Ralph Lauren. Tamar loved his walk and his confidence. However, today she needed answers and felt like clawing Taj's eyes out for whatever influence he may have had over Donovan.

"You look ravishing as usual," Taj said. He leaned in for a kiss on the cheek, but Tamar pulled her face away and placed a halting palm up to him.

"We need to clear the air first before we exchange kisses," Tamar told him.

Taj shrugged and stuffed his hands in his pockets as they prepared to walk along the trail.

"Taj, what did you do? And please don't bullshit me," she asked him.

Taj took a deep breath, smiled and then erased it quickly. He could sense that Tamar was watching his every movement, trying to gather some sort of indication that would help her piece together her new and broken life.

"Let's just say I knew that Donovan wasn't right for you."

Tamar stopped and grabbed his arm before she yelled, "I told you *not* to bullshit me! Now tell me what happened!"

Taj was stunned by her aggressiveness and also turned on by it. He looked into Tamar's pleading eyes and decided to come clean with her. Besides, if he exposed Donovan for who he was, perhaps it would clear a path for them to be together.

"I made him an offer and he accepted it."

"What offer?"

"Tamar . . .," he tried to stop her.

"*What offer?*" she nudged.

"Money and a new woman."

Tamar looked down at the ground. She had no words in response to something so meaningless. In just those few moments she summed up that Donovan was what Celeste referred to as a *user*. Tamar felt shitted on and unloved. She knew that Donovan worked hard, but had no idea that he was the type of man that could be bought. Tamar could feel her heart breaking all over again, but she was done crying. She had given herself one day to cry and then it was over. It was back on her grind and business as usual. It was one of those things her mother taught her.

It's no use sitting around feeling sorry for yourself. The world doesn't care if you are sad, so take a moment, dust yourself off and get your head back in the game.

"How much?" she asked.

"Tamar, don't. It's not that important."

"*How much*, Taj?"

Taj sighed again as if it pained him to say. He reached for her hand and gripped it slightly. He bit his lower lip and closed his eyes for a moment for effect. He sucked his teeth and then shook his head as if it were a crying shame.

"$30,000," he softly nodded when he told her.

"Bullshit Taj. He's got more than that in his fucking checking account! How much?"

"Okay okay, you busted me. It was $100,000. I swear it."

Tamar looked at him suspiciously. She may have just discovered that Donovan could be bought, but she knew for certain that buying that kind of a guy wouldn't be cheap. $100,000 was certainly a nice round figure, but it still gave Tamar pause.

"Why did you offer him money, Taj?"

"Just to see if he was the little shit that I thought he was," he caressed her shoulders as he faced her. "Let me take care of you, Tamar." He caressed her chin and looked deep into her eyes.

"Don't touch me!" She pushed his hand away from her and wiped her face to rid it of his touch.

"Tamar?"

"I can't believe you did that. We were trying to work on our issues and you just came in and destroyed it!"

"Tamar, I didn't act alone, did I? He could've said no, but he didn't, did he?"

"Why were you at my house?"

"What?"

"You heard me."

"I don't even know where you live!"

Tamar paced in a circle and took deep breaths to calm herself. Her cheeks puffed outward and sank back in when she inhaled. "I told you *not* to bullshit me! You were at my house when the movers were there and I want to know why!"

Taj had to think of a quick lie because Tamar was not letting up. He paused and looked out at the folks who congregated to play softball on the field below the raised trail.

"Why?!"

"I had to pay him that was the only reason. I gave him his money and left. That's it. It's over. He's gone, he's out of the way so you and I can be together."

"No," she calmly said as she shook her head in affirmation.

"What? No?"

"No. I don't want you. Not like this," she said. "You can't have pleasure at the cost of someone else's pain. You hurt me and I don't even want to know what you did to Donovan. He loved me. I know that he did. It's fucked up that he left, without a doubt, but I know what kind of man he is now. But you shouldn't have interfered. That was for me to find out in my own time."

"The time was now!"

Tamar shook her head out of pity for him. She rubbed his arm and looked saddened. She didn't know what else to say to Taj to get through to him that what he did was inexcusable and just flat out sickening.

"Well," she began. "You both got what you wanted then, right?"

"What?"

"You wanted him out of my life and I guess he wanted money," she was vexed. "Now I just want to be left alone – for good. Good bye, Taj."

*   *   *   *

There was no question that Tamar felt a complete void in her life without Donovan. She tried to fill her days as much as possible to take her mind off him. She dove into work, even though it wasn't as fulfilling to her as it once was. Tamar needed to fill the emptiness somehow. Her "go to" was in fact sex, but she wasn't feeling sexy anymore. Donovan made her feel sexy, Taj made her feel free, but with those two out of her life, she didn't have the energy to start over. If she were to connect with someone sexually, it would be nothing more than that. Tamar knew how to disconnect her emotions when it came to sex, but she had no intentions of even going through that for a while. She just wanted to be left alone as well as remain alone.

When she arrived back at work after taking the week off, she felt a slight sullen atmosphere but didn't acknowledge it. The receptionist wasn't at the front desk and she didn't see her legal aid either. Tamar thought nothing of it and stepped into her office. She booted up her computer as she flipped open her briefcase. Her computer was taking an unusual length of time to get started so she jabbed a few keys on the keyboard and sucked her teeth at its stubbornness.

Tamar's assistant stood at the entrance of her office.

"Ms. Woodruff?"

"Yes, hi good morning."

"You are needed in the conference room," she said and then walked away.

Tamar frowned because she knew that her assistant usually provided details before dismissing herself. She closed her briefcase and slid it underneath her desk before grabbing a pen and notepad. She grabbed a mint from the crystal jar on her desk and wondered what client was awaiting her legal advice.

The door was closed and Tamar leaned toward it in an attempt to hear what was taking place on the other side. It was silent with the exception of a few inaudible whispers. She turned the knob and entered. There were three people seated at the table all in black suits. Two men, one woman. The man and woman wore slicked blonde hairdos while the other man, who was black, donned heavy looking spectacles.

"Good morning!" Tamar said in a chipper tone while she smiled. She wanted to put them at ease while calming her nerves as well. They looked so official.

The black man spoke and Tamar instantly assumed he was the "leader".

"Good morning, Ms. Woodruff have a seat," he extended his hand toward the empty chair just across from them. "My name is Mr. Hughes how are you?"

"Fine. So what's going on?" Tamar slowly slid in the seat as it made an awkward noise. They sat as if they were about to interview her rigorously for a partnership. However, Tamar felt that this was something more than just a mere performance review. Not to mention she had never seen them before.

"We are part of a special investigation unit for the DC Bar Association. It has come to our attention that there were misappropriation of funds and excessive billing charges to clients for personal use."

"Yes."

Mr. Hughes looked over the rims of his heavy glasses and sat back in his chair. Blonde woman looked at him surprised, while Blonde man scribbled something on his notepad and scratched the back of his ear.

"Excuse me?" he asked.

"I'm aware of it. One of my clients brought it to my attention over a week ago and I researched the matter. My invoices had not been presented to my clients accurately and were inflated by someone else here at the firm. Not by me.

I have all of my statements that I provided to accounting and my system log files indicating the date and time of submission."

"I'm sorry . . . you knew over a week ago?"

"Yes."

Blonde woman finally spoke after she got over the initial shock about Tamar knowing. "Why didn't you say something at that time?"

Tamar thought for a moment, "Well, I didn't want to mention it here as I needed the entries to remain untouched. Secondly, I wanted to make sure that my entries hadn't been adjusted. Excuse me, but I had to cover my own ass. Is that a problem?"

"No, not at all," Blonde woman replied.

Mr. Hughes then sat forward again. "Well, Ms. Celeste Bacon's name was associated with almost all of the revised entries made through accounting and was arrested yesterday."

Tamar's mouth dropped, this apparently was more serious than she anticipated. She wondered who exactly Jameson called and what on earth he said because they worked pretty quickly. Even though Tamar was out of the office that week, if she were in any severe legal trouble, they would've come to her home.

Blonde man spoke now. "Why were you out last week?"

"I needed some time. I was dealing with a personal matter."

"May I ask what?"

"No," Tamar told him sternly, "you may not. But be assured it had nothing to do with this place or what is currently happening."

Blonde man shifted in his seat a bit perturbed that he may not ever know why Tamar was gone for a week.

"We understand," Mr. Hughes said as he looked over at Blonde man then back at Tamar. "Actually it was best that you weren't here. Our forensics team was able to verify your entries on your office computer during your absence. Your entries were confirmed, the hashes matched the submission and system log file. However the hash count changed a week before accounting generated its bills and those were linked to Ms. Bacon's machine. Her personal entry code, which no one else has and exit times were logged at the keypad outside, which matched. Not to mention, she flat out admitted making those entries when she saw the amount of evidence stacked against her."

"Wow," was all Tamar could say and quietly so.

"We take ethics very seriously as well as the service provided to anyone seeking legal assistance. The DC Bar has a zero tolerance for that sort of behavior. We thank you for your service, for researching the matter and you also may be called to testify when her trial comes."

Tamar swallowed hard as her heartbeat began to return to its normal pace.

"Well," Tamar began, "is there anything else that I can do?"

"We will be in contact," Mr. Hughes nodded and then smiled. "Thanks for speaking with us. We are done here and will show ourselves out."

Tamar stood, smoothed out her skirt and shook their hands before she left.

"Thank you," she told them. Tamar rose to let herself out of the conference room. The heat and wetness from her armpits resulted from her nervousness. She entered her office and closed the door. After it was shut securely, Tamar leaned against it and tilted her head back as if that were the hardest thing she had ever done. She then wondered for a moment what Celeste's mug shot looked like and how she was arrested. Tamar knew that her assistant would fill her in at some point. Tamar actually felt bad for Celeste because it was unnecessary for her to do any of that. Tamar was paid extremely well and she knew that Celeste easily pulled in twenty to thirty grand more a year than her. It didn't and wouldn't matter now.

Tamar's office phone rang. She picked up and her assistant told her it was a call from Switzerland.

"Ms. Woodruff here," Tamar looked puzzled.

"Tamar?" the male voice sounded so distant. "It's Jameson."

"Jameson? How are you? You're in Switzerland?"

"Yes! I wanted to call you to let you know that I contacted a good friend at the bar association to investigate those charges. I just wanted to make sure that you were okay."

"I'm fine actually. Apparently there was an arrest made."

"I don't take too kindly to people stealing from me."

"I understand. Why are you in Switzerland?"

"I'm still on my vacation. How is Donovan?"

Long pause.

"Hello?" Jameson asked.

"Donovan left me, Jameson."

"What? You're kidding, right? Is he crazy or something?"

Tamar smirked and nodded slightly, "or something."

"That prick."

Tamar giggled at Jameson's expression because he was always so refined whenever he spoke. She walked around her desk to have a seat. She tapped her keyboard and was able to log into her computer. She pulled out her briefcase and cracked it open with the phone tucked between her neck and ear.

"It's okay," Tamar told him. "If it was meant to be, it would've been. Life goes on."

"I love your resilience. I'm going to send you something, just a thank you for not trying to rip me off."

"Oh, please don't. I mean, I appreciate it, but since the investigation is still pending, it's probably best that I not receive any types of gifts. I didn't even bill any cases after you told me what you suspected."

"Understood," Jameson told her. "Look, I've got to go, we have a big day tomorrow and it's almost eight o'clock here. We're touring the Alps tomorrow. We are in Lucerne right now. I'll send you some photos and I'll save your gifts, eh?"

Tamar smiled slightly although she knew that Jameson couldn't see. "Sounds like fun and I appreciate it. Take care."

She hung up and stared at the phone as she placed her finger to her temple. She wondered what her life would've been like, if she had taken Jameson up on that dinner invitation on his boat two years ago. Maybe her heart wouldn't be hurting so bad now and she'd be touring the Swiss Alps with him tomorrow. Oh well, everything happens for a reason. Whoever the woman was, Tamar hoped that she was appreciative.

Shortly after Tamar opened her office door, her assistant tapped on it with the tip of her pen. Tamar turned, smiled and then took a seat.

"Good morning again," Tamar greeted. "So what happened while I was gone?"

The assistant came further into her office and closed the door so she could dish with Tamar freely. She felt a bit of relief that there was some sort of office gossip that she could share and possibly get details about. Her relationship with Tamar was so professional; it was nice for her to experience the "girlfriend" side of her for a change.

"They arrested Ms. Bacon, but wouldn't tell us why! She put up a bit of a fuss, but then she calmed down once they mentioned resisting arrest. Her secretary went with her and bailed her out soon after. They confiscated her machine, locked her office and everything. They called everyone in and asked questions. It was insane." Her flailing hands returned by her side when she was done explaining.

Tamar smirked a bit at her enthusiasm, but had to lead by example and set the standard for her subordinate.

"Well, we will have to wait on the official charges. The only thing we can do is speculate. But, let's not discuss this with any clientele or opposing firms. We clear?"

"Yes, Ms. Woodruff," she looked down for a moment and then back up at her remembering that it was indeed a law firm where they worked.

"But thank you for the details. I kind of wondered what was going on when I first got here, so I do appreciate it."

The assistant smiled again with that reassurance. "If I may, I'm just glad you are here. You have been a great mentor."

"Why thank you! Now let's see what sort of case loads we have okay?"

"Certainly," she stepped out and propped the door open as she left.

The girlfriend moment that Tamar's assistant attempted to have with her made her remember how it was to sit back, giggle and trade stories with her own girlfriends. It had been so long since she talked to Josephine. That was her shopping buddy. Since her marriage to Ian, Josephine had little time to hang out with her. She knew that they were trying to have a baby for a while, but wasn't sure if that had even occurred.

Tamar picked up the phone and called Josephine at her office. It rang twice and then she answered. Her voice was vacant and devoid of energy.

"Is this Josephine?"

"This is," I said blandly.

"Oh wow, what's going on with you? You sound terrible!"

"Tamar?" I asked. My voice perked up just slightly. "Oh my goodness, where have you been?"

"Same place as you, stuck at work then flying home to please my man just to go to bed to do it all over again," Tamar chuckled.

"And how is Donovan?"

"Gone."

"*What??*"

"Yeah. Josie, we need to get together. It's too much info for the phone. How is Ian?"

"Ian . . . well Ian has been interesting. I'm pregnant, but it hasn't been a pleasant experience. I just thought it would be a lot different with someone you love. But . . ."

"Well congratulations, I think . . .," Tamar told her. "Can you get away for lunch? You probably should. I can come to you."

"I do need to get out."

"Let's plan for twelve. I'll be there and we can – well *I* can have a drink while we chit chat and you eat for two."

"Three," I corrected.

"Oh hell!! We definitely need to talk!"

We met at Old Ebbitt Grill in Northwest. After Tamar finished her Donovan drama update she finalized her story by jokingly declaring revenge.

"If I could just get my hands on that fucker one last time!" Tamar pretended to choke an imaginary neck in front of her as her hands shook to show the struggle of doing so.

I laughed and dabbed my eyes after I settled down. I needed that laugh big time. I shared my story with Tamar about how Ian's last ultimatum was for me to give the kids up for adoption. Tamar almost went ballistic.

"Is he insane? What the hell is wrong with these men?" she asked me.

"I don't know, but Tamar, I love him. I can't lose him."

"Say what?" Tamar stretched her neck forward and tilted her head to hear me better.

"You heard right. I waited a long time for him and what I did was wrong. I have to consider his feelings and I didn't."

"Umm *huh*?"

"I mean really . . .," I began, "if the problem was with me, I would leave him if he went off and procreated with another woman just because he wanted kids. It's the same thing. I can't blame him for being upset."

"I mean . . . I *guess* I get it. But you are connected to those two lives growing inside of you, now you have to forget it? What in the world will your marital life be like going forward? He can't have children – that is *not* going to change. So he has one of two choices. Have you resent him for the rest of your life – and you will . . . or forgive you and show how much love he can give to these little ones and be their father. Yeah, it's fucked up, but it doesn't have to stay that way. I swear – people love to wallow in their mess instead of change it."

"You aren't wallowing?" I asked her.

"I did for a few days. The first day was the worst. But what can I change? Not a damn thing but myself. Yes, what Donovan and Taj did was more than jacked up, but it's over. They have to live with what they did just like I had to live with my choice for cheating on Donovan. It's done." Tamar waved her hands dismissing the whole wretched ordeal.

"I wish I had your outlook right now. I don't know how I'm going to get through these next four months. The doctor says I may even deliver early which is common with twins. I'm trying so hard not to be stressed, but I can't help it. Ian is not helping the situation. Every time he looks at me he rolls his eyes!"

"I *know* Ian is not being petty! I bet that changes when he sees those precious faces. I hope he gets it together for you and the sake of those babies. Lord knows we have enough fatherless kids. And now he just wants them to be given away? You are still the mother regardless. Think about it." Tamar patted my hand and gave a gentle smile. "It will be okay."

I wanted to believe her. Ian was in fact giving me hell and that needed to end. Even if I were to give up these babies for adoption, I didn't want them to be miserable souls because I had an emotional pregnancy. Tamar was right. The only thing I could change about this situation was me and I needed to reclaim my role as wife and new role as mother.

Ian and I are going to have a long chat when I get home this evening. I was sure it was going to get rather ugly.

32

I thought a lot about the conversation that Tamar and I had. She always gave it to me straight and I loved her for that. When we first started hanging out she told me, *if you don't want my honest opinion, don't ask.* Some of her words stung, but I never took it personally because if she didn't care, she would have never told me anything at all. One thing that resonated with me was that Ian had a choice to be despised or to be loved. I was the mother period. The twins came from my eggs and are living inside of me, so they are mine and I was not giving them up.

To my surprise when I arrived at home, Ian was there. I had a more difficult time getting in and out of the car these days as my belly was really the topic of most conversations whenever I went out to grocery shop or whatever. Actually, it was becoming a bit annoying. Most days I was more appreciative of the folks who just looked and smiled as an offer of congratulations. As irritable as the pregnancy was making me along with the stress from Ian, I just couldn't take the strangers wanting to know everything about me just because my stomach was inflated. Nor was that an invitation to offer advice or tell me about their pregnancy. I just wanted to get in and get out. Now, there were times where I welcomed the conversation, just not all the time. I needed to reach out to Hailey to see how hers was going as well. But not now, Ian and I had to have a heart to heart.

Slowly I walked inside. Ian heard the door and greeted me with a simple peck. He was getting better, but he wasn't back to where he was at all. That could take time or it may never happen, I just didn't know.

"Hey baby," he said.

"Hi," I looked around and noticed that he had made dinner. It had been a while for that as well. I was getting tired of microwaveable meals, salad and rice. I mustered a smile as I set my purse down. "You cooked for us?"

"Yes, I did. But I already ate. I left yours in there."

Ian turned his attention back to Sports Center. I gave him a damning look and sat my ass down. I knew he didn't think I was about to make my plate like a roommate and watch sports shows with him. After I sat, I cleared my throat – loudly.

He turned his head quickly in my direction and I tilted my head to prompt him to assist his pregnant wife.

"Oh! I'm sorry babe," he got up and I could hear plates and utensils being rattled around. It almost sounded as if he were cooking instead of reheating.

I struggled to kick off my shoes and find a comfortable position where it didn't feel like tiny limbs were pressing against my bladder. Oh goodness, I shouldn't have even *thought* about my bladder, now I had to go to the bathroom again.

By the time I came out, Ian had prepared my plate for me. Baked chicken with sautéed spinach and fingerling potatoes with rosemary – God I missed his cooking!

"How was your day?" he asked.

"It was fine. I met up with Tamar for lunch."

"Oh wow, that's a name I haven't heard in a minute. How is she doing? What was her man's name?"

"She is surprisingly well considering that Donovan, that's his name, left her."

"What?" Ian sat up from the shock of the news. He then slouched back, shifted in his seat and muttered, "She must've done something."

I stared at him for a moment while I chewed. He looked over at me with a trace of innocence in his eyes.

"What?"

"It was both of them, but more *him*!"

"Okay. I kinda don't care for real." Ian turned his attention back toward the television, or his personal idiot box. I finished eating and tried not to boil over since he had dismissed the conversation and me.

"Can you turn that off? We should talk."

I could see him curl his lips upward in objection as he readjusted his body against the cushions. He huffed and then aimed the remote toward the television. It zapped off and the screen went black.

"What's up?"

"Ian, I love you."

"I love you too," he said with no more or less enthusiasm as I had when I stated my declaration.

"And you know that I would do anything for you baby. I thought about what you said, about giving the babies up for adoption . . ."

He looked at me intently, "Yeah . . ."

I rubbed my belly as I leaned further back into the recliner. I looked down at my stomach and smiled at the lives inside as my eyes began to well up. I had no idea what these babies would look like, how their personality would be, if they would be a gift to society, one of the smartest kids in school or what, all I knew is that I loved them. I loved them with the same intensity as I loved Ian, but differently. I looked back at Ian and I felt as though he knew what I was about to say before I even said it.

"These are my babies," the tears rolled down my cheeks and onto my swollen belly. "I love them and I can't give them up."

"So you'd rather lose me?"

I wiped my eyes and wished we didn't have to have this conversation. It felt silly and I felt like a fool for believing him almost five years ago when he told me that his love was big enough for the both of us. In retrospect, it seemed like such a lie and a line.

"I think that is the question you should ask yourself," I rested my head sideways against the heel of my hand while I subconsciously told myself not to break down wailing at what his response could be. "Do you want to lose me and the babies? Or do you want to love and *have* love from all of us?"

Ian looked at me with compassion. A slight twinkle in his eyes that had gone dim for several months, suddenly sparked. I hoped that I had reached his heart enough for him to challenge himself to be the man that I knew he could be. I suffered for what I'd done and was still punishing myself for betraying his trust. I knew that it was going to be a long road back, but I was willing to endure it if I could have him and the twins in my life. I needed him to forgive me and then I needed to forgive myself.

"Josephine, I love you so much baby. I'm trying to remember what it was like to be in love with you. I don't know if my love will outweigh my anger. I'm trying. I'm trying. It's so hard for me. But baby you hurt me in a way that I never thought you were capable of."

"Ian, I'm so sorry for betraying you. Please find it in your heart to forgive me. I don't want these babies to be without your love and you without theirs. I love you."

"I know you are sorry, baby. I know and I'm sorry for making you feel less than my wife."

Ian got up and knelt at my feet. He rubbed my belly as he buried his face between my outer thigh and cushion. He turned his head back and forth as he allowed the movement to wipe his tears. His shoulders shuddered while he silently cried.

He sniffled before asking, "Will you forgive me?"

"Of course baby. I do."

"I mean for what I've done?"

"What did you do, Ian?"

"We can't be together, Josephine. I filed for a divorce last month."

33

Hailey called me a few times but I never returned them. It wasn't because I didn't want to, there was just so much going on with me right now that time and emotions weren't allowing it. I was still reeling from Ian filing for divorce and the fact that he did it a month ago. He knew then that he was done but didn't tell me. Maybe he was looking for a place to live during that time instead of having me throw him out on the street. I'm not sure why he waited so long to say something, but my heart would never be the same. I wish I could undo what I've done, but it's too late. I had to move on and I had to lift my spirits for the sake of my children. I was so involved in my own drama that I had no idea what was going on with Hailey and her pregnancy. When Hailey called me today at the office, I had to pick up and speak to her.

"Josephine! I've been trying to reach you!" she beamed.

"I know and I'm sorry, so much has been happening," I explained. "How are you?"

"I'm getting married!!"

"Really?" I livened up some because I know that Hailey had wanted to be married for such a long time. "Steve finally popped the question, huh?"

"Steve? No silly. Bryan!"

"Bryan? What?"

"Yes!"

I could hear Hailey smiling through the phone. If I had to guess, she was probably bouncing around in her office chair.

"He brought food up to my room and had the ring under the napkin! It was so romantic!"

"Aww Hailey! I'm happy for you! What does Steve think of all of this?"

"I haven't told him yet. But Bryan and I are going to get married right away. Like next week."

"What?" I couldn't believe my ears. I knew how much she wanted to get married, how was she going to do an edited version of a wedding? Something didn't sound right to me, but if it was what she wanted, who was I to say anything about it?

"Yeah, I was trying to get it done last weekend, but we have to wait for the license," she said. "I'll be Hailey Bryant. That has a nice ring to it."

"Well, I'm . . . I'm happy for you. I'm a bit shocked, because it's so sudden, but happy."

"Good! I'd love it if you and Ian would be our witnesses."

I gulped at the sound of his name and instantly became queasy. I tried to keep my voice calm and not give any vocal inflections as to tip her off that anything was wrong.

"I will talk to him about it. Just let me know when and where."

After they said their goodbyes, Hailey decided to reach out to Steve because he needed to know what was going on with her. After all, she was about to have a blended family and would need to have the guys co-parent and be cordial during the process.

He agreed to meet up with her after work at this Greek restaurant named Cava Mezze in Clarendon. She loved the food there and thought it would be a good place to talk and go for a walk afterward.

Hailey secured a nice table with a view of the other shops. Steve came in and stopped at the entrance while he tried to locate Hailey. Dressed casually, he looked a bit leaner than normal to her. In fact, he was looking rather sexy to her, but she quickly put those thoughts out of her mind. She was about to be married. When she noticed that he still didn't locate her, she waved and called out to him in a moderate tone.

"Steve!"

His head immediately turned in the direction of the voice and then he smiled when he saw her. As he began to make his way over to her, she stood to greet him with a one-armed hug as he kissed her forehead.

"How are you?" Steve asked with genuine concern in his voice.

"I'm better."

"Good. You sounded so bad the other week."

"I know. It was hard you know?"

"I would think so. Although I'm still not sure what that was about."

Hailey looked down in her lap and then back up at Steve. She could feel the tears about to form and fall from her eyes, but stopped them by taking a deep breath. She puffed her cheeks slightly and fanned her hands in front of her eyes to dry up the condensation as if she were a pageant winner.

"Talk to me," Steve said.

"Steve," Hailey began, "I'm trying not to hate myself."

"It's over. The abortion is done. There ain't nothing you can do about it now. Stop beating yourself up over it. I thought we talked about that part the other week. You just never told me why."

"I don't want any more kids, Steve. And as odd as it may seem, if I were to have more, I wanted them all to have the same father."

Steve shook his head and scoffed.

"What?"

"Fucking incredible," Steve said. "That's what."

"I beg your pardon?"

"You always want *what* you want, *how* you want it. You never give a damn about anyone else do you?"

Hailey was clearly confused by Steve's mild attack of her character. She backed up in her seat and crossed her arms in front of her.

"Look at you. And you *still* don't fucking get it," Steve muttered.

"Where is this coming from?"

"What's next, Hailey?" he asked.

"Steve please, I'm not *that* bad."

"Really?" he asked, to which she shook her head in response. "Well, did you tell him you aborted *his* child?"

"No and this is not what I came here to discuss."

"Well what? You made me burn my gas, is it about Alex?"

"No. Well in a way."

"Okay, hit it."

"Bryan proposed to me and we are getting married. Like . . . soon. As in real soon, like . . . next week."

Steve shook his head hard one time as his eyes were clenched shut. He looked back at Hailey in utter shock. "*What?*"

"Yeah."

"You are something else. Do you love him?"

"Of course."

"But you love me too?"

"Yes Steve, come on. You know that. I love you both."

Steve shook his head at Hailey's nonsense. Even though he was clean shaven, he rubbed his chin as if he had an itchy beard. She rolled her eyes up toward the ceiling and then returned her glare at Steve.

"What is it now?" she asked.

"How does that work? You know what? Nothing. I don't even know why I'm acting surprised. You don't give a shit. Only when you don't get what you want is when you start to care."

"That's so not true."

"You're serious? Hailey, you didn't want to give me any ass until you thought I was dicking another chick down. I tried to wait on you, but you kept messing around playing games. So you are going to marry this guy knowing that you aborted his kid?"

"Yes," she said. "I'm sorry you don't approve of my methods, but it's what I want. You talk about someone waiting? What nerve. I waited on you! You could never get your stuff together to marry me. Why were you taking so long? And *you* didn't want *me* until you found out I was with someone else! Don't hand me that bullshit and don't come off like you are the victim. We were together since college. So what was it? Really? Why didn't you marry me?"

Steve looked down and around the restaurant trying to avoid the question or think of a decent response.

"What? You didn't love me?"

"You know I did."

"Why did you cheat so much? I wasn't enough for you?"

"Not true."

"Well what?"

"I just wasn't ready! I can't put it any other way. You were doing your career thing and I was still finding my way. I wasn't about to let you take care of me. I tried to get myself together, but it just wasn't fast enough for you. I *wanted* to marry you. I'm sorry I didn't ask, but . . .," he took a deep breath and gulped hard, "I'm not sorry we *didn't* get married."

Hailey stared at him after his spiel and softly nodded. "Wow." She started to get her things together and dug in her purse for her keys.

"What are you doing?"

"I'm leaving. I can't believe you just said that. While you were running the streets with your boys and having your affairs I, like a fool, was being faithful. Taking care of you while you continued to be a boy. And you have the gall to sit there and say you are glad you didn't marry me because I had *one* affair? Fuck this."

Hailey stood up and secured her purse on her shoulder. She stuck her index finger through the key ring and rocked the keys back and forth on it. She waited for Steve to stand to walk her out.

"Oh, so what? You mad now?" Steve asked her as he stood.

"From now on, we don't talk unless it has to do with Alex. Understood?"

Steve shook his head and scoffed again. "Naa, 'cause it's not about what you want anymore, Hailey! We aren't finished. We will never be finished, you got it? Selfish ass . . . Do you even know what is going on with your friend?"

"Who?"

"Josephine!"

"What's going on with her?"

"Why don't you act like you give a shit and call her to find out? I'm out. I'll be picking up my son tomorrow. Do you just want to leave him by the curb with a bag?"

"Shut up, Steve!"

Hailey fumbled around in her purse to get her phone. Steve turned and walked out of the restaurant. Hailey tapped the numbers on her phone to reach Josephine.

"Josephine? It's me," Hailey began, her voice sounded rushed and out of breath. "I just met up with the ex-head case Steve. He said that I needed to call you. What's going on?"

"Oh no."

"What's happening girl?"

It took a minute to form my words to speak. "Ian filed for divorce. He's leaving me."

"No the hell he's not!"

"Hailey? Please," I started, "I can't have a 'let's-bust-his-ass' conversation right now. I just want to get some rest. Let's talk tomorrow, okay?"

"Oh. Okay. Sure," Hailey nodded as if Josephine could see. She then tossed the phone in her purse and looked around for Steve, but he was gone. Hailey thought that there was no truer love that she'd been personally privy to than theirs. Often times in the past, their relationship is what gave Hailey hope about her and Steve. It just seemed as if nothing was forever anymore.

34

Jameson, Camilla and Gabe were enjoying traveling Europe. Gabe was exploring new things and asking even more questions than ever before. Camilla even noticed that his speech was improving as his vocabulary was getting larger. Camilla came to realize that when it came to Gabe trying new foods, he was fearless. If he didn't like it, he'd spit it out; it was that simple to him. His tutor just loved him. She worked with him for three hours in the morning, again after lunch and again in the evening. Gabe and his brother would soon be three and already Gabe knew his alphabet, colors, shapes and could recognize several words. Gabe was always talking to the locals and Camilla would often have to tell him to wrap it up because he would talk anyone's ear off if given the chance. The locals spoiled him and always give him souvenirs. Gabe definitely had a way with people.

The trio made their way to Brussels, Belgium earlier this week. Gabe was fascinated when they toured the Royal Belgian Institute of Natural Sciences. Camilla had never heard Gabe say so many "ooo's and wow's" in all of his young life as he saw the dinosaur skeletons and interacted with the exhibits. Camilla had taken so many photos of Gabe's expressions that she didn't think her walls would be able to hold them all. His sense of discovery, his retention, and his fascination for life were all amazing to Camilla. Enjoying Gabe's presence, Jameson comfortably stepped into the fatherly role. Camilla knew that Jameson truly loved her son and more importantly her. He hadn't said it, but in her heart she knew. Afraid of being hurt by rejection, Camilla stopped herself from telling Jameson that she loved him. With just reason, Camilla guarded her heart but felt with Jameson that he would care and nurture it like a man should.

Jameson and Camilla were preparing to go out to dinner that evening and would be "dining in the sky". Despite not knowing the details, it sounded fun and interesting – it was probably some old abandoned fighter plane turned into a restaurant or something.

While they were getting ready for the night, Jameson noticed that Camilla was about to put on a full length dress and five inch heels. He stared for a moment at her attire, noting to himself how she always likes to over dress when they went out to dinner. He liked that aspect, but tonight if she wore that, she would be uncomfortable.

He leaned in close to her and whispered, "You may want to do a cute casual outfit and comfy shoes – just a thought."

Camilla frowned a bit and looked at her dress that was hanging on the door. She pointed toward it. "What's wrong with that?"

"Nothing, it's beautiful and I'm sure you look gorgeous in it, but not for this place. Trust me," he kissed her cheek and she put the dress back into the closet.

"Okaaaay. No dress – cute but casual." Thinking, she bit her lip as she sifted through some clothes. "Uhm, got it."

Once they arrived at the Mini Europe Park, Camilla was thankful that she changed her outfit to a more relaxing one.

"We have to bring Gabe here!" Camilla told Jameson.

"Of course! It looks cool at night, but sure, we can bring him during the day."

"He will probably try to push over this Mini Leaning Tower of Pisa," Camilla laughed.

"Or climb that Eiffel Tower over there," Jameson giggled. "He's a great kid Camilla."

"He is. I can't thank you enough for doing this. I would've never imagined this life in my wildest dreams."

"Well, it's happening." He pulled her in for a side hug as they continued to stroll around the park. "I'm just glad I have you to share it with. I've wanted to do this for quite some time, so thank you for trusting me to come along. I know it was a lot to pick up and leave like that."

"True. But I didn't feel like I was leaving anything behind. As long as we've been gone, I think I've only gotten one email from Josephine. Not even a call."

"Try not to take it personally. You said yourself that you guys weren't on the greatest of terms when you left, right?"

Camilla shrugged.

Jameson caressed her arm as they continued to walk slowly through Mini Europe. The detail on the miniature structures was phenomenal. They even had miniature tourists and of course most of the people who took photos were acting like King Kong or Godzilla. *How original*, Camilla thought but still managed to laugh at people's silliness.

Camilla noticed a restaurant in a tent near the exit of the park. She guessed that was where they would be dining. *So this is dinner in the sky*, she wondered. She guessed to herself that the theme probably originated because they were giants in Mini Europe.

"Is that the restaurant?" Camilla pointed and then rubbed Jameson's chest as they strolled.

He looked over in the direction that she pointed and chuckled. He shook his head and then kissed her forehead because of her inquisitiveness and incorrect observation.

"No baby," he kissed her forehead again. "We have a few more minutes and then we will make our way over to the Atomium."

"That's that sphere thing there, right?" Camilla pointed to a structure that connected nine silver spheres together. It was illuminated with purple lights and she saw several camera flashes in the distance of people capturing the structure. "Can you go inside them?"

"Uhh, five of them, yes. There's a restaurant in one."

"Oh! Okay! That's the dinner in the sky! How cool!"

Jameson still chuckled at her and dared not spoil the surprise. It was obvious that Camilla had no idea what "dinner in the sky" actually was. It was a table built for 22 people and in the center were three chefs who would be preparing their meals. No fire would be used of course. The seats are comfortable and the view is great. The view is great because the dinner table is lifted by a crane 180 feet in the air. Camilla of course, did not know that crucial tidbit about their upcoming dining experience. The chairs are also bolted to the base of the table, with enough space to get in and out upon entry and exit. Once in the air, you are securely strapped into your seat. This was a major dining experience and he hoped that she was adventurous and spontaneous like he thought. Jameson wasn't even sure if she was afraid of heights or not, but he really wanted her to step out on faith and trust him on this one. Actually, he needed her aboard.

"Camilla," he steered her toward the Atomium because the dinner would be near there, so they would have a bird's eye view of the upper sphere. "Are you afraid of heights?"

"Yes," she said without hesitation.

"Are you deathly afraid? Like would you do a rollercoaster?"

"Umm, a rollercoaster is fine. I probably wouldn't do hang gliding or a hot air balloon or anything."

Jameson gulped hard. If she just left it at the rollercoaster, he may have had a chance, but for her to throw in the hot air balloon was not a good sign. This dinner would be similar to being in a tethered balloon. Jameson suddenly got nervous. He didn't want her to freak out and he certainly didn't want them to dismiss the whole notion. He wasn't going to leave her on the ground for an hour while he ate. He hoped for the best, but had a backup plan just in case. Toucan Brasserie. They served seafood, caviar and the finest wines – but that was Plan B. Jameson crossed his fingers and hoped that elevated dining would win.

"Well, we are here," Jameson said as he led her to the area where the crane was situated. There were some other couples there waiting for the stragglers to arrive. Jameson and Camilla arrived about 15 minutes early so he had enough time to persuade her.

"Oh! Okay."

The operator greeted them and handed them a waiver to sign. Although they were fully insured and covered under the Fungroup, the owners and creators of Dinner in the Sky, they did not want to be held liable if someone unhooked themselves or horsed around.

"What's this?" Camilla said as she took a look at the paper.

"Well, baby, this is the dinner in the sky that I was telling you about. See the table and the chairs there?"

Camilla looked over and nodded. "Yeah."

"Well, we will be eating there, but we will be up there," Jameson pointed upward.

Camilla looked upward with her eyes first and then she tilted her head backward to see the top of the crane's neck.

"What?"

"I thought it would be something fun and exciting to try, you know? Please, Camilla trust me."

"Jameson!?" she said in an alarmed tone.

"Trust me."

"I just told you I'm afraid of heights!"

A lady interjected herself in the conversation and patted Camilla on the arm. It sounded like she had some sort of accent that Camilla couldn't quite place. Romanian or Scandinavian perhaps.

"I've been up at least twice. It really is secure and there is nothing to worry about. You forget once you are eating."

"I'm sorry," Camilla told her, "but *we* are talking. Can you excuse us, please?" The lady looked at her a bit offended and slowly backed away. "Thank you!" Camilla turned her attention back to Jameson while she awaited an explanation. "Jameson?"

"I know, I know. If you don't want to do it, I understand, but I wanted us to have a "first" together. I mean you did the Alps the other week. I just thought this would be a piece of cake for you."

"Oh . . .," Camilla pondered. "I don't know, you know? We were on the ground in the Alps. Here, we are dangling."

"I promise it will be fun and I will hold your hand the entire time."

"I can't, Jameson." Camilla looked up at the crane as it hung in the night sky. "It's dark."

"It will be lit up. This is important to me. Can you do it?"

"I don't know." Camilla rocked her body back and forth to calm herself. She alternated her weight from one leg to the other. Some of the other guests were getting strapped in and Jameson didn't want to miss out on two good seats.

"For me, baby. I promise it will be worth it."

Camilla looked into Jameson's eyes. He had protected her all of this time and she had no reason to doubt him now. Absolutely terrified with a ton of questions, she thought about her little Gabe. If something were to happen, he wouldn't see his mother again.

"Hmm," she winced.

"For me. I will make sure you are safe."

"Oh God." Camilla scribbled her name on the paper and took a huge breath. "You owe me big time."

"The biggest. I promise it. Thank you for doing this sweetheart. We will have fun."

The attendant strapped them in their seats and the one male assistant saw Camilla's anxiety. To him, it looked as if she were about to start crying before she closed her eyes. He patted her on the shoulder gently which caused her to open her eyes and then he smiled at her. Camilla tried to smile, but it came out as a frown. She looked over at Jameson who of course was seated next to her. She gripped his hand tightly. The safety specialist went over the rules of the dinner and told them that if anyone needed to go to the restroom, they could do so; it only took about a minute to be lowered down. Camilla silently prayed that no one would need to go. After the procedures and dining experience details were explained, the attendants stepped away and shouted all in unison.

"Ladies and gentlemen, enjoy your dinner in the sky!"

Camilla took a deep breath again. She reached for the napkin and covered her face with it to keep herself from crying. Jameson was stroking her hand and arm rapidly to get her to calm herself. The crane began to slowly lift and the other diners began cheering and clapping. The chefs spoke about the food they would be serving for the evening and made several corny jokes. They asked the different patrons where they were from and if this was the first time dining in this manner.

Camilla could hear all of this going on around her, but couldn't gather herself enough to participate. The chef asked Jameson about them.

"We are visiting from the U.S. Washington, D.C."

"Ahh! She covers her face zis one," the chef said in what sounded to be a French accent. "Is she shy?"

Camilla shook her head behind the napkin and Jameson patted her arm again to comfort her.

"Not shy? Uhh, your wife, she's nervous then, eh?"

"No . . . I'm not his wife," Camilla said in a moderate tone from behind her napkin.

"She will be," Jameson reached in his breast pocket and pulled out a ring box. He picked it up while they were in Amsterdam when Camilla was preoccupied with the cheeses and wooden shoes.

The patrons, who had since turned their attention to the couple because the chef had asked everyone where they were from individually, had all began whooping and cheering.

"She may want to open her eyes for zis one," the French chef said with a smile.

"Camilla?"

"Are we at the top yet?"

"Yes, sweetheart. Please look at me."

She lowered her napkin cautiously and noticed that everyone was looking in her direction.

"Why is everyone looking at me? I'm just a little nervous about the height, I will be fine."

Jameson placed the ring box on her empty plate in front of her. He tapped it lightly as he reached for her hand again. Camilla's mouth dropped and her eyes widened.

"I'm proposing that we get married, Camilla," Jameson said. "Would you do me the honor of being Mrs. Jameson Hedley?"

Shocked, she looked into Jameson's eyes.

"Oh my God. Really honey?"

Jameson chuckled, "Really! Did you take a look around? You see this beautiful view? Meeting you has put me on top of the world and I wanted to propose to you there. Will you?"

Camilla looked around, her shoulders hunched as she clenched the arms of her seat while doing so. The breeze from the night air was gentle and caressed her premature tears away.

"I will!"

Everyone clapped and cheered. Camilla reached over to embrace Jameson. Unbeknownst to her, the chairs were secured to the base of the table but swiveled around to about 45 degrees on either side. When hers turned, she wasn't quite prepared for the motion and she screamed.

"Oh my blessed, God!!"

She gripped Jameson's arm tightly, but only after hitting the plate that held the ring. Her startled movement caused the plate to flip downward in a see-saw motion, which caused the ring box to flip out and down 180 feet below them.

"Oh no!" someone shouted. "The ring!"

Jameson, still allowing Camilla to cling to him looked over as the ring box went sailing downward. Fear and disbelief engulfed his eyes as he peered down in terror.

"Oh shit!" he managed to yell.

Camilla sat straight in her chair and didn't even want to look over her shoulders at all. She turned her head and looked at Jameson. "Baby, I'm so sorry! I had no idea these chairs moved!"

One of the safety attendants radioed down to the folks on the ground to see if they could locate the ring. They were in a controlled space where no tourists were allowed underneath so he assured them that it would be retrieved.

"Oh my gosh! Oh my gosh!! Jameson! Oh no! I ruined your beautiful proposal!" Camilla apologized. Her eyes began to fill with tears. "I'm so sorry!"

Jameson gulped hard and then looked down at the ground again. He wanted to make sure the ring was safe. Thankfully she hadn't opened the box yet and he hoped it remained closed.

Jameson decided then he would never do anything that dealt with heights anymore with Camilla. Instantly feeling bad for convincing her to board, he realized that he shouldn't have pushed. A proposal that was supposed to be something different and memorable now turned into a mess.

"Don't worry about that. We will find it. Are you okay, sweetheart? You scared me!"

"I scared myself! I'm okay now. I just wasn't expecting that. They have to let us down."

"They are looking for it. Let's just enjoy our dinner okay? They will find it. I know it. Let's have a good time. Chef, a glass of wine for everyone, okay? Sorry everyone, she's fine."

They all clapped and cheered while a few made some jokes to lighten the mood. One guy mentioned marriage by skydiving would not be an option while a few laughed. Someone else said if that was a "yes", they wondered what her "no" would've been. They didn't take it too much to heart though. Jameson, while he tried to have a good time couldn't think of anything other than them finding that ring.

They just had to find it, he thought.

35

That evening, Hailey could barely take all of the information that Josephine gave her regarding Ian. It was hard to believe that Ian had been behaving so terribly toward her even after she apologized so immensely. After hearing Josephine's heartache, Hailey instantly began to feel bad for being wrapped up in her own drama so much that she didn't realize what was going on around her. She asked and hoped that Josephine forgave her, which she did. Having her own drama as well, Hailey filled Josephine in on what was going on with her, Bryan and Steve as well. She explained to Josephine that she knew Steve was trying to move on, but having Alex as a bond, it would be hard for him.

"He did not seem too happy about me and Bryan getting married, but hey, Steve had plenty of opportunities to step up. He had time to cheat, so he could've made time to marry me," Hailey barked.

"Sad, but true," I replied to her.

"Enough of that. Girl, you sound exhausted, try to get some rest and this thing with Ian will work out. I'm sure of it. He loves you too much to be this stubborn."

Just then, Hailey's doorbell rang. She rose from her comfortable position and made her way over to the door.

"I gotta go. Besides, I have to find out why Bryan keeps stalling the wedding and why he shaved! He's back to his old look. I will stop by tomorrow, okay?"

"That's fine," I told her before I hung up.

"You're late!" Hailey said as she flung the door open and yanked him inside. "We don't have a lot of time. Get in here!"

Steve walked inside with a sinister smile perched on his lips.

"You should already be undressed."

"Just hush Steve."

"You really *are* bad."

"Excuse me?" Hailey said as she began to get undressed. "You're here, so what does that make *you*?"

"Horny," Steve slipped out of his pants and pulled off his shirt.

"And willing!"

"I told you that I would do anything for you, because I love you. This just takes the fucking cake, but I love it. I get to fuck you still, impregnate you and the kicker, I get to look at Bryan's face knowing that you didn't want his child, but you wanted mine. That's one hell of a gut punch to his ass. Classic."

"Steve please. Don't be a dick about it."

"You think this will work?"

"Yes!" Hailey said, lying back on the couch. Steve looked down at her naked body as he rubbed his erect penis. His eyes were low and seductive as he thought of how sweet the initial insertion would feel to him. It had been over a year since they had sex together and he remembered how much Hailey drove him wild.

"No, not here," he said to her as he reached for her hand and pulled her up to her feet.

"What?"

"I want to fuck you in your bed."

"No!"

"Did you say *no*?" Steve asked with a wry smile. Hailey looked in Steve's eyes and gave him an evil stare. She shook her head and tugged him toward her bedroom.

"You make me sick," she muttered underneath her breath.

After a little over an hour, Steve reemerged and had gotten dressed. Hailey was still in the bedroom taking a shower. Steve made his way to the kitchen and fished around in her fridge for something to drink. The searched stopped when he looked in the lower bin and saw some beer. He grabbed it, slammed the fridge shut and popped the top off with the opener. In a little less than five minutes, he downed the entire beer. He belched, rubbed his stomach and tossed the bottle in the trash.

He wandered out of the kitchen and began looking at some of the photos of her and Alex. Steve wondered where were the photos of him with Alex or if Bryan didn't want to see them and asked her to put them away.

"Ass," Steve mumbled at the thought.

Steve had no problem being used because he felt as though he was getting the better end of the deal. He knew how ominous Hailey could be if she put her mind to it, that's why he tried to stay in her good graces. He never intended for her to find out about his affairs, but when she did, she quietly got her revenge with Bryan.

Hailey had a way of convincing men to do things for her and Steve was no different. However, he silently wondered how long it would be before Hailey would realize he had no intentions of getting Hailey pregnant. He did however, have every intention of fucking her until she maybe – just maybe thought there was the possibility that Steve had gotten a vasectomy shortly after Gabe and Alex were born.

36

By now I was at the start of my eighth month and I couldn't take it anymore. I wanted these kids out of me! I loved them, but they were making me miserable and sleepy all of the time. Ian was still in the house even though he told me over a month and a half ago that he had filed for divorce. I was beginning to think that he was just telling me that to prompt me to give the kids up for adoption. I made my position clear that I would never do that. Having cried enough, it was now time to focus on my children who were going to be here in another month. I had grown tired of his stubbornness and downright nastiness when it came to me. He only did the bare minimum for me, but at least he still did some things for me. After all, I was still his wife.

I hadn't heard too much from Hailey since we last talked. She mentioned something about Bryan getting cold feet or stalling or something. I just couldn't concern myself with that at the present. My stomach kept churning and the kids just couldn't keep still it seemed, so I took a much needed day off. Every time I found a comfortable position, I was soon shifting to find another. Even lying on my back was uncomfortable after a while.

For the first time in a long time, Ian arrived home extremely early today. It was only about one or so and naturally I was surprised to see him. Surprised as well, or maybe perturbed, he gave me a puzzled look from the threshold as he stood with the door open.

"Hey," he said, "you didn't go in?"

"Isn't it obvious?"

He smirked and closed the door behind him. I didn't mean to be sarcastic; it just came out that way. It irritated me when people asked dumb questions. Besides, I was just giving him a taste of his own medicine.

"Are you hungry?" he asked.

"I'm uncomfortable right now," I told him as I shifted around on the couch some more. "I will probably be hungry in a few."

Ian lifted my feet and sat beside me. The rocky motion of his sitting disturbed everything that I just settled. I winced at the discomfort and gave him a scolding look. He put my feet in his lap and patted them gently as a form of an apology.

"Well, I haven't told you often, but you look really great pregnant."

"Thanks," I responded flatly. For me, it was a bit late for compliments. I needed them in months two through eight.

"Did you get your pictures back from the photo shoot?"

"Not yet," I covered my eyes with my forearm as my head rested on the arm of the couch.

"I'm sorry I couldn't take you that day," his apology was beyond tardy. I went to the photo shoot almost two months ago. I didn't want to be too much of a balloon when I went, so I thought five and a half, six months was a good time to go. The photographer was taking an unusually long time but warned me that he was backlogged from several weddings. The anticipation was making me anxious to see how the photos turned out, but more anxious to meet my twin babies.

"I miss us so much, Josephine."

With that, I sat up and flipped my eyes up toward the ceiling and then back at him. He hadn't been this nice in several months, so I was wondering what his angle was.

"Ian, what is this?"

"What is what?"

"That's three comments of concern. What do you want? Why are you attempting to be nice to me?"

Ian clicked his teeth, "Probably because I realized how bad of a husband I've been."

I smacked my lips, "Well, don't worry about it. I've gotten used to it and moved on from it."

Ian began rubbing my feet. "I don't want you to get used to it. I was wrong, Josephine."

"You still are wrong." I lifted my arm and looked at him through one eye. I pulled my feet away from him. "Get away from me, Ian. You stressed me out during this whole pregnancy. I want the last month in peace."

Ian was a bit taken aback by the new attitude of his wife. She was no longer giving into his demands and was prepared to carry on without him. Ian knew that she needed him in the past, but if he had no purpose in her life now, he would feel useless to her. He liked the idea of being needed and being the provider. He took some time to think about the whole pregnancy and her betrayal. Ian tried to get past it on his own, but each time he felt as though he was making forward progress, he just couldn't fathom what she did to him. As a result, his thoughts brought him right back to a deeply treacherous place that was difficult to claw out from.

"I know this has been hard," he said to her.

"You have no idea and you obviously don't and didn't care. So tell me why should I, huh?"

"Josephine, do you even understand the magnitude of how your actions affected me?"

"Yes and I apologized over and over and over again. I've asked you what I need to do so we can move forward and your *only* solution was to get rid of these babies. Are you kidding me? So we are just supposed to act like they don't exist and move on with our lives? Is that it? What soap opera are you starring in baby because it doesn't work like that in the real world!"

"Sweetheart . . ."

Before Ian could finish, I sat up as my face contorted with pain. I held my hand on the side of my belly and rubbed it gently. The pain felt like a huge cramp as I exhaled heavily and began taking quick short breaths.

"Whoa," I said while I continued to breathe. That didn't feel quite right to me.

"You okay baby?"

"I think so," I said and continued to soothe the little ones inside by caressing my stomach.

"You need me to do anything?"

There were several responses that I could've provided him at that moment, but I decided not to hit him with another sarcastic zinger. The only thing I wanted was for the discomfort to go away.

"If that happens again, time it okay?"

"Got it. Where is your bag just in case?"

"It's packed and at the foot of the bed."

"Doctor's number?"

"On the fridge and by the front door," I kept breathing and humming one of Beyonce's latest songs that I never quite knew all of the words to. She seemed to crank out more albums than Prince did in his heyday. I started to break out in a light sweat and my mouth was getting drier than a geek's jokes. *Right now?* I asked myself. Ian and I were about to have it out – it was going to be a major argument. There were some things that needed to be said – things that I didn't say before because I was too sad that he wasn't being supportive and loving. In a way, I was glad the pain came when it did because I was about to throw Ian out of the house. The sheer irony of it all was that I needed him now.

"Do you need anything?"

I thought for a moment and tried to get myself off of the couch gently. Ian rushed over to help me. He stared at me and watched every ginger step that I took as he took them with me.

"I think we should go to the hospital. I don't feel right."

"Okay!" Ian raced upstairs to get my bag. It sounded as if he missed several steps because he was up the stairs in a flash. Returning with the bag, it looked like he took one giant leap from the top of the steps down to the landing. "You ready?"

"Yeah, while I still can. Don't forget the doctor's number. Uh oh!"

Hearing the splash of liquid hitting the floor, my water broke right there in the foyer.

"Oh hell!" Ian yelled.

"Ian! Please," I said in a calm and slightly alarmed tone, "if you start tripping, I will too. We both can't panic right now. Grab that towel from the powder room and put it on the floor. Grab another for me to sit on in the car. I don't have time to change anything!"

Ian stood for a moment frozen as he stared incredulously at the liquid puddle on the floor.

"Ian!" I shouted to bring him back to reality.

He jumped at the sound of my voice and snapped into motion.

We got settled into the car for our journey on the beltway. Ian was carefully rushing to Holy Cross hospital in Silver Spring. Luckily it was mid afternoon, just shortly before the traffic started to become a nightmare. My contractions had gone from five minutes to every two. I was trying to concentrate on my breathing and not on the life threatening pain that was to come with having these twins.

Thankfully, the doctor was close by and ready to get the party started. The doctor administered the epidural after the final sonogram. I was in some serious pain! It felt like someone shot me, stabbed me and then shot me again. I was fearful that the epidural wouldn't fully set in by the time the munchkins would make their appearance. Either way, they were on their way and they were about a month early. What if they hadn't finished developing? I was getting nervous all of a sudden and then I just started crying.

Ian tried to comfort me as did the nurse.

"Don't cry. What's wrong?" Ian asked me.

Between breaths I managed, "They're early. I'm scared."

The nurse, a big boned woman with a vibrant smile, reassured me. "It often happens with twins. You and they will be fine."

My labor didn't last too long, only about an hour and a half. Ian was in the delivery room with me and almost fell three times. If I wasn't so busy concentrating on delivery, I probably would've laughed at him. The first near fall was by far the funniest. His knees buckled and then he tried to straighten up before he hit the floor but his back slammed against the wall instead. Even the nurse glared at him with a smirk.

The first arrival was the baby girl who I named Locke. It was such a powerful sounding name to me, like she could be a superhero. It would be a cool name for her as a child and teen and would transform to a sexy name when she became an adult. About a minute and a half later, my baby boy Hunter arrived. His name was strong to match his loud cries that had an ounce of bass in them. They were the most beautiful babies I'd ever seen. Locke was a tad smaller than Hunter at six pounds and two ounces, while Hunter weighed in at seven pounds even. I was in love.

My tears were ones of happiness as I could hear the cries and whines of my babies. It was mainly Hunter though. I lifted my head to peer over to see them being cleaned up for presentation and noticed that Locke was rather quiet. She flailed her arms around a bit; my guess was she just wanted the cleaning to be over with. Hunter finally settled down after all of the rubbing and probing was completed.

Ian stood out of the way and didn't want to cut any cords at all. He barely even looked at them. The nurse thought his actions were more than strange and she smirked at him with a bit of disgust every so often. I saw Ian wipe his eyes a few times before he clenched them tightly together. After the crying from the babies settled, he tiptoed out of the room. The nurse stared after him eagerly and then turned back around with some confusion in her eyes.

It hurt, but I had my children to comfort me as I comforted them. The doctor placed both in my arms and I couldn't take my eyes off of either for too long. They were settled and quiet, their eyes slowly blinking to adjust to the over head lights.

"Mommy's here," I told them, "and she loves you both so much!"

Just outside of the waiting room, Ian called Steve on the phone.

"Steve here!" he boomed.

"It's Ian man, Josephine just had the twins."

"Aww man! Congratulations! It must've all went down pretty quick, Hailey didn't hear anything!"

"It actually did."

There was slight silence.

"How are you feeling?" Steve asked Ian.

"I don't know."

"Were you in there with her?"

"Of course. I just . . . I couldn't look at the actual birth though."

"Yeah, understandable. That's some sci-fi type shit." He laughed at his own joke. "The kids are fine?"

"Yeah."

"What'd you guys name them? Don't say Jack and Jill, or Romeo and Juliet. I hope y'all didn't do that twin bullshit."

"No, she named them. Locke and Hunter."

"Okay, okay. Well which is which?"

"Locke is the girl, Hunter is the boy."

"Aww man, that's hot. I like those. Sounds like a detective show that comes on every Thursday at nine. Locke and Hunter," he chuckled.

More silence.

"What's up, man?" Steve asked.

"They aren't mine, man!"

"Do you think those babies know that? Or even care?"

Ian took a deep breath and a long pause. He nodded, but Steve of course couldn't see. "I gotta go." He disconnected the line and paced the hall for a few moments.

Ian wanted to call Josephine's mother, but she couldn't stand his guts at the moment. The last time he talked to her, she knew about him not wanting to be involved with Josephine's pregnancy or the twins and she unleashed all sorts of expletives that he had never heard from her. The only thing he could do was quietly pass Josephine the phone. Recalling that tongue lashing, he decided to send her mother a text instead. It was less evasive and she couldn't curse at him, at least not where he would hear.

Ian fired off a text to her: Twins arrived. Locke and Hunter. Mother doing well. Holy Cross Hospital, Silver Spring.

He locked his phone and tucked it back in its holster and headed toward the delivery room. The nurse came out and restrained him from going back inside.

"You should wait in her room. We will be taking her and the kids there momentarily. Go." She said as she scooted him in the direction of her room.

Ian looked down at the nurse a bit miffed, but he slowly began to oblige her request. He thought on it a bit and figured it may have been because of the germs or something. However, it was the nurse's approach that Ian had a problem with. Realizing that it was the same nurse that looked at him strangely in the delivery room, he opted to address her.

"Something bothering you?" he asked her.

She was clearly bound with deciding to give a blanket response or offer an honest opinion. She gnashed her teeth and huffed before she spoke.

"She needs you and you seemed very unattached. I've seen men pass out in the delivery room, but then they get it together and are supportive, you were just absent. Childbirth is the hardest thing a woman's body endures. I'm sorry, I didn't want to say anything, but you asked."

"Well, I asked because you were shoving me and said "Go". Do you do that to everyone?"

"Sorry," she said and quickly headed back to the delivery room.

Ian sauntered into Josephine's room to wait for her. He thought about what the nurse said to him – *unattached* and *absent*. Indeed because he felt as though he contributed nothing to the lives of Locke and Hunter, which was none of the nurse's business. First off, his pain had not ended in that aspect, and his feeling of betrayal was a close second. Ian pulled out his phone and tapped the face of it several times. He inhaled and exhaled deeply and then pressed the button to send the message.

About twenty minutes or so later, the nurse, the same one that voiced her opinion to Ian, wheeled Josephine in the room. There was another nurse that wheeled in the babies.

"Alright daddy," the first nurse told Ian, "mommy needs some tender loving TLC, okay?"

Ian glared at her and moved out of the way of the gurney. When he saw the babies making their way into the room, he turned slightly away from them.

I noticed that Ian had done that each time the threat of making eye contact with them was present. He didn't even want to see them. The nursed fussed over me a bit more and then she smiled.

"Congratulations!"

I smiled back at her and she closed the door behind her as she left.

"Well, uh, you doing okay?" he asked me.

"Surprisingly, yeah."

"Anything else you need?"

"You act like you have somewhere to be."

"Well, no. It's just I texted your mom so she may be on her way in and I know she doesn't want to see me."

The babies cooed and stirred to which Ian turned to look out of the window.

"Ian? What are you doing?"

"What?" he said, his attention still at the window.

"Do you want to hold your son or your daughter?"

Ian's head dropped in an attempt to cease his thoughts. It didn't help.

"They aren't mine!" He raised his voice a bit and I gasped from the shock.

A knock was heard at the door and Ian turned toward it. I tried to gather myself and prayed that no one heard his statement.

"Come in," he said in a stern tone.

A small framed man entered. He had on a rather loose fitting gray suit that looked like it was over another suit.

"Josephine?"

"Yes, that's me? Do I know you?"

He handed her a wad of folded papers and said, "You've been served."

"What?"

The loose suited man walked out and I looked in Ian's direction. His head was bowed and eyes cast downward as he rubbed his chin. Stuffing his hands in his pockets, he sighed.

"You do this today? Right now?" I asked him. He couldn't look at me or respond. "That's it. I'm not going to subject myself to you making me feel guilty every day while we are married for something I keep apologizing for. You won't even look at these babies and they need you. I need you! If you want to go, you get your ass out now and don't ever come back. Ever!"

I started crying and couldn't catch my breath. I heard Locke beginning to whine a bit before she began to bawl gently. A new mother and I didn't even know what to do to comfort her while I was breaking down myself.

"Josephine?"

"You're heartless, just get out! I can't take it anymore! Go now!" Just then Hunter began to cry as well. I really wished Ian would've cradled his son and whispered to him that everything was going to be alright, that he would always protect him and teach him the ways of becoming a man. I wanted Ian to be Locke's first love and blueprint for what to look for in a husband. The dream was over now. It was up to me to do the best that I could and I didn't know where to start.

Before Ian headed out, Hailey and Bryan rushed in with presents and balloons cheering for us with smiles that matched their enthusiasm.

"Hi Mommy! Hi Daddy!" Hailey boasted. She leaned over and gave me a hug. I tried to smile behind the tears that she barely noticed. Hailey just wanted to get her hands on the babies.

"Look at her! Shhs, don't cry sweetie," she told Locke.

Bryan extended his hand to Ian to offer congratulations, but he brushed passed him and walked out of the room. Hailey stopped her bouncing and humming once she noticed that he left.

"Where is he going?" she looked at me and then called after Ian through the door toward the hallway, "Where are you going?"

"Hailey? No. He's gone."

"What?"

"Is everything alright Jacqueline?"

"Bryan," Hailey interjected, "for the last time, her name is Josephine. Why do you keep calling her Jacqueline, baby?"

"I'm sorry! I don't know why that name is stuck!" he told me.

"Go get some practice, get her baby boy over there and be careful honey."

Bryan carefully walked over to Hunter and scooped him up gently, being careful to support his head.

"What happened?" Hailey said as she continued to cradle Locke who was now silent. "What did he do now?"

"He had me served."

Hailey's eyes bucked from the surprise.

"Right here," I told her and her mouth dropped, "today, just now."

"No he didn't."

"Served? You guys are divorcing?" Bryan jumped in the conversation.

"Bryan?" Hailey said as her head tilted a bit to indicate that this was girl talk. He mouthed the words 'sorry' and continued coddling Hunter.

"Yes, he did. I told him to go and never come back. I can't do it anymore Hailey. I apologized, several times. I'm not giving my babies away to a stranger. No. He can have us in his life or be alone! Those are his choices. My only choice is to take care of my kids."

I reached for Hunter because Bryan looked awkward with him. He carefully walked over to me and placed him in my arms.

"I'm done."

"Wow," was all Hailey could say, "I would've never expected this from Ian. I still think he will eventually come around though. He won't find anyone better than you."

"I appreciate that," I told her. "But for now I have to figure out how to be a single mother."

37

Once Hailey and Bryan had their fill of coddling the twins and comforting Josephine, they headed home. It took a while for Josephine's mother to arrive because she lived in Fredericksburg, Virginia. The traffic during the time of day that she was traveling was horrendous to put it mildly. Hailey stayed at the hospital to keep Josephine company until then, especially when she discovered that Ian had served her divorce papers right there. Once the nurses took the twins away, Josephine immediately signed the papers. She quickly double checked to make sure she didn't miss anything. Hailey knew that Josephine had signed them out of anger and strongly felt that she would change her mind. She more so hoped that Ian would change his and stop being bullheaded about the situation.

After their hospital visit, Hailey picked up Alex from the sitter and they all headed home. Alex was still asleep from the ride from the sitter's so Hailey immediately rushed him upstairs before he awoke.

"Those were the cutest babies," Hailey told Bryan after they both got settled.

"They were. Locke, is that her name?" he asked and Hailey nodded with a smile. "She's a small baby."

Bryan went into the kitchen and opened the fridge. He whistled some Jamaican song he remembered the locals used to sing regularly as he got a cold bottle of Corona. He fished around in the utensil drawer to find the bottle opener. Once he did, he cracked the bottle open and downed the suds until he drank about half.

"Ah!" he uttered after swallowing it down. He didn't realize how thirsty he was for a beer. He walked around the kitchen while he sipped the remainder of the beer. He looked around at nothing in particular – just passing time.

In an instant, he froze in his tracks. As if he realized that he forgotten something urgent, he put the bottle down and swung open the refrigerator door. He yanked the drawer open and noticed four Corona's left. He exhaled, nodded his head gently and closed everything back to its original state. He poured the rest of the beer out and tossed the bottle in their recycling bin.

Hailey entered the kitchen and stood behind Bryan. She wrapped her arms around him and caressed his chest and moved down to his midsection. Bryan turned around and looked down at her smiling face.

"You have time for me?" she asked in a seductive manner.

He continued to look down at her with a rigid expression.

"Whoa. What's that about?" She pulled away from him and took a step back, her hands still on his waist. "Are you okay?"

"Is there something you want to tell me?"

Hailey stepped even further backward until her back was pressed against the oven door. With concern in her eyes and silence on her lips she looked at Bryan puzzled. She folded her arms and said nothing.

"Well?" he asked.

"Bryan," she began, "I have no idea what you think I need to tell you."

"Oh yeah?"

"Yeah."

"Well, let me ask. How is your pregnancy going? When is your next appointment?"

"Oh! Uhm, it's next week. Why?"

"I think I'll go with you. I should be more involved."

"Well, you don't have to. There's really nothing to it, a poke there, swab here. Nothing really."

"I should be involved in our child's development as much as possible. Even if it means as early as the womb. Don't you think?" he folded his arms and smiled a bit.

"Yeah, why not?" Hailey reached in the fridge and grabbed an apple. Bryan watched her closely as she washed it off in the sink and made a loud crunch when she bit it.

"Why are you looking at me?" she chuckled nervously.

"Nothing."

Hailey took another bite from her apple and smirked at him to indicate that his actions were a bit peculiar to her. She headed toward the living room but looked back at him with her eyes tapered slightly before doing so. She shook her head and exited the kitchen. He followed her.

"Well," she said, "I've been meaning to talk to you. I know we discussed going to the courthouse to have the marriage done quickly, but that was a while ago. Are you getting cold feet?" she chuckled.

"No. I just don't think it's time yet."

Hailey looked at him confused.

"What I mean is, what's the rush?" he told her.

"Well, I thought we were trying to do it before I got too big for a dress?"

"Why would you get too big?"

Hailey gave him another perturbed look.

"From drinking beer?" he asked.

"What?"

"Beer. I just bought a six pack about a week ago. I haven't had any until tonight, but there's only four bottles left."

"What are you talking about?"

"Go check it out. I know I didn't have any beer last week."

Hailey disappeared into the kitchen. Bryan could hear her fumbling around in the refrigerator before she closed it. She took a moment to come back into the living room. Bryan thought she was probably thinking of a lie or some elaborate story to tell him about the missing Corona.

"So what? Are you sure you didn't drink it?"

"I'm positive! I had wine last week. *Not* beer!"

"Well, I don't know then."

"Did my *pregnant* fiancé drink one?"

"What?" Hailey's voice climbed an octave when she asked. "Of course not."

"Well if you didn't have one, who did?"

"What are you saying?" Hailey weakly defended her case to Bryan. She knew her and Steve had been together last week and he must've gotten one before he left her. She wanted to give Steve a piece of her mind for being so careless, but it wasn't his fault. Bryan was being insecure but she knew that he had every right to be.

"Well, let's see . . . what am I saying? Okay, let me just take the simple route and ask an easier question. Who drank my damn beer?"

"No one, okay?"

"Hailey."

"I took a sip. I was feeling nostalgic and poured the rest out. I didn't want you to know, okay? Sorry!"

Bryan shook his head and scoffed.

"Damn," he said. "You are good. You really are. I wish I had part of your skills. And you do it like it's nothing. Second nature."

"What are you talking about?"

"Lie."

Hailey guffawed and raised her hand slightly in his direction. "I'm certainly not alone there, huh?"

"Me? You're suggesting that I'm a liar?"

"Yeah."

"Excuse me?"

"Did you tamper with that condom, Bryan?"

The inside of Bryan's mouth turned ice cold. He swallowed hard and his knees felt wobbly. Wondering how on earth she could have possibly known, he suspected she had hidden cameras in the house.

"What?"

"Mmm, that would be a yes," Hailey confirmed her own accusation. "I understand why though."

"You understand?" Bryan grew a bit concerned that she was not upset by the discovery or with Bryan's answer.

"I understand that you want a child. You thought Alex was yours a few years ago. You ran away when he wasn't. Now that we have the chance to reconnect, you wanted to make sure we'd always stay that way, huh?"

"Come on," was all Bryan could say followed by a nervous chuckle.

"Okay, so I'm wrong?"

"Hailey, please."

"Yeah, that's what I thought," Hailey said as she began to walk upstairs to dismiss him and the conversation. Bryan began to follow her and then halted. He did not know where this conversation was going to lead, but it needed to happen tonight. Watching her with anger in his eyes while she ascended the stairs, he shook his head, took a deep breath and followed to confront her.

"Unlike you," he yelled, which startled Hailey, "I don't have to lie!"

She clutched her chest to calm herself from the shocking volume in his voice. Her eyes were widened as he slowly approached her.

"Yeah, I did. I messed with the condom because I wanted us to finally be *us*. I'm fed up with Steve and you both actually. I hate that he gets to come around and still has a piece of you. I love you more than anything and he loves you out of obligation."

"Why did you do that, Bryan? That's so unfair! You don't have to carry a child! Your body doesn't undergo any type of physical stress like mine. You can't make that decision *for* me!"

"Well it doesn't matter now, does it!?" Bryan yelled.

"What?"

"You had a fucking abortion so it doesn't matter now, right?"

Hailey covered her mouth as she gasped. Her eyes began to water before she could even think of stifling any tears. She was bereft of utterances as she looked at Bryan with fear and remorse. She shook her head slowly in disbelief that her wretched action had been found out by him. However, she had no idea how he knew.

"How . . .," she choked on her words, "how did you know? How?"

"It's true?"

She slouched down on the edge of the bed and softly nodded her head.

"You weren't going to tell me?" he rubbed his chin roughly. "Were you?"

More tears flowed from Hailey's eyes as she shook her head. She looked up at Bryan, her eyes watery and apologetic. He clenched his jaws tight and glared at Hailey.

"So what were you going to do? How were you going to fake that pregnancy?"

Hailey covered her face with her hands as she silently sobbed behind them. "Bryan, please."

"Don't lie to me anymore!" his voice boomed and Hailey shook from the intensity. She looked at him, eyes crammed with anxiety. He stood over her, his hands by his side, chest protruding. He huffed quickly as his brows angled downward toward his eyes.

"Fine. Fine. I was going to tell you that I miscarried but I thought that would've been too much for you and that you'd want to try again. So," she stalled, "I was going to get Steve . . . to get me pregnant and pawn it off as yours. I'm sorry, but I don't want mixed matched children and different baby's fathers! I didn't even want any more kids!"

"Wait, wait . . . you said that you were going to have Steve fuck you until you got pregnant and then tell me it was mine?"

She sighed and looked up at Bryan from her seated position on the bed. She didn't want to relive her confession by repeating it.

"That's what I *thought* you said," Bryan told her. He turned slightly; the pain of the news wrenched his stomach. He looked back at Hailey and spread his hand wide and backhanded her across her face. Hailey rocked back a bit on the bed and she tried to regain her seated position. She placed a comforting hand on her face as her mouth was agape from the shock.

"Get out motherfucker!" she yelled at him. "Get out!"

Bryan did not offer an apology. Instead he looked at Hailey, his eyes requesting forgiveness once he realized exactly what he had done. He reached for her but she smacked his hands away.

"Go!" she yelled at him again.

Understanding the severity of his actions, he became upset with himself for letting his temper take over to the point where he would be physical with the person he claimed to love. He wanted to hold her and tell her profusely how sorry he was, but he knew in his heart that it was forever over with Hailey. The only thing that he could do was respect her wishes, try to forget about her, and leave.

38

Jameson, Camilla and Gabe were now headed to Lille, France which wasn't too far from Belgium. Thankfully, the ring was recovered and it looked stunning on her finger. Jameson admitted that he had never been so scared in all of his life. Not because of the height of the dinner, but because he thought that something so precious that he took his careful time to find for her was forever lost. Camilla thought about calling Josephine, but it would've been too awkward. They didn't speak too much before she left and now to call back to say "I'm engaged", was a bit lame in her opinion. There certainly was no need to tell Hailey. Their kids were brothers but other than that they had no real ties to one another.

Jameson had timed the trip perfectly so that they would not miss the Lille Festival. Several concerts and dance presentations were held among other arts and cultural events. There would be a lot to do and even more to see.

When they arrived at the festival, there were all sorts of musicians in one area and a ton of vendors selling arts and crafts in another. It was in a large square and Gabe wanted to see it all. Jameson hoisted Gabe up on his shoulders so he would get a bird's eye view of everything. While he sat atop Jameson's shoulders, he rattled off all of his questions. There were festival goers that stopped to talk to Gabe and as usual, they gave him gifts for some reason.

Jameson turned to me after the third person gave him something and said, "Maybe he will be president or something."

"I will have to buy him some hair dye. You see President Obama's hair? It's almost all white! He went in with thick black curly hair, now it's white and thinning!"

"Well look at Bill Clinton, he didn't come out looking the same," Jameson said.

"He went into office, fine and sexy and walked out looking like George Washington. It's a shame."

Jameson looked at Camilla for a moment before he started to laugh. He settled down from the ridiculous vision and noticed that Camilla was looking at some sari garments. She held one up toward the sky and smiled. It was blue with gold trim. Jameson watched her adoration for Southern Asian culture and smiled. She then held it up to shield her nose and mouth, revealing only her eyes. Camilla turned to face Gabe and Jameson. Jameson was instantly turned on by how sexy she looked in that moment.

"Ooo Mommy is pretty!" Gabe said.

"Yes Gabe, she certainly is," Jameson told her, his stare intensifying.

Camilla slowly dropped the cloth and smiled to herself. She folded the material up and placed it back on the table.

"Why don't you get it?"

"Oh no, I mean it's beautiful, but no."

"You know, why don't we just get married in Paris?" Jameson asked her. "We will be headed that way soon, and then it's down to Italy. I was hoping we'd be man and wife before we got to Venice."

"Wow. We've been gone for almost six months now. I just can't believe how beautiful and how generous you've been to us."

"Well, you know why right?"

Camilla grinned and then shook her head.

"You don't?" he asked and she shook her head more elaborately. "It's because I love you both."

Camilla blushed.

"I love you too, Mommy!" Gabe chimed in.

"What about Mr. Hedley, Gabe?" Camilla asked him.

Gabe put his little hands on top of Jameson's head and lightly patted it. "Yes, I love him too."

Camilla looked down at Jameson because she wanted to savor the look on Jameson's face. He could barely keep his feelings in check as he knew that Gabe genuinely meant it. Jameson knew that these were two people he needed in his life and that where ever they were, it was home.

*   *   *   *

Within the next week they had settled into Paris. Camilla never thought that she'd get a chance to see the Eiffel Tower up close. She thought her traveling days were over since she had Gabe, but Jameson made her dreams a reality. They ate tons of bread, cheese and drank the tastiest wines. They visited the Sacred Church and burned candles near the altar. Camilla prayed silently that this feeling would stay with her, even during the rough times of their relationship. She loved this man with her whole heart and never thought that she had the capability of doing so after all of the failed relationships she'd endured.

Just as Jameson had wanted, they were going to be married in Paris. Of course they would have to have an official license once they returned to the states, but the immediate desire was to wed in a romantic setting. Jameson flew his clergyman over and he brought his wife with him. Those two had never been to Paris, so they were absolutely enjoying the tours, the chocolate and the shopping.

Even though it was getting a bit cooler, the couple still wanted a simple outdoor wedding. Camilla wore a modest gown and Jameson wore linen. Even though they were in Paris, they dressed Bohemian for the affair. Little Gabe wore his linen slacks and loose fitting shirt. He was overjoyed for his mother even though he didn't fully understand what marriage meant at his young age. To him it was just like having a huge birthday party. They wed at the Chateau de Versailles. Its manicured grounds were designed in an intricate design over acres of greenery. They were able to find an area to have the nuptials with a bit of peace, although there were other visitors of the park that stopped to see the ceremony. Even though Camilla knew nothing about the people who stopped their tour to see a couple's vows exchanged, she felt as though they were their guests. To her, it was how it was meant to be and she would not have had it any other way. Because these strangers stopped by, she knew that those people wanted nothing but the best for her and Jameson. The positive thoughts would transcend through the life of their marriage and that was exactly what she needed.

That evening, before the consummation of their marriage, Jameson knelt in front of Camilla and began massaging her feet. She closed her eyes tightly as his fingers molded to the arch of her feet and felt warm on them. She smiled as his hands moved from her ankles to her calves. He kissed her shins tenderly.

"Mrs. Hedley?" he asked.

She opened her eyes and smiled wide. Her hand caressed the side of his face and trailed to his shoulder. "Yes honey?"

"Did I tell you today that I love you?"

"Yes, did I?"

"You did. But I will tell you again. I love you."

"I love you too, Jameson."

He leaned back on his knees and took a deep breath. "I have something to tell you."

Camilla's facial expression changed from joy to one of concern. His tone did not necessarily put her at ease because she couldn't imagine what on earth he would say to her – especially now.

"Okay," Camilla exhaled softly and squared her shoulders as she sat more erect. Because of all her bad relationships, she was expecting some terrible blow to her ego – something that may make her heart explode for good this time. Was it that he had another wife, he also loved men, he had several children, he just wanted to see if she would marry him . . . Camilla had no idea what treacherous news awaited her. She was not prepared to feel duped because she left her life in D.C. to follow through on an opportunity for a whirlwind romance that led to marriage. For her, there was no turning back and she wasn't emotionally equipped to deal with yet another disappointment.

"What is it?" she asked. She pulled her hands away from him and put them in her lap.

"Do you remember our first date, on my yacht?"

"Of course," Camilla was still emotionless.

"Why did you sign that document?"

"What document?" Camilla had forgotten for a moment and then remembered. "Oh, that. I didn't want any of your money that's why. I just wanted you to love and respect me. That's why I signed it."

"You know that it entitles you to nothing if I pass away?"

Camilla sighed. "Yes, I know that. You've been stolen from before?"

Jameson nodded. "The other women loved my money not me. I guess like you, I just wanted to be loved."

"I do love you."

"I know you do. Not because you signed the document, but you never brought it up again. You let me love you and you let your son love me. I wanted to tell you . . .," Jameson started and held her hands in his, "I tore up that document. The same night you signed it."

"What?"

Jameson shrugged and scoffed, "I just knew you were showing me who you were and that was all I needed to see. I'm sorry that I put you through that. I just needed to make sure."

Camilla caressed his face again, "It's okay. I'm here for you and I know you love me. Let's just make this a great marriage."

"Well, you know when we return, there may be some interviews and cameras, right?"

"Bring it on!" Camilla giggled and planted a firm but moist kiss on Jameson's lips. He lifted her and placed her more comfortably on the bed.

He kissed the slope of her neck as she threw her head back in ecstasy. He massaged her breasts gently and nibbled on her shoulders. Camilla rubbed his shoulder blades in a circular motion and caressed the narrow part of his back.

She helped him out of his pants and he helped lift her dress over her head. She wore white lace underwear with a matching garter suspender belt that secured her white thigh high stockings on her legs. Jameson sucked air between his clenched teeth making a slurping sound when he looked at her laced-donned body.

"Oh my God," he whispered.

"You like," she asked seductively.

"I love."

He kissed her chest and down to her stomach. Camilla arched her back as her body became limp with anticipation. Jameson carefully unfastened her garter clasp from her stockings as Camilla bent her body forward and raised one leg after the other to slowly slide off her hose. Jameson knelt between her legs. He kissed her ankles and calves yet again to show his pleasure. When she was free from all of her garments, Jameson buried his face between her legs and Camilla's eyes closed in delight. Moments later he climbed on top of her, his breath caressing her mouth before he kissed it, and consummated their marriage.

39

Since Donovan blindsided Tamar and left her home, she continued to submerge herself into her work. The idea of her going to any happy hours was becoming more and more obsolete. She attended a few live jazz sets at Blues Alley and hung out a few times at Half Note. Being as attractive as she was, she certainly had no problems drawing the attention of men and a few women too. Even Taj sent her a text the other week just to see how she was doing, but Tamar promptly deleted it. She had nothing else to do with Taj and certainly had no intentions of ever speaking to him again.

There was talk at the law office that Tamar may possibly make partner, but she wasn't so sure about that. After all that happened over the last several months, she wanted to relocate. She was already looking at taking the bar in several other states. Arizona was a consideration – Scottsdale to be specific. Tamar was torn. She knew that her friend Josephine needed her after Ian decided to leave her to care for two children on her own, but Tamar needed to regenerate. With barely an appetite for food or life, she needed to get back to her old self. She still hadn't gotten over the way that Donovan left and she had no closure. With the distinct possibility of never receiving that, she tried her best to press forward. The process was taking a lot longer than she had hoped.

Even though Tamar wouldn't wish for anyone's career to dissolve, she didn't have to worry about Celeste any more. Celeste was disbarred for misappropriation and unethical use of funds. Apparently, the company car and inflated salary wasn't enough for her. The percentage over what she billed the clients, was going into an off-shore account and on her lavish wardrobe to include purses, jewelry and shoes. They were all confiscated and she had to pay a $250,000 fine. She was ordered to serve a two year sentence in a minimum security facility and another two years of parole afterward. Greed may satisfy a temporary desire, but the desire wasn't worth the consequences.

Oh well.

There was a meeting at the law office regarding cyber-attacks and Tamar got to thinking about doing some checks and balances of her account. She had almost all of her bills set up on auto pay and her payroll deposited automatically. She had an idea of course of what her balance should be, but she neglected checking it as often as she wanted. After the meeting, she logged into her account online and checked her balance.

She typed on the keyboard as her eyes scanned the various screens to reveal her account balance. When she reached the final screen, her jaw dropped and she sat back in her chair because her torso fell limp.

"What?!" she quietly uttered. "No. That can't be right."

With this Celeste conviction and inquisition, the last thing Tamar needed was a ridiculous bank account that could raise suspicion. Tamar snatched the phone from the cradle and called the bank. When the service representative answered, Tamar hung up and thought it would be a bad idea to call from the office.

"I'll call from my car. Oh my goodness."

Tamar could barely concentrate on her briefs as she could do nothing but think of her account balance. When her day was over, she headed to her car and called the bank.

"Yes, I'm calling to check well . . . to verify my balance please," she asked the representative.

"Okay, let's see. It is . . . my computer is a little slow right now. Hold on," the rep told her. After a few long seconds, she came back to Tamar. "Okay, my apologies for that. Let's see. As of midnight yesterday, your available balance closed at $1,437,962.58."

"I'm confused," she told her.

"Uh, let's see," she tapped a few keys on her computer and reaffirmed. "No, that's correct. There were three deposits from another account with this bank.

All for equal amounts. For the deposit amounts we had to verify the transactions twice and yes, they are fine."

"From who? I'm still confused," Tamar chuckled.

"Uhm, it doesn't give me that information. Just an account number and unfortunately I'm prohibited from providing those details. But yes, that is the correct balance. Is there anything else that I can help you with today?"

"No, thank you for checking."

Tamar still had no answers, but she felt that it would be revealed to her soon. With nowhere to go and nothing to do at the moment, she went straight home, still figuratively scratching her head at the deposits. She checked her mailbox and sifted through the few pieces of mail as she headed up her driveway. Her feet were stuck as she saw a piece of mail addressed from Donovan.

"What?" she said to herself.

She closed the door behind her and tore the letter open while she stood in the foyer. Her purse and briefcase were still hooked on her shoulder while she read.

Tamar,

I'm so terribly sorry about the way that I left you. I wanted to see you the very next day but I knew that we were being watched. After Taj paid me to leave you, he threatened harm if I reached out to you. You know that I would not leave you or leave in that way. But I'm begging for you to forgive me. I want to be with you and only you. Since things have cooled off a bit, I will be at the Annapolis Marina every day this week from six to eight in the evening if you want to talk. I will explain everything. I love you and I miss you.

Donovan

Tamar's mouth became dry and her eyes watered. She wanted so much to believe the words on the paper. She didn't know what to do. She wanted to see him and get an explanation. She wanted to smack his face and beat his chest while she screamed to him how bad he hurt her. The other side of her wanted to make him suffer by not seeing him so he could wonder about her for the rest of his life. Obviously, she was still hurt, but was relieved that he hadn't forgotten about her. Tamar had some thinking to do and she would make a decision only after she had played out all scenarios in her mind.

Tamar contemplated for a few days. She wasn't trying to brush him off, she was merely wondering how the conversation would go and if she was ready to confront him without having any contact with him for over a month. She speculated if he had done anything different to his appearance, like shave off his hair or grew a moustache. He didn't seem like he would be the type to do anything drastic, but then again, he didn't seem like he would've left her for money either.

She read his letter at least 100 times if not more, wondering if there were any hidden messages buried beneath his words. There were a few things that tripped her up in the letter that she was curious about. The fact that he knew they were being watched and that Taj threatened harm was the major thing that concerned her. The other was since he wanted to meet in Annapolis, was he still in the area or did he leave completely and came back? He said that he would explain everything, but the impression she got was that he would explain it only if she met up with him. She only had a few more days.

This Friday morning started no differently than Tamar's others – a shower, getting dressed, a cup of coffee before she left her home to go to work. The office seemed fine; the cases were trickling in slowly despite the bad press they had received regarding Celeste. That was another reason why Tamar was hesitant to accept a partnership there.

She sat at her desk, counting down the hours, still wrestling with herself emotionally if she wanted to see Donovan or just leave well enough alone. At quitting time, she decided to just head home, take a nice long bubble bath and drink a bottle of her favorite wine. Yes, the whole bottle.

She drove home in silence, only listening to the roll of the tires against 495's pavement and barely realizing how she'd made it as far as she had. This was the last day to see Donovan according to his letter. She didn't think that he would stick around past Friday, she just assumed today was it. Tamar steered her car over toward the right lane as she was a bona fide left-laner whenever she drove on the beltway. In the next half of a mile, her exit was approaching. She tried to take her mind off of him for just a moment when she turned on her radio.

Alicia Key's song "If I Ain't Got You" was playing. Not only that, it was on the chorus.

Some people want it all. But I don't want nothing at all. If it ain't you baby. If I ain't got you baby. Some people want diamond rings. Some just want everything. But everything means nothing. If I ain't got you, you, you!

Alicia's words, coupled with the loud huskiness of her voice, bore holes through Tamar's soul. It was as if she was pleading for Tamar to not be so stubborn but to see this man and hear his explanation. If afterward, she decided to go, then do it after speaking her peace to him.

Just as Alicia began to moan before beginning the chorus again, Tamar stayed on the beltway and headed toward route 50 for Annapolis.

"What am I doing?" she mumbled to herself.

This wasn't like her. Tamar was so used to letting men go and never looking back, but this time it was different. Her heart ached for him and her body yearned for his touch. Tamar always loved Donovan, it was because she was in love that she couldn't find the off switch to her emotions. She needed an explanation, but most of all she needed him.

She barreled down route 50 and made it to Annapolis in half an hour. She looked at her dashboard clock, it read 7:26. By the time she found parking and headed toward the marina, it was 7:53. *Please be here*, she thought to herself as she walked quickly toward the pier area where the benches flanked either side. She stretched her neck to try to see several feet in front of her, maybe to catch a glimpse of his silhouette to give her hope that he may still be there. She trotted toward the pier and saw no one.

Her shoulders dropped with defeat and she looked in all directions, anticipating a tall figure that may be walking away because the wait was too long. She glared at her watch, 7:59. Just as she looked at it, the time changed to eight.

Feeling defeated, she rested on the bench; staring in the distance at the well lit restaurants, jealous of the couples sharing intimate moments together.

Her fingers fiddled with one another as she rested her hands in her lap – her eyes looking down on them while she contemplated what to do. She'd missed her opportunity. If only she'd come the day she received the letter. Or perhaps it just wasn't meant to be. This was the universe's way of affirming that they were not soul mates. Despite the hard times, the games and the deception, they were able to move past it. At least she had memories and a million dollars added to her bank account. But it still wasn't enough or what she wanted.

She rocked backward to give her leverage before she stood. There was no use hanging around, she had to fight the traffic headed back to her now lifeless home. She slowly walked down the pier back toward the loading area, her head down, which was something she rarely, if ever, did. She made it to the grassy area and still looked around but there was no sign of him. It was 8:10, and Tamar figured by about 7:30 he grew tired of waiting and left anyway. That sinking feeling she had when he first left, returned around her sternum again. She patted it lightly to soothe it as she stifled her tears.

"Hey sexy!" he called to her.

Tamar stopped in her tracks and then turned slowly in the direction of the voice. When she saw him, she exhaled slowly. He smiled and then erased it. She wanted to run into his arms but told herself to play it cool. *Gosh, he was fine*, she thought.

"I thought you left," which was not what she wanted to say.

"No, I was on another pier." He stopped in front of her and smiled tenderly. He wanted to grab her, kiss her and make love to her, all right there.

"So, I got your note."

"I'm glad that you did. You want to have a seat?" he gestured toward the benches.

Without speaking, Tamar walked toward the benches with Donovan close behind her. She parked herself and folded her arms in front of her.

"Your note said you wanted to explain everything. So go."

Donovan realized that this was not going to be a loving reunion, no matter how bad he wanted it to be. He clearly saw the disappointment in Tamar's eyes and he adjusted his demeanor accordingly. Meaning, he wanted to touch and comfort her, but understood that she may not want that.

"Uhm, first of all Tamar, I'm so very sorry that I left like that. You know that is not what I'm about."

"It's the money then?" Tamar told herself that she wouldn't interrupt him, but couldn't resist. She sighed and held up an apologetic hand. "Sorry."

"No, no. I deserved that. So you saw the deposit I take it?"

"Yeah. Why did you do that?"

"Babe, you know we are Bonnie and Clyde, George and Weezie, thick and thin all the way. You really think I was gonna let some Bollywood, Calvin Klein model reject dude keep me away from my baby?"

Tamar crossed her arms tighter and stared at him, unable to comprehend what he was speaking of. "I'm lost."

"Tamar, this guy offered me two million dollars to get out of your life. I know how his type operates. And I bet he tried to offer you the world in return to make up for paying me to leave you, am I right?"

Tamar just stared at him and continued to listen. He was right, but she didn't want to tell him so.

"Wait . . .," Donovan reared back a bit, "are you guys together?"

"Negative."

"Okay. I just needed to ask. But . . .," he chuckled, "as far as I'm concerned that fool just gave me two million dollars. Well gave *us* two mill."

"Say what?"

"Yeah. Think about it. He flexed his puny muscles, well . . . his bodyguard's muscles, and tried to keep me away by saying 'you're being watched'. I realized after a few weeks, that he wasn't watching me. The damage was done. He played me, I'll give him that, he used money to make me leave and in a manner that I wouldn't, just to piss you off and keep you angry with me. I get it. I just can't believe that fool gave up two million that easy. But I figured if I contacted you and he tried to kill me or whatever, at least you'd be taken care of with the mill. I don't care about the money, Tamar. All I ever wanted was you."

"Hmm. Well what about that woman?"

Donovan chuckled and shook his head. "I never met her, he couldn't produce her, he never mentioned her again, nothing. He just wanted me away from you."

"I just . . . I don't know what to think."

"It's not about thinking, what do you feel?" he reached for her hands and held them tightly. He looked in her eyes and awaited a response.

After a moment, Tamar peered back at him, her eyes filled with water. "You hurt me."

Ashamed, Donovan bowed his head and let her continue.

"Never . . . never has anyone made me feel like I wanted to die than live without them. I don't want to feel like that again."

"I understand," he said.

"What do you want from me?"

"I want you! Just you!" he pleaded. "I really want you to forgive me, but I want to come back home. I miss you and I love you so much. Please."

Tamar shook her head as her tears flowed freely. "I can't," she muttered.

"What? You can't what? You can't forgive me? I can't come home now? What?"

"I can't be with you," she sniffled and inhaled uneasily.

"What? No. No. We belong together."

"Do we?" her hurt turned serious expression penetrated him. "You still did it! You let someone else use you like a puppet. Just like Celeste did. Just like my old boss!"

Donovan tried to contain his response by tensing his jaws.

"You let people control you and I'm always there when they are finished with you. I can't do it this time. I just needed an explanation from you. Now that I have it, I'm good." Tamar wiped her eyes with the heel of her hand and stood up. Donovan got up quickly and stood in front of her.

"I'm here! Right now, I'm here. I'm not going on another day without you not being in my life. I need you Tamar. I do!"

Tamar gazed at Donovan, giving him the same empathetic look she gave Taj, because it was now Donovan for whom she felt pity for. She rubbed his arm, caressed his face around to his neck and pulled him in for a kiss but he backed away sharply.

"No!" Donovan turned away. "No. We're *not* doing this."

"Donovan!"

"No!" he pulled away from her again as she tried to calm him.

"Donovan! Listen!"

"I swear to God, I will jump off that damn pier." He pointed toward the water at the edge of the pier. "I'll do it. I'm not going to be without you. I fucked up, but I don't deserve *that* punishment. Tamar? No."

"Don't do this!" she pleaded.

"Fuck it." Donovan walked away from her and headed down the pier.

"What are you doing?!" Tamar waited for a moment as she thought he was being overly dramatic for effect. She knew Donovan couldn't swim and wouldn't dream of getting his expensive clothes muddied by the Chesapeake Bay.

"Tell my folks I love 'em."

He stomped further down the pier. When he approached closer to the end of the pier Tamar realized that he wasn't stopping. Her eyes widened and she ran down the pier to stop him.

"Donovan!" She ran faster when his pace remained constant. "Stop!"

"For what? If I can't have you, there's no reason to be here!" he yelled over his shoulder, his pace quickening.

"God dammit, Donovan! You better stop!"

He stopped when he reached the edge of the pier - his chest heaving up and down quickly. He turned to face her, his eyes seemed absent of a soul when he looked at her. His mouth became dry from the impromptu workout he had endured.

"What are you doing?" she asked him.

"Tamar, I mean it. I'm not living without you."

"So instead of not getting your way, you'd rather terminate yourself, but leave me riddled with guilt? That's love?"

"Love is you forgiving me and we get back together!"

"And love is not forcing me to!"

She held his arms with her hands and stroked them gently. Her bowed head pressed gently against his chest as he slowly raised his arms to hug her. He caressed her back up and down with his hands as his entire body began to stiffen the more aroused he became. His heart beat faster and Tamar could feel it against her forehead. He was nervous and so was she.

"So I saved your life?" she whispered.

"You saved *our* lives," he corrected. "You have no idea how much I love you and how hard it was to stay away. I'm never leaving you again. I mean it. Never."

"Never say never . . .," she warned.

40

Hailey was busted. Torn. Alone. She needed to feel validated because she couldn't excuse physical violence and refused Bryan. He hadn't tried to contact her, it was as if he already knew the verdict of their relationship when he left. Never did she think that he would be capable of doing that, let alone doing that to her. He was so refined and always carried himself at a higher standard. But Hailey knew, as with all people, that Bryan had a breaking point and she flirted with it far too many times. She did the only thing she felt she could do in a situation like this. She called Steve.

"You ready to make baby number two?" Steve joked when he came over to see her. He reached for her hips and pulled her toward him. Instead of falling into his embrace, she pushed him away slightly. Dumbfounded, he released her and waited for some sort of explanation.

"What are we doing?" she asked.

"You called me!"

"No, I mean what are you doing?"

"Again, you called me. You want me to give you a kid so you can say its Bryan's," he said and then scoffed. "Which is fucking nuts."

She stared at him after he murmured the last part. She folded her arms and jutted out her hip preparing to give him attitude.

"What!?" he defended when he saw her negative reaction to his comment.

"If it's so nuts, why did you agree to do it?" her neck meandered when she spoke.

"Are you kidding?" Steve smiled.

"I just want to know."

"A chance to sex up the woman I used to love for free! Why *wouldn't* I do it?" He still smiled, but when he saw that his words pained Hailey he smirked and closed his eyes for a moment immediately wishing he could take them back. He reached for her, but she lifted both arms to shun him and walked over to the other side of the room.

"Wow."

"Hailey, I'm sorry."

"For free . . .," she repeated his words through shallow breaths.

"I didn't mean it that way."

"Yes you did."

"Hailey, it was your idea!" he said. She quickly whisked away a single tear and tried to laugh the whole exchange off.

"Yeah, it was, but you agreed."

"So what's wrong now? Why are you crying because I know it's not because of what I said or what we're doing?"

"It's over between us. Me and Bryan that is. He hit me and I told him to go."

Steve clenched his teeth and balled his fists. Hailey could tell that he was increasingly seeing red as he paced and mumbled expletives. He pounded his fist into the open palm of his other hand and faced the wall for a moment. Hailey tried to calm him by placing her hands on his shoulder.

"When?" Steve said. When Hailey didn't respond quickly enough, his voice got louder and he turned toward her, "When!?"

"Let it go! He apologized and he's gone. He slapped me. I'm not saying it's right, but it wasn't a great conversation we were having at the time. He was upset. Very upset." She held her head down and shook it slightly as she relived the terrible memory and condemned herself in that moment for making up an excuse for his behavior.

"I'll kill him," he declared.

"No! You won't. Alex still needs you, so you put that crazy thought out of your mind. Don't worry about Bryan. It's over."

Steve calmed down a bit and caressed her shoulders and upper arms roughly as he looked around in a bit of a panic. Hailey knew that Steve was more than upset by the news and his actions indicated to her that he still wanted a piece of Bryan.

"Come on, sit down," she told him as she guided him to the couch. His body was stubborn as he resisted going down, the more she eased him into the seat the looser his body became. Once seated, he relaxed a bit more.

"What do you want from me, Hailey? Why am I here?"

"I want you to hold me."

Steve hesitated for several seconds which caused Hailey to place his arms around her to simulate how she wanted to be held by him. His arms fell limp and she placed one of his hands on her shoulder and the other on her hip again.

"Hold me!" she quietly ordered. He held her and she snuggled up to him. He tilted his head slightly away from her.

"Hailey?"

"Yes baby," she moaned.

"What do you want from *me*?"

"Let's just do it, Steve. Let's have another child. Let's move back in together and if everything goes well, let's just get married. I've thought about this for a while. We just need to stop all of this and do it."

Steve grunted out of frustration and took his hands off of her. She leaned away from him to get a full view of his face.

"What?" she asked innocently.

Steve shook his head and sneered.

"What? Why did you do that?" she asked him as she put her finger under his chin.

Steve wanted Hailey years ago and he couldn't get the memory out of his mind when she tap danced on his heart and turned a deaf ear to his apologies and pleas for forgiveness. He had to endure counseling for what she had done. Several years and hundreds of dollars later, she could still turn him to mush just with a glance. He had to make his own decision and not be coaxed into making one that would not only be detrimental to him, but to her and their child.

"Hailey, I can't help you there," he said.

"What do you mean?" she continued caressing his chin and added a few pecks to his face for good measure. He cringed slightly and moved his face away from her lying lips.

"I had a vasectomy the week after I found out both boys were mine."

Hailey gritted her teeth and pushed Steve in the chest with her hand. "You did what?!"

Steve lowered his eyes and turned his head away from her.

"Steve you . . .," she started but then stopped herself. She shuddered at the deception and reclined further into the couch. "So you were just going to keep having sex with me knowing I'd never get pregnant?"

He looked up at her and then lowered his eyes again. At the time, it was a genius of an idea to him, but he realized now how callous of a person it made him. He was going to sell her a dream that she was all too ready to grasp onto until it became reality.

"You bastard," she said with a laugh. "That's good. I'll give you that one."

"I'm sorry."

"Don't be." She looked at her wristwatch and said, "I gotta go pick up Alex." She stood and Steve rose as well. Because of her cool response, he didn't know what to do. Whether to go with her, offer to get him or stay behind until they both returned. She looked at him, expressionless. "Okay."

"Okay what?"

"I gotta get Alex," she repeated.

"Don't do this," he said as he tried to hug her, which she let him, her arms were stiff by her side. "Let me ride with you to get him."

"No. We are done Steve. I'm going to the courts next week and let them decide a visitation schedule and appropriate monthly stipend."

"No! Do not do that! Don't!"

"I've had enough of us!"

"Now hold on! You twist the game and fuck people's minds with no remorse, then get pissed when it's done to you? Get the fuck outta here with that Hailey."

"I gotta go."

Steve gripped her shoulders and steered her toward the couch and pushed her down into a seated position.

"You stay your ass right here. I'll go get him and we are going to discuss this later. You're not going to punish me and Alex because you can't get your way. Not this time. You stay here."

Hailey sat there, unable to move as Steve walked out to pick up their son.

About an hour later, Steve returned and Hailey was still seated on the couch. It seemed as if she hadn't moved at all the entire time. Alex ran in the house and jumped into his mother's arms

"Mommy!"

Hailey's saddened demeanor transformed to glee when she saw her baby boy. She smothered his face with kisses and he hugged her neck. "Hi my angel!"

Steve slightly smiled at the love his son had for his mother. He was a bit jealous because it seemed as if Alex was the only human Hailey was capable of loving unconditionally. He wanted that love from Hailey but knew it could never be that way with her. She was too scorned and he finally understood why. Although she loved Alex, every time she saw him, it was a reminder that Steve had conceived with another woman and given her a child as well. He understood that she needed to move past that pain. Steve was unsure if she ever would as he'd hoped, but it would have to be when she was emotionally ready. He would be there for her, but was not going to be separated from his son. He felt as though he lost his other son and ached during the separation from Gabe. Each time he had a Skype session with Gabe, it seemed to be from a different setting. Figuring that Camilla was nearby, she rarely stayed visible during the session. Camilla never interrupted them, which he was grateful for, but he couldn't wait to see and hold his son again.

He wouldn't allow Hailey to take Alex from him.

That evening, he stayed with them. Even though he wasn't that great of a cook, he prepared a meal for the three of them. They shared stories with one another and acted like a nuclear family for the first time in a long time. He wouldn't trade that moment for anything, but he knew it may be a while before he had that feeling again.

Without question, Hailey was the primary care giver. Consequently, she held all the cards. Steve could only pray that she would not go to court. He knew if she did that to him, his visits would be cut from being whenever he wanted to see Alex, down to a single weekend a month. How could he pack a month's worth of love for his son in three days? He wasn't going to allow it, but he knew Hailey. She had to be victorious no matter what, that was just her nature. It was too bad that Hailey didn't realize that her decisions sprawled to those around her like a spider's web.

Steve could only hope that this web she'd spun wasn't as delicate and fragile as her heart.

41

Camilla packed up their belongings for their return journey home. It was without a doubt one of the best moments of her life. She was grateful that she had the chance to spend it with the two people she loved the most. Not only was she returning to the states as Mrs. Hedley, she was returning to Washington D.C. secure in her relationship. Knowing that she was loved and not just going through the motions with random men anymore was exhilarating. Felix had finally given up on calling her, well she guessed.

For the last time overseas, she whipped open her laptop and decided to check her email. She found a comfortable position on the comfy bed that her and her husband occupied for the past week in Tuscany, Italy. The windows were open and the air was a bit crisp at about 7 a.m. She was already dressed as they had a late morning flight back to the states. To her surprise when she checked her email, there was one from Josephine. Camilla opened it and began reading. It was short, but had a lot of detail included within. Not everything incorporated were things that she wanted or even needed to hear, but she was appreciative for the broadcast. Josephine's email said that she had given birth to twins, which Camilla didn't even realize she was pregnant. The pictures attached of them yielded gentle adoration from Camilla. She instantly fell in love with them and couldn't wait to see them. Josephine apologized for not being there like she should've been because she was dealing with a divorce. Camilla's jaw dropped as she couldn't fathom Ian and Josephine splitting. Camilla didn't know the circumstances, but in most instances, she speculated that infidelity was involved. Josephine also mentioned that Donovan and Tamar were on the outs and Bryan had left Hailey.

Everyone is separated, Camilla thought.

Before she left the states, she knew that Bryan had come back, but hadn't seen him. Frankly, she had no reason to. At the end of Josephine's email, she mentioned that she wanted Camilla to call her when she had a moment.

"You almost ready?" Jameson said as he entered the bedroom.

Camilla was typing her response when he entered. She looked up at him and smiled. "No, but yes," she joked.

She continued clicking away on the keyboard. Jameson walked further into the room.

"Replying to Josephine," she casually mentioned and he nodded. In her email, Camilla said that she would reach out to her in about a week.

Preparing to leave, Camilla took one last look around. She noted the rustic walls which were cracked gold and peach colored. The floor to ceiling beveled doors had brass knobs that desperately required polishing. The hardwood floors were dark but sturdy. The linen drapes danced as the wind flowed through and passed them. Uneasy and missing the country already, she wished she could stay there with him forever but literally, the honeymoon had to end.

On the ride to the airport, Gabe of course was falling asleep. Camilla tried to keep him awake to see the sheep and the herdsmen on the rolling green hills that almost looked as if someone colored them with a crayon. The tops of the pale white towered buildings looked like old cigarette butts, except they held more history and flattered the country canvas. This was the most she felt at peace; she just wanted to cling to this feeling for as long as she could. As they drove through the city, it seemed like houses were stacked on top of houses. The home's colors of beiges, rusts and oranges were all vying for the sun's attention when it rose and set. Camilla vowed that they would have to come back there and spend their anniversary except this time, *she* was going to take him.

They arrived at the airport, too soon she thought, and she scooped up Gabe.

"Come on, Creepy," she whispered to him and she hoisted him up on her hip. Jameson grabbed the carry-on bags and the driver loaded the rest.

"Is he going to be awake during the plane ride?" Jameson asked.

"Not sure. I doubt it. You know motion lulls him into a REM stage," she chuckled.

*   *   *   *

They arrived late that night and when Jameson opened the doors of his home, he stopped at the entrance. He nodded proudly as he looked around.

"Glad to be home?" Camilla asked as she came up behind him. Jameson quickly turned to stop her.

"No! Wait, don't walk in!"

"What?" Camilla fumbled in her tracks and she immediately looked toward the floor, thinking there may be some bug or other critter he needed to exterminate before she entered.

He set the bags down and supported her back and leaned down to place his arm at the bend of her knees. He scooped her off of her feet and Camilla yelped in surprise.

"I have to carry you over the threshold!"

"Jameson!"

"Come on, girl. You don't weigh a thing. I could carry you all the way upstairs and back."

"And be in an Epsom salt bath all day tomorrow!"

After they entered he placed her on her feet gently and planted a loving kiss on her slightly parted mouth. The nanny came in with Gabe sitting up in his stroller. He was wide awake and Camilla struggled with how she would get him back on Eastern Time.

The couple spent the next few days unpacking and incorporating her and Gabe's things into Jameson's home. She would often ask him where she could put her items, or if she could add an extra mirror or some other piece of furniture in a section of his house. He corrected her after about the fourth time she asked.

"This isn't my house, Camilla," he told her, "it's our house. Make it ours."

She went through another one of her boxes and noticed the figurine she'd swiped from Felix's house earlier this year when she was disgusted about his impromptu threesome. Camilla was going to toss it until she remembered Felix saying it was valuable. As a reminder of what types of men were out there and never to stray, she decided to display the figurine in their bedroom.

"Oh nice," Jameson commented.

"You like?" She asked and then emphasized her pronouns, "Well it's *our* figurine and it's going in *our* bedroom."

Her phone rang. She looked at it mysteriously as it was the first time in two and a half weeks that it rang. She looked at Jameson, shrugged and answered.

"Hello?" she said and then cheered up some, "Josephine! Hi! How are you? You did what? I know . . . my phone hasn't had service in a while. I'll come see you in the morning. Can I bring Gabe? He wants to see the babies. Okay. 10ish is good."

The next morning, Camilla packed up Gabe and headed for Josephine's house. Jameson had an early business meeting. His executives found a spot for the supper club and had begun the design while he was away. It would be finished in a few months. He was still thinking of a name for the lounge and told Camilla she would be the first to know.

As she drove somewhat in a daze, she realized just how long it had been since she was gone. She almost forgot how to get to Josephine's. However, the car seemed to drive itself as Camilla began to remember all of the intricate turns and side streets she used in order to get there. Almost every weekend Josephine's place was one of refuge for Camilla when they both were single, as well as after Ian came into the picture.

Camilla made her way up the steps to ring the doorbell, which Gabe insisted upon doing. She lifted him up, he seemed heavier than she remembered and his little finger pressed the doorbell once. He heard the way it chimed and pressed it about six more times.

"Gabe, come on baby, no." She set him down on the ground and shook her head at his silliness.

Josephine opened the door and Camilla was instantly shocked by how large Josephine's breasts were! Camilla remembered when hers protruded, which was the main thing she loved about her pregnancy and afterward. It only lasted a year even though she gained a cup size out of it.

"My God!" Camilla said as she opened the door to let herself inside. "Your boobs!"

I laughed. "I know. They don't stay full for too long when they are doing double duty. I would've preferred the hair length that you got though!"

We hugged and I stepped aside to allow them entry.

"My boyfriend!" I beamed when I reached down to pick up Gabe.

"Hi *Aunt Joe-feen*," he managed in between all of the kisses I slathered on his face.

"I've missed you sweetheart!"

"I miss you too. Where is *Uncle In*?"

"*Ian*," I pronounced with a smile as I pinched his cheek, "is out right now." I kissed him again.

"Let's see these babies," Camilla diverted.

They were now two months old and getting some size on them. Locke was at ten pounds and looked like a little butterball turkey. Hunter, who ate much more than Locke, weighed in at thirteen pounds. Camilla gasped when she saw them quietly sleeping in their crib.

"Oh my gosh, Josephine, they are gorgeous! Locke and Hunter. They are so precious!"

"Mommy those are babies!" Gabe said loudly.

Camilla playfully covered his mouth and made an awkward face for his outburst. She whispered, "I know, but they are asleep, so we have to whisper."

"Oh," Gabe whispered, "Mommy those are babies."

I shook my head with a smile, "Still Gabby Gabe. Come on in, take a load off and let's chat."

Gabe settled in the play room and familiarized himself with a lot of the baby's toys. He managed to keep himself busy while the Baby Einstein cartoon learning series played on the flat screen.

"How long?" Camilla asked.

"It's been almost three months. He served me the day the babies were born. So it's like now while I'm celebrating their birthdays in the next several years, I'll always have that bitter reminder."

"That motherfucker," Camilla said. "I'm sorry, but what a rotten way to do that."

Josephine contemplated telling her secret. After a while she did. "Camilla, those aren't his babies."

Camilla nearly fell backward in her chair as they sat and had Mimosas at the kitchen table. "You cheated!?"

"No! No. Well, not in the traditional sense. I went to a fertility clinic and he wouldn't have known until I found out that he himself was infertile! He knew we were trying and didn't say a damn word."

Camilla shook her head and took another sip of Mimosa. It helped her swallow down her comment on the whole ordeal. After taking a few more large sips she just said, "My God."

"So that's the meat of it. We talk every now and then, but he hasn't seen the babies. He refuses to. He can't get over what I did. I won't push him because he is the one carrying that pain, but I don't want them to be three years old and wondering who *that man* is. That would break my heart. I can't believe he chose solitude over receiving unconditional love from three individuals."

"Damn, when you put it that way, it is a bit crazy."

"So you . . . what's been happening? You are glowing! Now where have you been? Phones disconnected, car gone, house abandoned."

Camilla could barely contain her smile as she began blushing at the very thought of being the one to glow. "I told you about Jameson."

"Finally! And just a little. Not much." Just as I said that, I noticed the rock on her left hand. My eyes protruded with surprise and I had to catch my breath from the excitement. "Wait! No way!! You guys are married??"

Camilla nodded as I reached for her hand to inspect the diamonds. Plural.

"Hot damn! Jameson finally got to put a ring on it. I don't know a whole lot about him but I knew he was ready for marriage. Go 'head, girl. You got a rich, handsome, smart man."

"I love him so much, Josephine. This man accepted me where and as I was. That's all I ever wanted. He's the best and Gabe loves him to pieces."

"Aww! So the torch for Bryan is out finally?"

"It was out a year after he," Camilla imitated a Jamaican accent, "*went down to de island where man 'im belong wit de coconuts!*"

They laughed hard at her impersonation and continued to swap stories about Camilla's travels, the engagement ring debacle and dinner in the sky. She shared with her all of the sites they took in and how much fun Gabe had even though he won't remember it when he gets older. Camilla shared a dozen or more of Gabe's stories of charming the natives to the point where he was loaded down with gifts from every country.

"He is a great kid, Camilla. I love him to death."

"He is something." Camilla looked at the time, "We'd better go! I have a ton left to do and I know the munchkins keep you plenty busy. I gotta run to the store to pick up some stuff for Gabe too. You should come by just to get your mind away from things for a while."

"I will," I laughed, "I may be over there tomorrow!"

We laughed again, but I was serious.

"Well, that's fine too." Camilla scribbled down the address on my white erase board that I kept on my refrigerator. It was bogged down with post-its and reminders for me and the twins. "You're welcome there any time!"

She hugged me and patted my shoulders for extra measure. I tucked in my bottom lip to suppress the feeling of abandonment and then managed a smile. I nodded at her invitation. "Thanks, Camilla."

"Either way it's going to work out for you. Believe that."

"I know it will, I just miss him," I confessed.

"Once he sees those babies, he will be hooked and he knows it. That's why he doesn't want to look at them. He's being stubborn but it will work out."

I nodded again. I didn't want to say anything because I could feel my emotions about to erupt into an explosion of tears. Crying was just as much a part of my life now as changing diapers. I needed a release soon. Camilla patted my shoulder again gently and stepped away to get Gabe from the playroom. I checked on the twins, whom were still asleep. I rubbed their soft arms tenderly and kissed them both. I checked on Gabe and Camilla in the playroom. Gabe was curled up on the floor in a fetal position, with a large stuffed Snoopy tucked under his arm. Camilla kissed him and scooped him up carefully.

"He sleeps a lot!" I whispered.

"Girl, I don't complain at all," she laughed. "Maybe he will be a very busy man in the future, so he's resting up now." She shrugged and followed me to the front door, I gave her another hug and she mouthed the words "Call me." I kissed Gabe on his forehead and waved to her.

Camilla loaded Gabe in the car securing him in his seat and headed for the grocery store. She needed to grab a few snacks and school supplies for Gabe. By the time they arrived, Gabe was awake but just barely, his eyes were still heavy and he was strangely quiet.

"You okay, Creep?"

He nodded. She loaded him in the basket and pushed him around the store. She had a few items loaded and was surprised that Gabe was so quiet. He must have been tired from the nap still. Camilla tickled his chin with her fingertip and looked at him closer.

"You okay, baby?"

He nodded again, yawned and rubbed his eyes. Gabe peered around Camilla's shoulder and stared.

"What's wrong?" she asked him as he continued to stare without blinking. She turned. There he was – looking the same as he did on the day he walked out of her life. Camilla gulped and she swore her heart skipped.

"I thought that was you," Bryan said as he slowly approached her. Camilla backed up slightly and placed a securing hand on Gabe. Bryan looked at Gabe and waved. Gabe stared at him as he knew it wasn't Mr. Hedley or his Daddy. He wasn't sure what to make of him really. Until he could, Gabe reserved his hellos until he could figure out what this exchange was about.

"Bryan Bryant," Camilla said with little enthusiasm. By then she had a moment to catch her breath and steady her heart rate.

"So that's him," he said. "He's a handsome little fellow."

"He is."

There was a bit of an immovable silence that hovered between them. Bryan looked at Camilla noticing how nicely she filled out, how much her hair grew and how sexy she looked.

"Are you in a big hurry?" he asked.

"Why?"

"I thought we could talk for a minute. I won't keep you long," Bryan smiled and then caught a glimpse of the massive rock on her left ring finger. He nodded and pointed toward it. "You took the plunge, huh?"

Camilla nodded.

"There's a uh, café next to the bakery over there if you want to sit for a few." He noticed the look of contemplation on her face and reassured her, "I won't keep you and your son long. I promise."

Bryan led the way and Camilla wheeled Gabe behind him. He still looked good to her, but the butterflies she once had for him weren't there anymore. Seeing him reminded her of the hurt and how much he made it clear to her that they would be nothing more than fuck buddies. She wondered what he wanted to discuss. They found a table and sat. Gabe remained in the front of the cart and Camilla kept her hand on him as she spoke with Bryan.

"So I heard you were looking like a bit of a Rasta. What happened?"

Bryan chuckled and nodded, "Yes, I was. I cut it off a few months ago. I didn't need that look anymore and I'm returning to work next week."

"That's good."

Gabe watched Bryan closely.

"So, what's on your mind Bryan?" she asked.

He thought for a moment before he spoke. "Camilla, I had two years to think while I was in the Caribbean and I won't lie, I thought a lot about Hailey, but I thought a bit about you too."

"Is that what you wanted to tell me?"

"No. Camilla, I'm sorry. I treated you badly and you never did anything to me. You just wanted to be loved."

She nodded, "I told you that very early on."

"I know and I wasn't listening. I only wanted what I wanted. I used you and I'm sorry."

Gabe hung on every word that passed through Bryan's lips. He read his mother's gestures and expressions as well. Gabe wasn't fussy even though he was getting a bit restless in the front of the cart. A few people walked by and waved to him and smiled.

"Bryan, you didn't do anything that I didn't allow you to do. You were being who you were. The signs were there, I just ignored them. I knew you weren't into me, but I wanted it so bad that I couldn't see it."

"It's still not right," he told her. He reached for her hand and caressed it. "You are a good woman and I just wanted to tell you that I was sorry. I don't want to keep you." Bryan pointed to her ring again, "I know he's a very lucky man."

"He is," she said and winked at him. She added a smile. "But I didn't do too bad either."

Camilla stood to indicate that this discussion need not go any further. She accepted his apology and forgave him long ago. However, she was appreciative that he acknowledged his role in their failed relationship. It offered closure and validated that she did nothing wrong. If she were guilty, she was guilty of wanting love at any cost. Bryan stood as well and hugged her.

"You look fantastic by the way," he smiled and gave the gratuitous up and down longing stare.

"Thanks. I had a lot of frustration and anxiety to work off in the gym. Well and some baby weight," she chuckled.

"Whatever you're doing, it's working . . . well."

Bryan reached over and held his hand out for Gabe to shake it. Gabe stared at him and then at his hand for a moment.

"Take care of your mom. Okay? She's a beautiful woman," he told Gabe.

Gabe reached for his hand and smiled.

"We can go now, Mommy," he said.

Bryan looked surprised at his comment and smiled gently. Bryan was obviously impressed with how mature he was at his age. Camilla nodded with a smile and rolled her eyes around a little.

"I know," she shook her head and rolled her eyes around a bit. "He's an old man."

"He's a good kid. If you need anything or just to talk, I'm at the Post."

"Thanks for that, but I'm good," she said with a smile. "Thanks again, Bryan."

"Good bye, Camilla."

She wheeled Gabe toward the checkout counter. Gabe leaned over to watch Bryan as they left. He lifted his tiny hand and waved at Bryan, who returned the gesture.

Bryan was glad that he saw Camilla and was able to speak his peace. He knew deep down that he messed up by seeing those two women. One was playing him, while he played the other. Bryan thought that perhaps in some perverse way, this was Camilla's blind justice. Bryan was without Hailey, the one he thought he loved who did nothing but use him to make someone else jealous years ago. Now Hailey used him again to outrage the same man who she supposedly stopped loving.

Hailey had so much going for her, but she was a manipulator. Camilla, had a lot going for her, but was also a victim. Bryan knew that now. She was happy and with that, he was happy for her. Still he wondered . . . if he chose Camilla, how would his life be today? If only he could go back in time and do it all over again. Life just may have been different.

42

The winter months were bitter. Those cold dark days were long and unyielding with a few inches of snow each week just about. I was still on maternity leave with the children and dare not take them out in the weather unless it was necessary. Ian would bring groceries or medicine if we needed it, but he never stayed long. Sometimes he would just leave it by the door and call me to let me know it was there. The lengths that he went to ensure he wouldn't see the twins were in the least, ridiculous. By now, I had gotten used to the cold weather and his cold shoulder so much so that none of what he did bothered me – much. I was sad for Locke and Hunter because they didn't deserve it at all. My mother often stayed to help out since she was just in Fredericksburg. Her job was to spoil them rotten and if it were a contest, she would win first place. Early on, she absolutely hated Ian for abandoning his family, but now, her focus is to love the babies, as is mine.

My friends had even fought the bad weather and traffic to come and help out when I needed. Tamar was a huge asset during this time. It was nothing for her to hop in her car and go. She spent a lot of time visiting me during the month of December. We cried together, laughed together and stuffed our faces. She and Donovan were going to give it a go again, something about his dramatic attempt at suicide resonated with her, but she knew Donovan. Tamar always felt that he was calling her bluff that night. Donovan was too in love with himself, had too many custom suits to leave behind and was a millionaire thanks to Taj – there was no way he was going to leave all of that behind. Tamar was cautiously moving forward with him because Donovan was always bringing the drama. Her fault was merely reacting to it. I asked her if they considered getting married still and Tamar said marrying Donovan was the farthest thing from her mind. He had a lot to show and prove moving forward, she told me. Maybe they will be okay.

Hailey, Steve and Camilla were in messy custody battle hearings all winter long. While they were running to and from City Hall, I had turned the third bedroom into a small gym and worked out to ease the pain of me and Ian's separation. All of the frustration helped to chisel my body the way it was meant to be. I looked better than *before* I gave birth. Every time I wanted to stuff my face with ice cream, I did fifteen minutes on the elliptical. When I felt like crying over Ian, I did fifteen, when I was upset with Ian, I did fifteen. When the babies slept I cleaned and cat napped. I barely ate or rested during those first four months. Adjusting to Ian not being there was hell. We still weren't divorced because we had to be separated for a year. I didn't even know where he lived or if he was seeing someone. Because Hailey wasn't really talking much to Steve, I couldn't get Intel on Ian's life – which was probably best.

Although I stayed away from that custody madness, I received constant updates about the proceedings. According to both Hailey and Camilla, Steve was upset that his life was being orchestrated by them. So instead, Steve decided not to go gently into the night. Sadly for him, it didn't go too well. The second time they arrived in court, Camilla brought her husband Jameson along, which was pretty much a wrap for Steve. They had more space – much more, had a nanny, a private educator who taught Gabe two languages in addition to English, and they had money. Steve didn't stand a chance. However, he was able to retain his current visitation. The cool part was that even though Steve drug Camilla to court, which she thought was because of Hailey, she didn't go after him for child support. She asked that he be even more involved in his life and contribute whatever he could monetarily – she would just put it in an account for him. Camilla told me that he didn't have enough soap and water to clean the egg from his face.

Now Hailey on the other hand had a rougher time. Because she aborted Bryan's baby, which came out in court, the pro-life judge did not look too favorably on that. The hearings continued almost until Christmas and the irony of it all was that he still had the same visitation he did prior to when they started this custody battle. He just acquired three more days, but had to pay a tad more in child support based on his salary. The judge told him to get his priorities straight. Funny, I remember Hailey telling him that exact thing several years ago.

With that winter drama out of the way, it was springtime, where all things were new and coming back to life. The flowers were budding for bloom; the birds were building their nests for their young and the best part, no more cold weather! It was time to clean and get the twins out in the sun. Even though Ian still hadn't laid eyes on them, I tried not to harp on that too much. I needed to move on and with haste. My body craved sex, but I know those days would have to be put on hold for quite a while. Being with someone new wasn't a thought, but with Ian gone there was no other alternative. Relish the thought, but it may be five years before I rode in the saddle again. By no means was I okay with that at all, but it was my new reality.

I packed up the munchkins, the double stroller, and headed to the National Harbor to get in a decent walk before dinner. I packed up water, goodies, diapers and wipes because I was going to make the trek across the bridge. I heard the view was awesome and the breeze was even better. I put extra sweaters on the kids because it was only in the low 70s.

By the time I parked and nestled them in the stroller, I took a moment to stretch. The babies were cooing and having a raspberry blowing contest. Dreading the clean up, I knew the dribble was going to be massive. It made me laugh because Hunter blew first, then Locke had to prove that she could do it as well and that was how it started. It went on for at least ten minutes.

I wheeled the stroller around, ready for a light jog when I saw Ian sprinting down the trail. He looked good. I guessed he spent a lot of time working out during the separation too. My heartbeat grew faster and I was at a loss for words. He didn't realize that I was there as he was clearly in a zone.

He trotted by us at first and I turned and saw the rear of him. *The nerve!* I thought. *He could've at least said hello!*

He slowed his pace and stopped in his tracks. Quickly he turned, I guess realizing that he just passed his wife on the trail.

"Oh shit!" he said. "Josephine! I'm sorry baby!" He walked quickly toward me and gave me a hug to which I kept my arms down by my side.

"Hi." I flatly said. He stood behind the stroller and didn't see the kids.

"I'm not used to seeing you out and with the extra everything," he awkwardly said as he flailed his hands around when he said it. "How are you? You look good."

I could tell that he was nervous and clearly wasn't expecting to see the three of us. The twins started the raspberry blowing contest again.

"I'm making it. It's tough doing double duty, but I'm managing."

Ian looked down at his feet for a moment as if he were looking to find a response down there. After a few seconds of an uncomfortable silence, he rubbed the back of his neck nervously and looked up at me.

"Um, look Josephine . . ."

"Don't . . .," I stopped him. I really wasn't in the mood for excuses or an empty apology. I put my hand on the stroller and began rocking it back and forth to comfort the babies. He nodded and looked away. "So what have you been up to? Dating anyone?" I asked. I needed to know right away before engaging him further.

He chuckled and shook his head, "Of course not."

"Well, I don't know. I've been hearing from you less and less."

"I just thought you wanted space. I think you said something like, if I leave to never come back."

"I said that to someone who was cold and heartless enough to serve me divorce papers right after delivery!"

"I don't want to argue!" he said and they quieted down. Just then I heard Locke. It sounded as if she was humming to herself. Then I heard Hunter in an equally soothing tone as he stole Locke's spotlight.

"Da da da da da da da."

Ian's eyes diverted to the stroller. He still couldn't see the babies because he was at the rear of it. He swallowed hard, and rocked on his heels a bit before looking up at Josephine. I was surprised as I ran to see Hunter.

"Hunter!"

"Da da da," he dribbled.

Ian took a step backward, obviously touched and speechless. I tickled Hunter's chest and smiled.

"That's the first thing he's said that sounded close to a word!" I laughed a bit and tickled him some more. "Isn't that right?" I asked Hunter as he continued cooing and kicking his feet around.

"Really?" Ian asked, still standing a distance away.

I nodded and giggled with Hunter for a few seconds more. I looked up at Ian and tilted my head a bit to indicate he was being a bit silly at this point.

"Come on, Ian. Your son is calling you."

Ian shook his head softly before bowing it. "But he's . . .," he began and I interrupted.

"Your son." I pleaded with my eyes. "Come look at these babies who are longing for you."

Ian stood still for several seconds and took one step forward and then hesitated. His shoulders rose and fell as the anxiety mounted. He took another step and I looked at him giving him a welcoming smile. I nodded again to let him know that it was okay. He stepped forward and peered into the stroller. I could tell that when he saw those faces looking up at him that he had immediately fell in love. Locke looked up at him and bent her brows for a quick second and continued humming her personal song. Hunter stared at Ian for a few moments without expression and then smiled. Ian smiled and looked up at me.

"He smiled at me!"

"I think he has a feeling of who you are. Whether you think so or not."

Ian looked at me and I caressed his arm tenderly. Ian smiled and cast his eyes downward for a moment then looked at the babies again. He stroked their tiny hands and Locke latched on to his index finger.

"She's got a strong grip!" Ian told me.

"You wanna hold 'em?"

Ian nodded and reached for Hunter first who had gotten heavier over the past few months. Hunter patted Ian's face and continued speaking baby gibberish. I reached for Locke and held her close to Ian. She reached for him after a few moments.

"Wow," Ian said when he realized that he couldn't hold them both at the same time. "Are we switching now?"

I giggled, "Sure." We swapped babies and Locke looked deeply into Ian's eyes. She blew another raspberry that soaked the lower part of Ian's face. He reared back a bit from the saliva mist and laughed. Locke smiled and repeated the act.

"Locke!" I softly scorned.

"No," Ian said, "it's okay." He stared at Locke with pure love in his eyes. He kissed her balled fist and nuzzled her chubby cheeks.

"So . . .," I began, "where were you on your way to?" I didn't want to terminate his meeting the twins prematurely, but didn't want to hold him up from anything either.

"Home."

"Oh," I looked down for a quick second, not knowing how to respond to that.

"With you," he looked at me after breaking his gaze from Locke. "Can I come back home?"

I could feel the waterworks coming as my vision blurred a bit from the tears that begun to form. I smiled and nodded. "Of course you can. It's our home."

"Jose', I'm so sorry baby. I love you."

That was the first time in a long time that he called me Jose' and it warmed my heart. "I never stopped loving you. Never."

He continued to securely hold Locke in one arm and rubbed my back with his free hand. Ian mouthed the words, "Let's go."

He helped me secure the kids in their car seats. It took a long time doing so because he couldn't stop staring at them. I watched quietly as I saw the love overwhelm him. Then Ian started to talk to them a bit.

"Y'all are so little," he said. "I'm gonna take good care of you guys okay? We will have a lot of fun. Ready?" Ian double checked the buckles on the car

seat to make sure they were secure. He shoved a few stuffed animals in the seat
with them and stepped out of the rear of my SUV.

"They good?" I asked.

"Yeah. So this is new?" He patted the roof of it and I nodded. "It's tight.
Uh, okay. I will follow you over there."

"You forgot the way already?"

Ian laughed, "No, I just like watching you from behind."

*   *   *   *

When we got home, Ian immediately leapt from his car and ran to the back
door of my SUV to check on the twins. I smiled and "gold-starred" myself for
knowing that he was going to be this type of father – caring and overly attentive.
Ian unlatched Hunter from his car seat and I scooped up Locke. Hunter was
extremely comfortable with Ian and Ian loved how this small life clung to him.
Ian looked like such a natural with them as he talked to them, kissed them and
nuzzled his face against theirs. Not only did he look like a natural, he looked
sexy as hell doing it.

His body had a lean hardness that contrasted against the innocent tender
flesh of the baby. Frankly it was driving me wild. All of those feelings that I
thought I'd never experience again for years had returned all in an instant. He
grabbed the diaper bag and tossed it on the opposite shoulder in one swoop.
Hunter grinned at Ian and he ate it up of course.

"You like that, old man?" he said to Hunter who cooed and babbled. "Yeah,
I used to be a superhero."

I fished the keys around in the lock and let us all inside. This was the feeling
I had longed for every since I met Ian. Family. My own family. I wasn't proud
of how it happened, but I don't regret the decision that resulted in Hunter and
Locke. All I needed was my husband, it was all that I prayed for and now he's
here.

"Are you hungry?" I asked Ian.

"No I'm good for right now. Speaking of that, I know you don't cook, what
have you been eating? You look pretty fit and lean."

"I've been working out a lot and I've only been eating rice and tuna."

Ian shook his head and mumbled, "You sound like Steve. You want me to cook you something? What do you have in here?" He peered in the refrigerator.

"Tuna," I said plainly and he laughed. "I have to get them fed, they will get fussy in a few. Do you want to help?"

Ian stopped peering in the fridge and looked back at me. He smiled and nodded. He closed the icebox and began washing his hands. "Of course, babe."

After we fed the babies, we rocked them to sleep and laid them in the crib. Ian stood over the crib for about five minutes just watching them. I slowly crept out of the room allowing him to bond with them as they slumbered. He couldn't take his eyes off of them. I collapsed on the couch and kicked my shoes off. It was a little after five and I made a mental note to wake them again at seven. I didn't want them awake all night. After a long while, Ian emerged from the rear bedroom and came to sit beside me. He placed his hand on my thigh and patted it lightly.

"They are something. A lot of work."

"Yeah, and that was just two hours," I joked.

"Those rascals work together I noticed."

"Yes," I laughed, "they do."

"Josephine, they are beautiful. I'm proud of you baby."

"Thank you my husband."

Ian looked down and then reached for my hand. He rubbed it roughly and then gently kissed it. "You still want me to have that title?"

I turned my body toward him and took his other hand in mine, "As long as you don't leave again. We need you, Ian."

"I need you guys too. I love you so much, Josephine. I had a lot of time to think and not that it wasn't fucked up, but I could've handled it better. I shouldn't have turned my back on you and the babies. I should've just told you what was wrong with me and we could've gone through it together."

"I messed up too and I know it. I'm sorry that I didn't consider your feelings first. Can you forgive me?"

"I already have."

Ian pulled my body close to his and kissed me like he never had before. His lips were so soft against mine, his mouth was cool and his tongue uncontrollable. The pinned up passion was unfastened and released from him and all over me. He squeezed me so tight and close to him that it almost hurt, but I loved it.

He moaned as he discovered how different my new body felt in his hands and he stiffened.

"Hmm, baby," he said while his mouth was in the crease of my neck. "I've missed you."

I parted my legs to let him know that I was more than ready for this. My body needed him and I wanted to feel his nakedness next to mine. We kissed uncontrollably and he was caressing me so frantically that at times it felt as if he had an extra pair of hands.

"Now!" I demanded.

"Right here?" he asked as he looked down at me. I didn't even realize he was on top of me.

"Where ever you want me baby," I panted.

"We need a soft surface because I'm going to wear this out."

"Well let's go!"

He tucked his hands under my bum and lifted me in one motion as I straddled him. It was never a problem for him to lift me before, but now with the weight loss, he lifted me as if I were a feather. I was soaking with anticipation and felt his stiffness rubbing against my inner thigh. I kissed his neck and shoulders as he carted me off to wildly reunite.

He tossed me backward on the bed and I bounced slightly. I smiled at him because I knew this was going to be incredible. He tore out of his shirt and quickly stepped out of his warm up pants. I slipped out of my clothes with the exception of my panties. When I started to slide them off of me he stopped me by putting his hand over mine.

"Let me," he suggested before removing them.

He climbed toward me like a predator in the wilderness, leaving moist and hot kisses on my calves and thighs along the way up to my belly. Caressing my waist and hips, he kissed my stomach as his hands slid behind my back. He lifted my upper body toward him and began kissing my breasts one from the other as he lie on his stomach in between my parted legs.

All I could do was tilt my head backward in between stealing a few glimpses of him enjoying himself with me. He lifted up on his knees and looked down at me. One hand rested on my lower abdominals while his thumb teased my clit. His other hand was stroking his penis, which he knew turned me on. His muscles and ripped abs drove me insane. I massaged my breasts while I watched him and licked my lips seductively while I waited.

"Turn over on your stomach," he said – his words cutting through the soothing bass of his voice.

"Anything for you," I moaned.

"Yeah?" he asked. "Well I want to hear you scream."

"Make me."

As soon as I turned over, he positioned my ass in the air with one swift motion and popped one ass cheek firmly. The sound rang in the air as long as the rap stung my flesh.

"Ooo," I said, sucking air through my teeth afterward.

I lie there on my stomach, back arched from having my ass slightly lifted in the air, waiting for contact of some sort. Suddenly, he buried his head between my ass and began eating me from behind. His hands were settled in the trench where my thighs and pelvis met. My legs, bent at the knees slid around on the surface of the bed, my feet swinging about in response to his tongue flutter. I couldn't retreat forward, because his grip firmly locked my hips in place. I wiggled about as I knew my lower body was about to erupt all over his face. I reached for a pillow, buried my face in it and released a loud orgasmic scream.

He lifted his face and popped me on the rump again.

"My naughty wife didn't let me hear that scream, huh?"

"Didn't . . . wanna . . . wake . . . the babies," I said through light gasps.

He popped my ass again for being disobedient and pulled me up on my knees by my waist. I felt his hardness against me as he rocked his hips from side to side – teasing me as I became wetter. His fingers spread wide on the fleshy part of my hips as he poked and prodded below.

He entered slowly and I had an orgasm.

"Ooo, nice and tight," he mentioned.

He stroked me gently with a steady rhythm that drew several orgasms out of me. I reached for the pillow each time to verbally release them there. Each time I did that, Ian popped my rump firmly. Of course, that just made me cum again. Several moments of being pleased in that position, Ian turned me over on my back.

"I need to see my beautiful wife's face," he said.

I smiled and soothingly palmed his face before kissing him deeply. He loved me with his stroke and kissed me passionately. He nibbled on my neck in between. I rubbed his back, chest and kissed any part of his body that I could reach.

"I love you," I moaned.

"I love you more," he said.

His rhythm increased and I knew that he was about to burst from the friction. I tightened my muscles and his stroke intensified.

"Ah!" he moaned just before. "Baby!" He pulled my body toward him and unleashed his orgasm. His body shook all over as did mine.

"Oh God!"

He turned over on his back and caught his breath. My eyes remained closed and I could feel myself drifting off into a light slumber. His hands touched my body lightly as he covered his eyes with his forearm.

I heard Locke whimpering a bit and sighed.

Ian chuckled, "At least her timing is good."

I laughed and used my elbows to prop me up.

"You want me to get her?" he asked.

"No," I told him, "I got her, Hunter will be up in a bit too. Let me wash up before they both really start singing."

Ian got up and followed me in the bathroom. We kissed again and I tossed on my robe. This felt so right and I was glad that he was coming back home. I stopped in the twin's room and checked on them. They were quiet and lifting their heads up trying to look around. Hunter had his hand on Locke using her for support so he could see a bit further upward.

"Hunter, you're just all over your sister," I lifted him and kissed his cheek. I bent my leg to support him and I scooped Locke up with my free hand. She was facing downward. I had to alternate this carrying method between the two and I think the last time Locke was upright. It was hard to keep track.

I sat Hunter down in his rocker and lifted Locke up for a kiss since I owed her one as well.

"Hungry guys?"

Ian passed the room and stopped at the threshold.

I pointed to the mini fridge in the corner of the room and asked him if he could grab two bottles and warm them up for me.

"Sure baby, how long?"

"Minute and a half, minute forty five."

He grabbed the bottles and headed toward the kitchen. While the milk was warming, Ian looked around the kitchen, remembering different aspects about it as it had been several months since he had been there.

He peered over at her pile of mail and noticed one addressed to her from the fertility clinic. It had been opened. Ian lifted it and flipped it over from front to back and then back to front. He bit his bottom lip and placed the letter back on the counter. He stared at it some more and reluctantly picked it up to open it.

From the nursery, I wondered what was taking Ian so long as he should've been back with the bottles by now. I went into the kitchen and noticed that he was reading a piece of mail.

"What's that?" I asked him.

Ian looked up at me, his eyes burning with fury. "It's from the fertility clinic."

When he said that, my heart sank to my ankles. I could hear the children getting fussy, but I couldn't tend to them at present.

"Is this a joke?"

"No. I just . . . I had no idea. I got it this morning and I'm just as surprised as you."

"Him? He's the father of our twins?" he asked. I looked down and nodded softly. "You gotta be fucking kidding me!"

"I said the same thing. I mean, what are the odds?"

"Did you tell him?"

"I haven't told anybody."

Ian reached for a book of matches on the counter that was next to the candles. He struck the match and lit it on fire. The flame continued down the paper, flickering as the air fueled it. When it was close to his fingertips, he laid it in the sink and watched as it burned completely.

"And we won't," Ian said. "No one must ever know."

www.ingramcontent.com/pod-product-compliance
Lightning Source LLC
Chambersburg PA
CBHW030013180626
46810CB00001B/7

* 9 7 8 0 9 8 3 2 4 9 2 2 1 *